The Angel of Lust

BY THE SAME AUTHOR

He Marvelous Story of Claire d'Amour
The Call of the Beast
Priscilla of Alexandria
The Mystery of the Tiger
The Poison of Goa
Lucifer
The Blood of Toulouse
The Albigensian Treasure
Jean de Fodoas
Melusine
The Brothers of the Virgin Gold

The Angel of Lust

by
Maurice Magre

Translated, annotated and introduced by
Brian Stableford

A Black Coat Press Book

Visit our website at www.blackcoatpress.com

TABLE OF CONTENTS

Introduction

This is the fourth volume of a twelve-volume set of translations of Maurice Magre's prose fiction. It contains translations of the novella, *La Vie amoureuse de Messaline* (1925), as "The Love Life of Messalina," the novel published as *La Luxure de Grenade* (1926), as "The Angel of Lust," and the chapter from *Magiciens et illuminés* (1930) entitled "Christian Rosenkreutz et les Rose-croix," as "Christian Rosenkreutz and the Rosicrucians."

Volume One, *The Marvelous Story of Claire d'Amour and Other Stories*, contains translations of early short stories, including the collection *Histoire merveilleuse de Claire d'Amour suivie d'autres contes merveilleux* (1903) and six other stories from various sources, published between 1901 and 1913.

Volume Two, *The Call of the Beast and Other Stories*, contains translations of his first three works of prose fiction in volume form, *Les Colombes poignardées* (1917), as "Stabbed Doves," *La Tendre camarade* (1918), as "The Tender Comrade" and *L'Appel de la bête* (1920), as "The Call of the Beast."

Volume Three, *Priscilla of Alexandria and Other Stories* contains translations of the original version of the story collection *Vies des courtisanes*, first published in *Oeuvres Libres* 23 (1923), as "Courtesans' Lives" plus the additional story added to the version published in volume form in 1925, and the novel *Priscilla d'Alexandrie* (1925), as "Priscilla of Alexandria."

Volume Five, *The Mystery of the Tiger*, contains translations of the novella *Le Roman de Confucius* (1927), as "The Story of Confucius," and the novel *Le Mystère du tigre* (1927), as "The Mystery of the Tiger."

Volume Six, *The Poison of Goa*, contains translations of the novel *Le Poison de Goa* (1928), as "The Poison of Goa," and the prose poems contained in *Le Livre des lotus entr'ouverts* (1926), as "Lotus Blossoms."

Volume Seven, *Lucifer*, contains a translation of the novel originally published under the same title in 1929 and the novella *La Nuit de haschich et de l'opium* (1929), as "The Night of Hashish and Opium."

Volume Eight, *The Blood of Toulouse*, contains translations of the novel *Le Sang de Toulouse* (1931), as "The Blood of Toulouse," and the chapter from *Magiciens et illuminés* entitled "Le Maître inconnu des Albigeois," as "The Secret Master of the Albigensians."

Volume Nine, *The Albigensian Treasure*, contains translations of the novel *Le Trésor des Albigeois* (1938) as "The Albigensian Treasure," and the collection of vignettes "Communication avec la nature" from *La Beauté invisible* (1937), as "Communication with Nature."

Volume Ten, *Jean de Fodoas*, contains translations of the novel *Jean de Fodoas: aventures d'un Français à la cour de l'empereur Akbar* (1939) as "Jean de Fodoas" and the chapter from *Magiciens et illuminés* entitled "Le Mystère des Templiers," as "The Mystery of the Templars."

Volume Eleven, *Melusine*, contains translations of the novel *Mélusine, ou le secret de solitude* (1941) and the collections of vignettes "Le Côté d'ombre des âmes" and "Révélation des mondes invisibles" from *La Beauté invisible*, as "The Dark Side of Souls" and "The Revelation of Invisible Worlds."

Volume Twelve, *The Brothers of the Virgin Gold*, contains a translation of the novel *Les Frères de l'or vierge*, first published posthumously in 1949.

The two works of historical fiction featured in the present volume follow on thematically from Maurice Magre's first long work of historical fiction, *Priscilla d'Alexandrie*, and are closely associated with it in their narrative strategy, tone and content.

The earlier novel was expanded and transformed from a short story contained in *Vies des courtisanes* (1923), which describes how the eponymous heroine, tricked into taking part in the murder of the neo-Platonist philosopher Hypatia, attempts to expiate that sin in an unorthodox manner, by becoming a prostitute in Constantinople, and subsequently decides to avenge Hypatia, initially by cutting the throat of the leader of the murderous mob when he visits her brothel. After having returned to Alexandria, she hires a sorceress to employ black magic to murder Cyril, the Bishop of Alexandria, who instigated the murder.

The expanded version not only offers a much more elaborate account of Priscilla's life and quest, but an extravagant account of the ideas of the neo-Platonist philosophers of Alexandria, giving center stage to three hypothetical exemplars, one of whom eventually becomes a solitary ascetic, while the second sets forth to find the wisdom of the ancients in a document which he believes to be contained in the tomb of Alexander the Great, buried under the city by an earthquake many years before, and the third sets off for India to follow in the footsteps of Apollonius of Tyana, as detailed in the "biography" of that sage by Philostratus.

The introduction to Volume Two of the present series suggested that the lurid and horrific imagery abundantly imported into the longer version of *Priscilla d'Alexandrie* was partly a response to the fact that Magre had recently being diagnosed with syphilis, contracted during a long period of obsessive promiscuity, to which his marriage in 1913 had not brought a conclusion. The effects of that diagnosis are not only reflected in the imagery of disease and decay imported into the novel, and the narrative's continual juxtaposition of sexual intercourse with nightmarish visions and death, but also in its intense interest in philosophy and "ancient wisdom" as a possible route to spiritual enlightenment and transcendence.

9

It was inevitable that the transformation of Magre's attitude to sex would be coupled with an intensification of his interest in the spiritual, in opposition to and conflict with the carnal, and in the long history of attempts by great thinkers to determine and map out the proper intellectual mission of human beings. The diagnosis of syphilis also coincided with Magre burgeoning interest in and involvement with the abundant Parisian vestiges of the nineteenth-century occult revival, and it was probably equally inevitable, in consequence, that it was largely to unorthodox accounts of spirituality and history that Magre turned in search of inspiration for a way through his own existential predicament.

In his subsequent non-fiction Magre sometimes referred to Philostratus' biography of Apollonius of Tyana skeptically, seemingly fully aware of the fact that it is a work of fiction. Nevertheless, he was more than willing to adapt its fanciful account of Apollonius' life not only into his fiction, as a useful narrative device, but also into the non-fiction he soon began to produce in abundance, some of which is scholarly fantasy offering an unorthodox account of the history of human thought and occult wisdom. Philostratus' account of Apollonius ultimately supplied the first chapter and imaginative bedrock of Magre's idiosyncratic and commercially successful account of the imaginary "Hermetic Tradition" in *Magiciens et illuminés* [Magicians and Illuminati] (1930), and other candidate elements of the imaginary secret history that he was in the process of building play important roles in both of the works contained in the present volume.

One of the supernatural motifs prominently employed in *Priscilla d'Alexandrie* is the Ark of the Covenant, ostensibly removed to Alexandria when the Romans destroyed the Temple in Jerusalem. In the plot of that novel it has to be saved again when Cyril institutes a pogrom against the city's Jews, and it is transported into the desert under magical protection. The protection is question seems to be strangely limited, however, and even more strangely selective, illustrating a perennial problem that writers of supernatural historical fiction and inventors of supernatural secret history always face: that of explaining why, if great talismans commanding occult forces really exist, they seem to be so mercurial and idiosyncratic in their effects. The Ark crops up again in *La Luxure de Grenade*, where it is credited with even greater power—a move that reinforces the problem of explaining why it does not appear to have played any role in known history since the fifteenth-century, in which the novel sets its hypothetical rediscovery.

Magre's interest in the various philosophies contemporary with early Christianity, and their elimination by Christian ideological monopolism, elaborately displayed in *Priscilla d'Alexandrie*, is further reflected in *La Vie amoureuse de Messaline.* The latter novella might have been written after *La Luxure de Grenade*—which is advertised in *Priscilla d'Alexandrie* as a work in progress entitled *L'Ange de la luxure*, a much preferable title that I have restored to the translation—although it beat it into print by a few months, appearing in December 1925. A previous translation of *La Vie amoureuse de Messaline* was published in New York by Louis Carrier in 1929 entitled *Messalina, Roman Temptress*, as an element in the "naughty library" of books, mostly of French origin that were sold under the counter or via mail order. Although that edition is not particularly scarce, it seemed worthwhile to make a new translation for the present series.

As with the sources of the earlier novel, the anecdotes attached to the scandalous life of the wife of the Emperor Claudius are pure fantasy, concocted long after her death by the highly unreliable Roman historians Tacitus and Suetonius, who had a strong political interest in blackening the emperor's reputation. Precisely because they were designed as scabrous slander, however, their inventions offered an account far more exciting than anything that the real woman could actually have accomplished, and presented an immensely useful gift to future writers of melodramatic fiction. Magre's greatly-elaborated version of the story has no scruples about ramping up the melodrama by a further order of magnitude. His introduction of a bizarre cult into which the future empress is initiated in her teens echoes the spell cast on Priscilla as a child by the witch Khepra in the novel version of her story, which eventually renders her a victim of raging lust, although Messalina is far readier to comply with that destiny than Priscilla.

In much the same way that Apollonius of Tyana is introduced into the earlier novel, *La Vie amoureuse de Messaline*, introduces one of his contemporaries, alive and active in this case, thanks to the earlier temporal setting. The character in question is Simon Magus, the Gnostic messianic candidate briefly mentioned in the *Acts of the Apostles*, whose story is more elaborately told, is a hostile and deliberately slanderous fashion, by such Christian apologists as Irenaeus and Justin Martyr. Both those writers relate the legend that Simon traveled with a prostitute whom he represented as a reincarnation of Helen of Troy and a mystical embodiment of Ennoia, or Sophia: an incarnation of divine wisdom. That legend, not unnaturally, is what drew Magre's fervent attention.

Magre must have been familiar with several previous literary dramatizations of the life of Messalina, especially Alfred Jarry's *Messaline* (1901; tr. as *Messalina*) and Félicien Champsaur's *L'Orgie Latine* (1904; tr. as *The Latin Orgy*), both authors having been associates of the Symbolist Movement and with both of whom he had been personally acquainted, at least slightly, when the relevant books were published. Doubtless he wanted to make his own version sufficiently different from theirs for there to be no suspicion of imitation—and he succeeded—but he must also have been concerned to fit his account of Messalina into the evolving historical pattern sketched in his fiction to date. He did that too, especially in his unusual development of the character of Valerius Asiaticus, whom he reinvented as a philosopher cast in a pantheistic mold that was to be elaborately developed in his subsequent works: a model of the sages whose celebration is the purpose of the secret history he formulated, and the antithesis of the embodiment of carnal lust that Messalina becomes, in spite of the prophetic warnings issued to her by Simon.

Simon Magus was to crop up again in Magre's work in the back-story of *Lucifer*, in which he is said to have distributed powerful talismans around the Mediterranean, including the south of France, for the use of subsequent generations of magicians and seekers of divine wisdom, and an elaborated version of the legend of Helen becomes a basis for re-enactment by the black magicians features in the plot. That association of Simon with the forces of evil was, however, the prelude to his subsequent relegation from Magre's version of the great hermetic tradition, and the role as an ancient distributor of hidden talismans in the Midi attributed to him in *Lucifer* was eventually taken over in the back-story of *Mélusine ou le secret de solitude* by Apollonius of Tyana.

Magre's Messalina is possessed by Miphileseth, a version of the god Priapus, and thus becomes an incarnation of lust. The equivalent role is taken on in *La Luxure de Grenade* by Isabelle de Solis, also based on a real historical individual, the daughter of a Castilian nobleman who was captured by raiders from Granada and sold as a slave after her family refused to pay a ransom for her. She became the concubine, and subsequently the consort, of the Sultan of Granada referred to in the story as Abul Hacen; she converted to Islam, took the name Zoraya or Soraya, and had two children by the Sultan. When she was captured during a civil war in 1482, the Sultan gave up his throne in exchange for her life. After his death she and her sons reconverted to Christianity. Her adventures made her famous and she is featured in several literary works subsequent to the present text.

For dramatic purposes, Magre collapses the time-scale of those events in the novel, which finds the fictitious Isabelle still in Seville long after the real one had been in Granada for some years, his plot conveniently obliterates her children and offers a very different account of her life following the strife of 1482. In Magre's story, Isabelle, aided by magic, becomes a powerful symbolic embodiment of Lust, always threatening to seduce the novel's protagonist, Almazan, away from the philosophical studies that he has commenced with Christian Rosenkreutz—studies that are under threat anyway because of the hired assassins that the Spanish Inquisition, headed by Tomas de Torquemada, is sending out to murder the leading freethinkers of Europe.

The plot of *La Luxure de Grenade* might well made up as the author went along, although it might simply have changed direction in the writing; either way, several mysteries and plot-threads deliberately introduced in the early chapters are either forgotten or fizzle out tamely, and Magre seems to have had particular difficulty in following through the supernatural improvisations of his plot. Having brought Christian Rosenkreutz into his story, and imagined a great conflict between rival fraternities dedicated to good and evil, had difficulty determining what might be done with such sweeping elements. The motif of some such ongoing covert conflict was to recur again in his work, most notably and most extravagantly in *Lucifer*, but whenever it comes to specifying how the members of either organization actually spend their time, he seems to have run into limitations of imagination.

When he had finished *La Luxure de Grenade* and looked back at it, Magre might well have seen all too clearly that the most successful episodes, artistically and dramatically—the kidnapping of Princess Khadidjah by lustful lepers and the bloodbath that follows the conclusion of the siege of Malaga—were incidental to the novel's presumed central theme, and that there was very little, in the end, that Christian Rosenkreutz and his pupils could actually do within the presumed framework of known history except remain in hiding, effectively invisible.

Magre was prepared to take the story of Christian Rosenkreutz's foundation of the Order of the Rose-Cross, as detailed in the anonymous scholarly fantasies *Fama Fraternitatis* (1614) and the *Confessio Fraternitatis* (1615) seriously, and to find the character, unlike Simon Magus, entirely appropriate to recruitment into his secret tradition of spiritual wisdom. In order to adapt him to a crucial role in his own scholarly fantasy, as outlined in *Magiciens et illuminés*, however, he changed the chronology adopted in *La Luxure de Grenade*, moving Rosenkreutz's life-story back to the early fourteenth century in order to connect it up with the history of the Albigensians, or Cathars, who had been extirpated in the south of France by a crusade launched by Pope Innocent III.

Magre's version of that crusade became a crucial element of his secret history, imagining the Albigensians as the heirs and prolific employers of the authentic ancient wisdom, which the Church was determined to stamp out at all costs, in order to protect its dogmatic monopoly. Christian Rosenkreutz was made into one of the Albigensians' direct heirs, which required the adjustment in his chronology. I have added a translation of the relevant chapter from *Magiciens et illuminés* to the present volume as an informative appendix, which helps to fill in much of the presumed back-story not spelled out in *La Luxure de Grenade*, albeit in a significantly different variant version.

Like *Priscilla d'Alexandrie* and *La Vie amoureuse de Messaline*, *La Luxure de Grenade* is a violent erotic melodrama, combining the imagery of sex, horror and death in much the same fashion. Although the three works show a certain progressive loss of energy and intensity—an inevitable result of reiteration—*La Luxure de Grenade* is still replete with extravagantly dramatic tableaux possessed of a fine excess. The climax of Princess Khadidja's story is brilliantly effective, easily equaling the similar tableaux in *Priscilla d'Alexandrie*, and its aftermath, in which Emir Daoud unwittingly ferries the Ark of the Covenant to its appointment with destiny, is similarly overwrought in its flamboyance. The portrait of Torquemada offered in the final chapters, although brief by comparison with the portrait of Bishop Cyril painted in Priscilla d'Alexandrie, is deftly effective. It is, however, not surprising that after its slightly faltering conclusion, Magre moved on from that cluster of works to attempt projects of a different kind.

The reasons for that change of direction were undoubtedly connected with changes to Magre's attitude to "the angel of lust" occasioned by the diagnosis of his syphilis, but the inevitable corollary to his change of attitude to the lusts of his inferior self was a corresponding change of attitude to the spiritual quest of his higher self. *La Luxure de Grenade* bids an equivocal farewell to the angel of lust, as personified by Isabelle de Solis, and the protagonists in Magre's subsequent works all prove more resistant to the wiles of her deceptive successors, albeit rather reluctantly in some cases. All of those subsequent works offer their protagonists a more fruitful relationship to true wisdom, as conceived and gradually transformed by Magre, than the one that poor Almazan eventually contrives to attain, and their exploits mirrored a more determined effort to draw constructive lessons therefrom, in spite of the difficulty of so doing. In its fashion, however, *La Luxure de Grenade* laid important groundwork for those works, as well as completing a strange trilogy of exotic erotic fantasies begun by *Priscilla d'Alexandrie*.

Like the tales of disenchantment collected in *Histoire merveilleuse de Claire d'Amour suivie d'autres contes merveilleux*, *La Luxure de Grenade* is a marginally nihilistic work, reflecting in gaudy fashion the *désespoir* that Magre eventually characterized as the ground-state of his soul in the opening paragraph of *La Beauté invisible*. That despair is, however, countered within the text by Christian Rosenkreutz, who is never in any danger of the kind of capitulation to the treacherous beacon light of amour suffered in the earlier story by the cynic philosopher Bigorneau. As well as a conclusion to one phase of Magre's literary productivity, therefore, *La Luxure de Grenade* represented the beginning of another, in which the possibility of intellectual progress was not denied, even though its difficulty, in opposition to everything for which Tomas de Torquemada stood, was fully recognized.

The translation of *La Vie amoureuse de Messaline* was made from a copy of the 1925 Flammarion edition. The translation of *La Luxure de Grenade* was made from a copy of the 1926 Albin Michel edition. The translation of "Christian Rosenkreutz et les Rose-croix" was made from the London Library's copy of the 1930 Fasquelle edition of *Magiciens et illuminés*.

Brian Stableford

THE LOVE LIFE OF MESSALINA

I. Messalina's Face

How can the facial features and corporeal form of Messalina be recovered? What painter could render us that mask of ever-unsated pleasure, the superstition that did not fear justice, but only the thousand divinities prowling in the air and under the ground? Who could resuscitate the long and delicate body, the breasts that, we are told, were high and firm, the inexhaustible loins, and that surge of the entire being toward the physical enjoyment of life?

Her effaced image, which one can seek to divine in cameos of the time, we imagine between two dragons—doubtless lust and death—extraordinarily childlike, rounded, bright and feminine, but with a basic angularity of the face, a solid jaw, not bestial but the jaw of a terrestrial creature, made for eating, biting and shouting. One is also struck by the astonishing luxuriance of the hair. It is a forest that has scarcely left room for the face, which consumes the forehead, and which from the root of the ears, springs forth, overwhelms and undulates, attesting to the fertility of the blood, an unaccustomed richness of nature.

Her quest for rare perfumes, the care she put into composing them herself, the quality of the baths she took, her love of mirrors—of which she had a collection of all forms—attest to an extreme refinement, and the fact that she worshiped her body. The liking for having numerous men as lovers, who were sometimes vulgar, is consistent with the preciosity of her form, and might even be the consequence of it.

As if the animality that she possessed intimately had wanted to mask by its seal the translucent skin imbued with aromas, she bore on the interior part of the right thigh a little tuft of hair that the pomades of all the physicians of the Roman Empire could not succeed in removing.

She was a delicate being whom sensuality held by its chain.

There is no synthesis more perfect than a woman's face. A country, a race and a time are fixed in mobile features, eyes that change and a mouth that creases. But the divine synthesis is partly effaced, nothing remains to us but a reflection. We cannot read in the intensely green eyes, it seems, the secret that all beings hide, which we do not learn sufficiently from the actions of Messalina's life. Did she carry within her the admirable anxiety of true lovers, or did she only pursue the satisfaction of her senses? If she gave herself to so many men, was it because she was seeking one man, the double that one has lost without ever having possessed, the one that ought to render the peace of the heart, fill in the ocean of desire and aid you to realize yourself? Or did she only expect a new form of pleasure from each of them? Did she have elevated goals beyond those that can be reached by the quest of lust? Did she attain the superior secret that certain souls sometimes obtain from the excesses of the flesh?

She was not the monstrous being that legend has created. Her name has remained for us a symbol of evil passions because we are accustomed to consider extreme sensuality, unjustly, as a quality in a man and as a vice in a woman. But the ancients had a conception of amour very different from ours, and if chastity was respected, so was immodesty, and it even had a religious character in certain cases.

Several of Messalina's lovers were poisoned on her orders, others were condemned to open their veins. But it is necessary to remember that, in all times and in all peoples, supreme power has engendered in sovereigns the desire to cause the death of those who are inconvenient to them, especially those they have loved. In any case, everything is relative, and after that of Tiberius and that of Caligula, the reign of Claudius and Messalina appeared to the Romans to be full of justice.

Who will render us the gaze of Messalina, in which there must have been cruelty, the hope of pleasure, scorn for those who were ignorant of its refinements, and perhaps the kind of ingenuous gleam that women have who often fall back into the puerility of enjoyment? Green and black, assuredly, mortal to those that were lost there, pitiless to those who turned away from it, the color of death and of joy, but with perhaps, far away, the light that there is in the eyes of every creature amorous via the senses, the light of the flesh that nevertheless transmits a little of the spirit.

II. The Temple of Priapus

It is beyond the transtiberian region, beyond the quarter of vagabonds, acrobats and animal-exhibitors, that the Temple of Miphileseth[1] is found. To reach it, it is necessary to pass not far from Hadrian's Mausoleum, to emerge from Rome's enclosing wall through the Aurelian Gate, follow the narrow paved road bordered here and there by a few tombs and wretched buildings and turn right on to a stony pathway. That path climbs a woody hill between cypresses, goes past a pond, and ends at the very door of the temple.

No one hid any longer in order to go there, although it was publicly notorious that on certain nights the obscene rites of the god Priapus were celebrated there under his Asiastic personification. The times of the consul Posthumius[2] had revolved and the virtuous measures taken two centuries earlier against the initiates of the Bachanalia were no longer in vigor.

The temple was rather compact and circular in form. It was built in white stone and had a singularly low door that was not precisely in the middle of two columns of disproportionate height. Externally, the statues were disposed of six priapic genii, servants of Aphrodite: Tychon, Conisatus, Orthanes, Lordon, Cydbasus and Pyrges. In the cella of the temple was the god himself, a little to the left, as if a deliberate

---

[1] The 1758 *Dictionnaire historique, géographique, critique, théologique, moral et portative de la Bible* asserts, in its entry on Priapus, that this Hebrew term, found in the scriptures, refers to that god; the same paragraph refers to Priapus' function as a scarecrow. Magre appears to have been the only subsequent writer to have made use of these dubious data.

[2] Posthumius Albinus was consul in 186 B.C. when the Senate took action to suppress popular Bacchic cults, probably for political reasons, although Livy asserts, in justifying the suppression, that cult members had perpetrated horrible crimes.

asymmetry had been the rule to which the ancient architect had conformed.

The god, on a granite pedestal, was carved in the wood of a fig-tree, painted red. He was covered with a goatskin, and necklaces of vine-branches were passed round his neck. He carried a staff in his right hand as a reminder that he had originally served as a scarecrow in the gardens to drive away birds and thieves. The naïve sculptor, who had wanted to give the face a cheerful expression, had only succeed in putting a sad bestiality therein, and, such as he was—the head sunken, almost devoid of a neck, with his enormous phallus, his deformed legs scarcely sketched outside the wood of the tree—he appeared the very symbol of generative matter, of physical amour in its primitive form.

In the posterior vestibule of the temple there was a stairway that led to a basement of sorts. That basement, greater in dimension than the temple, had once served to shelter the mysteries of the Bacchanalia in the time of the persecutions. It now served the priest as a storeroom for offerings, which were numerous.

The priest was a Jew named Chilon. He had repaired the abandoned temple. He had kept the god, but he had given him the name he bore in Palestine, Miphileseth, in order to attract the faithful, for foreign gods were supposed to have more power than the Roman gods. He said that he was the sole representative of the cult founded by Maacha, mother of Asa, King of Judea.[3] In reality, the mysteries of Miphileseth were nothing but a reproduction of the ancient Roman Bacchanalia, but Chilon had created the belief by clever propaganda that he held secrets of pleasure from the Orient and that he could render women fecund or sterile at will. He had grouped around him a small community of men and women who, under the color of religiosity, came to the temple on certain nights to

---

[3] Maacha, the daughter of Absalom and wife of Rehomboam, mentioned in I *Kings* 1-14 and also in passages in *Chronicles*, is actually said there to be the grandmother of Asa of Judah.

satisfy their sensuality. That community included people of all classes—rich and poor, gladiators and pederasts, even senators and matrons, and among the latter was the beautiful Lepida, the wife of the noble Messalla Barbatus, cousin of Claudius.[4]

It was the hour when the boatmen of the Tiber were beginning to light their lanterns among the willows of the river. The setting sun inflamed the monuments. On the field of Mars buccinas resounded, preceding a passage of cataphracts. The sound of chariots, the cries of litter-bearers pronouncing the name of their master in order to cut through the crowd more rapidly, the groans of the sick awaiting their cure under the columns of the temple of Aesculapius, the appeals of tennis-players and discus-throwers, spheromaques, throwers of the arenaire and the triagonal, were all confounded into a single powerful rumor that was about to die down with the descent of dusk.

A flame caused the enormous crystal ball posed like a diadem on the tomb of Agrippa to sparkle. On Caelius Mons, the muses of Thespis and the marble Venus in front of the temple of Felicity were tinted red. The temple of Volupia seemed to enveloped with a more profound silence the mysterious goddess Angerona, who was honored there and whose worship had for its object the silence of the true name of Rome, which ought not to be pronounced.[5]

A light floated for a few seconds over the map of the world that Augustus had had engraved on the portico at Pola,

---

[4] Domitia Lepida (c 5 B.C.-54 A.D.), probably married Marcus Valerius Messalla Barbatus in 15 A.D. or thereabouts; their daughter, the future Empress Valeria Messalina, would have been born a few years thereafter, but the exact date is unknown.

[5] The temple of Volupia, the goddess of pleasure—also known as Volupta—on the Via Nova, where sacrifices were offered to the protective goddess Angerona, is mentioned by several classical authors, including Pliny the Elder and Macrobius, but without further explanation.

to trail thereafter over the Porta Ratumena at the extremity of the Capitoline hill. The colossal statue of Apollo, and those of Jupiter Proedator, Jupiter the Thunderer, Marsyas and Romulus were animated by a luminous life that was communicated to the thousands of statues scattered over all the crossroads and squares and in front of all the temples. Then the shadow seemed to rotate around the umbilicus of Rome and the ruminal fig-trees. The enormous veil of dust that rose from the city like an exhalation, started to fall back slowly.

It was then that, in a stola of somber hue, with a veil hiding her facial features, Lepida emerged from her house of porphyry at the base of the Palatine hill, not far from the Circus Maximus, followed by her daughter Messalina, then aged thirteen, whom she was about to enable to live the first day of her life—for, according to the secret rite of the little temple of which Lepida was a priestess, life only commenced for a woman at the moment when she lost her virginity.

A single slave accompanied them, the one who was to bear the torch without which the return journey through the dark streets of Rome would have been very difficult.

They passed over the Tiber at the Palatine bridge and hastened past the tomb of Numa, because that was a meeting-place for prostitutes and thieves. Sometimes, a passer-by called out to Lepida, mistaking her for a woman seeking to prostitute her daughter. Her rapid stride and the forbidding face of the slave following her corrected the misapprehension immediately.

By the time the stars began to shine, they had passed though the Caesarian woods, left the fortress of the Janiculum behind and were climbing the little path between the cypresses to the temple of Miphileseth.

The priest Chilon was waiting for them on the threshold. He appreciated the full value of the living offering that was about to be brought to him, but he knew everything that he was giving in exchange by means of his intervention with the god. The one whose virginity had devolved to him would know nothing of amour but pleasure. A faculty of enjoyment would be born in her that ought no longer to run dry. She could, by the force of her will, obtain fecundity or sterility, and if it pleased her to be fecund, to have a male or female child, as she wished. She would not know the resistance of a lover. A magical force would incline toward her anyone she might desire.

Near the genii of the threshold, men and women were seated who were chatting and laughing together. Almost all of them knew one another, being regulars, but they had not seen one another for several months, for it was April, and those festivals had not taken place during the winter. They were pouring one another large cups of satyrion, a beverage with aphrodisiac virtues prepared by Chilon.

The cella of the temple was only just large enough to contain the whole crowd, but everyone had to come to touch the statue of the divinity with a hand in order to be penetrated by his force. A dense human warmth soon reigned. It was necessary for several people to go out in order to allow in the donkey, the goat and the rabbit that were to be sacrificed. Two dancing girls began to spin without pause around the statue, accompanied by an Egyptian cithern and singing a kind of amorous lament.

Chilon sacrificed the animals and poured a part of their blood into an immense bronze cup, after which their remains were dragged outside; but an insipid odor had spread. The movement of the dancers became increasingly rapid, and their shriller lament seemed calculated to shred the nerves of the spectators.

Then Chilon took the bronze vase between his knees and made a sign. Lepida handed him a solid gold needle, which she brought every time and left as a present. The members of the audience approached one by one, lifting up their tunic and holding out their bare arm. Chilon pricked each arm slightly and mingled their blood in the vase with that of the donkey, the goat and the rabbit.

One drop sufficed, for in the slightest parcel of blood there are countless magical beings that multiply in being separated from a man, whose power is amplified in being mixed with another blood. Those magical beings are then possessed of a strange life. They act in a singular fashion on the man to whom they belong, actively directing him according to their own law, and because they mingle in the bottom of the bronze vase with the magical beings of other men, they impel their former possessors to come together and fuse. And the blood of the animals, in addition to the pantheistic symbolism, is there to communicate genetic force and bestial instinct.

When everyone had accomplished the rite, Chilon stirred the contents of the bronze vase with a rod made from a mandrake root, and began to pass it from hand to hand. Some with a sensual avidity, others with a pious gratitude, all of them without disgust, drank a mouthful of the red liquid. There were some who wanted to drink again, and from whom it was almost necessary to snatch the vase by force. There were some did not wipe their lips and remained in ecstasy, their eyes raised to the heavens, their limbs seized by tremors.

A few were gripped by sacred fury even before having drunk. They fell to the ground and writhed there, prey to spasms, or went out precipitately and started twirling round a cypress, imitating the chant of the two cithern players.

Night had fallen completely and only three oil-lamps, combined with the serene light of the spring stars, illuminated the temple. Then Chilon launched a ball of colored metal against a gong suspended from a column. Dominating speech and stifled cries, the result of that was a plangent sound with unexpected vibrations, which seemed to penetrate the members of the audience. The laughter became hysterical, veils and tunics were ripped from top to bottom; hair was suddenly loosened, traversed by hands, emitting supernatural sparks. The crowd abruptly poured outside. Lepida felt a strong, familiar hand in the nape of her neck, drawing her away. The exhausted dancers had fallen to the ground, and the noise of their panting breath was audible.

Chilon had kept Messalina beside him. She had remained calm and staring beneath her white veils. He grabbed her arm sharply, but he did not have to drag her. She marched beside him with a firm tread, without suffering from the priest's ugliness, his vile smile and his eyes, so small that no gaze could be encountered there. He took her into the posterior vestibule of the temple and, illuminating it with a lamp that exhaled a nauseating odor of burnt oil, he took her down the few steps to the basement, in order to complete the rite.

The slave who accompanied Lepida and her daughter had attached a sand-glass to his belt. He had lain down on the ground at the place where the sandy path between the cypresses met the road, When the sand had run out he had the mission of lighting a torch and waving it. Thus, doubtless because of the excuses she had furnished to her husband, Lepida was obliged to measure her pleasures. Anxious, but respectful nevertheless of the majesty of the sexual god, she had waited for her daughter crouched before the genius Pyrges.

In the same way that it is irresistible, physical lust is essentially brief. At present, bewildered couples were motionless under the pines. Several were seen who were stretched out on the ground, asleep. There were men wandering, head bowed, as if searching for some lost object.

When Messalina appeared on the threshold of the temple, Lepida ran toward her and covered her shoulders with the flap of her stola. Then they descended the little path swiftly, for the slave was waving his torch in the distance.

A man followed them on all fours, imitating the leaps of a hare and the grunts of a goat, and pretending to deliver thrusts of imaginary horns with his head. When they arrived at the bottom of the path, it was necessary for the slave to drive him away, threatening him with his staff. Then, still on all fours, he started imitating the braying of a donkey, interminably.

Next to Lepida and Messalina walked the two dancing girls and cithern-players. They were glad to take advantage of the protection of the slave, for the streets were unsafe. They chatted together, and Lepida sometimes addressed a benevolent word to them.

Messalina felt an immense pride in having become a woman. She lifted up her veils. She would have liked the dancers to see the blood she had on her knees. But by the latter's conversation, she understood that they were chaste. They had come to Rome with a dance-teacher from Alexandria and were hired out cheaply. They had not participated in any way in the festival of Priapus. They had only seen it as an opportunity to earn the few sesterces promised by Chilon

Messalina was seized by scorn for them, and then anger. If she had dared, she would have ordered the slave to strike them.

In the distance, on the Tiber someone was singing an old Etruscan song. Rome was in repose. But as they passed over the Palatine bridge again, it seemed to Messalina that it was a new city that she had before her eyes. The colonnades of the temples were rows of phallic emblems. The Carmental Gate opened before her like a stone vagina. The statue of the bronze bull in the Forum Boarium reminded her of the animal sexual potency that she had just worshiped and to which she had offered her virginity. The obelisks standing outside certain patrician houses seemed to become animate and to extend toward the cupolas of monuments. She seemed to perceive, in the great display of stones, in the superimposition of porphyry, syenite and orichalcum that was the sleeping city, the voluptuous quivering of the mineral. The frozen splendor of the city was only apparent; the triumphal arches, the porticos, the sacred altars, the temples of the gods and the innumerable dwellings of humans were animated by the same life that warmed her adolescent blood.

And with the same spontaneous gesture, when they passed before the temple of patricienne Pudicitia, they veiled their faces while turning their heads, and extended their left hands with three closed fingers in a sign of aversion.

III. The Emperor Claudius

Claudius was one of those men who can find a precise median between an extreme dementia and an extreme sagacity, an extreme generosity and a boundless cruelty, a superior virtue and a sincere love of evil.

Since his childhood, all his relatives had judged him somewhat feeble-minded. His mother Antonia said that she had only brought into the world a sketch. His sister Livilla, when she heard it said that he might reign one day, deplored the destiny of the Romans, Augustus recommended that he was not to watch the circus games in the imperial box, because he would not have failed to attract attention by his ridiculous postures. He had been struck by all sorts of maladies, which had left him with many defects. His excessively frail legs could not carry his stout body, and he always gave the impression of tottering. His feet were abnormally long, to the extent that when he rendered justice and descended from his tribunal, it was his feet that certain advocates seized in order to retain him. He was precociously bald. His face sweated incessantly. He had large eyes and thick lips—at least, that is what can be distinguished on one of the rare busts of him that we have, which served for a long time as a counterweight in the clock of the church of the Escorial.

His notorious imbecility protected him from the fury of his nephew Caligula, but the latter spared him no insult. He threatened to deprive him of nourishment if he arrived late for supper, and forced him, by way of penance, to run around the triclinium. He was accustomed to fall asleep after meals, when people threw olives and dates at him, and as, when he was woken up, he rubbed his eyes, which were gummed up, people attached worn sandals to his hands in order that he would bear them to his face.[6]

He grew old in the midst of the disdain of his relatives, in the perpetual fear of being assassinated, struggling amid the greatest financial difficulties. But destiny had admirable adversities. In addition to Messalina, Claudius was to have for his wives and mistresses the most beautiful women in the Empire, and when he reached his fiftieth year he was, to his own great surprise and everyone else's, proclaimed emperor.

It was the ninth day before the kalends of February, toward the seventh hour. Caligula, with his friends and freedmen, were going to the theater. He had a stomach ache and he was walking with a slight stoop, which was a bad sign. He stopped in a gallery of the palace where the children of noble Asiatic families were practicing mimes for the theater. He addressed a few familiar words to them; but, the leader of the troupe having said to him, doubtless for the sake of saying something, that it was cold, he felt cold and wanted to go back. As he turned round, the tribune Choerea, who had drawn a concealed sword from his garments, struck him a rather maladroit blow, which only cleaved his jaw. He fell to the ground. Cornelius Sabinus had everyone driven away and dispersed by a few centurions, accomplices of the murder. He came back to Caligula, who was screaming without getting up, and pierced his heart. Then other conspirators, in order to be more certain of his death, approached and struck him thirty times.

There was great disorder in the palace. The Germans of the Caligula's guard came running and started striking at random those whom they supposed to be his murderers. The con-

---

[6] Author's note: "These details are reported by Suetonius." Suetonius was one of the "historians" who did everything possible, for political reasons, to blacken Claudius' reputation some time after his death, including inventing all the scurrilous myths that made Messalina's name notorious, and for which there is no contemporary evidence at all, so this description is highly unreliable.

spirators ran hither and yon, announcing the Emperor's death and pursuing his partisans. A tribune of soldiers, Julius Lupus, had run to kill the Empress Caesonia. Grabbing her four-year-old daughter by one leg, he smashed her head against the wall.

Claudius was among those accompanying Caligula. He fled, but running was difficult for him. He traversed a garden, perceived a little belvedere, and hid therein. His natural pusillanimity must have got the upper hand. Either he was not thinking or, like an ostrich, he was only concerned with shutting his eyes. His body was hidden under the belvedere, but his immense feet stuck out into the garden, under the floating curtain that served as a door. A soldier named Gratus, who was passing by, perceived them, marveled, and pulled them out of curiosity. He recognized Claudius. The latter fell to his knees and begged him to spare his life, but the soldier, who was involved in the plot against Caligula, and had often heard Claudius mentioned with regard to the Emperor's eventual succession, ignorant of what had been decided on that subject and finding himself unexpectedly in Claudius' presence, also fell to his knees, with the result that they found themselves kneeling face to face, both in an imploring attitude.

The soldiers placed Claudius in a litter and transported him to the camp, where he spent the night in dread. But that dread developed the qualities of peasant cunning that he had. Summoned by the Senate, he refused to emerge from the enclosure of the entrenchments, where he found a certain security. He thought that his life was worth more than the treasures of the Empire and he promised fifty thousand sesterces to each of the assembled soldiers, for it is sometimes necessary to engage the future without hesitation in order to save the present. He was proclaimed Emperor and carried in triumph to the Capitol.

Then, at the moment when he had supreme power, he caused his modesty to burst forth as an ordinary man expands his pride. He refused the forename of Imperator. He affected not to decide anything without the advice of the Senate. He witnessed its procedures as a simple assessor. He stood up during spectacles when the magistrates arrived. He celebrated the betrothal of his daughter privately, without any fuss, in order that there should be no talk about him. But the display of a quality as unexpected as modesty rendered him extraordinarily popular.

In any case, modesty is easy in a man of fifty who is dominated by other passions than pride and who has every facility to satisfy them. He had a passion for eating and drinking, and he did so without restraint, at all hours of the day, in accordance with the capacity of his forceful nature. He had a special service of boats that brought him rock lobsters from the costs of Africa, which he preferred to those of Minturno. Sea bass had to be fished in the Tiber and not in the open sea, because going upriver those fish gave their flesh a delicacy of which he was very fond. It was necessary that pheasants came from the frontiers of Phaeacia, goat-kids from Ambracia, tuna from Chalcedonia, moray eels from Tartissus, sturgeons from Rhodes, sausages from Gaul, salted pork from Sequania, and walnuts from the isle of Thassos. He often had salmis of nightingales prepared, but that was out of superstition, because he thought that the flesh of those birds developed the spirit of vigilance necessary to someone who renders justice. He lay down on his back after meals, blowing hard, and a slave had the mission of caressing his throat with a feather to relieve him.

He had, to an astonishing degree, a physical passion for women. He was married four times to wives renowned for a love of pleasure similar to his own. The sagacity of Messalina caused her to offer him new mistresses incessantly. She ordinarily chose beautiful but stupid ones. She preferred them to be slaves recently arrived from Alexandria, Tyre or Antioch, who only knew their native language. Claudius said himself that he did not want to talk to them, but only to touch them. Thus, Messalina kept away any foreign influence.

He loved brothels and often visited them. Although he did not conserve the one that Caligula had installed inside the imperial palace, it was only because of the insistence of his

33

freedmen. He claimed to be certain that women had no soul, as men did, and added that that was what made their bodies so desirable. Having once gone to see a brothel-keeper of his acquaintance in order to see a woman from Armenia whom he visited sometimes, he did not find her in her cell. He sat down on a stool and waited all day and part of the night without showing any sign of impatience.

He had an excessive fear of everything. After a riot, Camillus having written him a threatening and insulting letter in which he exhorted him to renounce the Empire, he immediately summoned an assembly of citizens in order to deliberate as to whether he ought to obey. As soon as he learned about a plot he talked about abdicating. He considered dreams as presages. While he was exercising the functions of judge, a plaintiff came to take him to one side and explained to him that he had seen him in a dream struck by an assassin. Shortly thereafter he designated his adversary in the case as the assassin in the dream, and Claudius immediately condemned that adversary to death for having wanted him dead. He had all those who came to visit him searched rigorously, even the young women, in fear of a weapon hidden under their garments. Once, he ordered that a slave he had in his bed be whipped because she had squeezed his neck slightly during a caress, and he had had the idea momentarily that she wanted to strangle him.

He was very distracted. Several times, he invited to supper men he had recently condemned to death, and, not seeing them arrive at the appointed hour, sent messengers to them to discover the cause of their absence. As he was taking part in a serious debate in the Senate, he suddenly cried out loudly, following a thought of a gastronomic order: "I ask you, can one live without eating eels?"

He was literate. He cited poets and he wanted three letters added to the alphabet, but their utility was only realized during his reign. He judged his life and all things with a certain philosophy, and said that it was in his destiny to have immodest wives.

He loved Messalina for her immodesty and her beauty, and because she was able to subjugate him entirely to her will and thus render him to his veritable destiny, which was to be a slave rather than an Emperor.

IV. The Tiber Boatman and the River Monster

When Messalina was seventeen years old, she acquired a violent taste for the marvelous—for the world was full of prodigies. There was no power or death of an emperor that was not announced by signs. It was asserted that the tower of the lighthouse of Capri collapsed of its own accord in order to inform people that Tiberius would soon perish. That Emperor had had another confirmation of his death in gazing at his fireplace, where extinct and cold ashes had shone all night long, as if they were ablaze.

The story was still told in Rome of the ship's captain Thamus, whose ship had been immobilized one night by the absence of wind not far from Sicily, some distance from an island he did not know. He was eating and drinking on the deck with a few passengers and is crew when he heard a voice calling him by his name: "Thamus, are you there?" He replied that he was, indeed, there. Then the voice said: "Announce this news to men: Pan, the great Pan, is dead!" And a noise of sobs and laments resounded. There was a gravity and a despair, and such a great mystery, in that voice that Thamus and his companions were struck by terror. A breeze having risen, in the morning they interrogated the wretched fishermen who lived on the island. They did not know the name of Thamus. Furthermore, the distance of the ship from the island had been too great for a human voice to cross it.

Thamus concluded that he had been summoned by a god. The story he told of the event flew from mouth to mouth and soon became the object of all conversations. The Emperor Tiberius was very impressed by it. He ordered an investigation in order to establish the veracity of the event. Two senators retraced Thamus' voyage and scholars were consulted as to the meaning of the prodigy. They simply concluded that Pan, the son of Mercury and the nymph Penelope, was dead, and had wanted to communicate that death to the mariner Thamus in order for him to spread it throughout the world. The latter had done that, so all was well.

Those who did not believe in the personal existence of nymphs and gods smiled. There was an Egyptian miracle-worker who recommended navigators to pay the most extreme attention when the winds dropped and the stars appeared, because at the same hour, in the evenings to come, many other gods were about to die.

But it was around her, above all, that Messalina heard talk of supernatural events. Her mother Lepida was the most superstitious and the most credulous of women. When she went out into the garden in the morning and looked to the right and left, it was as if she were reading an open book. A broken branch, the slime that a snail had left on the sand of a pathway, everything she saw, had a meaning. In the company of Tryphene, an old Thessalian woman who had been her nurse and Messalina's, she devoted herself to magical operations. All of them were performed with the objective of obtaining happiness, and above all wealth, for Messalla Barbatus was almost ruined.

The operation that she pursued with the greatest ardor was the birth of the mandrake. For that she took the egg of a black hen, which she pierced, and from which she let out a quantity of albumin equal in volume to a broad bean. She replaced that albumin with sperm and blocked the hole in the egg by allying a piece of virgin parchment to it. Then she buried the egg in a cemetery and covered the soil with the dust of human bones. It was necessary that that be done on the first day of the moon of March and, in the thirty days that followed, she came every day to pour the milk of a she-donkey and vinegar over it.

On the thirtieth day a little monster ought to have emerged from the egg, with a vaguely human appearance, which had to be nourished on lavender seeds, and the possession of which would assure the realization of all desires. Tryphene affirmed that in her youth, in Thessaly, she had succeeded in achieving the birth of many mandrakes; but Lepida, either because the egg was poorly sealed or because the bone dust came from people who had died too recently or too long ago, never succeeded in making a little monster emerge from the soil on the thirtieth day. Her imagination being vivid, she believed in it as much as if she had seen it, and Messalina shared her faith.

In any case, the stars, interrogated incessantly, announced a brilliant destiny. One day, when she went into the temple of Fortuna, Lepida had seen very clearly, in the half-light that reigned there, a statue of Apollo bend a knee before her, which was not a gesture habitual to gods, and had to presage great things. One morning, when she picked up her mirror in order to do her hair, it sent back to her, instead of her own image, that of heaps of gold coins and jewels. She had summoned Messalina immediately so that she could observe the prodigy, but when she came running, the mirror had become normal again and she only saw her young daughter's teeth, avid for pleasure, shining within it.

Even her father, Messalla Barbatus, a limited and precociously aged man, had the apparition of a familiar genius, which he claimed to be similar to that of Socrates. The familiar spirit only came to converse with him when he was alone and drunk on wine. Because of that he drank a great deal, and, for want of any other protection, he was at least able to see the cessation of his wife's recriminations because of his intemperance.

Only Messalina was not visited by any genius. When she passed by, statues remained inanimate, and no supernatural voice called out her name when she was writhing in her bed. Prey to the initial fevers of desire. She even slept the heavy slumber that youth and health procure, and that slumber was never traversed by any prophetic dream. She suffered from that incapacity to perceive invisible things, which was perhaps nothing but a lack of imagination. She sensed aspirations of an elevated order. She thought about entering the college of Vestals, and in order to make her renounce that project it was necessary to remind her that she was not a virgin and that young women who were found to have deceived the pontiffs in that matter were condemned to be buried alive.

Sometimes she went, crowned with verbena, into the Temple of Venus Libitina, which was near the city wall in the quarter of monumental masons, near the place where people went to register deaths. She sometimes stayed there for an entire day, formulating vague prayers, in a disturbance that had no cause.

Finally, one evening, perhaps because she had drunk a beverage prepared by Tryphene, perhaps because there was a full moon and she had gone to sleep with its pale light over her body, she had a dream.

She saw herself in a mute and uninhabited Rome, a Rome that seemed dead, going along the Tiber. She was walking with a sensation of extraordinary lightness under immeasurably magnified temples, alongside theaters and tombs of fabulous proportions. She saw a boat painted red that was coming down the Tiber, and, standing in the prow, a boatman in a black toga, whose face she could distinguish, who was very pale, long and somewhat emaciated. With his right hand he was plying the unique oar attached to the prow, and with the left he was making a gesture that seemed to be telling her to follow him.

Impelled by an irrational force, she started to run. The boat was moving rapidly and she had difficulty not losing sight of it. The landscape changed. There was no longer a city around her; the Tiber plunged into melancholy valleys populated with cypresses and large white stones with inscriptions in a language that she did not know. Then the river narrowed, and in spite of the faster current, Messalina went into the water in order to reach the boat.

She distinguished the face of the boatman more clearly and saw that it had an attractive and noble beauty. His eyes were fixed upon her, but he was still manipulating his oar. Then, as she reached out toward him, the waters opened up and she saw an enormous head surging forth, part-human and part-fish, with lips that hung down over its torso, large webbed hands that seized her under the breasts, and an obscene body that pressed against her own. She did not experience any physical horror, and allowed herself to be tipped back on the sand of the shore.

She was still looking at the boatman, who was rowing away, and she was gripped by a delicious sensation that invaded her on contact with the river monster that was embracing her. Her mouth was crushed beneath a fleshy mouth, and scales doubtless agitated over her delicate body. She dissolved in a carnal wellbeing that she had never known. Her loins sank voluptuously into the sand and the warm mud. In the distance, a fantastic setting sun bathed the horizon with crimson, and before closing her eyes, she glimpsed, one final time, a somber silhouette over the water and a hand that was beckoning to her.

V. Simon Magus

Perhaps it is true that the entire design of an existence shows itself to you in the first years, and the days of the life that flow past subsequently are like the thread that is placed on the template of an embroidery already traced. Perhaps it is true that by virtue of an inexplicable play of destiny, you have around you, at the age of twenty or thereabouts, all the individuals that are to play a role, good or bad, in your existence. They might disappear for some time, in order to return later, and one cannot tell whether they will be minor actors of heroes, but all the characters of the drama or the comedy of which one is to be the center come when the curtain rises to present their faces and state their names.

Thus, it was given to Messalina, shortly before she turned twenty, to see, gathered at the same supper, those she was to love, those she was to hate, and the future emperor that she was to marry.

A man called Simon, who had been nicknamed the Magus, happened at that moment to conquer a great celebrity in Rome because of the prodigies he accomplished.[7] Almost nothing was known about him except that he had come from Gittes in Samaria and that he possessed immense wealth. He lived in a splendid house near the Via Appia, not far from the tomb of Cecilia Metella, where he was served by Syrian slaves he had brought with him, and who seemed to venerate him like a god. Moreover, he said that he was a god, and there were many simple people who believed him, because he accomplished marvelous feats before them.

---

[7] The Christian apologists Justin Martyr and Irenaeus both record that Simon Magus performed magical acts in Rome during the reign of Claudius, and was honored in consequence with a statue on an island in the Tiber whose inscription declared him to be a god. It was the same two authors who laid the foundations of the story of his companion Helen.

41

He was Jupiter in person, some affirmed; but others thought that he was an Asiatic charlatan, so many of whom came to Rome in order to exploit public curiosity. It is certain, however, that he had the faculty of rising into the air by mental effort alone. It was also certain that he did not ask for any money for the cures that he operated, simply by the imposition of his hands, and that if he received any without asking for it, it was only in large sums.

A widow named Calpurnia claimed that, under the pretext of enchantments, he had caused her to give him all her jewels, among which there were pearls from India and emeralds from Persia. She had a great deal of difficulty getting them back, because Simon had assured her at first that a redoubtable genius, which he had evoked, had carried them all away. She had insisted, threatening to bring him before the law. He had then returned larger pearls and emeralds, because the genius had been mistaken in taking them away, and he had advised Calpurnia to keep silent regarding the affair, whose outcome was so fortunate for her. But all the jewels had been found to be fakes. It is true that Calpurnia's life was full of complicated stories of that genre, and one could never derive an argument from what she said.

He was also reputed to have acquired the house in which he resided by exploiting the folly of an old man. The house had belonged to a certain Cethegus, who had grown rich trading in grains and had talked a certain amount of nonsense since the death of his daughter. Cethegus had come to find Simon soon after his arrival in Rome because of his reputation as a miracle-worker and had asked him whether he could resurrect his daughter, whom he had lost the previous year.

Simon had replied that the operation, without being easy, was nevertheless quite realizable. He told him that he had seen it done, when he was young, in Bethany in Palestine, by a Jewish prophet named Jesus, but that was a matter of a man, and he had only been dead for four days. As it was a matter of a woman, dead for a year, he could not proceed with the same rapidity as the Jewish prophet. He asked for time. It even appeared to be necessary for him to install himself in the house where the young woman had lived, in order that the magical practices to which he was about to devote himself would be more operable.

Cethegus went to live in a small villa he had outside Rome, where he waited impatiently for his daughter's return to life. To while away the time, he devoted himself to gardening. One morning, having climbed a fig-tree to collect figs, he fell so awkwardly that he broke his back. He had time, before dying, to give his house to Simon by testament, in exchange for which the latter would bring the work of resurrection to completion. He sometimes affirmed that he had done that, and that the young woman had been resuscitated from among the dead, but he did not provide any evidence of it.

Simon had for a companion a woman of extreme beauty named Helen. He did not hide the fact that he had found her in a brothel in the Paloetirus quarter of Tyre. He said that in an anterior life she had been the beautiful Helen who had provoked the Trojan War. He seemed to love her infinitely. However, the rich Lucius Agrippa affirmed to his friends, when he had been drinking, that he had spent an entire night with her in exchange for a thousand gold deniers. As proof, he gave details of the form of her body, which was splendid, and the pleasure he had obtained, which had been very great—but, apart from the fact that these details were not verifiable, the enormity of the sum paid rendered the story implausible, all the more so as Lucius Agrippa was very miserly. What is certain in that regard is that Simon Magus conceived of amour in a manner different from that of other men. He allowed his mistress to appear almost naked at suppers and sometimes undressed her himself in order to have the guests admire the pure lines of her legs and breasts.

Opinions were therefore divided on his subject. Philosophers who had argued with him on the nature of the gods claimed that there was no man more learned or wiser. One compared him to Pythagoras, another to Plato. A third recognized in him a man who had received the highest initiation in the temples of Egypt. Others said that he was merely an eloquent charlatan, a conjurer more skilful and better endowed than the others.

The numerous cures of sick people that he performed among the poor gave him a great popularity. All of Roman high society sought him out, but he did not seem to desire the company of the rich. He sometimes invited to his home a small number of privileged individuals, and the difficulty of being in their number was extreme. Then, in conversation, he gave very precious prescriptions. One of them made the fortune of the keepers of the wild beasts in the circus for some time. He had indicated, as a remedy against tumors, a grease found on the forehead of lions between the eyebrows; but no dead lions whose skins were removed had any grease in that location. He replied to those who complained that the grease did indeed dissolve immediately as soon as the lions quit the desert.

He also affirmed once, in the market of the Equimelum, that he had caused a woman to enter into an egg, and he had brought her out and given the egg to a member of the audience to eat, to demonstrate that it had not been damaged. Thanks to him, many people knew their future, several madmen had become sane again, and a eunuch had recovered his virility.

One evening, Messalina came to the house of Simon Magus with Lepida. She was to see the image of her destiny there. At that moment Claudius was thinking of marrying her. He had mentioned it to his cousin Barbatus. The latter, whom drunkenness rendered stupid, had left the concern of deciding to Lepida. Lepida hesitated. Should she push her daughter to marry an old, stupid, debt-ridden man of dissolute mores, who had no other title than that of being Caligula's uncle?

Claudius desired Messalina for her beauty, but he knew that he was a mediocre catch. Furthermore, he was feeble and devoid of the will-power to realize what he wanted. Things were at that point when he encountered her at Simon's house.

What struck Messalina most of all when the ostiarius had closed the cedar-wood door again, and when she had traversed the prothyrum and the atrium, was the large quantity of un-known gods that were offered to her sight. They were of all sorts, represented in paintings, sculpted in marble or bronze, or molded in baked clay. Apart from those of Greece and Rome, there were images of Isis, in a transparent robe enam-eled with sapphires, in order to evoke by their blueness the principle of amour that they symbolized, and of Osiris radiant with intelligence. There were images of Horus, raising a magi-cal lotus; Anubis with the head of a jackal, guardian of the places where the dead live; Amon-Ra, the god of the planets; Hermes with his golden wand; and Nephtys, the goddess of damp regions, holding an open seashell.

There was an immense Phoenician Baaltis and a very ti-ny Carthaginian Tanit. She also saw a golden calf similar to the one the Jews had worshiped; a Melkarth with a cunning face; A Set Typhon with stupid features, and the group of the primitive Babylonian trinity, formed of Anu, Sin and Bel. The bird of the tempest, Zu, in bronze corroded by time, swung at the end of a wire. With his twenty-one arms, a Hindu Savitar seemed to be trying to seize her; a Siva fixed her with his thir-ty-three eyes; and a Mongolian Erlik-Khan was dreaming un-der a forest of hair that emerged from all parts of his cranium. And there were also crude idols, animal gods, half-fish and half-bird, gods that were no more than a beak or a tooth, and others that scarcely had any form. There was a conical stone adored by the Thracians, and a red pebble worshiped by the Getes.

When Messalina and Lepida penetrated into the triclinium, Simon Magus was speaking. He had a forehead so high and prominent that he seemed deformed, and little eyes, by turns laughing and grave, in which one could not determine whether they were animated by the most sublime intelligence or the endless desire to seduce. Helen was lying on the same bed as him, and he sometimes parted the jewels she wore around her neck in order to caress her nape. Her hair formed a profound mass around her milk-white face. Her body had a great linear beauty. She was slim and seemed indolent. A slight vulgarity in the joints was the sole defect in her perfect form.

At their feet, on the same bed, was a bizarre being whose sex Messalina could not distinguish at first. He had short curly hair and an adolescent body where, under a violet stola, one thought one could see the rounding of a woman's cleavage. The face was also feminine, but the shoulders and arms were hose of a young man. He could not have been older than fifteen. The hermaphrodite's head reposed between Helen's knees, and he sometimes pressed them with his blue-painted fingernails.

A murmur of sympathy greeted the arrival of the two women. Claudius tried to get up, but could not do it. He had already drunk to excess, and the disturbance he felt on seeing Messalina was not sufficient to allow him to recover his mental grip.

Messalina sensed, posing upon her at such length that it eventually became an embarrassment, the gaze of Caius Silius, a young man who was not yet twenty and was famous in Rome for his beauty. It was a severe, icy gaze, in which an irrational antipathy was manifest. She perceived that antipathy and returned it, forcefully. She was seeing Caius Silius for the first time, of whom she had heard talk, and was glad to find that his reputation for beauty was unmerited. How could she have thought then that the man she started to hate with such force would be the same one that she would love a few years later, to the death?

Valerius Asiaticus saluted them almost without seeing them. His thoughts gave the impression of being far away, and what impressed Messalina was the extraordinary serenity that was disengaged from his entire person. He had just reached his fortieth year, and he had stripped himself of his passions like a tree that, at the beginning of autumn, allows its leaves to fall around it. He had loved life ardently had had enjoyed it in all its forms. Several times a consul, he had had the satisfactions of power. He had known the glory of commanding Roman legions victoriously in Britain and on the borders of Persia.

His fortune was immense and he loved justice. In the name of that justice he had been one of the instigators of the murder of Caligula, and that had contributed to rendering him very popular.

Without him being able to define its origin, however, wisdom had suddenly come to him. The love of women, luxury and the pleasure that success gives had ceased to have any value in his eyes. He only took pleasure in speculations regarding the nature of things or future existence. He had become sober and chaste. It was claimed that he had changed as a consequence of a great disappointed amour for Poppea, the wife of the venerable Scipio, but there was no evidence to support that rumor.

There were also others round Simon, including Theogonius, who had made a semblance of being an imbecile for fear of Caligula, but, by virtue of simulating imbecility, had really acquired it.

Apion, the most learned man in Rome in philosophy and the natural sciences,[8] which he professed before numerous disciples, was holding his chin in his bony hands and staring at him with red eyes, radiating jealousy. The facility he had in expressing himself in all subjects and the science that seemed to be innate in the magician devoured his heart with more force than Prometheus' vulture would have done.

Amaryllis, the aged wife of a senator, known for her gaiety and her extravagance, was fanning herself with a large fan made from ostrich feathers. She sweated perpetually and was prey to surges of heat. She was very assiduous in Simon's regard because she had been struck by the experiment of the woman and the egg and keenly desired, she said, to be enclosed in the little oval palace of calcareous coolness that the interior of an egg must be.

---

[8] Apion (c20 B.C.-c48 A.D.), who taught rhetoric in Rome, did indeed have this reputation. The earliest version of the story of Androcles and the Lion is found in one of his works,

A prince named Arbaces, the companion of the king of Armenia, Mithridates, a refugee in Rome, gave the impression of a bronzed young athlete, who understood nothing of what was said but nodded his head perpetually, while staring at Helen with naïve eyes full of concupiscence.

And that evening, Messalina heard words that were to influence her life forever.

"I don't understand," said Valerius Asiaticus to Simon, "why you tell simple folk that you're Jupiter. You thus make yourself, without any advantage, pass for an impostor among intelligent folk."

"I am Jupiter for those who believe that I am Jupiter," replied Simon, smiling. "There isn't only one truth. There are a great number, in fact, and we ought to present ourselves to men under aspects that differ in accordance with their intelligence. I perform miracles for the simple, I utilize unknown forces for average minds, and for you, Valerius Asiaticus, I merely put my mind in communication with the universal mind. I don't suffer at all from passing for a charlatan, for the opinion of men is of scant importance and I only take account of my own, which is favorable to me. I have been initiated in a temple in Memphis by Pentaour, who had initiated Plato several centuries earlier. He was near to his death and he bequeathed to me the last wave of his wisdom.

"Afterwards, I was part of the community of the thirty disciples of Dositheus in Arabia. I lived among them the life of an ascetic, nourishing myself on herbs, sleeping on the sand, with a stone for a pillow, and seeking divine ecstasy. It was there that I heard talk of a sage in the community of Essenes who performed miracles in public and revealed all the mysteries. It was then that a light came to me. I had learned in my cell in the desert that the nourishment of herbs is poor, that a stone is insufficient as a pillow, and that the ascetic life is not the best one to fortify the spirit.

"I knew that I needed to go into the world in order to teach that the Essene Jesus was mistaken, that men were not yet sufficiently developed to receive the verities that he was revealing, that it would only be much later, perhaps in thousands of years, that the mind would be able to disengage itself from matter and attain, directly, what he called the kingdom of God. I knew that it was important to proclaim that there is a divine path, slower but as certain, in the normal enjoyment of life, which permits the drinking of wine according to one's desire, the admiration of the light of the sun and the extraction of sensuality from the bodies of women.

"I quit the desert, having learned the ingratitude of its sand, and went to find Helen, in order that she would be the instrument of my own pleasure. Thus I am, with her, a perfect example of the truly virtuous man who brings out the moral beauty of joy."

"But how did you know that it was really this one, and not another, that you ought to encounter?" Apion interjected.

"By the knowledge of the secret teachings of Pythagoras, from which almost all our true science comes to us, I learned the means of rediscovering my former incarnations and those of the woman I shall call my double, and who is linked to me in the course of my different lives. I can say that I have known Helen for many centuries. We have made one another suffer mutually under other corporeal forms in Persia, in Chaldea and in lands that have now disappeared beneath the sea. I was only about to be born when her beauty unleashed the Trojan War, alas—one cannot encounter one another in every life.

"In her following incarnation, when she was the beautiful courtesan Parthenis, in Corinth, I was the old philosopher Cleisthenes, already close to death. I was ninety years old when her renown reached me. I lived a long way from Corinth and I had myself taken toward her dwelling in a litter, retaining the breath of life that was escaping me. I remember that I perceived, far way, under a sunlit portico, the patch of her orange veil against the white marble. In vain I pressed the porters. I died without having seen her face, for destiny laughs at us. And she did not understand who the old philosopher was when someone came to deposit me, dead, before her.

"But our ages have coincided in this life. I went to her in a hovel in Tyre where she was prostituting her body—only her body, for her soul had remained purer than the mineral dust that reposes in the center of a diamond. And it is since I have been at her side that my spirit has veritably taken flight, for a fluid escapes from the flesh of a woman, from her color and her odor, which nourishes the spirit of a man."

The wisdom of the ancient ages, however," said Valerius Asiaticus, "has always informed us that it is chastity that is fecund, that the substance of the mind is the same as that of amour, that one only has within one a certain sum of wealth that can be transmuted into thought or sensuality. My personal experience has confirmed that wisdom. For the two years that my campaign in Britain lasted, I acquired the habit of no longer sleeping with a woman. I was also sober in my nourishment and I abstained from wine. It seemed to me that I lost a thick envelope with which I was covered. I have become less material. I think with greater ease and force, and my thoughts have been of a more elevated nature. I am striving to remain in Rome what I was in Britain and I believe that I am better and more intelligent."

"Once again," said Simon, "there is a truth for everyone and even a truth for every age of a man. Perhaps you have only profited from your abstinence and chastity today because you abandoned yourself previously to your passions, in the same way that I had to be an ascetic in order to penetrate the mystery of pleasure. There are two roads toward perfection: that of knowledge and that of amour. Neither the beauty of the substance that one cherishes, nor the moderate satisfactions of the body, is an obstacle to attaining either of them. On the contrary, the love of the material, if it is properly understood, leads to intelligence via the desire to penetrate the laws of what one loves, and to the veritable love of the spirit.

"That is why I surround myself with precious metals, paintings by great artists and fabrics in beautiful colors, I burn Oriental perfumes and have myself served the most savorous wines and dishes. Every day, I admire the beauty of the human body in its most perfect expression, which is that of Helen's body. I rejoice in the joy that she obtains, and same wave of amour that traverses her also penetrates me. Thus I approach more closely the rhythm of life, and I sense that I am more superior every day to what I was the day before."

Many other words were spoken that evening, to which Messalina listened avidly without understanding them completely. She only discerned therein that Simon Magus was glorifying amour and she thought that there was something sublime in the instinct of her body.

The night was already advanced when Simon, having made a sign to Lepida and her daughter to follow him, quit the triclinium. He took them along a marble corridor, raising in his hand a little lamp that cast a blinding light, to a square room open to the sky, the walls of which were covered in fabrics. On one side of the room there was a small ivory door. The room only had two seats, a gilded chair and a silvered chair. On a tripod there was a bronze tray with several colored bottles and powders that cast a phosphorescent light.

Then, Simon having said that he was ready to respond to her, Lepida interrogated him about the projected marriage, about Claudius and about her daughter's destiny.

"I read the future in the images born of perfumes," said Simon, "although one can read it by many other means, if one knows how to measure the relationships that exist between all things. But previsions are never absolute. Human will incessantly modifies events, and one only sees events to come when that human will has already pronounced upon their cause."

He lit a little flame on the tripod and he threw several pinches of powder upon it, which were contained in the bottles. An extraordinarily acrid perfume spread through the room, to the point that Lepida and Messalina could hardly breathe. A thick smoke rose toward the sky. It changed color, becoming green, blue and then blood red as the perfumes also changed, becoming sweet, bitter and violent.

His head tilted back, Simon gazed at the sky and he smoke that was rising toward the tranquil stars. There were confused images, human faces, tumultuous assemblies, chariots launched at top speed, gladiators striking one another, armies on the march, which passed through the swirls of smoke and disappeared, over the changing tableau of the future.

Then, slowly, the smoke became less thick, and dissipated. Simon was now sitting on the ground. Sweat was pearling on his forehead as if he had made a great effort to see the images and to choose them.

"I distinguished Claudius clearly," he said. "He will be Emperor. The causes have existed for a long time, and I would have been able to predict it several years ago. He ought to know it himself. An eagle has announced it to him by alighting on his shoulder in the forum when he was a consul for the first time. For every man is informed of his destiny by a material sign; but he almost never understands it. You, Messalina, I saw less clearly. I don't know whether you were enveloped in crimson or in blood—perhaps both. The six priapic genii were around you and you seemed to be their plaything. Above the head of every woman there is a golden lotus, but they are unaware of it and allow it to perish. Yours was hidden by a sword. You will be fatal to those who love you, unless you have enough strength in your soul to set aside the sword and enable the golden lotus to shine."

The twilight that precedes the dawn bathed the statues of the atrium. Simon's guests were standing up, ready to depart. The voices of slaves were heard who, woken from their sleep, were bringing litters to the door.

Messalina did not take her eyes off Valerius Asiaticus. His slightly blanched temples gave his face a noble gravity. He was gazing upwards at the stars, which were beginning to pale, and did not sense Messalina's attention so ardently posed upon him. It even seemed that he did not have the notion of her existence, for he had talked familiarly to everyone, including Lepida, except to Messalina, and he was standing beside her as if she were invisible.

She conceived because of that a resentment mingled with desire, which only aggravated the disgust in inspired in her by the tottering Claudius, whom it was necessary to sustain by the shoulders in order to get him to his litter.

The young Armenian prince was now walking under the pilasters of the atrium, holding Helen against him. At times he hesitated, and his naïve face was seen looking toward Simon with an expression of anxiety. But Helen was allowing herself almost to fall against him, with an abandonment of her entire being, and her gaze was full of security. Then he squeezed her shoulders, kneaded her breasts with his clenched hand, and sometimes both of them paused to unite their lips, swooning to the point that one might have thought they were about to fall over.

"Nothing is more beautiful than the embrace of two beings who desire one another," said Simon Magus, pointing at them.

And as Messalina was on the threshold, she heard the gross Amaryllis, who was laughing and panting, promising to send him during the day, via his steward, the hundred thousand sesterces that she had promised him in exchange for a pomade against transpiration.

VI. The Nuptial Nightingale

On waking up on the morning of her marriage, Messalina observed that it was raining, and she wept. For her, everything was a presage. The gods, hostile to her union with Claudius, were manifesting it by according it the least possible light. But a butterfly came to make a circuit of the terrace overlooking the garden. It had iridescent wings. That consoled her a little. It was a messenger from Venus. Furthermore, the rain stopped.

She felt a great discouragement at the thought of the night she was about to have. So, all the dreams of pleasure that she had formed ended with this! She belonged to a drunkard, almost an old man, for the sake of a chimerical hope. For Simon Magus might have been mistaken, or said no matter what, according to his whim. How could people think of taking a man like Claudius for Emperor!

Lepida and her old nurse Tryphene came to look for Messalina. An old custom dictated that before the marriage, the young woman should deposit the playthings of her childhood on the altar of the house. The gods were supposed to receive that which she had loved until now. Either by derision or because it was the symbol of her thoughts, Messalina offered a little bronze phallus.

A few hours later, the ten witnesses were gathered before the same altar for the marriage ceremony. The grand pontiff and the flamen Dialis united the hands of the spouses. Messalina felt that Claudius' was soft and slightly moist. Valerius Asiaticus was one of the ten witnesses.

A young woman immediately handed the bride a wheat loaf, honeyed wine and milk, in order that she could make an offering to Juno. Then a ewe was brought, which the grand pontiff sacrificed, and the bile of which he threw before the sacrarium, to signify that all bitterness must be banished between the two spouses.

The house was filled with guests, who could not weary of admiring Messalina's beauty. Beneath her white veils and her crown of verbena she had a tranquil and virginal appearance, but she imagined within herself how Claudius would be during amour; she had the obscene vision of the gestures that he would make, the pleasure that he would take, and the pain that she would endure.

He stared at her occasionally with his glaucous eyes, like balls devoid of light, in which desire struggled with the natural timidity that was the foundation of his nature. He smiled benevolently at the ancient rites of marriage that were accomplished before him, in which he did not believe, but which he respected, as he respected all old customs.

The bride having brought her veil back over her face, three young patricians, designated in advance, approached her and pretended to snatch her from the arms of her mother, who pretended to retain her, one of them raised a whitethorn torch, as a sign of the happiness to come Two young women presented a distaff and a wicker basket. Then all the women began to clap their hands, crying: "Talassio!"—which was the name of a basket for storing wool. The cry was to remind the wife that she must spin for her husband all her life.

All that was done while laughing, as a pleasant game, for the nuptial ceremony had lost the pious gravity that it had had in the early days of Rome.

They waited until the star Venus was visible over the horizon. A servant, who as examining the sky from the roof of the house, shouted: "Stella!" and the cortege set forth through the streets, toward Claudius' house.

The servants were grouped in front of the door. Messalina was presented with a pine torch, an emblem of the hearth, and a vase of water, in which she dipped her fingers, an emblem of purification before a new life. She hung a strip of white woolen cloth from the door catch, which signified that she would be a good spinner, and she rubbed the hinges with a perfumed ointment, which had the property of repelling evil spirits and destroying malevolent spells.

The husband threw a few handfuls of sesterces to the children and beggars who were gathered, and then lifted Messalina in his arms, for the feet of the bride ought not to touch the threshold of the house when she enters it for the first time. But Claudius, who was never very solid on his legs, ridiculously thin for his stout body, and who was troubled by the attention of which he was the center, staggered and was about to fall on to the mosaics with his burden.

Everyone ran forward to sustain them, and it was Valerius Asiaticus who extended his hand to Messalina. She disguised her anger. She squeezed the hand that had taken hers. She tried to plunge her gaze into that of Valerius—but no; he was looking elsewhere, above her head; he was holding her hand but he did not see her.

Then the meal commenced. It was served in the triclinium but, as there were more than eighty guests, the tables and beds extended on to a terrace that overlooked the garden. Lanterns were suspended from the trees and rose petals covered the ground. The meal was made up of several courses, which rendered it extremely long. The rarest dishes succeeded one another without pause, and a very old Falernian flowed inexhaustibly from amphorae.

Claudius smiled at everyone blissfully, but he was trembling internally. The desire to possess Messalina, and the emotion that the thought of her young body caused him to experience, were replaced in him by the dread of his own awkwardness. The purity of her face, under the flammeum, and the disdainful attitude that she affected, completed his disturbance. He could not help thinking, on seeing so many guests assembled around him, how the simple whores that he was accustomed to frequent gave him a pleasure more exempt from preoccupations, less noisy and more certain.

Valerius Asiaticus was placed almost facing Messalina. He did not drink and scarcely ate. Two or three times, Messalina spoke to him, and he replied politely, but seemed not to bring any interest to that response, from very far away, and without meeting her gaze.

Meanwhile, spirits warmed up. As they poured the wine, the slaves joked with the guests, as usual, and the latter replied to them. One Greek slave, renowned for his joy and his coarse sallies, and also for his special mores, went from table to table amid laughter. Cymbal players chosen for their beauty and who were scarcely clad, had the mission of waking up, by striking their instruments, those guests whom good cheer had rendered drowsy and who were falling asleep. They ran hither and yon, spreading sensuality as well as noise, by the movements of their bodies.

Then came the moment when the actors and jugglers hired to cheer up the end of the feast appeared on the part of the terrace that was still free. First there were the Homerists who took turns in reciting Homer's verses; but that was too grave a distraction and they were rapidly dismissed. Then there was a dancing bear; but the beast was too close to the beds and a few women were frightened. Then came the Cinedians, a little troupe of dancers reputed for their grace and beauty; they danced, and everyone exclaimed, for the end of a meal predisposes one to admiration, and they were offered wine in the cups that were on the tables.

Narcissus, one of Claudius' freedmen, had reserved for the end the young Syrian Ithamar, who was only twenty years old, whose body was marvelously well-made, and who possessed the talent of imitating a nightingale to perfection. He laughed innocently and showed dazzling teeth. His imitation unleashed enthusiasm and he was made to repeat it several times.

The guests began to get up and spread out in the garden. Abruptly, Messalina understood what it was that attracted her to Valerius Asiaticus. With his pale and long face, his simple and somber toga, he resembled the Tiber boatman in her dream, who had summoned her with his hand and had drawn away in his boat. Had the dream not had a prophetic quality, and was not Valerius the man to whom she should have attached herself?

She was now standing in the triclinium, full of tumult. She took a few steps to catch up with him, wanting at least to exchange a few words with him. She was close to him and she said to him, in a low voice: "Valerius!" Perhaps he did not hear, for he drew away without responding.

A rage seized her. She respired forcefully the aromatic odors that the day's rain, followed by a heavy, stormy heat, had caused to emerge from the soil of the garden. Spilled wine, the buzz of speech and the ambient drunkenness intoxicated her. She pictured with clarity the frightful mouth of Claudius, who was about to moisten his lips, his thick, naked body, which was about to crush hers. She was possessed by a blind fury for pleasure, for immediate satisfaction.

She arrived at the extremity of the terrace and her quivering fingers touched the sculpted spindle trees that bordered it. Then she remembered the god to whom her mother had once consigned her, and the temple after the path through the cypresses, on the hill. In a low voice, she formulated a prayer.

"O Priapus, to whom I offered the young blood of my virginity in the person of your priest, you who preside over couplings, you who makes beasts in rut cry out in the spring and young women writhe with desire beneath the deerskin of their beds, you who are rustic because you are symbolic of the force of the earth, you who are hairy and horned because an animal genius is within you, you whose attributes are as enormous as the unlimited desire of the inflamed bodies that summon you, O Priapus, grant my prayer! Give me today the pleasure that I need! Let me be tipped back, folded, rolled and penetrated in the arms of a young man whose skin is smooth, whose teeth are healthy, and whose breath is pure. If, by a miracle, I obtain what I desire, I will confess that you are the greatest of gods, I will make an offering to you of my days and I will, as a pledge of my fidelity, give my body once again to your old priest, on the beaten ground, in the basement of his temple, where he has already had the first movement of my loins."

Lepida had approached her. The epithalamium was being sung. Messalina followed her mother into the nuptial chamber.

But Claudius had desired so much to acquire courage by the absorption of Falernian that he had, in fact, acquired it. He talked loudly, his eyes bulging, seemingly ready to fall over. He staggered as he walked, in the midst of his friends' discreet jokes, leaning on the shoulder of his old companion in debauchery Athenodorus, who exhorted him in a low voice to put on a good face and not to appear drunk.

In the chamber, between a statue of Juno and a statue of Venus, the bed was set on an ivory pedestal. Claudius had forgotten the words that he had promised himself to pronounce, by which a tender delicacy would have been translated. He simply took off his toga, and then his tunic, and sat down on the bed, drawing Messalina to his side brutally and tipping her backwards.

She had the part of resignation that all women have, whatever their nature, at such moments. But Claudius, with his bald cranium and his fat belly, appeared to her so ugly that she closed her eyes in order not to see him.

She felt his large hand, which parted the folds of her stola and brutally, with a single thrust, tore her linen chemise from top to bottom. Then that hand moved over her, caressing her breasts, and it had the effect on her, with its moist softness and its slowness, of a huge slug moving over her. But to her great surprise, the caress of the hand became slower, more inanimate; there was something mechanical about it, something dead. It became heavy, and eventually stopped.

Messalina opened her eyes slightly. Claudius was asleep.

All the sounds of the feast had ceased, one by one: first the epithalamium, then the laugher and the adieux of the guests, and then the calls of the slaves, the barking of the dogs and the clicking of doors.

Messalina got up, animated by a confused hope. She went to the window and respired the warm night air avidly. The lanterns in the trees were extinct. Only the light of the stars cut out the shadows of the trees over the sand of the paths.

There was a birch whose white trunk was gleaming near the fountain, and that moved her, as if she had seen a melancholy young woman walking beside the water with an anxiety similar to her own.

She made sure that Claudius was profoundly asleep. His respiration was heavy and noisy. She threw the pleats of her stola over herself and leaned on her elbows, contemplating the glimmer of the coral pink powder that had been sprinkled on the gravel of the paths.

A nightingale started to sing somewhere in a tree and she lent to that music a tone of sadness that she had within herself.

But in an opposite direction another nightingale started to sing, and she shuddered. There were two nightingales in the garden, but the voice of the second was not exactly similar to that of the first. It bore a strange resemblance to the imitation of the bird's song that the handsome Syrian had made during the meal.

Messalina leaned over and scrutinized the garden. In the direction from which the second nightingale's song was coming, she distinguished a human figure propped up on the lawn. Doubtless the young Ithamar, inconvenienced by the heat, had emerged from the slaves' room, where the performers were spending the night, and had come to lie down in the garden. He was awake, and imitating the song of the nightingale. But his voice did not have the sadness of the voice of the bird. It was like a magical appeal, an incantation of all nature, a hymn whose meaning Messalina perceived.

O Priapus, it's you who are granting my prayer! she thought.

The young man had been sent by the god.

She opened the door very quietly, but without excessive precaution, since Priapus was protecting her. Semi-naked, she walked into the garden.

She did not say a word. She set aside the veil that scarcely covered her and lay down beside the Syrian, placing her two white arms on his bronzed shoulders. She drew him toward her and weakened on sensing the warmth of the man's blood against her breasts.

And there was only one nightingale singing any longer on Messalina's wedding night.

VII. The Chain of Lovers

She submitted to her husband's caresses. She grew accustomed to them. She sought better ones. She had two children. By means of those children, by the science of pleasure that was innate in her and that which she was able to acquire, she dominated the feeble Claudius.

Then circumstances brought the latter the Empire.

It requires a marvelously tempered soul to resist the sudden advent of power. A individual struck by success thinks that his own value has been previously misunderstood and, instead of being astonished by his good luck, he convinces himself that immanent justice has just become manifest.

The certain sign of baseness is the rapidity with which one becomes accustomed to immense wealth or immeasurable power that has just suddenly come to you. A true sage suddenly borne to a throne would surely keep his simple mores and modesty.

It was not satisfied pride by which Messalina was intoxicated, but the joy of satisfying all the caprices of her flesh. The Empire was, for her, a means of enjoying the men she desired, of having by terror those who might have refused her, and of savoring in complete security the amour of those attracted by the prestige of her incomparable beauty.

She was twenty-five years old and she exerted the kind of fascination that bodies ever avid for the enjoyment of amour emit. It was like a material fluid spread around her, a wave that bathed those who approached her. The green light of her eyes had lost its original softness and had taken on a hard gleam. She looked all men in the face, even old men, with an embarrassing insistence, as if to estimate the quality of virility of which they might be susceptible. She had become imperious and violent, but she had crises of weakness, moments when she became similar to a child, and when she had an irresistible need to be commanded, and even struck, by the strong hand of a master.

She also had great surges of tenderness. Then she desired affectionate words, a shoulder against which to huddle, and she wept for a long time with the regret of not having belonged to one man all her life. But she was ashamed of those crises afterwards and hated those in whose company she had had them.

She wore the nail of her index finger very long, painted with care, and had the habit of rubbing it incessantly, especially when she was bored, with a little golden brush that was in a case suspended around her neck. She liked to stripe the skin of her slaves with that fingernail, playfully, or that of her lovers, lustfully

She did not depilate her body, with the exception of her armpits, in accordance with the Greek fashion then in usage, because she had heard a Jewish physician say that human vitality breathes in the air through the down.

Hundreds of female donkeys were maintained for her in the palace. She bathed in their milk, which, she believed, gave her skin firmness.

Her nurse Tryphene was charged with composing aphrodisiacs for her. She drank them and made others drink them, but never found their effect on men efficacious enough.

She instituted a strange competition among painters and men of science with a large sum of money as a prize. It was a matter of finding an ointment that could completely efface from her skin the streaks and bruises that she loved to see imprinted there by those to whom she gave herself.

She only liked women in the measure that that was necessary to distract Claudius. She made them think that she loved them and gave the impression of sharing their pleasures, but it was only to avoid sharing that of Claudius. She was never jealous of their beauty because she felt that her own was always more perfect. She only attached two slaves to herself, Calpurnia and Cleopatra, by both of whom she was loved, but who were nevertheless to betray her. She often said to them, in moments of confidence, that the only thing that made living worthwhile is the moment when a man is on top of you, uttering the grunts of a savage beast, while he takes his pleasure.

She had Narcissus for a lover, but only once, even though he was neither handsome nor agreeable. The reason was that he was incessantly around her to take her orders, that he was obsequious and approved her in all things. Having retained a bad memory of that experience, however, she often mocked him for being a poor lover, for which he bore an eternal grudge against her.

She gave herself to Lucius Vitellius, who inspired disgust in her, because of the admiration he had for her. He had asked for one of her brodequins, which he always carried on his breast, to which he addressed his prayers. She only found out later that adoration was a form of dementia in Vitellius. When he had returned from Syria, where he was governor, he had only dared approach Caligula with his head veiled, had circled around him three times and had fallen down, as if dazzled. He sometimes lay face down before Claudius in spite of the latter's protestations. He had little gold statuettes of Messalina and Claudius in his house, which he worshiped, and he even had the freedmen Narcissus and Pallas sculpted, whom he worshiped in the same way.

She gave herself to Pallas because, by dint of administering and stealing the wealth of the Empire, he had become its richest man, and he rendered her services.

She gave herself to a lanista of gladiators because of his strength, to Vinucius, Claudius' nephew, because he was paltry, to Sabinus because he had long hair and she liked the perfume of verbena that it gave off, to another because of the color of his eyes, another because of his hands, which had the particularity of always being hot, another because he had a hairy body, and another because of his smooth skin.

At Baiae, after having bathed in a solitary spot in the presence of her maidservant Livia, she gave herself to a passing fisherman, because he was passing.

And yet she never stopped thinking about Valerius Asiaticus. When she closed her eyes, she saw his pale face emerging from the shadow. She imagined how he would be, losing his noble gravity in her arms. She took advantage of every embrace with a new lover to enjoy in imagination the familiar lover that she had not had.

She wore a long Greek chain in sculpted gold around her neck and marked one of its links every time she had experienced a man's caress. She laughed with Livia when she put it around her neck and she exclaimed "How light it is! What a little thing pleasure is!"

It was only later that she was to experience its crushing weight.

VIII. The First Encounter with Death

Mnester was the man that Caligula liked to kiss on the lips in the hippodrome, in front of the assembled people. His celebrity in Rome was very great, and did not only come from the amour that he had inspired in the Emperor. Phoenician in origin, he had learned the art of dancing in Tyre and Antioch, and that of pantomime. He was both a clown and an actor. He danced on a rope, executing perilous leaps, and excelled in the art of producing laughter by grotesque imitations of the illustrious heroes of literature and history. He had composed little scenes in which he was by turns Ulysses, Achilles Menelaus and even Helen. He appeared, dressed as a woman, covered in jewels, and mimed the gestures of amour.

As laughter is the great of forces, he was adored by the people, especially by the crowd of courtesans, procurers and all the servants of debauchery who lived in Suburra and the outlying districts. He was carried in triumph after performances. Several women had died of amour for him. He was rich and he lavished his money freely on parasites and catamites.

He was cynical. He did not hide the exclusive amour he had for men. Many had ruined themselves for him. He had never been handsome, but over his face, with its overly prominent nose, after a bored lassitude, passed a vulgar joy that was fascinating. He was past thirty and becoming sensibly fat, which was driving him to despair, when Messalina saw him and desired to know him.

At that moment she had just had a house furnished not far from the Circus Flaminius that was supposed to belong to her servant Livia, but was actually to serve for her rendezvous. It was there that she received Mnester.

She knew his reputation and doubtless did not expect too much from him. Mnester did not count on vanquishing the repugnance that the feminine form inspired in him. He glorified the beauty of the Augusta without attempting to profane it. Messalina treated him as a prince of vice. The two of them, passionate for flesh, obsessed by the same sexual image, found that they were close to one another by virtue of the community of their desire. A kind of amity was born between them, based on the mutual services they could render one another. Messalina did not seem to be offended by Mnester's physical coldness for her. She was charmed by his cynicism, and by the stories of his debaucheries. She confided in him, and a sort of pact was concluded.

Mnester returned to Messalina's house a few days later, before sunset, with young Titus, of the family of Domitius. Titus was scarcely fifteen, and had no great intelligence, but had a troubling beauty that Mnester appreciated.

Mnester offered Titus to Messalina as one offers a present to seal a nascent amity. All three remained together late into the night, and it was necessary for Livia to insist to remind her mistress of the necessity of returning to the Palatine.

She had Titus return alone thereafter, and took a liking to his youth. She even had an attachment for him, of short duration.

But it happened that Titus, who had no experience of life and was dazzled by Messalina's beauty, denied the tastes that had driven him thus far to seek out adolescents of his own age and had taken him into the arms of Mnester. He proclaimed to his friends the discovery he had just made of the woman, boasted about the body that she had revealed to him, omitting no intimate detail, and taking pride in the woman's illustrious name. All the young debauchees in Rome were soon informed of that liaison. Mnester, whom Titus neglected, informed Messalina of the danger she was running by virtue of those rumors, which might reach the ears of Claudius. At the same time, Lepida, who had been warned, came to find her daughter and beg her to be careful of her safety.

Messalina thought she was in danger. She deliberated with her mother as to what to do, and they fell into agreement that the best means of putting a stop to everything was to make Titus disappear.

There was then in Rome, living on the first floor of a commercial street in the vicinity of the Aventive hill, a widow named Locusta, who was the perfect image of the Roman middle class. She had a life regulated to the point of appearing manic to those who knew her. Either to economize on lamp-oil or by force of habit, she went to bed exactly an hour after sunset. She made an exception to that rule twice a week; on those days she received her lover, who was as punctual as her. He was a functionary in the administration charged with receiving notification of deaths, and lived on the far side of the city. Twice a week he came to take the evening meal and spend the night with his mistress. Invariably, both of them went for a walk the next day in the Forum Pistorium, and they went as far as the Porto Navale, at a slow pace. Then they separated, and Locusta went to buy vegetables at the Favaria market: the beans and chickpeas that composed her exclusive nourishment.

In the middle of the day, she went out for another hour with her dog, but—something that surprised her neighbors—the dog was often different. That perpetual renewal of the dog was characteristic, the only singular thing in such a settled existence.

However, that slave to the rule she had traced for herself, that lover of habitude, that good employee of life whose closed visage reflected neither curiosity nor hope, exercised, with method, application and intelligence, the curious profession of poisoner.[9]

---

[9] The alleged career of the ancient Roman poisoner Locusta was detailed—long after her supposed death—by Tacitus, Suetonius and Cassius Dio, but the later accounts probably copied the first. Her name became legendary in nineteenth-century France because Alexandre Dumas used it as the nickname for the poisoner featured in *Le Comte de Monte Cristo*. Typically, Magre's characterization is greatly embellished.

Who knows where she had learned it, and the origin of that particular genius? Perhaps the desire to see the disappearance of her first husband, who had beaten her and ruined her, was the basis of her science. Perhaps a taste for extinguishing life by means of herbs and powders was innate in her.

Her clientele, initially not very numerous, only increased. She had important protections, for those who made use of her had no interest in her being disturbed by the magistrates. When she was in vogue she demanded high fees, but only from the rich. She was good to the poor and concocted poisons for next to nothing when those who came to find her had no fortune and appealed to her good sentiments.

She prepared beverages of all sorts. There were some that provoked death in an instantaneous fashion, but that was not always what was requested of her. In many cases, a slow death that appeared to be natural was preferable.

For the cruel, to whom the death of an enemy seemed insufficient, she had found a blue powder that caused frightful suffering without attacking the sources of life. For women jealous of the beauty of a rival, she had a paste that it was necessary to have them chew in a bonbon, and which deformed the jaw after having made the teeth fall out. She had one perfume that provoked blindness and another that communicated the vital properties of a dog when it was breathed in, which made one walk on all fours, bark and raise a paw like the animal in question.

She claimed that certain minerals had a hidden force within them that, if one succeeded in disengaging it, rendered a man similar to them by virtue of a law of analogy that she was seeking. She said that she would soon find a tenuous powder that would change those who respired it into a kind of soft stone. It was by means of a poison of that nature—at least, so she said—that the woman mentioned in Jewish books had been turned into a pillar of salt. She did not have time to perfect that discovery.

The functionary who registered deaths only found out about the mysterious activity of his mistress later. How did he explain the visit of a peasant woman carrying a box of scorpions and various pebbles? How was he not chagrined by the incessant deaths of the dogs that he walked in the morning? Doubtless he was an insensitive man devoid of curiosity. When, because of the numerous visitors who came, Locusta no longer hid from him what she did, he showed the courage of a hero in continuing to eat, drink and respire perfumes in her company.

He had no reason to complain. The functionary nourished the dreams of wearing jewels. He had rings on all his fingers. He became an important man. No malady without a cause and no deformation of the jaw ever afflicted him. That was because he was beloved, and knew it.

It was the violet powder, the one that transmitted instant death, that Messalina obtained from Locusta.

Tryphene came that day to the house near the Circus Flaminius. In growing old she had acquired a hideous appearance. When she opened the door to Titus, the latter thought he was seeing Death in person, but he did not run away, and he went into the room where he expected to find Messalina full of desire.

She was accustomed to wait for him, stark naked, on the crimson cover of the bed. In order that he would not suspect anything, she had not changed that habit. She welcomed him with the same smile and a more lascivious movement of the body, but she never lost sight of two cups that had been prepared, one of which contained the poison. She remembered stories she had heard told in which, in analogous circumstances, by virtue of mistaking the cup, it was the one who wanted to give death who received it, as if divine justice had wanted to punish him.

In order not to make a mistake, she insisted that Titus drink right away, in spite of the pleasure she would have had in embracing him.

To her great surprise, the effect of the beverage was not immediate, and before she had had time to reflect, the young man had taken off his clothes and thrown himself upon her. She abandoned herself to him with a furious lust that was full of horror, but without neglecting to protect her mouth from his because of the poison that he might have communicated to her in his saliva.

She had never yet attained the voluptuousness she experienced. She had never surrendered to it profoundly. She sensed it, and redoubled her ardor, and it seemed to her that her soul was magnified because she was playing the role of divinity for someone. She was the Fate who has marked the inexorable hour of destiny. She was the divine Aphrodite who changes dolor into pleasure, pleasure into joy, and embellishes the last minute of the man who has loved her.

Titus disengaged himself from her arms and sat down on the bed, bent double, his head almost touching his knees. He did not have time to speak. He gasped several times, as if he could no longer breathe, palpated the air with his hands as if to recapture the life that was fleeing him, and fell to the floor, having suddenly become astonishingly heavy. His face was very red and an immeasurably swollen scarlet tongue emerged from his mouth.

Tryphene who was listening, heard the noise of his fall. She considered Titus, sniggering, leaned over him, pointed her bony finger at his face and said: "Aha! There it is, the tongue that talked too much."

Scarcely had she pronounced those words than Messalina seized a solid gold amphora, half full of wine, and brought it down on her head swiftly. Tryphene having made a movement, the sculpted handle of the amphora, instead of her skull, which it would have broken, collided with her neck at the birth of the shoulder, and she fell, stunned. Messalina leapt upon her, put a knee on her chest, and squeezed her throat. She contemplated the old woman's face momentarily, rendered more hideous by fear, and then her free hand seized the cup from which Titus had drunk, in which there was still a little wine, and she tried to introduce that wine into Tryphene's mouth, saying; "You won't insult anyone with your tongue anymore."

The other, understanding her intention, struggled with the strength of desperation, and they both rolled over the dead young man. Messalina, who was still completely naked, sensed the body of her lover, still warm, on her skin.

Her nudity, the dead man sticking out his tongue, and the old woman who was struggling, suddenly filled her with disgust and fear. She perceived the horror of the situation and released Tryphene, who got up and fled, without crying out but making a noise with her chattering teeth.

Then, a kind of modesty gripped Messalina. She picked up her stola, which had fallen on the floor, and, as far away as possible from Titus' body, flattened against the mosaics of the wall, she wrapped herself in the folds of the fabric, her eyes staring at the face from which beauty had fled forever.

IX. The Friend of Flowers and Trees

The Gardens of Lucullus were enveloped in mystery. Above the high walls that surrounded them, the foliage could be seen of a singular tree such as had never been seen in Rome. It was said that there were temples to unknown divinities there in which prodigies were accomplished, kiosks whose doors opened and closed of their own accord, and statues that could descend from their pedestals, walk and run.

At the back, behind an enclosure of centenarian oaks, it was known that there were immense aviaries from which clucking, croaking and chirping emerged incessantly, mingled with the flutter of innumerable wings.

The gardens enclosed all the essences of plants and flowers that grow on earth. In order to seek out certain seeds and bring back certain cuttings, voyagers had traveled the burning deserts of Africa where lions live in thousands and savage men have never seen the fascia of Rome. Others had traversed Germany, far beyond the region of icy forests.

The gardens were superimposed in stages, they had terraces, staircases, flower-beds that made deigns, impenetrable arbors and paths between old box-trees that intersected so eccentrically that one could wander there for a long time without finding one's location.

Valerius Asiaticus, to whom they belonged, had Greek and Egyptian gardeners to cultivate them, and had even brought a family from the banks of the Euphrates who had conserved through the ages a Babylonian tradition for the cultivation of lilies and giving them an extraordinary grandeur. He loved his gardens passionately, as one loves beauty. Sometimes he walked there for entire days, listening to the life of vegetal forms, admiring the lines that he had succeeded in giving them. In the evening he had his ivory bed carried under the portico of his house, and contemplated indefinitely the long rows of yew trees, the sandy pathways that penetrated like silver streams between the dark spindle trees, and, further away, the mass of cedars, plane trees and ebony trees that made a noise like a multiform and multicolored sea, endowed with its own soul.

He remained there, solitary, long into the night, and after a life agitated by wars and by amour, he was reputed to be detached from all things and no longer to have in his heart anything but the infinite tenderness that his gardens inspired in him.

The mystery of the gardens, into which Valerius Asiaticus only admitted very rare intimates, only augmented the desire that Messalina had to get closer to the man about whom she now thought incessantly.

Claudius found Valerius boring, because he ate little and did not drink. He was intimidated by his gravity and refused to invite him to the palace. In vain Messalina had gone to the baths to Baiae hoping to encounter him. Scarcely had she arrived than she learned that Valerius had just left abruptly for Rome, and someone had given, as a reason for that return, a renewal of his amour for the beautiful Poppea, the wife of the old senator Scipio, whom he had once loved.

She was seized by rage at that idea. It was as if the sea and the sky had faded before her eyes. She went back to her palace on the Palatine rapidly.

Poppea was one of the most beautiful of Roman women. She was married to an old man who pushed timidity and mildness to the point of imbecility, and who adored her. She was reputed to have lovers and to seek pleasure. Her name alone was a cause of irritation for Messalina because she knew that she was compared to her, when people discussed the perfection of a body and the beauty of a face.

The slave had scarcely announced to Valerius Asiaticus that the Empress wanted to see him than she was standing before him.

Introduced into the room that Lucullus had called Terp-sichore's Room, where there were seven pillars whose base was rounded in the form of a lyre, instead of waiting for the slave she had followed him and had reached the terrace behind him.

She therefore took Valerius by surprise, and she was able to see that he was weeping.

The pretext that she had chosen for her visit was the recent decision that Valerius had made not to return to the armies in Germany and to disinterest himself henceforth from public affairs. She had come to express an official regret on behalf of the Emperor, but she was no expert at dissimulation. She immediately asked him the cause of his tears.

And Valerius Asiaticus, his eyes staring far above Messalina's head, replied: "I'm weeping because I've glimpsed the truth too late. I know that I've lived until now in error, and I also know that I don't have time to repair my faults during my life."

"What error and what fault?" said Messalina, putting all the warm tenderness into her voice of which she was capable, and making it understood by the creasing of her eyelids and the moue of the lips that in her, everything was forgiveness for him.

"In the confines of Syria and Persia, and then in Britain, I became illustrious in war. You must know, like everyone in Rome, the extent to which I risked my person. At the head of a century of cavaliers, I departed as a scout, without a breast-plate and lifting the vexillum high, which made me the target of arrows. I excelled in striking with the lance and, by an ever-renewed coincidence, I killed at the first stroke. I remember the surprise and delight that the fall of a man gave me, his last cry, and the blood that I saw dripping from my weapon.

"I organized the ballistas and scorpions personally before besieged towns, I place the first of the ladders against the ramparts, and when I fought with the sword, each of my thrusts carried. By virtue of negligence and fatigue, I did not prevent my legionaries from burning innocent women and children along with houses; by virtue of ennui I witnessed tortures of prisoners so cruel that pain made a visible aureole around their bodies, like the one seen around the priests of Eleusis at dawn when the mysteries have just been celebrated.

"But now, all the actions of which I was proud are a subject of remorse. I'm ashamed of having struck men and having taken their lives, and I feel as different from the man I was then as water differs from stone and a forest from a sandy expanse."

"There is a legitimate joy in killing one's enemies, and I don't see why you regret having done so," aid Messalina, drawing closer to him and smiling at Valerius' puerility. "I was raised in the fear of the gods, but every time I have heard philosophers in dispute. I remember that they always concluded that the pleasure we obtain on earth is the only certainty. I love pleasure. One can only attain it with two, and there are so few men with whom I would like to attempt that pursuit!"

They had advanced, while talking, as far as the balustrade of the terrace. Messalina leaned on it. She seemed to be dreaming, and placed her hand negligently on Valerius' shoulder, as if that familiarity were unconscious.

But Valerius, following his own thought, said: "It's in Asia that I received the truth, as one receives a precious stone of which one does not know the value, and which one carries on one's person believing it to be a vulgar pebble, until the moment when one looks at it in the sunlight and its light dazzles you. With my legions, I had surpassed the Euphrates and attained the confines of Mesopotamia. An old man was brought to me who walked stark naked, leaning on a staff, and whom the majesty of the Roman camp had not frightened. He claimed that there were certain men, marked with an invisible sign, who had been charged with announcing certain verities, and he affirmed that he recognized me as one of them. I only listened to him because I liked to learn about the mores of barbaric peoples, and one can even learn those mores by talking to madmen.

"His words seemed to me to be vain absurdities. But afterwards, like seeds that have been sown and that flourish, they reappeared in my soul, imposed themselves upon me and became the conduct of my life. I was seized by the desire to develop my spirit and reestablish it in its purity. Now, it is in the contemplation of trees, in the constant observation of the changes of their color and form, their burgeoning, that the human spirit finds its own wisdom. I have always loved these gardens that you see unfurling before us, passionately, and that love has caused me to be nicknamed, in Rome, the friend of flowers and trees. But when I saw them again on returning from my lat campaign in Britain, they spoke to me in a new language. I remembered the words of the old ascetic that came to me in Mesopotamia: 'Watch the trees grow, and in the end, you will see your spirit.'

"I have watched for days and nights, and a new man has been born in me. Everything that had agitated me once, the love of women, the pleasures of the senses, the satisfaction of pride, appeared futile and vain to me. I am not ambitious for a greater happiness than leaning over the young shoots that swell in spring, seeing the color of flowers and the outline of foliage agitated by the wind."

Messalina started to laugh, only taking Valerius' words for poetic imaginations. She even thought that he was trying to say in a roundabout manner that no woman occupied him.

"Do you remember," she said, "the supper at the house of Simon Magus? It was the first time that I saw you, and immediately, my youthful thoughts went toward you. But I'm a woman now and I find that sympathy is so beautiful and so rare that one owes it frankness. I have not yet encountered a man who has understood me. Oh, if you wished, Valerius, what great things there are to accomplish in the Empire for two individuals like us!"

She was speaking to him very closely now. She strove to lean her breasts, which were palpitating, against his chest, and her extended leg brushed his. She moved her head in order that gusts of aroma would escape from her hair, and he had the warmth of her breath on his cheek.

In spite of the effort she made, however, she could not succeed in plunging her gaze into his, in order to test the effect on him of the sexual magnetism that she emitted via the eyes, and whose power she had often verified. In the end, as he remained silent and even drew away gently, impatiently, she seized his head in both hands and drew it close to hers, to the point that they were almost touching. She plunged the green light of her eyes into Valerius' pupils in order finally to possess the gaze that he refused to surrender to her.

Then she had a clear consciousness of the fact that Valerius' gaze did not pause either on the beautiful lines of the face not the grain of the mat skin, nor the curve of the eyebrows, nor the velvet of the eyelids, nor the green gleam of the irises, but that it passed through her without seeing what her form was, to contemplate the arborescent syringas, the prostrate willows, the upright yews, and the entire landscape of the beloved garden that was unfurling behind her.

She suddenly sensed the indifference that she inspired in him, that she had always inspired in him. She recoiled. She would have liked to have a weapon with which to strike him. A savage hatred warmed her blood, against that pale and calm man who, at that crepuscular moment, resembled even more the Tiber boatman she had seen in a dream and whose image haunted her. She looked around; she would have liked to demolish that house, because he lived in it, and those gardens, because he delighted in their beauty.

A flood of filthy words came to her lips. It was because of Poppea that he disdained her. She knew full well that they were both coupled by a community of debauchery, an equal amour of young boys that drained the brothels of Suburra on their account. The Petra brothers lent their house for their rendezvous, but Poppea was an insatiable woman. She had other lovers of whom Valerius was unaware. While he watched his trees grow, she prostituted herself to gladiators. All Rome knew that. He was an object of mirth, and a subject of indignation at the same time, because he was making a fool of the noble Cornelius Scipio, who was his friend.

Valerius raised his slender hand slowly. He would have liked to respond to her and calm her down; but a light wind rose and agitated the foliage with a profound undulation. Coming from far away, from the infinite Orient, he thought he could distinguish mysterious words, scarcely formulated.

He remained silent before Messalina.

To the right and the left almost everywhere on the terrace, white birds settled. They smoothed their plumage. They were not afraid. They advanced almost to Valerius' feet.

At that moment, a slave appeared, carrying a mass of breadcrumbs on a silver tray. Valerius took a handful and threw it toward the birds.

"Excuse me," he said. "It's the hour of the doves."

Then, with a shrug of the shoulders, without looking back, Messalina went away.

X. The Death of Valerius

There was then in Rome a certain Suilius who, in exchange for money, took responsibility for carrying an accusation to the magistrates. He thus made a commerce of false testimony. For five thousand sesterces, he had been witness to an adultery, and for twenty thousand he had seen a murder with his own eyes.

It was with him and with Lucius Vitellius that Messalina organized her vengeance.

She thought at first that she would only have to open Cornelius Scipio's eyes for him to repudiate his wife, but the old man, very gentle, had always been clear-sighted. He was illuminated by Poppea's presence around him, and had pardoned everything in advance to such a beautiful creature; he would have given his fortune, and even his life, for her to be happy. He knew that Valerius Asiaticus had loved Poppea shortly after he had married her, but he also knew that the loyal man had departed for Asia in order to forget that amour, and that, exceptionally, Poppea had not given herself to him, perhaps for lack of opportunity and perhaps because women who have many lovers do not like to become the mistresses of those who love them too much.

To Suilius, who had come to find him to expose the scandal to him and to speak to him about the honor of his name, Cornelius Scipio simply replied that he was careful above all of the honor of his soul.

Messalina therefore thought of addressing herself to Claudius in order to doom Valerius and Poppea at the same time. But it was difficult to talk to him about anything whatsoever. That was the moment when, after having abandoned literature for a long time, which he had cultivated before being Emperor, he returned to it with passion. He was writing a history of the Carthaginians, and, under the pretext of profiting from the inspiration that was within in, he was doing so almost without stopping. The freedman Evodus, to whom he dictated, scarcely quit him, even by night. A slave was also required to be beside the Emperor during his hours of inspiration, in order to tickle his nose with a feather, for he fell asleep while dictating. Apart from the Punic Wars, he did not want to hear mention of anything. His cook had orders only to serve him dishes whose recipes came from Hannibal's cooks, for he thought that would enable him to obtain a Carthaginian soul.

Although he neglected all affairs of State, he remained sensitive to fear. That was what Messalina exploited.

Valerius Asiaticus had woven a conspiracy against him. It was an established fact. He was about to depart for Germany and he was going to raise an army, making use of the relatives he had out there. He was an intelligent and audacious man, whom the legionaries loved. Furthermore, in the name of justice, he had participated in the murder of Caligula. The honest Suilius knew his accomplices and had collected their confessions.

The faithful Narcissus also begged Claudius to take measures for his safety. Finally, Lucius Vitellius himself, who had been Valerius' intimate friend and companion in Syria, denounced him as a traitor to the Emperor. It was necessary to strike him without delay and include in the punishment his mistress Poppea, who added to the crime of treason that of dishonoring her husband by a scandalous life.

It was morning, when Claudius awoke. He felt the assassin's daggers in his breast, suffered the terrors of translation, and was agitated by the convulsions of poison. He thought about being precipitated from the height of the Tarpeian Rock. He was bathed in sweat and full of uncertainty. He was persuaded that the danger was so pressing that it was necessary to act immediately and by surprise. Soldiers went to find Valerius, bound his hands and took him before the Emperor.

Claudius was half-lying on his bed. He was holding a page of the history of the Carthaginians, lifting it toward the sky from time to time. Messalina was beside him.

Valerius knew what a wretched individual Suilius was. He would have had little difficulty disculpating himself if evidence and good faith had counted for anything. He thought about maintaining a scornful silence in the midst of the baseness by which he was surrounded, but he thought about Poppea and wanted to save her. He therefore spoke. He reminded Claudius of their old friendship, the services he had rendered him, and he did so with so much eloquence, put so much sincerity into his voice, that Messalina felt tears rising to her eyes and was obliged to go out in order to stifle the sobs that were shaking her.

Meanwhile, Claudius allowed himself to be persuaded. He was seized by the imperious need for justice that he often had. Then it happened that the bonds tying Valerius' hands came undone. The latter, continuing to speak, sensing that his right hand was free, made a gesture to support his speech. That gesture, perhaps a trifle abrupt, gave Claudius the sensation that Valerius was throwing a javelin dissimulated in his garments. He held out the page of the history of the Carthaginians like a shield, and ducked. He perceived his error a second later, but the emotion he had suffered had caused his taste for justice to fly away. He asked Vitellius for his advice, saying that he would rely upon a man so sage and so devoted.

And Vitellius, forgetful of former amity, squeezing Messalina's brodequin, which he carried beneath his toga, in order to steel himself against his treason, declared with an apparent emotion that he certainly took account of what Valerius had done for Rome, what was owed to his courage and years of fidelity, and that it was appropriate to leave to him the choice of his genre of death.

The case was heard. Valerius turned his face way. He was already looking toward the country where the injustice of men only appears as the effect of a known cause, and not the power to cause suffering.

On the afternoon of the same day, Valerius Asiaticus had a pyre built in his garden of branches of sandalwood, which he had recently brought from the Orient in large quantity. For he knew that the perfume of that wood favors, after death, the separation of the double from a man and from the matter of his burned body.

He made is adieux to a few friends and his servants. Then, shortly before dusk fell, he walked through the pathways of his garden for a mute adieu to his other silent friends, the trees. It was the middle of autumn and the leaves were falling of their own accord, seemingly coming toward him.

As the sun began to disappear, he lay down on his ivory bed, which had been carried on to the terrace. But he got up immediately on perceiving that his pyre, which would be ignited to burn his body, would damage with its flames the vault of cedars under which it was placed.

The slaves began it again, a little further away, in an uncovered place that he indicated to them. Then he lay down again and one of his freedmen opened his veins rapidly with a razor. He extended his wrists over a golden vase placed to his right in order that the blood would not spread over him. He had asked everyone to go back into the house in order not to be troubled by a last adieu or the sound of a sob.

There was no longer anything more than the slight murmur of his blood dripping on to the gold. He filled his eyes with the vision of immense, moving, profound, amicable gardens that were clad in a majesty greater than the ordinary. He sensed his soul diminishing with the loss of his life, as if it were drawn by an unknown attraction. The sun poured a great crimson wave over the foliage and the motionless trunks, and Valerius verified then that, as the Asian sage had once told him, there is no greater wisdom than the one taught by the mystery of germination, and that it is from the birth of plants that the most beautiful and the most tranquil road emerges that leads a man to death.

Messalina terrified Poppea by having her told that Claudius had decided to reestablish for her the ancient punishment for adultery, long fallen into disuse. The adulterous woman was exposed naked on the straw in a prison with a small window to the street. The people were summoned by the public crier at sunrise. All the dregs of the outlying districts came running. Until nightfall she would belong to all the men who wanted her and who penetrated into the prison, in turn, after having received a number. The crowd had sometimes been drawn in greater numbers than by the circus games.

Poppea preferred to poison herself than submit to that torture. Cornelius Scipio wept for her bitterly, but his old age and his natural timidity gave him the courage to survive her and removed that of avenging her.

Some time after that, Claudius having finished his history of the Carthaginians, and gather his friends at supper in order to celebrate that event. He invited Cornelius Scipio and, as he was very distracted, he was sincerely astonished, when the latter appeared, not to see him accompanied by Poppea.

"Destiny has disposed of her," said the fearful old man, with melancholy.

XI. The Mystery of the Gardens

Behind the hill that the gardens covered, within the high wall, there was a small door of solid bronze, which served the friend of flowers and trees to leave home secretly. Messalina, who knew of its existence, had the key brought to her on the same day as the condemnation of Valerius Asiaticus.

She could not longer put off the pleasure of walking in the inviolate solitudes, of penetrating the mystery of the gardens, to which Valerius attributed a spiritual force. She mounted a chariot, accompanied solely by the negro slave Ahmes, and reached the little door at the same time as the slaves were placing the sandalwood branches on top of one another on the other side.

When the bronze had swung, she was penetrated by a sensation of freshness that came from the thick vault of very old and very tall oaks that grew there. She would never have thought that there could be trees with trunks as thick, with a form so majestic, and she was astonished that the garden, which she had believed to be perfectly cultivated in all its parts, had a wild aspect in that one.

She advanced deliberately, desirous of seeing the marvels that legend reported. She walked for a long time over thick moss, until the clumps of bushes gave the impression of being grouped in an orderly manner and she was treading on the gravel of raked paths.

The disposition of a few cypresses attracted her attention. She went past them and arrived at a small mausoleum of great simplicity. It was borne by four columns and surmounted by a roof like a temple. One reached it via two marble steps. In the middle was an altar where there was a place for an urn, dominated by a stele on which there was only a single ornament, which was a golden lotus engraved with a single inscription: *The Friend of Flowers and Trees*.

Messalina understood that it was in that place that Valerius had wanted his ashes to be placed. She recoiled. She knew very well that the mausoleum was still empty. If Valerius had killed himself during the day it would have been necessary to rub his body with perfumes that ought to hasten the combustion of the flesh on the pyre and, after the destruction of the flame, to seek the bones in order to deposit them in the bronze urn, with milk, roses and aromatics. In any case, she had not heard the sitines that were made to resonate as the concluding act of funerals.

She was impressed by the simple gravity of that little monument in the middle of the trees and by the golden lotus engraved on the stone of the stele. She drew away rapidly.

She had taken a path to the right that, she thought, ought to take her back in the direction from which she had come. But the places she traversed changed aspect. There were white statues shining in the arbors. Some clumps of bushes were reddened by the autumn, others had remained a bright green, and there were some that, with their leaves, black on one side and white on the other, presented the image of a noisy chessboard.

She dared not follow one narrow path because of two sphinxes that were positioned to either side of the entrance, and she had the sensation that a frisson had run along their ocher-stained stone backs.

She suddenly emerged into a clearing and her heart leapt in her breast because she was walking in blood. A red light seemed to fall from a dark garnet cupola, from which something like a pebble fell at intervals. Carobs were sadly flamboyant in the last rays of the sun. She crossed the clearing in a few bounds, instinctively lifting up her tunic in order not to be soiled.

Without turning round, sensing her soul weakening, she advanced very rapidly. A procession of young women, very tall and slender, appeared to be coming to meet her. She counted a dozen. She was about to make them a sign but she saw that their floating robes were only the white trunks of a clump of birches.

She stopped and looked round. The sun was declining further and further. There was no sound, and everything continued to be motionless. She was struck by the sadness that surrounded her. Trees collapsed in on themselves appeared to be twisting the knots of their wood and hiding desperate faces beneath their bark. Untiring tears wept in the foliage of high branches. There were smaller ones that slid over the trunks of spruces, rounded in white globules of resin, others that made pearls along fig-trees. Pines, like candlesticks, extended their thousands of needles, illuminated by the sunset for a funeral ceremony.

Messalina understood that she was walking through a mute mourning, a crepuscular festival of death, which the vegetables were celebrating silently.

She wanted to flee, and took a path between gray rosemary and tall box-trees. The path intersected with others, and turned back on itself, forming one of those labyrinths that incessantly lead the person following them back to the same place. She ran there for a long time, with the desire to cry out in fear, and when she finally found the issue, she allowed herself to fall on the grass.

She was at the foot of a strange statue, which was that of the goddess Pacht, who was venerated at Bubastis. She was remarkable for the thickness of her beasts. She had the head of a lioness and was holding an ansate cross in her hand, the symbol of divine life for the Egyptians.

Messalina did not know that foreign divinity. Because of the leonine head, however, combined with the very evident femininity, she thought she saw her own image therein. Her courage returned. She stood up and perceived that she had arrived at a place in the garden where the trees were sparser and where there were flower-beds. A little further away, she perceived a row of colonnades with a portico.

A rage overtook her at the terror she had experienced. As she marched through the xyste, she seized with both hands, at random, the flowers in the borders. She crushed them and threw them over her shoulder. On the pathway powdered with violet and she left a wake of periwinkles, anemones and roses.

Having reached the portico at the end of the path she found herself before the aviaries that were disposed in a gallery on three sides, surrounding two oblong pools. The aviaries were very numerous and multicolored. All the species of birds in the world that flap their wings were gathered there, from the northern fetish-bird that has a circular golden crown like a king to the blue bird of India, whose azure tail opens and closes like the fan of a princess.

All the birds were agitating, spreading their tails and deploying their wings, and that palpitation, in all the cages, mingled together, and an immense frisson of plumage rose up therefrom.

Slowly, animated by the same desire that had driven her to tear up the flowers, Messalina, as she passed before the cages, opened their doors with a rapid gesture. And in the same way that the blood of the roses and the snow of the periwinkles had fallen over her shoulder on to the violet path, behind her steps, birds with wings variegated by all the colors of the rainbow, flew over the great streaks of crimson of the sky, which was about to darken.

At first there was an extraordinary confusion around the cages between species from different regions, which had never encountered one another on the celestial routes before. The kingfisher ran into the murderous fieldfare, the marsh-sparrow with its black cap brushed the demoiselle crane with its beak. Parrots called to one another with human cries. Pelicans dragged their goiters toward the nearest grass. Barn owls and long-eared owls, seeing the realm of darkness familiar to them about to descend, were the first to take flight in a direction opposite to that of the setting sun.

Abruptly, there was a great upsurge of birds toward the heavens. The falcons and eagles brushed the turtle-doves and grouse. The tanager competed for speed against the impaled dove to stain the azure, one with its red, the other with its bleeding heart. The catbird uttered a screech like a mewl. The booby launched into a disorderly dance. The anhinga undulated, the *avis venatica* struck itself with its beak. The hummingbirds gave the impression of droplets of light floating in the dusk.

And when all of that winged life had dispersed, Messalina felt as weary as if she had flown with all the birds herself. Seeing the stone of a pool glimmer not far away she dragged herself there in order to rest. She sat down on the water's edge and dipped her fingertips in it. A large domesticated swan that glided toward her, impelled over the surface through the nenuphar lilies, came very close, and, as she did not move, posed its dazzlingly white neck on her bare arm. There was such a mysterious tenderness in that movement that tears moistened Messalina's eyes. She maintained her immobility in order to prolong the amicable caress.

Then, an evening breeze that had risen made the nearby sycamores rustle and brought a tenuous, almost invisible loud into the air. On the snowy plumage of the swan, on the marble arms of the woman and on the linen of her garment, a little bizarre dust fell, gray and sad. Messalina looked in the direction from which it was coming and perceived a dying redness. And, frozen, she remained there with the swan in her arms, receiving upon her, in the ash of the pyre, a little of the ash of the man she had loved.

XII. The Malediction

It is alleged that Simon Magus had the faculty of rising into the air after he had entered into a profound meditation, with his legs crossed and his head tilted forward. Fewer instances are cited of his power to transport himself distantly. However, he had that power and he made use of it several times, notably to save his disciple Palladus, condemned to death in Corinth, and also in the following circumstances.

"I want you to explain why he always looked at me without seeing me."

Messalina was before him. She had had the great surprise of seeing Simon open the door of his house to her himself. No porter, no servants. In the atrium, the statues of the gods had disappeared. Nothing any longer remained but the stone pedestals. One sensed that the house had been recently abandoned.

Messalina had followed Simon into the black marble corridor as far as the square room open to the sky, to which she had come a few years before. The hangings had been removed; there was no tripod or phosphorescent powders. Broken bottles were left in a corner.

Simon's face was closed and severe. He did not have the desire to please that normally characterized him. From his small eyes, beneath a forehead that seemed more monstrous, an irritated gleam emerged.

"Valerius Asiaticus doubtless never saw you," he said, "because the spirit, when it has attained a certain purity, traverses matter without being impressed by it. Once, in this same room, I told you that there was a golden lotus above your head. You have stifled it, instead of enabling it to flourish. You have fed the beast within you endlessly. You have misunderstood the elementary wisdom of equilibrium that wants us to arrive at perfection by developing the two principles that animate us equally.

"Woe betide the individual who causes one to predominate over the other! Woe betide the ascetic in the desert who has confined too narrowly the furious bull of the flesh, but above all, woe betide the creature in whom there triumphant flesh has killed the spirit. You are soiled by the ineffaceable crime, the one that is never forgiven, that of having killed your own soul. Woe betide you!

"You will move backwards in the human scale. In your next lives you will be a wretched whore, uniquely preoccupied with the warmth of your belly, a beast receiving men. As for the sage that your lies have killed, while awaiting reincarnation in a more perfect being, he is wandering in gardens more beautiful than those of Lucullus: the miraculous gardens of his thought, which are forever inaccessible to you."

Messalina, pale, her lips trembling, had recoiled all the way to the door. In the street, her chariot was waiting, driven by the negro Ahmes, escorted by a few soldiers of the Emperor's guard.

"I'll have your skin torn off in pieces, and red-hot iron needles plunged under all your fingernails," she said, and ran outside.

It only required a few seconds for her to summon the Praetorians. They searched the whole house in vain. There was no other exit than the one they were guarding, but they did not find any trace of Simon.

The Prefect made enquiries in Rome and the provinces. He was not able to learn anything certain. It only seemed that at the very moment of Messalina's visit to Simon, a woman whose description resembled that of Helen had embarked in the port of Ostia on a vessel belonging to her, and to which she had had great riches transported.

She was accompanied by an adolescent with a feminine face and wide hips, whose sex it was difficult to specify. She took great care of a man who had been seen the previous day in Ostia and who was carried on to the vessel fast sleep. According to the testimony collected, the man woke up at the moment when the ship set sail, and those who saw him were struck by the enormous width of his forehead. The time of the awakening and the ship's departure coincided exactly with the moment when Messalina was listening to the malediction of Simon Magus.

That made the Empress think that there could not be any connection between those travelers and the man on whom she wanted to avenge herself, and because of that she did not give an order to pursue the ship in the ports where it might call in.

She was not sufficiently knowledgeable in occult matters to suppose that it was only Simon Magus' double with whom she had talked.

XIII. The Vow

Messalina remembered the vow that she had made to the god Priapus on the day of her wedding, the execution of which she had put off. She feared that the god might take his revenge on her, and as it was an evening in spring, and the rites of Miphileseth were imminent, she decided to go to the little temple on the hill in order to offer her body to the priest Chilon.

With Ahmes, alone, to drive her chariot, hiding her face beneath her veil in order that no one would recognize her, she traversed the transtiberian region and emerged from the city through the Porta Aurelia, as on the evening when she had gone to shed the blood of her virginity joyfully.

She climbed the path through the cypresses, went past the six priapic genii and opened the low door between the columns.

In the half-light of the temple, Chilon was sitting beside the Miphileseth of fig-wood, mending a woolen tunic with a needle. He had aged; his nose seemed to have descended over his lips, his hair had become sparse and his beard was going gray He raised a hideous face toward her, on which amazement was painted, and then, recognizing her, he prostrated himself, his forehead on the flagstones.

Full of disgust, but determined to conclude the matter rapidly, she had him get up by touching his shoulder with her foot. He remained before her, stammering and frightened. She looked him full in the face and, taking the nape of his neck in her hand, familiarly, she pushed him toward the back of the temple and said to him that she desired to see the basement again where she had already celebrate the mysteries of the god.

He apologized for the disorder that reigned there, affirmed his despair at not having been warned about the imperial visit, and started running around in search of a lamp.

"It's Maacha who has protected you and given you your children," he said. "But you have raised yourself to the rank of the goddesses. I never fail to invoke your name when I celebrate the god's feast and cause the drops of blood to fall into the vase. It's for you that I immolate the donkey, only leaving to Miphileseth the goat and the rabbit, and I know that the faithful, when they are possessed by the animal forces and they embrace one another, imagine that they are clutching your divine body and obtain a pleasure a thousand times greater."

The lamp was lit and Messalina smelled an odor of rancid and burned oil that evoked for her in a gripping fashion the evening in her thirteenth year when she had followed Chilon into the same place. She thought she could hear the chant of the cithern players, the hysterical cries, and a human voice imitating the braying of a donkey. A kind of magic operated on her, as if those walls were the receptacle of sensual larvae, insatiable ephialtes that took possession of her body.[10] She advanced toward the stairway, animated by a horrible desire. In the same way as before, Chilon, curbed in two, raised and lowered his smoky lamp to illuminate the steps.

Down below there were empty gourds, the skins of sacrificed animals that he had not yet had time to sell, a cask of wine and formless objects.

Chilon dared not comprehend as yet the meaning of the imperial visit, but she let herself fall to the floor and drew him to her.

When Messalina reappeared at the door of the temple and she had breathed deeply, she raised her right arm toward the sky in order to summon Ahmes. The latter came up the path through the cypresses at a run. She went straight toward

---

[10] The term *ephialtes* was used by the Greek physician Galen to describe nightmares, imagined as caused by an incubus lying on top of a sleeper.

him and, taking his head in her hand, she gave him an order, whispering in his ear.

In his turn, Chilon had come out of the temple and was walking behind Messalina. Seeing that she had turned toward him, he put one knee on the ground and lowered his head in order to take his leave of her.

Before he had raised his eyes, Ahmes had delivered a blow of the fist to the nape of the neck, at the exact spot that the Empress' hand had touched it, with all his might. Then he took a small knife out of his belt, leaned over the priest, and rummaged under his garments with the blade. There was a frightful howl, interrupted by Messalina's curt voice.

"Throw that in the temple—it's my offering to the god, this evening."

A few moments later, the imperial chariot disappeared in the direction of the Porta Aurelia, and the old priest was moaning and shedding his blood at the feet of the six priapic genii.

XIV. Lysisca's Cell

Nothing can satisfy her any longer. Always desirous of new bodies, indefatigable, she only pursues the pleasure of amour. No human face retains her, no caress has any need to be repeated, she passes through all arms, only avid for forms that she does not know.

The blind Claudius is tormented by the cares of State and his literary works. He has aqueducts constructed to bring cold spring water to Rome; he has the port of Ostia enlarged; and he works on his memoirs. Messalina has put into his bed two Greek slaves whose beauty she has savored herself and whom she believes that she can trust. She enjoys an absolute impunity.

It was Mnester, who had remained her confidant and her companion in orgies, who suggested to her the idea of the night in Suburra that legend transformed, contrary to the most elementary plausibility, into a daily habit.[11]

Messalina was often tormented by the idea of imitating Cleopatra. She had gone several times to Caesar's former villa on the right bank of the Tiber, where the Queen of Egypt had lived during her sojourn in Rome, to dream about her there. She admired her ostentation and the choice of her pleasures. She had heard it said that on certain nights, disguised as a tavern servant, Cleopatra would run around the low dives of Alexandria on Antony's arm, and that seemed worthy of envy.

---

[11] Author's note: "Juvenal, Tacitus and Josephus are unanimous in claiming that it was almost every evening that Messalina took the place in a brothel of a whore named Lysisca. It stands to reason that the entire city of Rome would have headed for a place where the Empress could be had for a few sesterces. It is more plausible, as Cassius Dio says, that she only went there once, on the occasion of which he speaks."

She imagined surpassing those exploits and being, at least once, exceeded in her flesh.

In Suburra, in the vicinity of the Caelian hill, not far from the great marketplace, there was a brothel prostitute named Lysisca who bore such a great resemblance to Messalina that she had been able to raise her tariff in consequence to a silver denier. She was a harlot—which is to say that she only sold her body by night, after the evening meal, leading a regular life during the day.

Mnester took change of indemnifying her for a night of repose. He also warned the brothel-keeper that he would that he would bring a fake Lysisca that evening also resembling Messalina and susceptible of satisfying her clients with the same ardor. He had known the brothel-keeper, named Gnathoenion, who was a habitual furnisher of young boys, for a long time. Gnathoenion, initially the proprietor of a bath-house, had transformed his commerce almost involuntarily. Because harlots were taking advantage of his baths to bring back men that they solicited in the street, he had started charging a fee of three as per man. Afterwards, he had found it more practical to make a declaration to the aedile and to have women in residence. He had a tavern on the street and an atrium behind it with a pool connected to the former steam-baths, transformed into cells for prostitution.

Claudius was traveling. Messalina attended to her toilette as if she were going to meet the most delicate of lovers. She spread a fine violet powder in her hair, in accordance with the custom of the courtesans of Alexandria, and twisted it over her nape, securing it with a silk ribbon. She put a tear of carmine on the nipples of her breasts and enclosed them in a fine gold mesh so light that it was almost invisible. Her flesh was odorous with all the perfumes with which she was anointed. She did not put on jewelry in order not to be recognized, with the exception of a necklace with a phallus in very ancient gold, which came from Phoenicia. She wrapped herself, stark naked, in a large linen sheet, put on top of it a cucul of coarse cloth with a hood, and at the first hour of the night she left her palace on the Palatine by a hidden door, where Mnester was wait-ing for her.

It was summer, and outside the shops of Suburra sloven-ly individuals were seeking to aspire the nauseating air. The cries of drunken gladiators could be heard. Streetwalkers al-ready weary at the commencement of their round looked pass-ers-by in the face. Odors of the evening meal escaped from doorways. It was still the hour of nourishment, which was about to give way to the hour of amour.

Having arrived at Gnathoenion's house, for which a red-painted wooden phallus served as a sign, Messalina thought about going back, on breathing the odor of human sweat of a man who brushed past her. But she saw the handsome face of a legionary sitting in the tavern and she went in.

The chamber where Mnester left her was a little less sor-did than the others in the house. It was only separated from the atrium by a loose curtain, alongside which was written in chalk: *Lysisca, one silver denier*. Inside, the walls were cov-ered with crudely painted erotic images. Mostly, they repre-sented the phallus in the comical forms of birds, insects and fish. There were some with teeth, others on stilts, and others as long as snakes, but they were all veiled by the soot of the lamp and other stains.

The furniture consisted of a worn rush mat covered with a few cushions and a patched and hideously stained coverlet. On a small table there was a smoky bronze lamp, and there was a sandstone jar in one corner.

Messalina had barely thrown back the coverlet in disgust when her neighbor in the next cell drew the curtain and came to conclude a story doubtless commenced the previous night. She was a scrupeda, á woman who, after a night spent in a brothel, went to the cemeteries in the morning to satisfy men between the tombs. She laughed as she talked about her walks around the Pomoerium, rapid embraces with prowlers against the steps of a sepulcher in the shadow of a tombstone when dawn breaks. She recounted the simplicity of the market-gardeners who descended from their carts in response to her appeal, their coarse caresses and their generosity. She evoked dangers run, and a flight between the gray walls of the columbarium in the city of manes.

Voices resounded. A band was spreading out among the chambers. A young man had entered Lysisca's cell; he seemed handsome to Messalina, but he was timid. He stood by her side, in silence, and she had to make him sit down on the mat with her. She started to laugh when he held out the silver denier, and he left even more confused. Afterwards, one came who wrenched off the veil she had retained violently, seeming to consider it an insult not to find her completely naked. He rolled her on the ground unceremoniously, and kneaded her shoulders and breasts with his hands, almost striking her.

An adolescent who had drunk to excess swore to her that he had loved her for a long time and that he would even marry her if she wished. She heard him fall and vomit on the mosaic of the atrium when he had quit her. There was a madman who wanted her to prostrate herself at his feet in order to kiss them, while saluting him with the name of Jupiter; there was an old man who asked her to spread her hair over her shoulders and tried to cut off a lock; and a fop who patted her lightly on the cheek with his hand, promising to come back often to bring her the same pleasure.

Messalina was astonished by so much brevity in the caresses. Nothing of her natural pride subsisted any longer. Like the humblest of the establishment's whores, she submitted to the erotic caprices, or even the brutality of men. At one moment, the fetid mouth of an old man posed for a long time on hers without her daring to resist, in spite of the breath that was poisoning her, so completely did she identify with her role.

She sometimes breathed the night air on her threshold. The bacario immediately ran forward with is large jug full of water and poured its contents into the jar in the chamber. When the hour was late he no longer knew which way to go; everyone was demanding him, and Messalina was obliged to shout loudly for him several times. Sometimes, too, the ornamentary ancilla came to offer powders and ointments, and

99

the aquatoli ran hither and yon carrying trays laden with of drinks.

The night was well advanced when the frequenter of tombs started uttering howls so loud that Messalina thought that she was being murdered. An enormous gladiator had threatened her with a knife. He went away cursing. He was not handsome and his eyes had an evil glean. He went past Messalina and she looked him in the face, as she was accustomed to gaze at those she desired. He would have continued on his way but she seized his arm and drew him to her.

He was a man from whom an excess of strength emerged, as the same time as a force of evil. He possessed Messalina while insulting her. Then, having stood up, he uttered a little snigger of disgust and took a step toward the door to leave, having place three as instead of the silver denier that he owed her on the small wooden table. Messalina demanded them loudly, for she obtained a puerile vanity from having merited that salary.

He turned round and responded with a flood of insults. It was a dead woman, already decomposing, that he had just embraced. She was not even worth one as. He was being charitable in giving her three.

Then she caught hold of his tunic and shook his leather belt. She felt robbed. She wanted the silver denier that she had earned, and which appeared to her more precious than all the riches of the Palatine. She threatened to cry out and summon the brothel-keeper.

He seized her by the wrists and shook her as if he were about to smash her against the wall. Then, seized again by desire at that contact, he threw her on the floor and fell upon her with all his weight. The metal buckle of his belt scratched Messalina's breast. She thought for a moment that he was going to kill her. As she rolled over the soiled coverlet she turned her face away with disgust, He saw that movement, an in order to humiliate her, taking handfuls of her hair, he rubbed her face against the unspeakable fabric for a long time.

Satisfied, and still menacing, he picked up the three as he had given her, and left.

Messalina knew that the police of the watch were robust and that the local procurators rendered strict justice to women. She started to follow him, but she saw his back in the atrium swaying so powerfully on his solid legs that she stopped. She considered him as he drew away, bruised, finally weary, and infinitely indulgent to male brutality.

She called the bacario one hast time for water. The night ended. A drunkard was still singing in the tavern. Wrapped in a gray stola, the scrupeda went away, lightly, to provide other caresses in the region of the dead. Mnester was asleep on a bench. He had spent the night with a young fellator whom he had the custom of finding at Gnathoenion's, but fatigue had aged him, and he suddenly had the appearance of a feeble old man.

And going through the streets, leaning on him, the Empress dreamed of a unique lover, of an amour that would be pure, of the golden lotus about which Simon Magus had spoken to her, which flourished, she knew not where, in the unknown realm of the soul.

XV. Caius Silius

Caius Silius was reputed to be the most handsome man in Rome. He was a consul and enjoyed a great popularity. He loved virtue and defended it. He was the one who had asked the Senate for the execution of the ancient Lex Cincia forbidding advocates to receive money or gifts for pleading a case. That demand had been indirectly aimed at Messalina, who had bought the accuser Suilius and made use of him to doom her enemies.

Messalina was not unaware that Caius Silius incessantly raised his voice against the excesses of her life. Several times she sought a means of having him killed. She ended up loving him passionately. It came to the same thing.

One day, when Caius Silius was returning along the Tiber in the Mucian Meadows from an excursion on horseback, an arrow whistled past his ear and plunged, vibrating, into the trunk of a poplar. Another time, he received as a gift a basket of figs of extraordinary size. They were already on his table. A slave who had tasted one died in convulsions. So, when he was summoned to the Palatine by Messalina, he thought that his final hour might be near.

Messalina wanted to understand how there could be a man who resisted her beauty, audacious enough to speak ill of her, and so deprived of virile nature as not to desire her. She wanted to penetrate that mystery, which seemed to her to be virtue, and, by means of a frank explanation, to know the cause of Caius' hostility. She received him lying on the Tyrian purple of her bed, naked beneath light veils. Neither of them foresaw what would happen.

At first they conversed coldly, the Empress representing to the consul how imprudent it was to attack her and he defending himself without losing any of his natural arrogance.

But perhaps there was in Messalina a force of seduction that acted upon men even against their will. Perhaps the antipathy of Caius Silius had its cause in a hidden desire. Perhaps they were marked by destiny to give together a great flame of amour and to die.

At the moment when Caius Silius stood up to take his leave, Messalina, with a sad pout, suddenly hid her head in her folded arm, leaving one of her naked legs dangling outside the bed in an abandoned pose. Caius took her in his arms and they savored their union in a pleasure that they had never known before.

Then an amour commences that approaches frenzy. Messalina wants to see her lover at all hours, whenever she pleases. Although he is married to a beautiful young woman, Junia Silana, she sends for him if Claudius absents himself, even in the middle of the night. An imperious message sometimes summons him when he is in the Senate, and the messenger is ordered to bring him to her even if he is addressing the assembly. As soon as he arrives, as soon as they are alone, she throws off her garments furiously and tears off his.

If they go for an excursion in the country it is sometimes necessary to stop the chariot and hire a room in some rustic tavern in order to possess one another. Once, not far from Rome, Caius has to take her in a ditch, almost on the road. She marks his body with bites, in order that Junia Silana can have no doubt as to his treason. Soon, however, she cannot bear the idea of another woman approaching the man she loves and she obliges him to divorce.

That is not sufficient for her. She wants to efface all the caresses that Caius has received. She has an order given to a woman named Cytheria, whose lover Caius once was, to quit Rome immediately. She has another, who has boasted about having had him, poisoned. Her desire for possession is less sated the more she satisfies it.

And then, a singular desire comes to her to make her liaison known to everyone. In the guise of a joke she tells Claudius that Caius is her lover. He laughs. She gives him intimate details that she appears to have invented, but which are true.

"I'm going to meet my lover," she tells him when she leaves, and she does, in fact, go to meet Caius, and that gives Claudius a complete security.

She takes Narcissus, Pallas, all the freedmen, and Calpurnia and Cleopatre as confidants. She tells Vitellius, who continues to love her and suffer for her, about the pleasures she obtains with Caius, shows him her weary eyes, the shoulders that he has held forcefully, and the traces of fingers above her knees. In public, she affects to put her arm around the neck of the man she loves, whispering to him cheek to cheek. In the evening, when she crosses the forum to go to meet him, she would like trumpeters to precede her chariot and announce to the people the name of the man who is going to give her joy.

One evening, in her house near the Circus Flaminius, she makes Calpurnia and Cleopatra hide behind a curtain in the room where meets Caius, forbidding them to reveal their presence. She gives herself with more ardor than ever. The next day she heaps the two slaves with presents, because they have seen.

That obsession only increases. She would like public recognition of her amour. From that comes the extravagant idea of her marriage, which she realizes as soon as she has conceived it.

She had a limitless confidence in the stupidity of Claudius. She frightens him by telling him that a dream has announced her husband's death to her. Destiny, however, can be deceived, in such a way as to deflect the misfortune on to a new husband. Claudius does not say no, and in the meantime, he leaves for Ostia, where he goes to supervise the transportation of provisions for Rome that are arriving by sea.

Then Messalina, as if intoxicated by a bizarre desire to see her amour consecrated by public witnesses, hastens to press forward with the marriage ceremony.

She commences by having transported to Silius' house a part of the imperial riches: jewels, statues, even items of furniture. She gathers the witnesses, the Grand Pontiff, the Flamen Dialis, and has herself served wheat bread and honeyed wine.

In the midst of a large number of friends, in accordance with the consecrated rites, she married Caius Silius.

An intelligent and sane man sometimes accomplishes great follies because he believes in his lucky star and tells himself that chance will intervene in the danger. Caius Silius, who was related to the greatest families, a consul of Rome, thought that he would only get out of such a singular and dangerous adventure by killing Claudius. He thought of having himself proclaimed Emperor in his stead, but he only prepared for that insufficiently. In any case, he did not have a minute to himself in order to prepare for it. Messalina wanted to have him in her bed incessantly, and it was there that he spent almost all his days and nights. He abandoned himself to events, since pleasure did not give him time to organize them, and left his head empty, his spirit irresolute.

On the brazen tripods of the temples, incense and perfumed gums burn. Cavalcades of cataphracts ride along the Appian Way going toward the Palatine. In gala togas the senators, tribunes and aediles come to bring their felicitations to the Augusta's new wedding. No one really understands what is happening. Surprised glances are exchanged. Comments are made in low voices. People laugh surreptitiously. They wait. But it is noticed that Narcissus, Pallas and Vitellius are not present, nor any of Claudius' freedmen.

The people crowd around the palace, uttering acclamations. They cry: "Thalassio!" A distribution is made of sesterces and congii of wine. When evening comes, a festival rumor fills the air. It seems that the whole city is rejoicing and those cries suffice to give the newlyweds the security they desire. They want to persuade themselves that Rome is with them. In any case, they have plenty of time. They will put off the care of organizing the *coup d'état* until tomorrow. Who knows, anyway? Everything might work out for the best with the feeble Claudius.

The coral powder that has been spread over the garden makes it entirely pink in the sunset, like certain sea-shells. It is autumn, and Messalina has organized a simulacrum of grape-gathering in the garden of the palace, for the evening of her wedding. Vats and presses are brought out. The wine flows. It is spilled on the ground. A heavy odor rises beneath the trees. The women are dressed as Bacchantes; the men are only wearing animal-skins. The hymns of the feast of Bacchus are sung. Couples stray into the bushes or disappear briefly into the bedrooms of the palace. Animated by the same obsession, Messalina would like Caius Silius to possess her on the ground in front of everyone. He hesitates. Perhaps he will do it. But at that moment, Theogonius has climbed a tree, and a few people ask him what he can see.[12]

"A furious storm in the direction of Ostia," Theogonius replies.

Many people knew him, and know that he was a fake madman who had acquired the habit of folly in the time of Caligula, and had retained it in order to disguise his wisdom.

"It's raining," he said, having descended from the tree. "I'm all wet. I need to go home before the lightning strikes."

And he left. It was notorious that the weather was fine.

Everyone remembered the absence of the freedmen, and thought about a possible return of the irritated Emperor. In very little time, the majority of the guests had disappeared. The others sought excuses. The tribune Servinius, a simple man, who did not find one and to whom Messalina was in the process of talking, abruptly turned his back on her and fled at a run. In the palace, doors slammed. As if a signal of terror had been given and an invisible warning issued, the friends, and even the slaves, slipped away. There was a panic. Messalina and Caius Silius soon found themselves almost alone.

It was only later, during the night, that they learned that cavaliers had arrived, preceding Claudius. The Emperor was

---

[12] Author's note: "Tacitus says that is was Cectius Velens who climbed he tree; others name Theogonius. It does not matter."

on the road from Ostia. He knew everything and was running to take his revenge.

The two lovers were infected by the general terror. They wondered what they ought to do. But Rome was asleep. Caius Silius decided to go to the Senate at daybreak in order to impose upon it by his presence and deliberate with his friends as to the best course of action. Messalina lay down on her bed to sleep for a while.

They were not to see one another again.

The freedmen had wondered what they ought to do in the presence of Messalina's follies. They had thought of begging her to renounce her marriage, but that was dangerous. The Empress would have considered it a crime not to favor her amour. On the other hand, they feared the triumph of Silius, who would not have failed to get rid of them.

They departed in haste for Ostia, and Narcissus, who was the only resolute one among them, made a plan and took Calpurnia and Cleopatra with him. He counted on them for the first words, which would be the most difficult. He made them see that once Messalina had disappeared, it would be them who reigned over Claudius. Pallas, the richest man in the Empire, assured them of a fortune in exchange for their testimony.

Claudius needed women as much as nourishment. Installed at Ostia in a house that the Prefect of food supplies, Turranius, had on the harbor, he spent his time eating, but lacked women. His joy was great when he learned that Narcissus had had the amicable idea of bringing two women to whom he was accustomed to Ostia. It was the middle of the day. He sent everyone away, giving the order that they were to come to him immediately. And he lay down on his bed.

But it was no time for pleasure. Calpurnia spoke first and recounted everything that had happened. Cleopatra gave a further account. They also reported the scene that they had witnessed, hidden behind a curtain. Narcissus came and added, with a great surge of sincerity, everything that he knew about

Messalina's liaisons. But it was not the adultery that it was necessary to stop, he said, it was the danger that was pressing. The people, the army and the Senate might give Rome to Caius Silius at any moment.

Claudius lost his head completely. He wept and uttered howls of anger. He had the Prefect Turranius summoned, and Lucius Geta, the commandant of the Praetory, and then his freedmen and friends. He ran this way and that, livid with fear, and asked everyone whether Caius Silius was not the Emperor, since he had married the Empress, and whether he was now only a simple individual. The terror that animated him infected everyone. The greatest functionaries of the Empire, who were gathered there, thought of nothing but fleeing. Vitellius marched around, his arms raised to the heavens, and every time anyone questioned him he replied: "O crime!"—an exclamation from which he only departed when he had seen how events turned out.

Turranius talked about embarking on a ship for who knows where.

Narcissus, wiser, declared that it was necessary, at dawn the next day, to go to the camp to make sure of the Praetorian cohorts, and had the Emperor entrust him with the supreme command of the soldiers until all danger was averted.

XVI. The Dung-Cart

It was the silence that woke Messalina. She called out, and no one responded. Dressing in haste, she walked through the palace. It was completely deserted. The kitchens, the stables and the gardens were equally empty. Doors were open, forgotten cloaks trailing on the floor. Even the ports had quit the palace. The negro Ahmes was on the threshold, on the lookout for news. A peaceful dawn was rising over Rome.

The sight of Ahmes rendered Messalina a part of her courage. She ordered him to prepare a chariot with the fastest horse. She could see what had to be done. Nothing was lost. She had learned during the night that Claudius would leave Ostia at sunrise. She could not have lost her empire over him. She could arrange everything if she could meet him before his arrival in Rome.

But there was no longer any chariot or any horse. The slaves had made use of them to flee. It was necessary to hurry. Followed by Ahmes, Messalina left the palace by the back door. She retraced her steps, remembering that she had not reddened her lips with carmine and made up her eyes. The beauty of her face had never been as indispensable.

She marched through the streets in quest of a hirer of carriages. Ahmes knew of one not far away. He knocked on the door for a long time. No one responded, Messalina assumed that she had been seen through a loophole and recognized, and that no one was opening up because it was her. She had the sentiment of a general malediction that was enveloping her.

She drew away and wandered at random. At a corner she almost bumped into a large cart half full of ordure. The conductor was leading the horse by the bridle. He had just stopped and was picking up vegetable debris from outside a shop with a shovel. Messalina thought that Claudius might reach Rome at any moment, and that that wretched vehicle was better than nothing.

She gave the conductor the gold coins that she had in her hand, but the man was limited. He explained that the cart did not belong to him, that a functionary at the refuse tip would demand that he account for it. In her impatience, Messalina detached a diamond necklace from around her neck and threw it at him. The man did not know its value and continued to protest. Ahmes was obliged to knock him down with a blow of his fist. Then he cracked the whip that he had seized, and they finally set off.

The diamond necklace had broken and the stones were scattered in the street. As he got to his feet the conductor contemplated in surprise the fragments of stars that the goddess he had glimpsed momentarily had left behind her, having chosen his cart in which to travel through Rome at sunrise.

Ahmes thought about getting out of the city immediately and going round it via the Pomoerium, in order to go more rapidly, for while walking they had drawn away from the direction of the road to Ostia. But the horse was thin and tired and had difficulty trotting. The axles of the vehicle screeched with each rotation of the wheels, and Messalina, tossed about on her seat of dung, experienced all the horrors of the journey bitterly.

On the Tiber Island, which they traversed, the sun set the dome of the temple of Aesculapius ablaze. Strange forms emerged from it. Beneath hoods, Messalina distinguished enormous faces the color of milk, with eyes emerging from eyelids like tumors. Hands like damp tubers appeared under the cloth of cloaks. They were lepers who had permission, four times a year, to spend the night in the temple of Aesculapius, where the gods sometimes accorded them a miraculous cure.

As the cart moved through their troop, they perceived Messalina with her dazzling shoulders, which emerged from her tunic, and her face, where anxiety did not veil the gleam of the skin. They all extended their arms toward her, in a gesture of desperate supplication. Hoarse, inarticulate sounds emerged from their throats, by way of acclamations, and they started running behind the cart, staring at her with their bulging eyes, in order to retain for as long as they could the image of inaccessible beauty.

Ahmes drove them away with lashes of the whip.

The cart had traversed the square and moved on to the Pont Cestius when, in front of the phallic obelisk that stood at the corner of the bridge, Messalina recognized a stooped man leaning on a staff who appeared to be praying before the roseate granite phallus.

It was Chilon. Doubtless he had come to spend the night in the temples of Aesculapius in order to request the return of his lost virility. He had become a frightful old man. His unsatisfied desires were inscribed on his bestial face. He gave the impression of one of the shades of the dead whose desolation seers perceive when they attempt to satisfy a body they no longer have, in the company of the living.

Messalina saw the symbols of her life there, passed in the vain pursuit of pleasure. It was that frightful Jewish priest who had taken her virginity, and had informed her that there was no other god than the enjoyment of the flesh. It was that phallus of pink granite, reflected in the water of the Tiber an illuminated by the sun, the rigid, colored, immutable phallus, that had been the goal of her life. For the sake of swooning in beds, the strength of arms bending her back, the heat of her vagina, she had neglected the beautiful possibilities of the spirit, the world of which she had glimpsed without wanting to penetrate it.

Above the head of every woman there is a golden lotus, Simon Magus had said to her. Where was that gilded flower? She had perceived it on the stele in the mausoleum of Valerius, the wise man who had found the truth amid the life of trees. She had the knowledge of having killed something within herself, and that the crime was more serious than that of having killed the bodies of her lovers.

Her life appeared to her as a stupid error, a race for the enjoyment of her loins that had led to this triumph among lep-

111

ers, on this throne of ordure, on which she was like an empress of ignominy.

As a sign of humility she touched the detritus on which she was sitting with her forehead, and she wept.

Fearful of Claudius' changing moods, Narcissus had climbed into the carriage that was taking the emperor back, and also made the freedman Cecina and Vitellius climb in. Claudius had moments of tenderness. He recalled the beauty of Messalina and his past amour. Vitellius, on whom Narcissus had wanted to support himself, and whom he pressed to explain clearly, was still repeating: "O crime!" and then maintaining an ambiguous silence.

The cavaliers of the Praetorian guard who were preceding the carriage slowed their pace as they came in sight of Rome. A stationary cart was blocking the road and a woman, standing up, was making them an imperious signal to halt.

Narcissus understood that the moment was critical. With a gesture, he ordered the buccina players to sound their instruments in order to drown out the appeal he was beginning to hear. Then, as he made the painful decision, abruptly, to follow the truth to the end, he held out the tablets on which the names of all Messalina's lovers were written, and he indicated them with a finger, forcing Claudius to lean forward to read them.

The buccinas played.

"Is that possible?" said the Emperor, several times.

"O crime!" repeated Vitellius, but while making a movement that blocked the carriage door, which made Narcissus think that he could count on him and that the game was won.

XVII. The Dead Leaf in Valerius' Garden

Claudius was extremely popular because of an appearance of vulgar stupidity that he had, even when saying intelligent and just things, which the people adored because they saw their own image therein. He only had to harangue the Praetorian cohorts assembled at the camp to sense that he would remain the master of Rome.

Then again, a man who complains to other man about the turpitudes of his wife always encounters an indignant sympathy.

In a few hours, Narcissus had had Caius Silius arrested, along with the majority of his friends and all those suspected of having served his projects. Silius, sensing that he was doomed, did not defend himself and only asked that he be put to death rapidly. That wish was immediately realized. His accomplices were treated as if they had expressed the same desire.

Vibidia, the priestess of the Vestals, an aged and venerable woman to whom Messalina had rendered a few services, came to the Palatine to intercede on her behalf and to ask that she not be condemned without being heard. Narcissus did not let her see Claudius and assured her that the Empress would have every facility to defend herself. He also turned away Britannicus and Octavia, brought by Lepida, who would have implored mercy for their mother.

Toward evening the Emperor sat down at table, having rediscovered a certain tranquility of soul. He began to eat with abundance, as was his custom, and the first warmth of the wine caused him to regret Messalina. He turned to Narcissus and said to him: "Have the unfortunate Messalina come tomorrow to justify herself to me."

Narcissus knew that that word was his own condemnation if he did not act with the utmost rapidity. He went out and told the tribune of the guard and the centurion that the Emperor had ordered them to go and kill Messalina immediately. He summoned the freedman Evodus, a vile individual who was devoted to him and of whose hatred for Messalina he was aware, and he charged him with following the tribune and making sure of the execution of his orders.

Messalina had installed her mother Lepida in the house of Valerius Asiaticus, confiscated on the latter's death and now imperial property. It was with her that she had sought refuge. She had spent the afternoon in the garden, lying on the grass, awaiting news of events. Lepida tried to remind her that, according to the old wisdom bequeathed as a heritage in Roman families, it was necessary to look death in the face if it presented itself, but Messalina breathed in the autumnal freshness that came from the gardens of Lucullus and shivered, having never felt the sweetness of life so much. She was not yet in despair.

She thought she had heard a noise from the direction of the house. She got up and perceived a man running toward her. It was Evodus. He had come on ahead of the tribune and the soldiers, who were searching for Messalina in the rooms, and, having learned from a slave where she was, he had launched forth to insult her before her death.

When she recognized him she understood her destiny. Evodus had always hated her beauty, because he was dirty and ugly and had been unable to aspire to possess her. He served as Claudius' scribe and had rendered himself indispensable by his erudition and is faculty of writing quickly. He was literate and base of soul, which often go together.

Hatred made him snigger and prevented him from speaking. He arrived close to Messalina, and as her stola had slipped and uncovered her breast, he struck that breast, whose beauty had outraged him for a long time, with the back of his hand, with all his might.

Messalina could not retain a cry of pain, and fainted. Evodus grabbed her by the hair and shook her, shouting: "Bitch! Harlot of the Suburra!" and, trying to rip her tunic from top to bottom, he said to her: "Show us your body before dying."

But the tribune, followed by his soldiers, had just arrived. He thrust Evodus aside violently, making the observation that the justice of Caesar ought to be more measured and more silent. As Lepida had handed her daughter a dagger that she had under her garments, he stood some distance away and turned his eyes away in order not to be embarrassed by that supreme second. He made a sign to his soldiers to drag Evodus further away.

But it requires great courage to strike oneself with a pointed weapon. When one has sought pleasure all one's life, one is not prepared to give oneself pain. Messalina attempted several times to deliver a mortal blow, but only scratched herself lightly. The sight of her blood frightened her and, dropping the weapon, half-collapsed on the ground, she hid her head in her hands.

Then the tribune, full of pity, advanced stealthily behind her drew his sword, braced himself and struck her a mighty blow under the armpit, which traversed her clean through and killed her instantly.

Then, having made sure of her death, he drew way with his soldiers.

In the meantime, darkness fell.

Lepida had remained alone next to her daughter's body. There was a rustle in the trees of the garden of Lucullus, in the dense spindle-trees and the mortuary box-trees, and a dead leaf, which seemed to be carried by a light breath, fell on to the ardent heart that was no longer beating.

THE ANGEL OF LUST

I. The First Appearance of Lust

Almazan admitted it to himself, with astonishment: he was afraid. He did not know why. He experienced an anguish without any apparent cause, the expectation of an unforeseen event of a terrible nature.

He lifted the canvas door-curtain of the room where he was walking, traversed with firm tread the Andalusian patio where the moonlight put gleams over the multicolored azulejos and opened the narrow window that overlooked the quay.

He leaned out, with the sensation that a form sprung from the shadows was about to seized him by the neck.

Everything was calm. The suburb of Triana was at rest. Almazan could see the mass of the Golden Tower on the other side of the Guadalquivir, and the great ocher-colored rampart that linked it to the Alcazar.

The tranquil strength of the stones reassured him. The minarets that some houses had retained from the Moorish epoch were outlined in the sky like young women exalted by the warm night. To his life were the illuminated lamps of the ghetto of Santa Cruz, and further away the Moorish quarter, where the carders and weavers lived. The landscape that Almazan had before his eyes was familiar and peaceful.

In any case, what did he have to fear? Several years ago, the militia of Saint Hermandad had organized a nocturnal police, which rendered armed attacks more difficult. Was he not known throughout Seville? Since the Jewish physician

116

Aboulfedia had ceased, by an inexplicable eccentricity, to practice medicine, he was the one, in spite of his youth, whom everyone came to consult. He was loved by the poor people of Triana, whom he treated gratuitously. It was true that the Holy Office suspected him of heresy. He knew that he was hated by Doctor Juan Ruiz, the queen's counselor, one of the two Dominicans appointed by the Pope, who was directing in Seville the initial investigations against conversos and Jews. But he had powerful friends who would warn him in case of real danger. His soul was well-tempered and, until now, inaccessible to fear.

He closed the shutter of his window. The sound made him shiver.

He shrugged his shoulders. He was irritated by his weakness, He talked to himself aloud.

"Come on! Am I losing my mind?"

His voice resonated with an unexpected tone in the little stairway that rose up to his bedroom.

He was about to cry "Guzman!" but he remembered that his servant, who slept above the gallery overlooking the patio, had asked him for permission to go and see his mother a few leagues from Seville, and would not return until the next day.

In any case, what would Guzman be able to do for him? It was the excessive heat that was agitating his nerves. Perhaps he had read too much of the guide to the ramblings of Maimonides, of which a large folio manuscript written in Arabic was open on his table.

He traversed the patio again and stopped, open-mouthed, holding his breath.

Like a blade traversing him, like a cold sweat covering his body, palpable and mute, hallucinatory and invisible, terror had just gripped him.

Everything was silent. A leaf from one of the laurel trees surrounding the pool placed in the middle of the patio was detached with a small sad sound and fell into the water. Almazan had a desire to utter a howl in order to break the spell of fear that enveloped him. But his voice caught in his throat.

117

It is in such cases that prayer is useful to those who be-lieve, he thought.

His reason rebelled. He made a great effort of will. He remembered the words of his master and benefactor, the Archbishop of Toledo, Alfonso Carrillo:[13] "There are some-times hidden powers that deliver themselves to great combats around us, without our being aware of it. Fortunately, a dense material form covers our understanding and veils our percep-tion, for we would go mad in contemplating them."

Archbishop Carrillo was right. There were a thousand living forms around him. Some were beneficent, but others were full of hatred and terrible to humans. Had not that old insensate Aboulfedia given him a description of gray larvae that floated above certain evil places, deformed ephialtes that physical eyes could not see because they were composed of a matter more subtle than that of our bodies. All the alchemists and scholars with whom he had conversed were unanimous regarding the existence of the world that populated the ether. At certain moments of great intellectual exaltation, had he not glimpsed himself the ideal contours of ravishing but immateri-al young women?

He raised his eyes and looked at the somber blue sky, dotted with stars. Was not the end-point of all reason, the ul-timate wisdom of the Greek, Hebrew and Arabic books that filled his house, the cult of the human will? He had the great-est strength possible within him.

That thought rendered him calmer.

Come on! The best thing I can do is sleep, he thought.

It was then that he perceived the sound of light footsteps on the quay and the presence of a human being behind the entrance door of his house. Someone was now pressed against

---

[13] This character is based on Alfonso Carrillo de Acuña (1410-1482), who was appointed as Archbishop of Toledo in 1446. He was one of the main instigators of a bloody civil war in Castile in the 1460s. The details of the character's later life given in the story are all fictitious.

the wood of the door, someone who had come through the streets of Seville to spy on him by night.

Quietly, he traversed the vestibule, and thought he distinguished a friction on the wood, as if a hand were groping for the bronze knocker in order to lift it.

He waited, but the knocker did not resonate. An absolute silence followed. Almazan drew nearer to the door. He listened with all the force of his attention, but he did not know whether he could hear the breath of a halting respiration or whether it was his imagination that made him think that someone was breathing close by.

He had put his ear to the lock. He could stand it no longer. With all his might he shouted: "Who's there?"

No one replied. Presumably, a thief coming to assure himself of the solitude of his house, or a spy of the Holy Office, would have fled at that appeal. He would have heard footfalls on the quay. A sick or wounded man desirous of his cares would have knocked and shouted.

All the forces of his attention were alert. Fear had placed a passionate curiosity in his heart. The danger, if there was one, was of a human order and did not frighten him. A weapon was unnecessary; he had confidence in his strength. Slowly, he turned the key. He listened again. This time, the silence seemed absolute—there was no longer the slightest breath.

Then he leaned on the catch and opened the door slightly. A light push made itself felt, as if someone were trying to make the batten swing faster. Almazan maintained it momentarily, and then decided to open it abruptly.

"There's no need to push, you can see I'm opening up...," he began to say.

But at that moment he had the vision of a blanched and contorted face, with immeasurably wide eyes, of which he could only see the white, with a wide mouth stretched on the right all the way to the ear as if by a monstrous hilarity, a face of ceruse or chalk, singularly dappled by gray patches.

He did not have time to be astonished by that spectral apparition. The bearer of the frightfully livid face, who was a man of tall stature, let all his weight fall upon him.

Instinctively, Almazan extended his arms and seized the unknown man by the neck, but he did not have to fight. The man collapsed heavily, as if his feet were made of lead and were dragging him down. Almazan contemplated him with amazement, lying on the mosaic tiles of the vestibule. Tics were still running over his revulsed features. His mouth stretched immeasurably, almost climbing as far as his eyes. The expression of laughter become demonic, and froze.

Almazan put his hand over his heart and made sure that he was dead.

He closed the door. He lifted up the recumbent body and dragged it across the patio as far as the room where his books were. He meditated profoundly.

He had just recognized the man, who must have expired behind his door at the very second that he opened it. It was Pablo, the confidential servant of his master Alfonso Carrillo. By the white foam on his lips, the torment of his features and the milky whiteness of his face and hands, Almazan saw that he had succumbed to a mineral poison of rapid effect, which had disorganized his nerves and abruptly decomposed his blood.

But why had the Archbishop of Toledo sent his servant to him at this late hour of the night? Why had the messenger crossed the few leagues that separated Seville from the dwelling to which Alfonso Carrillo had retired on foot and not on horseback?

Almazan had announced his visit for the next day. He wanted to consult his master about the propositions he had received from the Moorish king Abul Hacen,[14] who was at-

---

[14] This character is based on Abu l'Hasan Ali, who was the Sultan of Granada from 1464-82 and again from 1483-85. He refused to pay tribute to the realm of Castile in 1477 and invaded the city of Zahara in 1481, which sparked a war against

tracting to Granada the poets and scholars of Morocco and Spain to be installed in the Alhambra. The Archbishop must have had a very powerful reason to see Almazan to want to bring his visit forward by a few hours.

What could that reason be? What had happened?

Almazan searched the dead man's pockets. There was nothing in them. The message was doubtless oral.

He had to leave immediately. It was necessary to inform the Archbishop of his servant's death. But could he leave the corpse alone in his house? When his domestic Guzman returned in the morning, would he not be struck by terror on finding it? Who could tell what unforeseen steps terror might drive him to take? Then again, the nearest hirer off horses in Triana was in bed and would not open the doors of his stables until sunrise.

Almazan sat down in his armchair and tried to reconstitute the sequence of events that might have brought that cadaver to him.

Almazan had not known his father and could scarcely recover the image of his mother in the earliest memories of his childhood.

He saw once again, confusedly, a bronzed face framed with long dark tresses, with ardent eyes, and heard an Arabic song that she sang at sunset along the ramparts of Almazan, which was inexpressibly sad. He bore the name of the city of his birth. He had quit Almazan when his mother died, never to return.

"It's a pity; he's too handsome!" Archbishop Carrillo had said, when he had seen him for the first time in Toledo, where he had been confided, in order to be brought up, to a poor family of laborers. He had never been able to obtain ex-

---

Isabella I of Castile. The latter events are juxtaposed in the story, and chronological liberties are taken with a number of other datable events, but the principal action appears to take place in 1481-82.

act information about his birth. Inigo, who worked steel for an armorer, hardly ever spoke to him, and his wife Juliana was a gossip who scarcely recounted anything but lies. He only knew that is mother was a Moorish captive and his father a foreign scholar who only stayed in Almazan for a few days after having gone to visit the Archbishop of Toledo.

The esteem that he had for the father had earned the son, on the part of Alfonso Carrillo, a protection that had never been belied. First he had given the order that he be taught the métier of arms, which was done. Inigo's brother, an old soldier who had made war against the Moors, the Portuguese and the French, taught him to handle the sword and the lance, and to make use of an arbalest. But Almazan, who had shown a precocious love of study, was sent to the University of Salamanca, where he followed the course of the Trivium and Quadrivium, which comprised the education of all the known sciences.

The Archbishop of Toledo's protégé seemed destined to follow the ecclesiastical path and to succeed rapidly therein, but to everyone's surprise, he was distanced from it by the Archbishop himself, who encouraged him to neglect theology and go to study medicine with Abiatar in Cordova,[15] and then Abouldefia in Seville, who was more alchemist than physician, was reputed to be a heretic, and whom the protection of Jewish bankers had difficulty preserving from the pyre.

Almazan followed his master's advice. He settled in Seville and had a rapid success there.

It was then that the Archbishop of Toledo, the violent, capricious and extravagant Alfonso Carrillo, henceforth neglecting war, the Church and women, which he had loved

---

[15] Abiathar Crescas, a Jewish physician and astrologer who became the chief astrologer of King John of Aragon, who reigned from 1458-79. He became famous for restoring the king's eyesight by means of a pioneering cataract operation. Aboulfedia is fictitious, and is not to be confused with the fourteenth-century Arab historian Abulfeda.

equally, underwent a singular evolution. Abruptly, he shut himself away in his palace at Alcala de Henares, no longer to emerge therefrom. Faith had withdrawn from his soul like a tide leaving a limitless strand uncovered. He had glimpsed a new world.

He had cartloads of Arabic manuscripts brought from Cordova and set about deciphering them feverishly. He discovered the extent of the heavens. Quickly, one of is envoys departed for Malaga and bought from the Emir of that city the largest astronomical telescope in the world, which came from the times of the Almobade caliphs and had once been on the Giralda of Seville.[16] He had a special furnace brought from Fez, of a considerable weight, for the cooking of metals. He chartered a ship in Valencia and charged a cleric to go and search for a college of Syrian Sufis in the Orient, which possessed, it was said, engraved on a copper plate, a copy of the Emerald Tablet of Hermes.[17] He gave money to all-comers for chimerical secrets and insensate discoveries.

His servants had orders never to go into the rooms where he worked and where he was sometimes perceived clad in a white robe and crowned with a strange miter that did not resemble that of the Church.

---

[16] Astronomical telescopes were unknown in Europe until the seventeenth century, but Magre consistently places them in remoter periods of history in his historical novels, and seems to have believed that they were employed in the Orient in antiquity.

[17] The legendary Emerald Tablet of Hermes Trismegistus was reputed to contain the secret of the transmutation of primal matter, and was regarded by European alchemists as the foundation-stone of their art. The extant text, which is brief and gnomic, dates from the eighth century or thereabouts and was translated into Latin in the twelfth century. Its subsequent translators included Roger Bacon, Albertus Magnus and Isaac Newton.

The inhabitants of Alcala murmured dully. In the evenings, they went to throw stones at his windows. There was talk of sorcery and necromancy. Cardinal de Mendoza, his personal enemy, had written to the Pope about him. In spite of that, his situation at Court was as powerful as ever. He had once been Queen Isabella's confessor. She manifested several times the desire to have the Archbishop of Toledo beside her again, for whom she retained her affection. He had not responded to her advances.

One night, without informing anyone, accompanied by his only servant Pablo, he had quit Alcala, his books, his telescopes and furnaces. He had come to reside a few leagues from Seville, in a dilapidated Moorish dwelling that he had bought secretly some time before. It was in that dwelling that rabbi Aben Hezra[18] had lived, the translator of Alfergan, the author of a mysterious book about the origin of the world, which his contemporaries had mentioned but which had never been rediscovered. A vague legend claimed that the book had been hidden in his house for three centuries.

Had he added credence in that legend and did he want to find that book? Had he left Alcala in order to escape a danger that threatened him, or was he only in search of solitude? That was what Almazan had asked himself when had learned of the Archbishop's arrival a few days earlier.

---

[18] Rabbi Aben Ezra, whose full name was Abraham Ben Meir ibn Ezra (1089-1167) was one of the most distinguished Jewish philosophers of his era. He was forced into exile from Spain by persecution of the Jews. His prolific writings included numerous astrological tracts. The "Alferan" whose work he is alleged here to have translated is mentioned by that name in the *Encyclopédie* as an Arab astronomer; his name is usually rendered Al-Farghani or Alfraganus, and he lived in the ninth century. Translations of his textbook of elementary astronomy became a standard reference book during the Renaissance.

With his head in his hands he reviewed the details of his last visit to the house of Rabbi Aben Hezra.

He had told the aged Archbishop that he could not continue to live in that ruin, the doors of which were shaky and the windows staved in. The roads were full of thieves and Cantillana, the nearest village, was a league away. In addition to the thieves, it was necessary to fear all the people at Court who, being anxious about his possible return to the Queen's favor, had an interest in his death.

But Alfonso Carrillo had smiled at the young physician's fear. For him, material danger no longer existed. He had confided to him that he had discovered an order of dangers far more redoubtable. He knew the secret of evil and invisible forces that oppressed humans. It was not with firmly-closed doors and high walls that one could be protected from those forces. But he also knew the art of directing the beneficent powers that opposed the evil. He no longer had any need of the books, apparatus and telescopes so patiently amassed in Alcala. He had decided to wander henceforth among the centenarian box-trees that surrounded the ancient dwelling with a dark green forest, clad in the white robe of the Greek philosophers.

In addition, he might be about to initiate Almazan into his secrets. He was still hesitant. He thought him too young and above all too handsome, with eyes that were too large and too dark. The beauty of the body, he said, was a redoubtable bond that draws us into the chain of the passions. There was no urgency. Almazan must come again. He had adjourned the revelations.

As they parted, he had placed his hands on Almazan's shoulders, saying: "Soon."

And as Almazan had drawn way along the path, Pablo had caught up with him and made him party to his fears. He thought that his master's discourses were becoming strange and that something disquieting was floating over that solitary house. Furthermore, an unknown man had come the day before and had spent all night conversing with the Archbishop.

Pablo had made a portrait of the man. He said that he was about fifty. He was tall, with a pale face and extraordinarily bright eyes. His black garments were simply cut, but had something Oriental about them. He was not carrying any apparent weapon, and that was what had worried Pablo the most.

Why, Almazan thought, *did he make me swear that solemn oath not to reveal his retreat to anyone?* Someone knew, though. Who could the visitor be? What could the urgent message have been, and who had poisoned Pablo?

The heat did not diminish as the night advanced. It even became increasingly heavy. The foliage of the orange-trees on the patio stood out against the moon with such clarity that they seemed artificial, carved in jade. The marble basin and the circular colonnades appeared to Almazan so pale that everything around the livid corpse had an unreal air, and he thought that he was meditating in a nightmare.

Suddenly, he leapt to his feet. Coming from he knew not where, a muffled voice had called: "Almazan!"

He looked at the body extended before him. Had the lips not stirred? Was it not him who had pronounced his name, and repeated it several times?

But no; the lips of Carrillo's servant were now pinched, so rigidly clenched that they seemed closed by leaden pincers. The dead man really was dead, and was reminiscent of a caricature in white wax.

It was from the street that the appeal was coming. The voice was alive, warm and impatient. It was a woman's voice. At the same time, someone knocked on the door of the house.

Almazan closed the door of the room where Pablo's cadaver lay, carefully. Perhaps a further envoy was about to clarify the mystery that preoccupied him. Perhaps someone had simply come to seek him for a sick person in the vicinity.

As he reached the vestibule and placed his hand on the lock, he heard: "Open up, I beg you! In the name of Christ!"

He opened the door. Someone rushed inside. It was a woman. She closed the batten of the door immediately and fell upon the bolts that sealed it. Then she threw her arms around Almazan and clung to him.

"They're after me. I don't think they saw me. One second more and they would have seen me. Don't move. Don't make a sound. They're capable of anything."

Almazan felt warm breath, a semi-naked body. The woman's panting respiration caused her firm breasts to stir; her abdomen and legs quivered against him.

Shouts resounded on the quay. Several men went past at a run. There was a heavier tread behind them, doubtless that of an older man. He was trotting, grunting, and sometimes uttering insults. Almazan heard: "Oh, the bitch! Catch her! I must have her!"

Rapidly, the woman quit Almazan's breast and blew out the lantern that was illuminated near the door.

They both stood there without moving. The pursuers drew away along the quay. They had doubtless turned left, for they could no longer hear anything.

Then the singular visitor uttered a cry of joy, simultaneously savage and childlike. Again she put her arms round Almazan's neck.

"Thank you! You've saved me!"

She started to laugh: long, forced, hysterical, bizarre laughter, as if it were a matter of an enormous and dangerous joke that she had brought to a conclusion. She leapt up and down with satisfaction and her laughter went on and on.

Almazan had drawn her into the patio and considered her in the moonlight.

She was almost a child. There was something delectably passionate, ingenuous and cynical in her features. The expression on her face changed continually and nothing remained fixed but the gleam of two drops of gold that she seemed to have in the depths of her pupils, which had the same tint as the flowing gold of her hair, twisted into a sheaf. That hair agitated, framing her with flame, illuminating her, with the appearance of having a life of its own, and the nuances of that living hair were varied, by turns ruddy and dark, like a silken conflagration, or wheat in the moonlight.

She was small of stature, which further exaggerated her appearance of extreme youth. The upper part of her body was wrapped in a shawl. Her only garment was a short sapphire-blue basquine with black fringes, and one sensed that the shawl had been hastily thrown around her neck at the moment when she had fled and that the basquine had been attached in haste, and was not securely attached. Almazan saw a bruise on her naked right shoulder, caused by a blow or an excessively prolonged caress. He remarked that the carmine of her lips had been crushed by another mouth and smeared, enlarging the design of her lips. A diamond attached to a gold chain was sparkling between her breasts and she wore enormous ruby on her right hand. She had a slightly animal perfume and something lascivious and fatigued was disengaged from her skin.

For a few seconds, she quivered with rage, her face turned toward the quay.

"You heard him panting and dragging his feet," she said. "That will cost him dear. I'll have him tied up one night and chastise him with my own hand."

Then, satisfied with the idea of that vengeance, she stated laughing again.

"What happened" asked Almazan. "Did someone want your jewels?"

"She shrugged her shoulders.

"My jewels? It's certainly not a matter of my jewels. You're naïve. Apart from little Rodriguez, who would gladly have stolen them to give to a fisherman in Guadalquivir, the others don't care about them. You don't know little Rodriguez? He has blue eyes and he's well made. The old man likes him too. My God, what a night! Here, would you like my ring as a souvenir?"

She attempted to put her ruby on his finger, and as he refused her gaze made a tour of the patio, and she thought about something else.

128

"I like your house, but I'd like to rest for a while."

She headed for the door of the room where the dead man lay. Almazan saw that she was tottering slightly. He overtook her.

"Not that way," he said. "Take that staircase."

But she was obstinate in laughing. No, it was that door she wanted to open.

"Let me go in. I'll give you my diamond too."

Then he lifted her in his arms and climbed the stairs. She did not resist. She rolled her head on his shoulder and he felt her hair against his cheek. Her loins folded in abandonment. She had half-closed her eyes and he could see two motionless golden dots through the quivering lashes. He put her down on his bed.

She was suddenly weary. She stretched herself out. She had undone her shawl and her breasts appeared, without her trying to hide them. In the movement she had made as she stretched, her skirt had ridden up above the knee, allowing her naked leg to be seen, the curve of which was perfect. She turned her head and there was a fleeting gaze beneath her mobile eyelids.

"I'll tell you everything," she said, with a spontaneous impulsiveness. "But you won't understand. There are such singular men. You see, everything happened because of Cariharta. A whore like that! She's filth! I'll gouge her eyes out. As for him, he's sure of his affair. I swear it on the Virgin!"

With her little fingers in mid-air, she made the gesture of cutting with scissors, and laughed again, childishly.

"But you doubtless know him. Perhaps he'll come to find you afterwards in order for you to care for him. Who in Seville doesn't know the fat Jew Aboulfedia?"

Almazan shuddered. It was a matter of the physician Aboulfedia, with whom he had worked. He was a man of great science, but bizarre and full of whims. He had departed for Rome once, in order to convert the Pope to Judaism. For a long time he had worked on a flying machine and dreamed of launching himself from the top of the Giralda and soaring over Seville like a swallow. As he grew old he had abandoned science in favor of debauchery. Almazan remembered rumors that had run around on his account, and to which he had never lent credence. There had been talk of sadistic scenes that unfurled in his house in the suburb of Triana, of a reconstitution of the ancient Sabbat, with the murder of children and the adoration of the Devil. Risible legends, surely. But it was certain that the procuresses of Seville obtained a great deal of money from Aboulfedia and that on certain evenings he received the dregs of the shady taverns of Triana.

"What are you thinking about? Perhaps you're wondering how I had the idea of coming to knock on your door? Don't think that it's the first time I've seen you. You don't recall having gone one evening to a little house in the Santa Cruz quarter to care for a woman who had a stab-wound in the thigh? I was in the next room, and while you were bandaging the wound I lifted up a door-curtain and examined you. You had a lock of brown hair that was falling over your eyes, and you were continually brushing it backward impatiently. It was impeding your vision. You were staring at my friend Juana's leg so intently that I was jealous. It wouldn't have taken much for me to wound myself in order that you'd stare at me with the same intention. That happened not long ago. A Moorish slave had gone to fetch you on my behalf. Do you remember? Isabelle de Solis?"

"Isabelle de Solis?" repeated Almazan. "You're Isabelle de Solis?"

"That's me. What of it? Has someone spoken badly of me to you? You don't think I'm as pretty as is claimed? Oh! Nights in Aboulfedia's house are tiring."

She had propped herself up on her elbow and was looking Almazan full in the face, as if she were challenging him.

Isabelle de Solis had supplied fuel for all the conversations in Seville. She was the daughter of the Alcaide of Martos and she had been enslaved by an adventurer the previous year. Her father, a severe and pious man, had sworn to kill her. He

130

had pursued her to Seville, but had never been able to catch up with her. Isabelle de Solis, abandoned by her lover, had caused the captain of law, a collector of royal customs duties, who had set so many ambushes in the path of the venerable Alcaide that the latter had ended up quitting Seville, in fear of his life. Isabelle was nicknamed the "hermosa hembra" because of her beauty and the tranquil audacity with which she showed off the jewels of the tax-farmer's family when she emerged from mass.

Almazan had perceived her at a distance and had admired her. The beauty of women impressed him, but he avoided them out of pride, fearing rejection. He had arrived at considering amour as a danger, a sensual chain that attaches us to what is material, draws us downwards, and diminishes our power of thought. He had decided to banish it from his life. How would he have been able to recognize the "hermosa hembra" in that semi-naked girl running through Triana by night?

He leaned over her. So Isabelle de Solis was in his house, on his bed! The most beautiful young woman in Seville had come to him of her own accord to request protection! And now, with an equivocal grace, she had let herself fall back on his pillow, closing her eyes as if to go to sleep, only to open them again suddenly and provoke him with an oblique gaze and an abrupt stretching of her supple loins.

"Be chaste, if you want to be great in intelligence," his master Archbishop Carrillo had often said to him.

He knew that the pleasure of the senses was rapid and followed by sadness. It diminished intellectual capacity, the faculty of loving life.

He had a kind of vertigo. A warmth departed from his feet and ran all the way to the roots of his hair. He had a desire to throw himself brutally on that creature, sent to him by a mysterious whim of destiny, and to possess her, willingly or by force. But she would not resist. He sensed a tacit consent in the abandonment of the legs, in the weight of the head sinking into the pillow.

He thought about the dead man lying directly underneath, in a position symmetrical with that of the bed. He thought about the danger that his old master might be in at the present moment. And, at the same time, he imagined Aboulfedia with his flabby jaundiced face, his fat belly and little legs, among naked whores, pale adolescents and the silhouettes of assassins in rut.

He was disgusted with his own desire. He stepped back two or three paces, and then left the room quietly. He went down to the patio.

Suddenly, almost ungraspable, an odor reached him. It was an odor he knew well, that of human decomposition. Almazan had heard it said that certain mineral poisons had an effect of instantaneous disaggregation on the organism they attacked, but he was amazed that the dead man could make its power of destruction sensible with such rapidity. That mortuary odor, which mingled with that of the orange-trees in the calm light of the pale moon, had something atrocious about it.

But was he not mistaken? He opened the door of his study room. He picked up the heavy bronze lamp that was burning there in both hands and leaned over Pablo's body.

The blanched face was now stained with streaks. The veins of the neck and hands were lacquer red. The lips were green-tinted. An intense curiosity animated Almazan before the mysterious molecular labor that was commencing.

Death, the termination of a temporary form, was the beginning of a more extraordinary activity than that which had made the body move when it was alive. The cells coordinated for the existence of a whole were resuming their autonomy, changing into liquids and gases. In that flesh and those bones, under the action of the destructive mineral, there were liquefactions, explosions, multiplications of parasites, the unfurling of populations on the march amid lakes in formation and on the shores of putrescence, and an incomprehensible life was seething there.

What a drama that was! How much time would humans require before having found the intimate secret of the substance of which they were molded?

He passed his hand over his forehead and stood up. He thought that it was necessary to make a decision, and the embarrassment of the situation appeared to him. It was not in vain that he had sensed invisible evil influences floating around him. His dwelling, once peaceful, now sheltered a dead creature and a living creature more dangerous than the dead one. What was he to do?

While he reflected, it seemed to him that the light was modified and that the dawn was already spreading its first tints.

He thought he heard a slight sound. He had the impression that someone might be looking at him through the keyhole and seeing the singular spectacle that he must form, standing next to the corpse in an attitude of anguish. He launched himself forward, ran up the stairs rapidly and opened the bedroom door. The bed was empty. He went down again immediately and looked behind the orange-trees and the laurels. He made a tour of the patio. An orange was detached and made a splash in the pool.

He perceived that the entrance door was ajar. He ran to it. He looked outside. On the quay to the right, already far away, in the shadow that the Golden Tower made, there was a woman of small stature drawing away.

She was drawing away slowly, without fear, without haste, indolently, as if nothing in particular had happened. Sometimes, she stopped, to respire the morning air, or to contemplate the first roseate hues of the rising sun on the walls of the Alcazar.

II. The Rabbi's House

Almazan was now riding alongside the Guadalquivir in the roseate light of morning. In exchange for a few reals, one of the hirer's grooms had had gone to sit on the steps of the house and wait there for the arrival of Guzman, with the mission of sending him immediately along the Cantillana road, to the dwelling of Rabbi Aben Hezra, where he would find his master. Almazan had his key in his doublet. No one could get into his house before he returned. He was tranquil on that matter.

But he was astonished not to be pressing his mount harder and not being more tormented by anxiety, remaining so detached from events. In spite of the corpse he had left behind him and the uncertainty of the danger that Archbishop Carrillo was running, he felt vaguely glad. He reproached himself for that obscure satisfaction, only to savor it again. So, Isabelle de Solis had thought of him! She had come to seek a refuge under his roof! He was accompanied by her affectionate presence.

The waters of the Guadalquivir flowed between their scorched banks like a promise of amour, and the line of hills bordering the horizon and extending a blue-tinted shadow in his direction seemed softer. He experienced an ardent joy in living, and found the word full of beauty

A kingfisher rose into the air, and he almost stopped to watch the wake of colored plumage that it made in the air. He had the sentiment the somewhere, around him, a childlike face framed by flame was gazing at him with mobile golden pupils. He respired forcefully the vegetal odor disengaged from the matinal earth and thought he could sense the human perfume of a body that he had held in his arms.

He saw a shepherd descending a slope. He crossed paths with a monk sitting on his donkey. He listened to a distant church bell. He urged his horse forward. Finally, in the distance, to the left, he perceived the somber mass that the gigantic box-trees of Aben Hezra's dwelling formed.

Those box-trees loomed up like a wall. They were menacing, tormented and blind. They evoked thoughts of solitude and renunciation. In order to reach them it was necessary to follow a long avenue bordered with poplars, and even when one drew near to two truncated columns, which indicated that there had once been a gate there, the house hidden by the centenarian box-trees still could not be seen.

Almazan leaned forward in order to see more quickly. He imagined that the Archbishop might be waiting for him at the entrance and that he might perceive his white robe in the distance. But an impressive silence covered everything. In the sky, a bird that was descending and gliding, gave the impression of a message sent by destiny. The truncated columns, with Arabic characters engraved on them, took on the significance of funerary steles. The immobility of the foliage, which seemed to be attentive, penetrated Almazan with an impression of anguish.

He passed between the columns and tried to utter a shout in order to announce his arrival, but his voice failed in his throat and the sound he emitted was low and hoarse, different from his own voice, as if expressing an internal terror of which he was not yet conscious.

To his right he perceived the open and empty stables. The horses had been stolen, then. He dismounted, observed that there was no trace of disorder there, and advanced on foot through the mute pathways between the box-trees.

It was then that a sound reached him. It was the clack of one object against another, or a door that had been closed abruptly, or perhaps the fall of a body. He could not make it out exactly. He advanced at a faster pace. The pathway turned, and he found himself facing the house.

It had been constructed in the time of the Arab caliphs, in an epoch of peace, when the police were efficient, and it did not have any kind of defense. The park extended behind it, on the hillside, among heather and rocks, and Almazan saw, at a

135

glance, how easy it had been to reach the house without being seen and without leaving any trace.

It formed a large square mass, whose whiteness the shade of the box-trees caused to stand out more, and which only had narrow opening for windows, placed very high and closed by wooden trellises. The door, which was made of iron studded with bronze nails, was open, and Almazan was struck by an ancient inscription that he had not noticed during his previous visits.

He went through the doorway rapidly and found himself in the interior courtyard. He took a few steps and stopped in order to look around.

The courtyard was vast, full of aloes and pomegranates, and weeds had grown between the paving-stones. It was surrounded by porticos that sustained a circular gallery whose sculpted wooden colonnettes had been eroded by time. Windows and doors opened to that courted and Almazan was surprised to observe that they were all open. He had the sensation that there were beings watching from the shadows of the rooms, on every side at once.

A singular life seemed to be circulating around him. Old wood paneling was uttering sighs, parquets were groaning, and the sound that he had heard before struck him again. He listened. A door had banged to his right. Another banged behind him. Perhaps the wind had just risen at that very moment and, in agitating the battens, was the sole cause of those sounds. But who had opened all the doors and all the windows like that? Had not Archbishop Carrillo always had an immoderate dread of air currents, to the point of having the keyholes in the rooms where he slept stuffed with pieces of cloth?

Even then, in spite of the extreme anxiety he was experiencing, Almazan saw the face of Isabelle de Solis for a few seconds, and delighted in the memory of cruel and childlike laughter.

He chased away that image and made a decision. He went into the large hall on the ground floor that had been the former Arab Mabeyn. The Spanish successors of Aben Hezra had crammed it which somber oak furniture, which stained the bright azulejos of the walls. The dust was so thick that that it seemed to have been cast like a layer of ash. Almazan did not pause in that room. He ran into another, passed under the ogive of an open door, and went through a long sequence of empty rooms full of echoes.

He could not remember the exact location to which Archbishop Carrillo had taken him when he wanted to see him. He retraced his steps. He visited other apartments. A breath of desolation and a mystery of solitude descended from the ceilings. The sheets of white marble, the paneling of colored cedar-wood and the faded beauties of Moorish art added, by virtue of their abandonment, to the bleak melancholy that filled the place.

He had arrived at the foot of the stairway. He climbed it. It seemed to him that the search would never end.

It was then that, having pushed yet another door, he found himself face to face with Archbishop Carrillo, seated in a large armchair, who stared at him with round white eyes. His long and powerful hand was placed on the table, where he was in the process of writing. That extraordinary hand had the appearance of being sculpted from a block of chalk, and it was by virtue of its lividity and the redness of the veins that snaked along it that Almazan realized that he was in the presence of a dead man.

He had died by the same poison as his servant. He had been sitting down at his table, and death had struck him while he was writing.

The features of the face were not distorted. The forehead seemed broader. The eyes were terrible. Almazan attempted to close them, but the eyelids resisted and rose again. He only succeeded in part, and the Archbishop seemed to be darting an oblique vitreous gaze beneath them.

Almazan saw his name on the paper on which the chalk hand seemed to be drawing with the nail of the index finger. It was a piece of linen paper hastily torn from a notebook that was beside it, and where part of the torn sheet could be seen, still joined to the others. He read a few lines in tortured handwriting.

I am going to die before you arrive, without having been able to tell you what it is necessary for you to know at all costs. These sheets I am placing in the table will inform you partially. I was insane to wait. One never believes that one will die. I could not know that they feared me to this extent. I ought to have realized that as I emerged from ignorance and the truth took possession of me, I would become powerful and, in consequence, redoubtable. But the essential thing is that you live, and for that it is necessary that you flee. Leave without reflection, immediately, and do not return to Seville, either to regulate your affairs or to bid farewell to your friends. This is my last thought. In Granada...

Archbishop Carrillo had stopped writing at that word. He must have made a great effort, for the last lines were tremulous and barely legible. He had tried to continue, but had not been able to succeed. Incoherent streaks indicated that his hand had ceased to obey his will. However, he had been able to gather his strength and he had succeeded in tracing a name at the bottom of the page—a name unknown to Almazan.

That name was *Christian Rosenkreutz*.

Almazan repeated it mechanically two or three times.

Then he remembered having heard mention from the Archbishop himself of a death that had occurred in analogous circumstances, and which had been marked by the same symptoms. Don Pedro Giron, grandmaster of Calatrava and Carrillo's nephew, had left Almagro a few years before, followed by a numerous escort. He had been going to the Infanta Isabella, accepted by her brother Henrique as her fiancé. He had stopped overnight in the village of Vilarubia, near Ciudad Real. In the morning, nothing had been found in his room but a cadaver, so white that the servant who was the first to enter had not been able to distinguish its whiteness from the sheets, and had thought the bed was empty.

From the depths of his memory Almazan tried to recover what he had heard the Archbishop say about that subject.

Abruptly, he leapt toward the door. He had been struck by a sudden thought. The poison had not been absorbed in food; it was in the air. He was breathing it in. He was about to perish by the same means as the Archbishop and his servant Pablo.

But he changed his mind. The archbishop must have suspect the manner in which an invisible enemy as attempting to reach him, and he had opened all the doors and windows in order to purify the air. The gusts that had animated the old Moorish dwelling, making the shutters and doors bang like appeals, must have borne away the mysterious mortal force.

Almazan went to the window and breathed in deeply. Then he examined the wooden shutter. He noticed a narrow opening, rounded in form, and freshly made. Someone must have come, at nightfall, along the gallery overlooking the courtyard, and made the hole, narrow in appearance but broad enough to allow death to pass through it. The poison must have had an effect all the more rapid because the chamber was hermetically sealed. Doubtless the Archbishop had summoned Pedro, the latter had come, and a few minutes, or perhaps a few seconds, had sufficed for him to respire the same death as his master.

Neither of them had imagined then that the dose of the poison absorbed was sufficient for their hours to be counted. Pablo had left for Seville. The Archbishop was so certain of seeing his servant come back with the man he called his son that he had not thought of writing down what it was so urgent to tell him. It was only at the end, either because of an onset of pain it by virtue of the singular perception that the spirit sometimes acquires at the moment of quitting its corporeal form, that he had traced those few enigmatic lines in haste.

Why was he, Almazan, under threat? What had he to do with any vengeance by which Archbishop Carrillo might have been pursued because of an existence that had been divided between violence and justice, folly and wisdom? Why that imperious order to go immediately to the realm of the Moors? Was the danger so great that all of Catholic Spain was forbidden to him? And by virtue of what confidence did the Archbishop exhort him to go to Granada, on the very day when he was to come to consult him about his eventual departure for that city?

Almazan reread the paper he was holding in his hand. Who was this Christian Rosenkreutz? What was the truth that had rendered the Archbishop redoubtable to the enemies to which he made allusion, and who were those enemies?

By crowding his mind, all those questions had annihilated his faculty of grief. He had never loved the Archbishop tenderly. He had been grateful to him, fearful of him and admiring. He was the man who had guided the development of his ideas and had orientated them in a direction very distant from the teachings of the Church. Almazan owed to the Archbishop his liberty of thought, and he had measured the inestimable extent of that benefit.

He approached the dead man with the intention of formulating mentally a speech whose magic would be powerful enough to resonate in the beyond. But he could not find the words. Could love alone inspire them? The Archbishop's face seemed to him to be formidably serene, but simultaneously imprinted with such a frightful solitude that Almazan remembered the faces of so many simple men that he had seen on their death-bed, and he wondered whether it might not be better to prefer an expression of pitying attachment to the majesty of a seeker of truth in the individuals one quits.

He took the Archbishop's hands and crossed them. In the course of that gesture a small metal object fell to the floor. It was a cross made of alchemical gold, but a singular cross with a thick rose in the middle, a cross that Almazan thought sufficient to have its possessor burned by the Holy Office.

He put it in his pocket. He took from the table the notebook that the Archbishop had placed there with his intention and left the room, under the vitreous gaze of the dead man, filtering through the half-closed eyelids.

And it seemed to him, at the very moment when he quit the physical form of his master forever, that Isabelle de Solis was at the door and making him a sign, laughing sacrilegiously and showing her bare breasts immodestly, outside her torn chemise.

III. The Archbishop's Notebook

As soon as he was among the shadows of the box-trees in the park, Almazan started leafing through the Archbishop's notebook.

There were notes devoid of sequence, often contradictory. Some of them had been written feverishly, others scrawled furiously. Sometimes, a few pages had been torn out.

In the same way that the spirit of good is incarnate in messiahs and prophets, the Antichrist descends into the soul of certain individuals to set an active perversity to work in order that the world goes backwards. That is logical; it is certain. One cannot imagine a medallion without a reverse side, pleasure without pain, light without darkness. That has always been hidden by those who knew. The colleges of the priests of ancient religions only revealed it in their Mysteries to Initiates of a superior order. Would the world gain anything from such knowledge? A few strong men would stand up to struggle with more ardor, but terror would curb the weak and they would be borne away by the attraction of evil. For evil possesses seduction and it is more powerful than good.

Thus I have been able to live for so many years under the reign of the Antichrist without being aware of it.

The Antichrist is not the man who sheds blood, he is not the man who kills the body, and he is not the man who burns churches, but the man who lights a flame at their summit to create the belief that God has descended there.

Why does the truth appear to some when they are young and capable of action, and to others only at the end of their life? How have I been able to be possessed to such a degree by pride, to expend myself for vain interests, to accomplish so many sterile and criminal acts? With the material and spiritual powers that were devolved to me, what tasks I might have been able to accomplish! Since the initiates who live in Damascus and Jerusalem knew me and chose me, why did their messenger not arrive sooner? How much time wasted! Christian Rosenkreutz has told me that it is necessary for every man to discover himself and extract the truth from his soul as a miner extracts a little gold from a subterranean seam, but that does not appear to me to be a sufficient response. They ought to have enlightened me, since they could. I criticize them from the bottom of my heart, but that is the effect of my nature. I once cursed the Pope, I have cursed God, and I am cursing those who are bringing me the truth. But is it really the truth?

According to many prophets the Antichrist ought to be a Jew of the tribe of Dan. Saint Jerome and Saint Anselm affirm that he will be born in Babylon. Saint Hippolyte represents him as merciful during the early years of his life, in order better to deceive men. He will travel the earth mounted on a donkey. His stature will be surprising and one cannot fail to recognize him by his astonishingly red and gummed-up eyes. What childishness!

I was struck, a few years ago, by eyes such as I had never seen. They were bright eyes, miraculously profound, which did not reflect hatred, or pity, or desire, or pride, but a strange certainty that made me shiver. The eyes in question were those of a prior of the convent of Santa Cruz in Segovia. He met me at the convent door, surrounded by Dominicans of his order. When he had kissed me hand, bowing respectfully, I thought that I was surrounded for a few seconds by a supernatural light, and I contemplated an apocalyptic spectacle of the end of the world. There were no extravagant abysms, no flames springing forth from the earth. The angels were not sounding their trumpets through the clouds. There was merely the sign of regression on the faces of the people surrounding me.

The old porter of the convent had taken on the expression of a faithful dog and the key he was holding in his hand resembled a bone that he was about to gnaw. The birdlike profile of one of my pages was emphasized to the point that he seemed overwhelmed by the weight of a beak. My guards, whose breastplates were gleaming like corselets, were insects raising their stings. A peasant on all fours before a stream was gulping water with a woolly jaw like that of a sheep. I saw leonine faces, supple bodies like those of snakes, hands on which talons grew like those of vultures, and others that were webbed like those of ducks.

The prior and the Dominicans had raised their heads and were looking at me with ecstatic eyes filled with nothingness. And I was obliged to make a great effort of will not to whistle, bark, croak or roar. I quit them in haste, telling myself that the Antichrist would have a similar power of emptiness in the depths of the eyes and that his reign would not be marked by any visible catastrophe but by an internal movement of the human soul toward the Beast, which is the supreme sin.

I learned not long ago that Tomas de Torquemada has been raised to the rank of the Queen's confessor.

The Rose-Cross! A secret order that has for its aim defending and transmitting intelligence. Are there men disinterested enough and pure enough to be part of it? And why have I been chosen? Am I worthy of it?

It was a year ago, to the day, that Christian Rosenkreutz came for the first time, bringing me the message.

The idea that there are individuals consciously orientated toward evil and that those individuals accomplish evil lovingly and logically, as a divine duty, has something terrifying about it.

He is right; evil almost always triumphs. What has become of the wisdom of the Egyptian priests? It is extinct, almost without leaving any trace. And that transmitted in the

Mysteries of Eleusis? Nothing left. The explanation of the world by means of numbers that Pythagoras taught has been lost. Since the origins of Christianity, the letter has stifled the spirit and the Pope would be astonished if anyone told him that his Church is only the shadow of a truth that has been deliberately lost. The Gnostics of Alexandria, the disciples of Nestorius and certain sects of Syria and Palestine also possessed that truth. They have disappeared like a lamp that is blown out. The force of evil!

I cannot understand why it is necessary not to employ force. I have an immense fief, soldiers and treasures. If, as I have been told, it is in this time and in this country that evil will be incarnated and radiate with a force unprecedented in the history of the world, why should I not struggle against it with the material armaments at my disposal? I am ready to fill my prisons and erect pyres in all the squares in Toledo.

Every member of the Order of the Rose-Cross must choose a successor at the moment of his death. Who shall I designate?

Should it be the cleric Ambrosio or Almazan? Ambrosio is more reflective and more laborious. Almazan is more intelligent—but he is handsome, and beauty is a trap that nature extends to humans to make them fall. Oh, if I had been ugly, what would not have happened to me?

It is true that he has Moorish blood in his veins. To the Moorish race, for eight centuries, Christian Rosenkreutz affirms, the guardianship of the world's intellectual treasure has been given.

I cannot believe that. When I remember his words on the subject, I began to doubt again. Christ's enemy race might be an elect race! The followers of Mohammed had a mission higher than that of the defenders of the Cross! Evidently, it is in Arabic manuscripts that I study philosophy, my palace in Toledo and that of Alcala were built in accordance with the rules of Arab architecture, and it is through the telescope constructed by the Caliphs of Cordova that I gaze at the color of the planets.

The rose and the cross! Amour and knowledge! I am a blind man for whom a ray of light is commencing to filter through.

The rules of the Order of the Rose-Cross:

To relieve suffering in a disinterested fashion. I have not relieved any suffering.

To love God, in the sense of wisdom and verity, above all things. I have loved my own self above all things.

To be patient, modest and silent. I have been violent, proud and loquacious.

To devote one's life to the progress of the spirit, in others and in oneself. I have not enlightened any man, and it seems that my ignorance had increased.

To gather once a year in a given place. I shall not go to Granada.

To choose as a successor a man of pure intelligence. Neither Ambrosio the stupid nor Almazan the skeptic. No one is worthy to succeed me.

I have resumed the Great Work. It will not serve any purpose. Putting the formulae that have been sold to me into practice has produced nothing but smoke. The majority of pretended sages are only charlatans.

I can no longer doubt. They exist, those whom Christian Rosenkreutz calls black magicians. They exist, they know that I know of their existence, and they have designs on my life.

Tomas de Torquemada…his ascetic youth…the unlimited passion for dolor…the void of the eyes…the mask of Satan…

Is he Satan incarnate?

There is a mystery in that Torquemada.

Christian Rosenkreutz is mistaken. It is necessary to bring about the triumph of good by force. I have just replied to the Queen. I shall set forth tomorrow to join her. I shall reform the Spanish Church.

How blissful solitude is! I understand here why the Arabs cherished box-trees and always planted them in their gardens. In their shade there is a kind of philosophical reverie, and the man who lives in their proximity thinks with more force. Arnaud de Villeneuve gives a recipe in his *Thesaurus Thesaurorum* for a beverage made with the root of the box-tree and a dozen ingredients that are violent poisons. Doubtless those poisons combat one another. Their mixture produces an incomparable spiritual exaltation, according to Arnaud de Villeneuve.[19] Fortunately, the *Thesaurus Thesaurorum* is among the books that I have ordered Pablo to put on his horse.

Christian Rosenkreutz had received my message. He has come. I have talked to him about Almazan and my hesitations. He replied to me that there is no urgency, since I shall doubtless live for a long time. I find his insistence that I go secretly to Granada singular. What if that hides some monstrous trap? We are at peace with the Moors, but the Archbishop of Toledo would be an invaluable hostage for Sultan Abul Hacen. Nor do I understand why Christian Rosenkreutz showed such great anxiety when I told him about a few intoxications procured for me by box-tree root and Arnaud de Villeneuve's twelve ingredients.

---

[19] The physician Arnaldus de Villa Nova (c1240-1311), called Arnaud de Villeneuve in many French sources, translated many medical texts from Arabic. Following his death he acquired the reputation of hang been an alchemist, and several well-known alchemical texts were falsely attributed to him, including the one cited here.

What has just happened to me is extraordinary. Just now I thought I heard a sort of rustle in the room next door to the one in which I read and sleep, like something soft rubbing against the wall. I picked up the bronze lamp, opened the door and looked out. I saw, or thought I saw, a giant rat with an extremely pale human face, which gazed at me for a second and fled through the other door of the room, which opens to the staircase. I set down the lamp and tried to pursue it, but I stumbled in the darkness. I heard its hairy tail brushing the stones. Then I remembered the Antichrist and his advent.

There is also a bat of extraordinary size that walks like a man over the gallery of the house. It is extremely fearful. At the slightest sound I make as I open the window it flies away over the roof. But when I extinguish the lamp it comes to adhere to the shutter and it listens for hours to my respiration. I regret not having a sword. I would deliver an immense thrust through the wood of the shutter and nail it. Yes, a sword, a sharp sword. I shall send Pablo to ask Almazan for one. It is necessary that I see at close range these first human exemplars, the annunciators of the reign of the Beast.

Since my arrival in this ancient dwelling, I have only conversed with Almazan and Christian Rosenkreutz. Pablo goes to Cantillana every morning to seek provisions. All three of them must know. Why have they not said anything? Are they afraid of the disturbance that it might cast into my mind? Have they noticed a commencement of the horrible evolution in my own features? There is only one mirror here, which is in the Mabeyn on the ground floor. It is an old, damaged mirror that only sends back deformed mages of which I cannot be proud. Last night, I contemplated myself in it at length by the light of a smoky lamp. In my philosopher's tunic I look like a great white owl devoid of wings. There was a disquieting quiver of felt around me. Do the bat and the rat also come to adhere to the mirror in order to see their increasing animality?

I have gone to the stables, unhitched the horses and chased them away into the countryside. Why should they be the slaves of their fellows? I saw a shepherd in the distance with a cloak of black feathers. He had a crow's beak and croaked as I approached. He fled, hopping on his feet, when I tried to seize him.

Jesus Christ said: Immediately after that day of affliction, the sun will darken and the moon will no longer give any light.

Now, the twilight has just been singularly brief, and the moon, which ought to be high in the sky, has not appeared. The unfortunate Pablo's eyes are strangely shrunken, and just now I heard him barking in the courtyard. A dog, a wretched dog!

It isn't worth the trouble of writing anything, for beasts cannot read.

Almazan almost let Archbishop Carrillo's notebook fall from his hands, so full of amazement was he. He formed new hypotheses. Perhaps his master had poisoned himself with Arnaud de Villeneuve's beverage, and it was the beverage that had troubled his mind. But he really had seen a circular hole in the shutter of the room. The Archbishop might have pierced it himself in order to keep watch on what was happening on the gallery. What about Pablo? Perhaps he had also made him drink the same poison with the aim of procuring him a salutary spiritual intoxication. Why had he sent him to Seville by night? Perhaps simply to satisfy his whim to have a sword in order to nail a chimerical bat to his shutter.

Christian Rosenkreutz remained, for Almazan, an enigma that he could only clarify in Granada—for he thought that, in spite of everything, his duty was to obey the Archbishop's last will and to do so with the precipitation that the latter had recommended.

Holding his horse by the bridle, he had arrived while reflecting at the end of the avenue of poplars that led to the road.

In the direction of Seville he could see someone in the distance heading toward him. It was his servant Guzman, coming to join him as he had ordered.

He brought him up to date with what had happened. Guzman was to go to Cantillana, where there was an officer of the Sainte-Hermandad. It was him, initially, whom he was to inform of the Archbishop's death. Afterwards, he would go back to Seville, go to see the governor on his behalf, tell him about the night's events and take care of Pablo's burial.

Almazan would head for Granada immediately, taking the road via Carmona and Marchena.

At the moment of quitting Guzman, he thought that his departure might seem inexplicable, and he gave his servant the piece of paper on which the Archbishop had written his supreme desire. Guzman was to put it in the hands of the governor of Seville.

In any case, Almazan thought that his voyage would not be of long duration, and that he would be able to return in a few days.

And the two men drew away in different directions.

The brick tower of Cantillana was still visible behind him when Almazan remembered that he had not eaten or slept since the day before. He went past a posada at the confluence of the Vir and the Guadal, where boatmen gathered. He dismounted and went in.

He sat down on a rickety stool and a brunette girl, thickset and dirty, served him. The cool shade of the low-ceilinged room and the sudden influx of wellbeing that nourishment gave him caused him to become involuntarily drowsy. With his forehead leaning on his arms, he struggled for some time but then let himself slip into a kind of torpor.

In the midst of that transparent slumber, the girl, whose head and torso he could see between two earthenware jugs, began to smile, and that smile displayed luminous teeth. She leaned over, and a beam of light coming from the door, which stood ajar, played over her neck, which was thin and milky.

She was not brunette. A bright gold flowed around her delicate head. She seemed to be reaching out toward Almazan and her smile had suddenly given way to an ardent expression. She advanced her lips lightly toward him and creased her eyelids, as if she were appealing to him before swooning.

He straightened up suddenly. He passed his hand over his face. He understood, by the light illuminating the room in the inn, that dusk was falling. The thickset girl had left the counter and was moving around heavily, her eyes dull.

He gave her a silver coin. He leapt on to his horse.

A delay of a few hours, he thought. *It's necessary for Aboulfedia to tell me where I can find her.*

He did not want to reflect. His instinct was driving him. And it was along the road to Seville that he returned, through the twilight.

IV. The Sabbat at Aboulfedia's House

Aboulfedia's house was situated in the Triana district, near the extremity of a side-street that faded away into waste ground. It was surrounded by a high white wall that prevented it from being visible from without. Aboulfedia had recently had the entrance door remade in wood of enormous thickness, as if it might have to withstand and assault.

Almazan was surprised, after he had knocked on that door, to see the guardian who came to open it manifest no astonishment at his nocturnal visit. He did not ask who he was; he took his horse into a dilapidated stable that was to the left, between a few palm trees, and, holding his lantern aloft, he preceded him into a pathway that led to the house.

It seemed to Almazan that the servant was one-eyed and powdered, and that his unique eye was fixed on him amicably. Having arrived at the perron and fearing that he had been mistaken for another visitor who was expected, Almazan stopped and said: "Go inform Alboufedia that his former pupil Almazan wishes to speak to him."

But no, there was no mistake. The one-eyed man made a slight movement of his shoulders, which meant that there was absolutely no need to inform Aboulfedia, and, as if to aid him to mount the three steps of the perron, he took Almazan by the arm, subjecting it to such a long and familiar pressure that the latter nearly sent him sprawling in the garden with a blow of his fist. But he contained himself.

The strange servant had just pushed him into a large room surrounded by columns, and had already departed at a run into the garden, doubtless to open the door to a newcomer, for distant raps had resounded at the portal.

The room that Almazan had just entered was dimly illuminated by two lamps that only emitted a confused light. There was stifled laughter, a rustle of fabric, and a form enveloped in a large chestnut-brown cape allowed a door-curtain to fall back and disappeared. Almazan only had time to see a white hand and the glint of a ruddy gemstone.

He was alone. He looked around. The walls were covered with precious hangings in laminated silk, which were faded and soiled. A disemboweled cushion had spread its feathers in a circle like the pale humor of a wound. In a corner, an empty pitcher had been forgotten, which must have contained wine.

Almazan waited for some time. In the end, impatiently, he approached the door at the back of the room. He lifted up the heavy cloth that covered it and was about to open it when it swung on its hinges and he found himself face to face with Aboulfedia.

He was clad in an Arab gandourah with broad sleeves, under which he was wearing a chemise in transparent pink silk, extensively ripped. His enormous and ridiculous belly could be seen through it, and even the graying hairs on his chest. His sparse jet black hair, recently dyed, was stuck to his temples by a moist cosmetic. He was puffed up, shiny with unguents, impregnated with aromatics, polished by massages and was trembling on the minuscule sticks of his legs like a painted gourd, in the midst of a perfume of Oriental rose and human fat.

He hastened to close the door behind him. His broad face had brightened at the sight of Almazan. He always seemed to be laughing because of the breadth of his mouth and the two wrinkles that framed it, but he seemed astonishingly sad as soon as one had perceived that that hilarity did not proceed from his humor but merely from the conformation of his features.

Immediately, he began speaking volubly.

He knew everything. News traveled more rapidly than cavaliers on the roads. People were looking for Almazan everywhere. An important individual whom he had visited that very morning had been found dead in the vicinity of Seville. Now he was in hiding. He had done well to think of his former master in medicine, the reproved Aboulfedia. Hs actions only concerned him. He was safe in that house in Triana.

Almazan could not help blushing, and thought for the first time how unusual his action was. He hastened to disculpate himself. He had nothing to fear. So many rumors ran around that had no foundation. The governor of Seville had a document in his hands that legitimated his absence. If he had come to find Aboulfedia...

He lowered his voice. He had a great deal of difficulty explaining the objective of his visit. He sensed its strangeness. And then, the atmosphere of the house, Aboulfedia's costume, the heaviness of perfumes, the dirty sumptuousness of things, were causing him a physical malaise.

The eyes of the old physician were blinking now with irony, and his prominent chin cleft his mouth even more broadly.

"It's with regard to this affair," said Almazan. "I've come to consult you about the power of certain poisons. Do you believe that the atmosphere of a room can be rendered mortal to the extent of bring about an almost immediate decomposition of the blood on the part of anyone who breathes that atmosphere?"

But Aboulfedia took him by the shoulders and shook him gently.

"Why this lack of sincerity? Have I not taught you all I know about poisons? When I went to Rome to make that foolish attempt to convert the Pope to Judaism, I leaned that the masters of the art of poisoning are the Italians, who can make people die simply by brushing them with a fingernail or a hair. Life is such a little thing. You know that as well as I do. Be frank. You don't care at this moment about the effects of poison on an old man who is dead. And you're right. You're only thinking about the joy of a young man who is alive..."

Almazan was about to protest. The old physician stopped him. He was sure of his fact.

"How lucky you are! You're thirty years ahead of me. It took me all that time to perceive that pleasure as the only certainty. When I was your age, I had such a great faith that I would gladly have been burned for no matter what idea that was dear to me. To the point of going mad, I adored the Jewish race, science, the Messiah. The messiah! I believed in him with all my soul. When the astrologer Avenar announced that he would appear at midnight on the second of March 1467, I recall that I had such a great spiritual intoxication that I had difficulty preventing myself from dancing. I fasted and prayed for three days in order to be worthy of receiving him, for I had no doubt that it was to my house that he would come first.

"All the Jews in the Santa Cruz quarter had left their doors open, and I saw their credulous faces and black bonnets in the tranquil night. I too left my door open. Well, when midnight chimed at the Giralda, who do you think came into my house? A poor prostitute that the alguazils were pursuing for some misdeed or other. I hid her and had her lie down in my bed while I continued to wait on my threshold. In the morning, I scrutinized the dawn anxiously, and the Santa Cruz quarter was full of square-shouldered men gazing at the sky. Avenar must have been mistaken by a few hours, and we waited during the following nights.

"Insensate that I was! I hadn't understood that it was the revelation of my destiny that the astrologer had seen in the planets, and that my Messiah really had come for me in the magnificent form of a whore. I was waiting at my door and the Messiah was in my bed. Years passed, and it was only when my face had become as jaundiced as a rotten orange and my belly had swollen in a caricaturish fashion that I realized that all powerful pleasure is in youth and that there is no God to forbid it to us, nothing but death to steal it from us forever."

Aboulfedia was pacing back and forth in the room and Almazan gazed in astonishment at his obscene costume, the deceptive gaiety of his youth and the desperate gleam in his little eyes.

"But you've come a long way," he said, suddenly. "You must be thirsty."

He examined his guest's dusty costume with a hint of scorn, and then opened the door through which he had entered by a crack, and called to someone whose name Almazan did not catch.

A minute later, a child scarcely twelve years old came into the room carrying a metal tray. Her thin arms and slender legs were naked. She had two brown tresses that fell over her slim shoulders, and her face was that of a little old woman. She looked at Almazan brazenly, almost under his nose, and started laughing. She was missing a tooth, and she had a double scar near her nose, like the trace of an animal bite.

At a sign from her master, she disappeared, waddling, making her short skirt ride up over her loins in order to show off her legs.

Aboulfedia filled two chipped cups to the brim with a dense wine, and emptied one of them in a single draught.

"Oh, you're right, Almazan," he went on, "to come and find me. There's the age of the senses, the age of thought and finally, perhaps, the age of wisdom. Woe betide the man who is wise too soon or who begins by thinking. You'll become my pupil again. But what I'll teach you is finer than the philosophy of Aristotle or that of Averroes."

Aboulfedia drew nearer to Almazan and spoke to him at close range, in a low voice, breathing the odor of the wine he had drunk in his face.

"There are secrets, yes, yes, and I know them. Carnal pleasure is never simple. If it isn't commanded by the brain it's nothing but a frisson along the body and a rapid grimace. The amour of a man for a woman is only child's play. Only debauchery is beautiful. It's necessary to penetrate into the accursed palace in order to know the enchantments of nature and savor the terrible intoxication. Once one has entered, there's no question of wanting to return. So-called debauchees who have become saints have restricted themselves to simply coupling in the manner of beasts.

"Debauchery! The ancients made a kind of religion of it, and they were right. They worshiped Priapus, Pilummus,

Tryphallus, Angerona, Genita-Mana, Tutana, Typhon and a thousand others, and the festivals of those sublime gods always served as a pretext for formidable scenes of collective possession. I've rediscovered in Byzantine manuscripts the description of the rites of certain mysteries.

"At Mendes, a hundred young women were locked in the temple on spring nights with the sacred goat, and it was necessary, in the morning, for the guards to bring whips to drag them away from the delights they had savored. At Byblos, people came from all over Syria to participate in the initiations of the cult of Cotylo, who was called the goddess of lubricity, but who was also that of intellectual penetration, for her priests taught the means of procuring divine ecstasy by means of the carnal spasm.

There were secret schools in Alexandria, Memphis and Heliopolis, where the confusion of the sexes was exercised by the confusion of embraces, and where, to the vibration of certain kinds of music and the intoxication of certain perfumes, one found a state of ideal voluptuousness with the vanishment of one's individuality. The Moabites and the Ammonites did better still in their worship of Belphegor, who was identified with the plant Mars. They lay down in hundreds at sunset in the sands of the desert, and when he first rays of the bloody sun brushed their bodies, the great cry of stupor that filled the dusk sent their spirits toward the god, and confounded them with the god.

The Rutrem of the Hindus, who had a lingam instead of a head, the Atis of the Chaldeans, who was represented with a vagina on the forehead, and the Anahita of the Persians, whose body was covered with breasts, demanded similar frenzied couplings in secret rituals. The Christian cult of the Devil, the Catholic Sabbat with its goat, the son of the old Egyptian goat, and its witches imitative of Bacchantes, is nothing but a reproduction of the ancient cult of pleasure of which humankind does not want to let go. And the principle is the same everywhere. It's the profanation of chastity, promiscuity in lust."

Aboulfedia's face had become hideous. Droplets of sweat were pearling on his temples. His fat hands were trembling. He let himself fall in the midst of cushions and stayed there is the attitude if a man witnessing an extraordinary scene.

Almazan considered him with disgust. He thought of the pure air of the highway. He stood up.

"Almazan," said Aboulfedia, also getting up, "You're an artist and you love beauty. Doubtless you've heard mention of the woman that I cast in the role of Lilith and the adolescent that I had so much trouble finding whose ambiguous form is that of Belial in person, the demon that incarnates the attractions of both sexes."

No, Almazan had not heard mention of any of those individuals. He did not want to know them. He had a desire to make the old physician ashamed, to remind him of his old love of science and the nights they had spent together leaning over the cadavers of men condemned to death, trying to decipher the mystery of the human organs. It was a prostitute that had come to Aboulfedia one night, instead of the expected Messiah. No matter! Was there not a Messiah who descended at every moment into the soul of those who sought and hoped?

But he kept silent.

It was up to him to preach morality to the old man gone astray. The image of Isabelle de Solis had just recoiled a long way, between the toothless girl and the powdered one-eyed lantern-bearer. She was merely a miserable instrument of a base orgy among the dregs of Triana. He no longer wanted to think about her; he no longer wanted to think about anything.

"Lilith and Belial!" murmured Aboulfedia, in a dreamy voice, as if he were talking to himself. "The prestige of demons who bear on their faces and in their corporeal form the forbidden beauty! It's pollution that makes the attraction of beauty and the mystery of faces only has a moving profundity if the lips are impure."

Almazan headed for the door of the garden, but Aboulfedia retained him by the arm.

"I want to show you Lilith," he said, and an expression of gravity passed over his features. "I don't believe there's a body more perfect in the whole of Spain. And God has put hair of flame on her to mark her with the seal of Hell. Follow me, but don't make any noise, because her fits of wrath are terrible, and then one can't do anything with hr. She's more indecent than a bitch in quest of a dog, but sometimes she doesn't want to let her little fingernail show."

Almazan sensed that curiosity was stronger than disgust and the followed Aboulfedia.

The room into which the latter had drawn him was entirely dark. Almazan took a few groping paces therein, wondering whether the faint sound of water he could hear was coming from—the intermittent sound of falling droplets.

"I imitate the sect of the Baptists of Byblos," Aboulfedia whispered in his ear. "First I practice the purification by water."

Almazan sensed that the hand that was drawing him into a corner of the room was trembling in his own.

"Look, and hold your breath."

Almazan almost uttered a cry. Aboulfedia had lifted a curtain, and through golden gauze whose mesh formed diamond-shapes, he saw the next room, which was bathed in a delightful turquoise light by a high bronze lamp. The walls were covered with blue faience, and to the right and left there were coverts covered with multicolored carpets and cushions. The middle of the room was a circular pool to which three steps led down.

On those steps Isabelle de Solis was lying face down, entirely naked. Her small breasts were scraping the marble and it was her that was making the irregular sound of water that Almazan had heard, for she sometimes filled the hollow of her hand and threw its contents negligently into the air. The droplets, as they fell back on her nape and back, covered her with a rain of scintillating pearls and caused a long frisson that suddenly made her tense and fold up.

Beside the steps, an open orange was placed.

It seemed to Almazan that Isabelle de Solis' eyelids had started to flutter more rapidly when he had gazed at her through the diamonds of the golden trellis, and that she made an imperceptible movement of the head. Could she suspect that he was there?

He was penetrated by surprise, admiration and a sentiment analogous to the one that the discovery of a crime inspires.

"Lilith was anterior to Eve, according to the Talmudists," murmured Aboulfedia. "The man loved her, with an ideal love, and the veritable original sin was the pollution of a virgin body that had been created for beauty and not for physical enjoyment."

Isabelle de Solis had raised herself up. She placed her head on her elbow. Her eyes could be seen shining like two droplets of phosphorescent water. She gave the impression of a panther waking up in order to go hunting or for amour.

And suddenly, she seized the orange that was beside her, tore away pieces of peel, and started throwing them in the direction of the cushions that were to her right, aiming carefully, her puerile face suddenly becoming full of attention.

Almazan perceived that there was a form lying among the cushions. The slender upper body of a very young man emerged. He smiled wearily; his features were taut and his immense eyes enlarged by kohl were moist and devoid of light.

But Almazan did not have the leisure to consider him. The curtain raised by Aboulfedia had just fallen back in front of him. The old man was panting angrily. He exclaimed: "I'll get you! Haven't I forbidden it? The son of a gypsy that I pulled out of the mud! Beggar! Swine!"

He agitated in the darkness, no longer able to find the door, stamping his feet. Meanwhile, on the other side, like a spring waterfall, like precious stones agitated by a goldsmith in an invisible casket the naked Isabelle de Solis' laughter echoed musically from the blue faience.

Aboulfedia traversed the first room and disappeared, doubtless to the room where the pool was, to chastise Belial for bathing with Lilith.

But Almazan did not follow him. He had seen enough. He no longer aspired to anything but going far away, to forgetting the old physician, the young woman and their obscene companions.

He ran into the garden, found his horse, made an imperious sign to the one-eyed servant, who was near the door, and fled.

The road wound between two rocky hills and on the horizon the twenty-four towers of the Alhambra appeared, solid, legendary and sunlit, like stone sisters amid walls of ocher.

They dominated a colorful accumulation of turquoise domes, mosques the color of mat pearls, flat terraces bordered by azulejos the color of emerald, and porticos the color of amethyst. Granada! The city was staged on the flanks of three open hills, like the streaming pieces of a pomegranate from which a torrent of precious metals, faiences and jewels was flowing, amid woods of laurier roses and clumps of pistachios.

Almazan looked around at the countless shiny irrigation channels that dated from the time of the Ommeyade Caliphs. Men were walking in the cultivated fields, Russet vines displayed their abundance. An impression of wealth and joy rose from the fertile plains.

Granada! Almazan recalled all that he had heard said about the old Arab city. There, poets and scholars were honored more than warriors. No one was persecuted for his religious beliefs. In the whiteness of palaces embellished by the art of centuries, the descendants of the race that had conquered the world remained, refined and subtle.

A young woman crouching in front of a low house, who was practicing playing a darbuka, made him an amicable hand signal from a distance. That gesture and the music that resonated were for him the material symbol of Arab hospitality and their love of beauty.

He hastened forward. He perceived the mass formed by the Puerta de Elvira on the horizon.

A horseman advanced toward him at a gallop. When he was a few paces away he stopped and considered him in a threatening fashion. He was a young man, scarcely twenty years old, with a complexion more bronzed than the majority of the Moors he had encountered. He was very handsome, but there was something unintelligent in his face, and even bestial. By the magnificence of his garments, Almazan thought that he must belong to a rich family. He had stopped too, surprised by the hostility of the young man, and he was about to ask him what he wanted when the unknown man, uttering a dull groan that lifted his chest, spurred his horse and drew away along the road at top sped.

Scarcely had he disappeared than another horseman arrived and, before Almazan had recovered from his astonishment, he dismounted and addressed several obsequious bows to him. He was an old man with large moist eyes and a certain plumpness.

"Please excuse him, Lord," he said. "You seem to be a stranger and you don't know him. Did he address some insult to you? Did he strike you? In that case..."

The old man put his hand to his belt.

Almazan was about to reply that if that had been the case he would have taken charge of punishing the young man himself, but the old man did not give him time. He touched his forehead with his finger and uttered a flood of words.

"Isn't it a great misfortune? He's not twenty years old, and what incomparable beauty! You can imagine the chagrin that it causes his father. But it's believed that there's no remedy. Everyone is aware of it in Granada, for he belongs to the greatest family in the city. He's an Almoradi. So the Zegris haven't failed to profit from it to spread all sorts of calumnies. It afflicted him at about the age of fourteen. From that moment on he thought of nothing but women. In principle, the Koran forbids them before marriage, but in practice it isn't a sin. The son of Ali Hamad could have any women he wanted. He doesn't want any of them! As soon as he gets close to a woman he's afraid; he starts to tremble and his teeth chatter. Note that he spends his days summoning them and desiring them. And in what a fashion! To the point that those who know him have nicknamed him the goat. The impotent goat! It's funny. How can it be explained? In sum, his mind has been disturbed by it. He no longer knows what he's doing. The greatest physician in Fez has come to see him and found no means of curing him. As he insults passers-by, his father, whose steward I am, charges me to follow him to apologize for him and pay compensation if necessary. Is it…?"

The talkative fat man held out a purse. At Almazan's negative shake of the head, he went on: "Personally, I think that it will pass one day without anyone knowing why. Evils come and go according to the caprice of Allah."

He had mounted his horse. He burst out laughing. "But today, it requires the woman to whom he addresses himself to be a very great lover to be able to satisfy him."

He was already far away, but Almazan could still hear his laughter, and he wondered why the young man he had just encountered, and even his servant, inspired such a great revulsion in him.

The Puerta de Elvira was encumbered by muleteers and beggars. By the roadside, on a bank, a man was seated. He looked at Almazan for a long time with soft and very bright eyes.

He stood up, approached him and said: "You must be Almazan, the physician from Seville. I've been waiting for you since this morning. Alfonso Carrillo might have mentioned me to you. My name is Christian Rosenkreutz."

And, not doubting that Almazan would follow him, he set about preceding him, with a slow tread, which gave the impression of hardly touching the dust.

V. Princess Khadidja's Secret

The gardens of the Generalife were disposed in terraces, and the whiteness of wrought stucco porticos and faience basins alternated there with the shadows of cypresses and those of spindle-trees arranged in squares, with the consequence that the gardens gave the impression, at a distance, of a succession of miraculous chessboards. It was there, among the pistachios, the laurier roses and the arborescent magnolias planted between clumps of box-trees, in accordance with the teachings of the gardeners of Bagdad, that Princess Khadidja came every evening to watch the sunset.

She took two or three more rapid steps in order to make a butterfly rise up, and Emir Daoud, who was accompanying her, thought that she was about to take off behind the insect.

She was tall, delicate and mobile, like the jets of water in the fountains amid which they were walking; she was as transparent as a vapor, leaning over like a lily whose flower is too heavy for its stem; and every time she moved, the emeralds with which she was covered made a precious music as they collided.

She had made the butterfly flee the pathway in order that it would be safer amid the clumps of orange trees, because she could not bear the idea of the death of a living being without weeping. Recently, she had stayed shut up in her room for two days, refusing all nourishment, because she had found the tiny corpse of a nightingale on her window-sill.

When the butterfly had disappeared, she fixed her immense green eyes, which were the same color as her emeralds, on the Emir, and said to him indulgently, as if in a dream: "Yes, yes, I like everything you say to me very much."

But the Emir knew that she had not heard what he said and thought that perhaps she could not even see him.

Princess Khadidja was always thinking about something else. She memorized poems by El Motannabi or Abou

Nowas,[20] who were her favorite poets, or she even composed a few lines herself, which she then copied out in a book of Samarkand parchment bound in gold, which had been sent to her by the Sultan of Egypt and illuminated for her by a celebrated artist from Damascus. Then, while walking and chatting, she glimpsed, she said, the confused and very beautiful images of certain beings that she called her Gennis[21] and with whom she conversed in thought. She attributed all her distraction, all her forgetfulness and all her moods to those Gennis, and no one knew, when she laughed and talked to them, whether she was serious or making fun of them.

It had only been a year since she had quit her father, the Emir of Malaga, El Zagal,[22] to come to the Court of her uncle, the King of Granada. As she was famous throughout Islam for her intelligence and her beauty, Abul Hacen had welcomed his niece with magnificence. He had given her thirty women to serve her. She had sent almost all of them away because of their disgraceful appearance and their ill-omened faces, and it had been necessary to search Granada and the neighboring cities for slaves that were agreeable to look at and also expert in playing musical instruments or reciting verses.

Abul Hacen had wanted to install her in the Alhambra in the tower of the Peinador, whose splendor was renowned and whose rooms of repose Sultan Hafside of Tunis had once visited as models of refinement. Khadidja had laughed at her

---

[20] Al-Mutanabbi (915-965) and Abu Nuwas (756-814) were two of the greatest Arabic poets.

[21] I have left this term as it appears in the original rather than transcribing it as djinn (the plural of djinni), because the text uses the term djinn at one point in another context and the idiosyncratic variant employed by the princess is clearly deliberate.

[22] The historical Sultan known to the Spanish as El Zagal [the valiant] (Abu'Abd Allah Muhammad al-Zaghali, 1444-1494), was not the Emir of Malaga in 1482, although he did become Emir of Granada briefly in 1485.

uncle's vulgar taste and the latter, confused, had accommodated her in haste, according to her own indications, in the palace of the Generalife, which was alongside the Alhambra and communicated with it via a succession of antique gardens.

She scarcely went out of that palace. She spent a part of her time there mixing the essences of flowers to compose perfumes. None of them satisfied her. She said that she wanted to rediscover Kyphi, the sacred perfume of the Egyptians, which permits one to see at a distance when one breathes it in. She also fabricated dyes, because there are harmonies between colors, perfumes and certain stones, and it was indispensable for her to compose a hue exactly similar to that of her emeralds. Her experiments were not always successful.

Once she had gone along the Darro mounted on a splendid horse given by Abul Hacen, entirely painted in a green that might have emerged from her eyes and her jewels. The King of Granada hid from her the immense hilarity that her passage had provoked among the inhabitants of the Albaycin, not knowing whether the delicate creature might die of shame or whether, on the contrary, it would incite her to have all the horses in her tables painted.

In any case, he preferred to see her as little as possible. He thus avoided the tyranny of her caprices, which he could not resist.

Khadidja walked with her face unveiled in imitation of Ouallada, the celebrated poetess of Cordova.[23]

She said that since the Ommeyade Caliph Al Mostakfi had permitted his daughter not to wear a veil over her face in the time of the greatest splendor of the Caliphate, she could be permitted to do the same. Unlike Ouallada, Khadidja was chaste and wanted to remain so. However, she glorified amour

---

[23] Wallada bint al-Mustakfi (1001-1091), daughter of Muhammad III of Cordoba, who was assassinated in 1026 and replaced by the caliph known in the Occident as Almanzor; it was not by virtue of her father's permission, therefore, that she refused to wear the hijab.

and she sometimes let it be understood that if she did not give herself, it was because of a secret that she would never reveal.

Emir Daoud hid his timidity beneath the glamour of his magnificent attitudes. He only spoke about his amour by means of allusions, but those allusions were so transparent that Khadidja would easily have understood them if she had listened to them. She did not pay any attention to them because she knew that the noble Emir had been in love with all the women he had approached, and was misunderstood by all of them, because of the evil destiny that had never ceased to harass him in sentimental matters.

He had a large fortune, he had been illustrious in the wars against the Christians and he bore the admirable title of Emir of the Sea, which conferred the command of all the King of Granada's fleets upon him, but amour was his only preoccupation.

He commenced by reciting the verses of Ibn el Dahane:[24] "Under the almond-trees in flower, she wept, and with her eyelid, she has wounded my heart."

But he stopped. He extended the flap of his white brocade robe, and attempted to make Khadidja take a path that turned to the right.

The rigid silhouette of Sultana Aixa had just appeared a few paces away from them. She affected nonchalance in order to disguise the angular character of her torso, and she was leaning on her son Boabdil, a young man of twenty with an abnormally large forehead, a false gaze and almost devoid of lips.

Aixa was nicknamed the Horra—which is to say, the chaste—because of the affected purity of her mores.[25] Ne-

---

[24] Perhaps the grammarian Ibn al-Daddan (1101-1174).

[25] Aicha al-Horra, known in Spanish sources as Aixa, is generally thought to have obtained the suffix al-Horra [the honored] because she was supposedly a descendant of the Prophet. Previously married to Abu l'Hasan Ali's predecessor, his mar-

glected by Abul Hacen, she had lived in solitude in the Al-hambra, devoting herself to her son whom she loved madly. All her life she had proscribed all adornments, pleasure and even amour from her vicinity. Once, she had nearly caused a maidservant, surprised by her in the arms of a guard, to die under the whip. But at the age of thirty-six, a belated coquetry had overtaken her, and when Khadidja came to Granada, she wanted to wear emeralds and dress in amaranthine veils in order to resemble her. She did not hide the admiration she inspired in her until the moment that admiration turned into an inexorable hatred.

Rather late one night, she had gone to render a visit to the young princess in the Generalife. Khadidja, joyful at first, had not disguised her ennui thereafter. Desirous of giving a small indication of her desire for solitude, she had extinguished a lamp and begun to undo her hair. Her gestures had undoubtedly been misinterpreted by Aixa.

"It seemed to me," said Khadidja, in recounting the scene to her friend Emir Daoud the flowing day, "that a crude wooden statue became animate before me. I was seized by coarse hands and two narrow pieces of ice posed upon my mouth while I respired in her breath an odor of dusty books and humidity, exactly the same odor that I had respired in Fez when visiting the library, where I was guided by a wise and holy Sufi, clad in very dirty garments. I uttered a desperate scream, my maidservants came, and I asked them to stay with us because the Sultana Aixa and I had just seen the most frightful of all the Gennis of the nocturnal air."

---

riage to her was a political matter—her dates are unknown but she was presumably considerably older than the thirty-six suggested in the text—and she was exiled from the Alhambra when the Emir fell in love with Isabelle de Solis. She sided with his rivals in 1482 in order to enthrone her son Boabdil (1460-1533) as Muhammad XII, at first temporarily and then again from 1487—when he refused to intervene in the Siege of Malaga—until Granada fell to the Christians in 1492.

And because of that confidence, Emir Daoud would have preferred that there was no encounter between Khadidja and Aixa.

As they crossed paths, the two women exchanged polite greetings but Aixa's bad sentiments floated around her like an opaque fluid. She claimed that Khadidja introduced into her room every night one of the Africans responsible for guarding the Alhambra. That calumny, always present in her mind, was reflected in her gaze and the curl of her lip. Young Boabdil, beside his mother, also betrayed his contained hatred, mingled with an obscure desire to humiliate her by possession.

"I'm quitting you with great regret," sighed Khadidja, leaning over slightly as if she were about to break. "I've forgotten a precious liquid—very precious—in an alabaster vase on my window sill. It's composed of delicate essences to which the slightest ray of moonlight is contrary, and the moon is about to rise."

"And what purpose does such a liquid serve?" asked Aixa, with a snigger.

Khadidja raised the smallest hand in the world toward the sky, with marvelously tapering fingers, in which the fingernails were mounted like jewels.

"Nature has such imperfections!" she said. "It's a liquid to bleach the skin of the hands and render it less coarse. I'll give you some, not for yourself, but for your maidservants—provided that the moon hasn't spoiled it."

Now, it was Aixa's despair that, in spite of the cares that she devoted to her person, she was unable to attenuate either the redness or the coarseness of her vulgar hands. In vain the masseurs of the Alhambra had kneaded them with unguents and bathed them in milk. Under the rings that hid them poorly they remained the visible flaw of a body that had not been made for beauty.

And Khadidja drew Emir Daoud away, showing him the crescent moon on the horizon, with a feigned dread, without even deigning to enjoy the expression of rage hat spread over Aixa's face.

As she went along a terrace that ended at one of the gate of the Generalife, however, she suddenly stopped and seized Emir Daoud's arm. That familiarity was rare on her part, and it filled the latter with pride.

Perhaps the poet is right, he thought. *Words of amour are like arrows launched by a hunter. The deer that has received them continues running, and one cannot tell immediately whether the wound is mortal.*

The terrace overhung one of the gardens planted with all the varieties of roses on earth. That made a stream, an accumulation of various colors. There were violet roses from Persia, cinnamon roses that are milky and greasy, Capuchin roses that incline like rusty urns, and Bengal roses that are the color of flesh, so that when their petals are plucked and strewn on the ground, one might think that naked young women were lying next to one another in order to sleep.

In the midst of that dazzle of roses, on the sand of a path, Sultan Abul Hacen was sitting. He had parted his robe of pink silk and undone his broad trousers of the same tender hue, which he wore in the hope of seeming younger, and he was displaying a wound that he had in the thigh. He cared for that wound by coving it with a piece of the raw meat of a lamb, for the wound was considered by the physicians as a living force that required to receive an aliment in order that it did not nourish itself on the flesh of the body. That injury had become a kind of obsession in him, the suffering of which was primarily mental, and he showed his wound, without the slightest modesty, to all the people he encountered, in the hope of receiving useful advice for its cure.

But the stifled cry that Khadidja emitted had not been caused by the disgust inspired in her by the sight of a bloody piece of lamb and a gaping wound on a man's thigh, amid the scatter of rose petals the color of the violet wound and the color of the pink flesh. She considered for a few seconds the unknown man who was standing next to Abul Hacen and leaning over him with a mocking smile. She put her hands to her breast as if to prevent her suave soul from emerging from a form to which it was scarcely attached, and she said: "Almazan! The physician from Seville! May the prophet watch over me!"

And she fell full length on the paving stones of the terrace—but lightly, as if invisible wings had attenuated her fall.

A few days later, everyone in the Alhambra knew that there was a secret that occupied the life of Khadidja.

Perhaps, following the example of so many Arab scholars, she was searching for the philosopher's stone.

Her room was cluttered with bottles, jars and powders. Someone emitted the hypothesis that she wanted to capture the force of rays of sunlight with certain glasses of a special form, and condense it into certain stones in order to make powerful magic talismans. She had sent for all kinds of lenses used in telescopes and had been seen extending them toward the sun and trying by that means to burn the light down on her arms. Or might she simply have a liaison with a perfumer, or even with a perfumer's apprentice?

Wrapped in the green silk of her albornos with silver spangled fringes, at the hour when the shops closed, she had slipped into the Albaycin and, by means of a long detour, she made her way to the celebrated street of the perfumers that ended in the Square of Bibarrambla, which embalmed the entire quarter with the effluvia of all known essences, She had emptied the Persian perfumer's stock. She had carried away all the unguents and all the pastes of the Arab perfumer and all the flasks of the Hindu perfumer. A negro slave, a Christian slave and a Tunisian child recognizable by his red fez marched behind her when she returned, carrying full coffers.

Abul Hacen had read an urgent message that she had addressed to him and the Sultan of Tunis, and had remained confounded by astonishment. She begged the Sultan to send her, without delay, willingly or by force, at a price of gold or by means of threats, an individual of dissolute mores named Hassan, who lived with the dregs of the people and exercised the decried profession of depilator, in which he was reputed to be very skilled.

Princess Khadidja had a secret of which she might die, but which she did not tell anyone. It was because of that secret that she had sworn to herself never to love any man.

She, whose constant effort tended to spiritualize her material form, who had a skin more transparent than the water of a spring emerging from a rock, who reflected by the bright green of her eyes thought in its ineffable essence, had in the groin a tuft of stiff, oblique hair, ugly and deeply rooted. It had grown without reason in her childhood, by the inconceivable mystery of some original pollution. It was the symbol of the Beast, the terrible link that united that ideal creature with matter.

She had resigned herself to bearing that seal of Iblis on her person. But now she had seen once again the only man she had ever thought she would be able to love, the physician Almazan, who had once come to her father's house in Malaga. He had accompanied a Jewish physician who had been consulted regarding the malady from which her mother had died. She and he had stood together for a few moments on a mirador turned toward the sea. She had been astonished that he spoke Arabic without an accent and he had replied that if one loved what one desired to know, one knew it immediately. Perhaps words with a double meaning! The conversation had been limited to that, and the insensate princess had devoted herself to that memory.

Against all expectation, the physician had reappeared in her path. Perhaps it was an effect of the protection of the Gennis or an obscure will of destiny. But what good would it do? No dream was realizable. There was no hope of ever reposing her fragile heart against a beloved breast, for the hairy shame was attached to the impeccable marble of her flesh.

Oh, what plant juice, what mineral with devouring virtues, what formidable and delicate corrosive could stifle at the root the living force of that thick hair?

And during the night, in the hot air that blew from the hills of Granada, Princess Khadidja, amid her cushions, shed the pearls of her tears between the emeralds of her necklaces, because of a little brown patch that she saw, a little lower down than the inflexion of the thigh, on the nacreous amber of her skin.

VI. The Automata

When Almazan emerged from the Alhambra through the Puerta de la Justicia, the blacks of the Moroccan guard who were squatting on the threshold got up precipitately and inclined their spears in front of them as a sign of respect.

They all knew the amity that Abul Hacen had for him since the wound in his leg had begun to heal. Almazan had replaced the bloody pieces of lamb with dressings of pure water, renewed every day, and the rumor was running around that he had the power of curing bodily harm by communicating his will to the water. Abul Hacen did not do anything without consulting him. He had lodged him magnificently in the Plaza de los Aljibes, near his Alcazar, and sometimes had him woken up during the night to converse about medicine and philosophy.

That evening, Abul Hacen had one of his habitual fits of melancholy, caused by the sadness of growing old, and he had retired to his apartments, determined to sleep for a long time because of the youth that repose gave to his features.

Almazan went down as far as the Darro, went along it for a while, and perceived Christian Rosenkreutz, who was waiting for him. They both plunged into the narrow streets of the Albaycin.

"I'm taking you to the house of Al Birouni," said Rosenkreutz. "He's a sage, and above all, a scholar.[26] Don't be astonished by his eccentricities or those of the other men who will be there. There are great differences between the races. Religious faith often leads to fanaticism. And it's a singular effect of wisdom only to penetrate into minds by troubling their equilibrium and bringing with it a part of error. But

---

[26] This character is obviously not the great Arabic scholar known in the Occident as Al-Biruni (973-1048) but might be modeled on him.

you'll see all the Rosicrucians present at this moment in Granada.

The sun had just disappeared behind the mountains of Loja, and from the heights of the radiant mosques, night had precipitated abruptly over the city in a cavalcade of shadows. There were still children playing in the dust of the crossroads, and because of the narrowness of the streets, the two men stood aside in order to let a mule pass with its silent conductor.

But Almazan, accustomed to the nocturnal life of Seville, where the spies of the Holy Office swarmed, turned round from time to time, and did not take long to perceive that someone as following them.

He remarked on it to Christian Rosenkreutz, who started laughing.

"Fortunately," he replied, "we're neither in Castile nor Andalusia. The police had maintained the organization of the times of Muhamad Alhamar, and after Alexandria and Bagdad, Granada is the city where one can wander by night with the greatest tranquility. Although our meetings are secret and our fraternity must not be divulged, it's not because we have anything to fear from Abul Hacen. He professes tolerance for all forms of belief and imposes that tolerance even on the most fanatical of Alfaquis. But the three wise men who founded our order knew that the possession of the truth and the love of good give birth, for those who acquire that possession and that love, to an immediate danger of death. So the three men who have summoned me to the Orient, since they sent me here, prescribed that the first duty of the Rose-Cross was to seal their lips forever with regard to the mission with which they are charged.

"That's what I can't comprehend," said Almazan. "Why not act in broad daylight? Why not spread thought like a light, around which all those who are struggling again darkness would immediately gather? How many evils might be avoided and how much time gained in that manner! Why remain an elite aristocracy who possess a spiritual treasure but who only deign to distribute it in parcels?"

175

The street that they were following climbed a slope between white walls, over which the foliage of pomegranates dangled. They could not be very far from the city ramparts. Almazan perceived behind him the soft footfalls of someone walking. He wanted to stop, but Rosenkreutz drew him on.

"All civilizations have perished," he said, "because the intelligent men directing them made use of their knowledge not for the grandeur of the spirit but for material enjoyments and egotistical ends. So long as men believe that their effort ought to consist of augmenting the wellbeing of the body, they will not glimpse the goal. Why give those insensates weapons with which to doom themselves? Are you sure yourself, Almazan, of making a usage of your intelligence that will not bring you backwards on the road to your distant perfection?"

As Almazan remained silent, Rosenkreutz stopped in front of a low door and signaled to him that they had arrived.

"All his life, Al Birouni has studied the laws of mechanics and sought perpetual motion," he said. "He has fabricated automata as a diversion and has achieved extraordinary results. The flying dove of Archytas of Tarente of which Aulu Gelle speaks, the iron fly of Regiomontanus and the Bronze Head of Roger Bacon are nothing compared with his creations. In addition to the science of mechanics he has sought the appearance of life and had succeeded in giving it. He has fabricated a naked young woman who is so beautiful that one of his slaves killed himself because he was in love with her. He has reproduced inside her body, with different metals, all the parts of the human organism; the liver in made of bronze and the heart of gold. He claims that he would have been able to making her pronounce entire sentences, but he suddenly lost interest in mechanics in order to study submarine flora and fauna with the same passion. He has had a glass bell constructed in Almeira and proposes to place himself in it soon and have himself lowered in the bell into the depths of the sea. You'll see other men no less astonishing in his company."

The low door had opened. Casting a final glance into the street, Almazan saw a silhouette outlined there. He wanted to point it out to Rosenkreutz, but the door had already closed behind him. He felt an impression of coolness. He was in the interior courtyard of an Arab house and around a jet of water, between pillars of bricks painted in different colors, a few men were seated, considering another man, motionless in the depths of the courtyard, staring at a large polished turtle-shell, as shiny as a shield.

Al Birouni advanced toward the newcomers. He was thin, with a narrow beard that, combined with his round eyes and a certain emaciation and disproportion in his shoulders and arms, rendered him similar to a night-bird that was also a scholar.

"This is Almazan, whom Carrillo designated when he died," said Rosenkreutz. "He will be the youngest among us, but perhaps he will be called upon to play the most active role, for the fortunate hazard of a cure has enabled him to become Abul Hacen's favorite."

A voice resounded. It was that of the man with the turtle-shell.

"Death will enter Granada. It is mounted on a white mule. It has adopted the disguise of lust. The marrow of men will become warm, and desire will possess them to such an extent that they will push women into the mosques in order to couple with them on the paving stones."

"That's Massar," said Al Birouni, moving his head up and down as if pecking with a beak. "He's in a prophetic vein. I suspect him of having absorbed too great a quantity of the green hemp that was brought to him from Persia. Let's listen to him. We might collect a verity among a thousand extravagances."

"What is he looking at in that turtle-shell?" Almazan asked Rosenkreutz.

"The future or the past. He employs a mode of divination used by the Chinese. A glimmer designs written words or images for him on the turtle-shell."

"Six cavaliers accompany her," proclaimed Massar, whose ascetic face expressed anger and disgust. May the

Puerta de Elvira not open! May the ramparts rise all the way to the sky in order to bar her route!"

The witnesses pressed around him, seeking to understand what he meant. He stared straight ahead, sometimes inclining his head as if to see better. He suddenly uttered a cry and began to snigger.

"Aha! The cavalier who appears to be the leader is plunging his hand between her breasts. He is caressing her. He is kissing her lips…they are walking entwined…she is laughing... Behold the Queen of Granada! Thanks to her the mosques will change into churches and will be covered with bells like abscesses of bronze. Thanks to her the Palace of the Alhambra will fill up with Christians like a swarm of lice in a stone head."

"Always these predictions of the end of Granada," said a man wearing a golden turban and a gandourah of orange silk embroidered with silver, the sumptuousness of which contrasted with the garments of the others present. "Soleiman also claims that Boabdil will deliver Granada to the Kings of Castile. I don't believe in clairvoyance or astrology, and yet I don't like to hear predictions of that nature."

That was Tawaz, one of the richest inhabitants of Granada. He made a profession of skepticism and was a poet and musician, putting art above everything. In his palace he had a collection of musical instruments used by all the people of the earth, and claimed that the quality of the sounds that one perceives influences the intelligence and duration of life, in such a way that a man living in a desert only brushed by certain qualities of sonorous waves, carefully regulated, might live for a least a thousand years and acquire an unusual degree of intelligence.

Tawaz was a disciple of Omar Khayam, the Persian poet who had lived three centuries before, and he proposed to depart soon on a pilgrimage to Nichapour and respire in the cemetery of Hira the flowers of a peach-tree that extended its branches over the tomb of his favorite poet.

Massar suddenly stopped prophesying and lowered the turtle-shell on to his knees. He had perceived Almazan. He exclaimed: "Bound together like Munkar and Nakir, the two black angels with the blue eyes who ask the dead what their religion was on earth! Bound together by the flame of lust! They do not believe in the Prophet. They make a semblance of hating one another as they make a semblance of loving one another. They will be like the male and female goat who die of exhaustion by virtue of coupling."

Massar spat in Almazan's direction and fell into a profound dejection.

Al Birouni and his guests immediately surrounded the young physician, making apologies. Massar was an uncultivated intelligence whom they only admitted among them because of a certain gift of seeing the future, which might have been wrongly attributed to him. It was necessary not to take account of what he said. In any case, the time had come to talk about more serious matters.

Conducted by Al Birouni, they all went into a room entirely covered with green mosaics and took their places on cushions of a darker green than that of the mosaics.

Almazan noticed a large wheel with a wooden handle, fixed to an iron shaft and seemingly activated by a metal cable that plunged into the wall.

The more intelligent the men are to whom one addresses oneself, Almazan thought, while listening to Christian Rosenkreutz speak and gazing at his interlocutor, *the more they reform the truth and misunderstand it when it falls from above.*

In accordance with to his personal ideas, and the ideas of the sect of Sufis to which he belonged, everyone had an objection to make.

Those who were Sabeans said that it was vain to preoccupy oneself with what was good or evil. The essential thing was to render worship to the first cause, which the planet Saturn symbolized because it was the most distant. For that

Tawaz had had a hexagonal temple constructed in his gardens in black stone, the proportions of which had once been indicated by Pythagoras, and in which the planet was represented as an old dark-hued Indian holding an ax in his hand.

Those who belonged to the ancient sect of Brothers of Purity founded in Basra by the blind poet Bacchar claimed that it was uniquely necessary to attach oneself to the destruction of dogmas and distribute treatises on the essence of matter and the universal soul.

Some invoke Avicenna, other Averroes, and there were some who burst out laughing when those names were pronounced. Spirits became heated. All sorts of opinions were emitted. It was prophets who had done the most harm to humankind by their pride. One old man affirmed in the midst of protests that the Buddha of the Hindus was the greatest of them.

"Was he not ignorant of Pythagoras' theory of numbers?" cried someone.

"There is only one prophet," said another, "who is reincarnated in successive human forms. He has been Pythagoras, Jesus Christ and Mohammed."

Clamors rose up.

"I've just heard him in Alexandria," said a man clad in a miserable brown robe and carrying a pilgrim's staff. "He's inhabiting the body of six-year-old child and preaching the law in the suburbs with more science than a doctor."

"What's the point of all this," murmured Tawaz, with a weary smile. "We're a part of a humanity that is mistaken, that has followed a retrograde path and is descending toward barbarity. A little music is superior to all philosophies."

Even when Rosenkreutz affirmed that it was in the kingdom of Granada that the civilization of the world had taken refuge and that it ought to extend from there into the Occident, there was a concert of protestations.

Some responded that Bagdad ought to remain the spiritual heart of the world and that it was there that it was necessary to go in order to draw from that fatherland of thought the strength necessary to sages. Others cried "What about Alexandria?" and one voice added "Let us return to India, our Mother!"

But the question was raised again of the goal of the Order of the Rose-Cross, to which they had initially adhered.

What was the point of enlightening barbarians like the Castilians or the Andalusians? And were not the others, those who were beyond the Pyrenees, even worse? Better to turn their effort toward the blacks of Africa. In any case, Rosenkreutz had promised to bring scholars and philosophers to Granada from Seville, Toledo and Salamanca. Where were they?

The explanations that Rosenkreutz gave cast a malaise into the audience.

Several eminent men of their acquaintance had risen above religions, had been rallied by his cares to the symbols of the rose and the cross. Out there they had titled themselves the Alumbrados.[27] They were to come to Granada to confer with their Arab brothers.

"Well? Well?" people said on all sides.

"Only Almazan has responded to the appeal," said Rosenkreutz. "The majority of the others have died in recent days. Perhaps it's an extraordinary chance that has determined that their lives ended at almost the same time, for causes difficult to explain. Perhaps, as I have hypothesized, there exists a group analogous to ours but which has evil for its ideal instead

---

[27] The alumbrados were Christian mystics who probably first appeared in Spain during the late fifteenth century, although history has little race of them until a later period than the one in which the story is set. They became targets of the Spanish Inquisition, which issued an Edict against them in 1525. Their beliefs appear to have had something in common with the Albigensians of France, who had been ruthlessly suppressed in the early thirteenth century. Magre puts Christian Rosenkreutz in contact with them in the biography summarized in the appendix.

of good—and by evil I mean, like you, hatred of intelligence, love of the material and the effort to turn back. If such an evil group of men exists, it is not retained by any moral rule and it must possess immense power. Its first preoccupation must be to suppress those who might pose an intellectual obstacle to it. If so, have not the Alumbrados of Spain been its victims?"

A heavy silence followed those words, and in that silence, a Sufi with a falsetto voice said: "If a secret group of men exists who desire evil and are the Rose-Cross in reverse, they'll never have a better opportunity than this evening to kill us all at the same time."

Laughter followed, but it rang false. They looked at one another and whispered. Was all that really possible? What proof was there?

"There's no formal proof," Rosenkreutz went on. "Only the alchemist Luis Percheco of Majorca collapsed at the moment when he was about to board a ship, struck by a sudden paralysis. He was old and paralysis is a natural malady. Guzman de Pilar, the celebrated professor of Salamanca was found dead in his little room at the University, where he was in the process of putting on the toga in which he taught. It's true that he had been suffering heart trouble for a long time. The man nicknamed the Great Samuel of Madrid, accused of heresy, was imprisoned by the Holy Office, and when a royal order was sent for his liberation, he was found strangled in his prison. I ought to say that his guard had a hatred of Jews that was pushed as far as madness, and had already murdered several. Finally, Alfonso Carrillo, Archbishop of Toledo, died in mysterious circumstances, about which Almazan can give you a few clarifications."

Anxiety passed through the assembly like a palpable current, a fluid devastating souls. People questioned one another in low voices. In the lamplight, the green of the mosaics became icy and sad, like the reflection of a tomb. Suddenly, like a signal of terror, the teeth of a pale old man began chattering. The noise seemed atrocious.

A few of those present turned their eyes toward the door.

Then that door opened suddenly and a servant irrupted into the room. He doubtless thought that he was entering a noisy meeting, for he called to his master in a voice whose pitch was singularly raised, which resonated in a terrible fashion in the midst of the silent assembly.

Al Birouni advance toward him calmly. The servant was an old man, and doubtless pusillanimous. He learned toward Al Birouni and explained to him in a choked voice what had happened.

As he did every night, he had made a tour of his house, which he was responsible for guarding. The house was surrounded by a garden and he was to maintain a particular surveillance over the large room in the form of a rotunda where his master's precious automata were kept. He had just observed that a window in that rotunda, which no one was allowed to enter and was locked internally, had been staved in and remained agape. He had passed through the garden an hour before and had not noticed anything abnormal. During the previous hour someone had introduced himself into the hall of the automata. He had come to notify his master immediately.

The Sufis had all come forward while he was speaking, and those who were nearest heard what he said. Others did not understand, and their common fear was aggravated by that. The anguish was modulated by the clicking of the bloodless old man's teeth.

There were a few minutes of confusion. Where was this rotunda? Was it the room that communicated with the one where they were? What as it necessary to do?

Al Birouni raised his hands, trying to reassure everyone. He went to the wheel that Almazan had noticed and began to turn it. Almost at the same time, a sinister cry resounded, a cry expressing an immeasurable fear, a cry so unexpected that the calm Al Birouni remained motionless, his hands attached to the wheel as if it were part of him.

The philosophers, suddenly deprived of their wisdom by the terrible strangeness of the cry, rushed for the door. They jostled one another, flowed into the interior courtyard of the house and reached the street, some leaving their turbans and others their staffs. They disappeared, uttering feeble cries, like a flock of timid birds.

Al Birouni had tried in vain to halt that unforeseen panic. He made a sign to those who had remained to follow him into the next room in order to take account of what had happened. Rosenkreutz and Almazan went forward first, but they stopped, nailed to the spot by surprise.

They had before them an immense room of which the ceiling could scarcely be distinguished. Close to the door, against the wall, a man was crouching, gasping with fear, his hands over his head as if to protect himself.

A naked negro advanced toward him with a large and measured stride, and when he was about to reach him, pirouetted, took a dozen large strides in the opposite direction, and recommenced.

An elephant was sweeping the air with its trunk with a regular rhythm, while its mahout leaned over to prick its flank with the same rhythm.

Two silent individuals, a Chinaman and a Persian, were making the gestures of playing chess on a little nacre table.

Above them, a screech-owl, to which Al Birouni had given the resemblance of his own face, deployed its wings, traced an ellipse in the air while making the sound of a meta bobbin unwinding, and returned to its perch, to depart again with the same deployment of wings.

A snake twisted its green-tinted coils; a pelican clicked its beak; an octopus extended its tentacles.

At the back, the color of milky wax to which the moonlight gave the appearance of flesh, a naked young woman raised herself up among cushions, waved a fan of feathers, hid her face modestly, and allowed herself to fall back with a voluptuous movement of the legs, like an invitation to pleasure.

The silence, only troubled by the grating of springs and the hiss of invisible wheels, added further to the phantasmal character of the assembly of automata.

"He is, I believe, merely an unlucky thief," said Al Birouni, making a semblance of not perceiving the admiration of his companions and leaning over the man shivering with fear.

"Or perhaps he's a curious individual who has heard mention of these marvels and wanted to contemplate them," said Tawaz.

Al Birouni's servant had brought the terrified man to his feet and shook him rudely. His master made him a sign to take him away.

They attempted to interrogate him, but he remained bewildered, his eyes staring. He stammered incoherent phrases.

"That teaches us," said Tawaz again, "that it's necessary not to demand philosophy from warriors, or courage from philosophers."

It was impossible to get anything at all out of the unknown man. A black slave had come forward and got ready to lash him with a long leather whip. Rosenkreutz opposed that.

Wearily, Al Birouni gave the order to throw him out.

The door to the street closed behind him and his rapid footfalls were heard as he fled. Only then did it seem to Almazan that the face of the man was not completely unknown to him.

Tawaz got ready to leave. He smoothed his orange silk gandourah, and then took a box covered with emeralds from his pocket and spread a light cloud of gold powder over his beard.

"There are some lute players in my house," he said. "Would you like to hear them?"

Christian Rosenkreutz's eyes had lost their gleam. He lowered his head. He seemed very tired. He leaned over Almazan's shoulder and said to him in a low voice: "What a melancholy spectacle to behold: after a meeting of sages, a meeting of manikins!"

The courtyard was full of slaves holding up torches. Before closing the door of the rotunda, Al Birouni had made a tour of it. From a distance, Almazan saw him lean over the

185

naked young woman and kiss her delicately on the forehead, perhaps the lips...

First light was beginning to blanch the terraces. Almazan went down the streets of the Albaycin alone. Christian Rosenkreutz had quit him suddenly at a crossroads with a vague gesture signifying: *When she we see one another again?* and he had disappeared, as if he had dissolved in the pre-dawn twilight.

Almazan walked solely, without haste. He thought that the doors of the Alhambra would open at sunrise, and that it would not be necessary to wake the Moroccan guards.

As he was about to reach the Darro he heard the sound of hoofbeats. He stopped. A few cavaliers emerged from a street that led in the direction of the Puerta de Elvira. He had nearly bumped into them, but he steps aside under a portal. Then he passed his hand over his face, thinking that he was dreaming.

It was Isabelle de Solis that he had just seen, mounted on a white mule, in the midst of several Moorish soldiers. The one who appeared to be the leader had his hand on her breasts and was laughing in a vulgar manner. Almazan noticed the slightly stooped back of the man and his unkempt beard. Isabelle de Solis was also laughing, and looking to the right and left with a puerile curiosity at the white houses of the city that she was penetrating for the first time.

The group was already some distance away along the quays of the Darro when the horse of a soldier who had stayed behind and was trying to catch up with his companions reared up in front of Almazan.

The latter took advantage of that to ask the rider: "Who is that woman? What is she doing with you?" And he added, authoritatively: "I'm the Emir's physician."

The soldier became anxious. Moors and Spaniards lived in peace, but it was impossible to prevent, on either side, raids on livestock, and incursions into villages in which women and children were abducted to be sold as slaves. Abul Hacen had instructed the Alcaides of the frontier towns to punish Moorish marauders severely.

"We haven't done any violence to that woman. She's a Spaniard, but the chief doesn't intend to sell her as a slave. She was hiding in a wood near Martos. It was her who appealed to us. She claims to be the daughter of the Alcaide of the city. According to her, her father would have taken her by force to Seville, had her whipped and locked her in his castle. Is the story true? One never knows with women. In any case, she showed us the traces of the whip on her back."

The soldier started to laugh bestially, and at a gesture from Almazan he departed in the direction of his companions.

The distant mountains were covered by a bloody light. On the highest tower of the Alhambra the silhouette of a Moor was outlined, whose head and shoulders were covered by a sparkling hood that removed the human character from his form and rendered it similar to a sort of fire-spirit. He sounded the trumpet several times and, as if they had been waiting for that signal, the first prayer of the muezzins were intoned at the summit of the mosques. The sky had the appearance of a vast torn robe and Granada awoke, sighing with enjoyment.

Then Almazan recalled the words of Massar, who was prophesying while gazing into a turtle-shell:

"Death will enter Granada. It has adopted the disguise of lust."

VII. The Slave-Market

For a long time Abul Hacen had been mourning his youth. He had not got used to growing old. Toward his fiftieth year, in a sudden and very rapid fashion, as if by a malignity of nature, his hair had begun to turn white. At first he had tried to dye it. But mention had been made to him of a certain Emir of Tlemcen who had gone blind because of the pernicious influence of the black coloring in the optic nerves. Since his childhood, it had been one of his weaknesses to fear incessantly the loss of his sight. He also feared dust and lightning flashes, and there was always a little lamp in his bedroom, in order that he would but have the sensation, when he woke up, of having gone blind. He had therefore retained his white hair and he sensed it on his cranium like the torturing force of time.

But he had begun to get fat. His chin hung down, his belly protruded, he panted when he walked. He did not admit it to himself. He felt that he would only be irremediably fat on the day when he recognized the fact. He continued to eat and drink enormously, lulled by the lies of his entourage, who said that in him, by a fortunate exception, nourishment did not cause plumpness. He further imposed that opinion by the terrible authority of his gaze, and the suggestion that he radiated when he asked, every morning: "Haven't I got thinner?"

And he interrogated the Hagib who came to talk to him about the affairs of the kingdom, the Alfaquis who wandered in his gardens and commented on the Koran, the guards at the doors, and even a mute who followed him everywhere and made approving signs while laughing as soon as he pointed a finger at his belly.

He had chosen for a companion in his walk Hamet Moktar, the grand master of the public schools, who was as fat as him and whom he mocked on that account. He made him walk rapidly and for a long time, so as to be able to say to him: "You're getting fat, my poor friend, you can't keep up with me any longer!"

Abul Hacen claimed that he liked to wander around Granada incognito, in order to listen to his subjects talking, in imitation of Haroun al Rachid in Bagdad. Modestly dressed, followed by Ali, the mute, he went through the bazaars with Moktar and to the markets, but as he was vain he could not help looking at the passers-by arrogantly, until they had recognized him and prostrated themselves. Then he feigned a great ennui at not being able to pass unperceived.

He was fond of directing his excursions to the slave market, because he hoped to discover an exceptional beauty there that he could immediately take to the Alhambra, for the desire for women tormented him all the more as he felt it diminishing within him. He attached himself to it as the surest proof of his manly strength. Women fatigued him now, but he sought them out anyway. He dreamed of new embraces that would procure him new ardors.

The slave market was held early on the Plaza de Bibarrambla. The slaves stood in tows, between which the buyers circulated. A few were sitting on a little wooden box that contained all that their former master had left them. Some laughed in order to appear sympathetic. The suppliers of the galleys examined their teeth with care in order to know whether they could chew the biscuit, which was very hard. Those who had fled from Spain in order to be slaves among the Moors and be better treated were recognizable by the scars covering their bodies. They made signs that it was indifferent to them whether they were sold to one man or another, finding themselves among people who would always be more humane than the cruel Christians they had quit. Some raised their hands in the air to show by means of the calluses by which they were covered that they were accustomed to laboring in the fields. And Africans, holding their knees between their arms, stared sadly at the sky, remembering the natal desert.

Almost all of them came from Tunisian and Algerian corsairs and had been brought from Almeria or Malaga by correspondents of the corsairs who, sitting on Persian rugs and covered with jewels, left the care of the sale to their agents and affected a great importance.

All that made a variegated crowd, sordid and magnificent, in which were mingled quarrels, haggling over prices and glorifications of the merchandise. But there were hardly ever any but aged or ugly women there, the pretty ones being kept in neighboring apartments by entrepreneurs who charged a ducat just to show them. They also kept overly handsome young boys destined for pleasure and ran right and left seizing passers-by by the sleeve and giving them descriptions in loud voices of firm breasts and opulent hips, hollow torsos and straight necks.

That morning, Abul Hacen cut through the crowd at a rapid pace. He was in a bad mood. He had heard a child designate him by the nickname that his enemies gave him: the Old Man!

Cries resounded in front of him. The market flowed away like a wave. The Kaschefs ran forward to restore order but, recognizing the Emir, they cleared the plaza before him with blows of the rod, so that Abul Hacen, increasingly furious, found himself involuntarily at the center of a gesticulating and vociferating mob.

A woman of short stature was in the middle, holding a dagger. She had snatched it from a frontier Adalide and was threatening him with it, as well as two other men whose rich embroidered gandourahs indicating the métier of slave-merchants.

It resulted from the clamors of the audience, the insults and threats of the woman and the protestations of the merchants that the Adalide had sold a Spanish woman as a slave, for a hundred gold mitcals, without having the right to do so, since they were not at war with Spain. The woman was shouting that she had confided herself to him freely in order to go to Granada, that she had been brought here by surprise without knowing where she was going, and that the sale was not valid. But almost all those who were present shrugged their shoulders and said that it was not worth the trouble of paying attention to the shrieks of a Christian. The two merchants had counted out the hundred gold mitcals and affirmed that the sale was definitive.

"Let this young man be the judge!" said Isabelle de Solis, throwing her dagger at Abul Hacen's feet. "I put myself under his protection."

Did she say that by virtue of a genius for the penetration of the human heart, or, as some witnesses later claimed, did she actually say "Let this fat man be the judge" and the word *fat* was misunderstood because of the Spanish accent she had in expressing herself in Arabic?

It seemed to Abul Hacen that the heavens had tipped over like a vast cup in order to let an embalmed liquor fall into his soul.

Silence fell. The Kaschefs were motionless, maintaining the crowd with their raised rods.

Abul Hacen darted a triumphant glance at his companion Moktar. He felt slim, light, just and omnipotent.

All the young woman's words were true. The Adalide's crime was flagrant. It was monstrous to try to sell a Spanish woman when they were at peace with the Christian kings. He would only pardon the two merchants on condition that their transactions would be marked henceforth with the seal of equity. The hundred gold mitcals would be paid by way of compensation to the offended woman. The latter was invited to go without delay to the Alhambra, to recount the whole story in detail.

Without any delay! Ali the mute was charged with not losing sight of her and conducting her.

The Kaschefs took the Adalide away and, while climbing the sloping streets that led to his palace, the Emir repeated, laughing to the grand master of the public schools:

"How you're panting, my poor friend. You can no longer keep up with me. And then, I'll wager that you'll lie down to sleep as soon as you get home, while I..."

It was the Hagib himself who took Isabelle de Solis to the Almocaden of the prison of the Alhambra.

A knowing smile brightened his jaundiced face.

He interrupted the Almocaden's surprise with a gesture.

Yes, the Emir had judged that it was necessary for the first functionary of the kingdom to introduce a young foreigner into the cell of an Adalide imprisoned the day before. But there was no petty mission for a faithful minister, and Allah was the sole judge of the caprices of the great.

The prisons occupied the bottommost floors of the Alcazaba and one reached them via a long spiral stairway.

The Almocaden marched ahead, holding up a lamp, and sometimes pointed out a worn step to the visitors. On the way he exchanged a few words in a low voice with the Hagib. They had treated the singularity of the Emir's taste in the matter of women and the rapidity with which he fell in love in spite of his age.

The Almocaden related what the Adalide had said in the prison about the person he was guiding with so much respect. The prisoner had declared that he believed himself to be authorized to sell her because of the facility of her mores. He had given details. He demanded to be heard by the Cadi, or even the Emir.

They had arrived at the entrance to a long corridor. The Almocaden opened a door and Isabelle de Solis questioned him with a smile: "Is the cell illuminated?"

"Yes, he replied. "There's a barred window overlooking the Darro."

The Hagib was about to ask whether she wanted him to witness the interview, but she had already slipped into the cell.

He and the Almocaden did not see anything of what happened. They supposed that on seeing the young woman, the Adalide, whose hands and feet were enchained, and who must have been sitting down, got up and prostrated himself, face down, to beg for mercy. They heard him exclaim in a stifled voice: "O Zoraya!"—meaning light of the dawn, a name that he must have called her at a very different moment.

Then, for a few seconds, there was a singular groan. They were about to push the door when Isabelle de Solis emerged, her eyelids fluttering and her lips pinched. She said imperiously to the Hagib: "We can go up again. I've punished that man for his calumnies."

And she launched herself on to the stairway.

The Almocaden darted a glance into the cell and saw that the Adalide was still prostrate, and would not get up again. A small dagger plunged into the nape of his neck had struck him dead.

He ran up the stairs shouting furious words, in which there was mention of justice and his responsibility with regard to the prisoners confided to him. He only caught up with the Hagib on the platform of the Alcazaba. The latter had turned round and in his black gandourah, in the sunlight, he was more jaundiced than usual.

He considered the Almocaden severely, and even with slight scorn. He gestured to him to shut up.

"Justice!"

With a movement of the head, he showed him the feminine silhouette that was drawing away rapidly, beneath her aureole of golden hair.

"Zoraya!"

VIII. The Nightingale's Tomb

Almazan could not sleep. Every time he closed his eyes and began to sleep it seemed to him that a being devoid of material form but warm, naked, mobile, animate and audacious covered him, enveloped him with caresses and bathed him with living breath.

He extended his hands and took account of the fact that there was no body beside him. What he experienced was a sensation of contact that was not localized and went beyond touch, from the roots of his hair to the tips of his feet.

Sitting up, he breathed in deeply, believing that he could scent a strange perfume in the room. It was none of the essences whose fabrication rendered Granada celebrated, nor was it the rose of Bagdad nor the aloes of Constantinople, of which it was said that the secret had been lost since the Turks had entered that city and had massacred the master perfumers. It was an insipid odor but very light, the odor of a woman who had just been kneaded by masseurs, an odor of washed hair and skin through which the first desire is passing. It was mingled with an unexpected taste on his moist mouth, as if the saliva of a kiss had remained there.

He got up, lit a high lamp that illuminated the room, looked at the cushions on which he slept, his Moorish garments spared around, and the manuscripts brought to him from the library of the Alhambra. He was quite alone.

He remembered what Aboulfedia had once told him about incubi and succubi and the pleasures that a man learned in magic could obtain from them. There are beings that have the power to disengage themselves from their body by night and send their double to other beings whom they desire. They enjoy them unawares, but one can, by an effort of will, become conscious of the pleasure one receives, with the consequence that in the formless world there are invisible embraces and caresses all the more voluptuous for being immaterial.

Follies of sorcery! Almazan said to himself. And yet...might it not be that another desire had responded to his own desire, might not a double bearing two droplets of bright gold in her eyes have come to plaster her breasts against him, the breasts that he had held in Seville, her precious breasts, which he had seen clasped the day before by a Moorish soldier?

The story of the stabbed Adalide and the Spanish woman that the Emir was keeping in his apartments had run around the Alhambra. Almazan knew that Isabelle de Solis—Zoraya, as she was now called—was a short distance away from him, lying in the crimson brocade of Khorassan that covered Abul Hacen's bed. Perhaps she had let herself fall amid the skins of white bears that came from the extreme north of Mongolia and was offering herself, laughing, to the King of Granada. Almazan's active and precise imagination painted a scene in which no detail was forgotten, where there was the design of mosaics that he remembered, the alabaster basin from which the nocturnal jet of water sprang forth, and the narrow body of the woman he had seen, with the fullness of its curves, the amber of its hues, its shadows, and even its down.

But no! The reality was more frightful. He knew, by virtue of the man's confessions to the physician, that old age, like a sad beast that never lets go, had attached itself to Abul Hacen's senses and was weakening them by the day. And he knew by virtue of amicable confidences, the words freely exchanged in the evening, everything that the blasé master demanded of women in order to achieve pleasure. Woe betide the woman who had pleased him! There was no repose for her.

Almazan could not bear the exactitude of his vision. He picked up a manuscript by Alvaro of Cordova and strove to continue reading it, having commenced that morning. But he quickly threw it aside, angrily.

Was it not those books that had stolen the possibilities of his happiness? What sterile efforts! Pitiless thought devoured the body. Would it not have been better to be an ordinary man, devoid of pride, who slaked the quotidian human desires and did not think himself diminished thereby?

He got dressed. He went out. Walking, he thought, would calm him down. The silence of the Alhambra was heavy. On the silvery towers a Moroccan sentry was intoning a chant. The stars seemed higher than usual, and as inaccessible. He took the path between the ramparts and the walls of the palace and had the low door opened that led from the Alhambra to the gardens of the Generalife.

Her advanced in the midst of magnolias and fabulous roses. He climbed marble steps between files of cypresses and went along flower-beds arranged in such a fashion as to depict verses from the Koran. Sometimes, the enamel of a kiosk glittered in the midst of box-trees. An awakened swan slid into pool, went around a belvedere and disappeared in the myrtles, like an abandoned dream.

Almazan stopped, hearing a very soft music reaching him. It was a female voice singing plaintively while making the strings of a darbuka resonate. He had arrived on the ninth terrace at the entrance to the path of the Fountain of Laurels.

He looked in the direction from which the song was coming. A few paces away, beneath a minuscule cypress, a woman was sitting on a panther-skin. At first, Almazan could only make out a delicate face beneath an immense green turban, and the suavity of long, tapered hands. Seeing that the woman was not wearing a veil, he turned round and was about to draw away, but she looked at him without sketching the slightest gesture to hide her features. The emeralds on her fingers and those of her eyes darted equally incomparable gleams, and their glare enabled Almazan to divine that he was in the presence of Princess Khadidja.

She had experienced a great chagrin when she had found the little cadaver of a nightingale on her window sill, and she had increased that chagrin by virtue of the influence of her chimerical scruples. According to her, the nightingale would not have flown into the magnolia where it was singing except

196

to please her. It had found new harmonies in her intention. When it had sensed that it was dying it had come to tap on the shutter of her window with its beak. But she, a coarse creature, had been sleeping heavily and had not heard anything. She accused herself of ingratitude. She suffered from remorse.

She had attached an enormous emerald to the bird's neck and had buried it secretly beneath the dwarf cypress not far from the Fountain of Laurels. And every night, at the hour when, she thought, the bird had suffered from her abandonment, she came to sing, by way of expiation, a little poem of her own composition, accompanying herself on the darbuka.

Almazan had heard mention of Khadidja's fantasies and he had already turned into a lateral path when she suddenly got up and advanced toward him. Her features reflected both discontentment and sadness. She spoke, without giving Almazan time to apologize for his presence.

"I knew that you would come, but why is it at this hour, which belongs to a memory that is dear to me? But why, above all, have you not come alone?"

Almazan looked around, in surprise. The pathways were empty and silent.

"There's a Genni that accompanies you, and we cannot reach an understanding, it and I. It appears that you have acquired a great science since we talked together on a mirador facing the sea, in Malaga. You cure the wounds in legs, but perhaps you're quite ignorant regarding certain subtle wounds of the soul. Assuredly you'll laugh when you know that I am rendering homage to an incomparable nocturnal artist, a delicate poet that loved me, a musician exalted by the lunar dew and the wine that the night decants into the calices of lilies."

Weakly, she lifted her darbuka as if to take the stars for her witness.

"Yes, nothing but a nightingale! But my thought rises toward it as lightly as a prayer between the holy hills Safah and Mervah. Go away. Even if that poet, returned to life, had resumed its place in the magnolia that shades my window, even if that prince had resumed its plumage of molten gold

197

and burning slate, even if that musician resumed tapping the crystal with the pearl, you would not understand what it was saying. Perhaps, another day, I shall have the pleasure of conversing with you, but this evening, go away, quickly."

She spoke as if she had received an insult, and she drew away without looking back.

And Almazan thought, as he returned to the Alhambra, that there might be certain very sensitive creatures who can see the sort of gray nimbus that carnal desire makes around men.

IX. Female Combat

The power of hatred that one bears within oneself is un-limited. It can multiply indefinitely, and become a reservoir of forces so great that in the end, those forces of hatred spread out, and poison the souls around them.

The hatred that Aixa had for Khadidja because of her beauty and her purity did not diminish; on the contrary, it in-creased the hatred that she had for the Emir's new favorite, the Spaniard Isabelle. But that hatred, instead of reposing like a poison that one does not use, began to agitate, to burn, to live.

To begin with, Aixa had repeated, all alone, in her bed-room the name of Isabelle, as if the sounds of the syllables might be as many dagger-thrusts that she was delivering in the invisible.

Afterwards, it was with her son Boabdil that she enumer-ated interminably the reasons for complaint that she imagined, the grievances that grew in her mind with more force than nettles in the fields.

Boabdil bore above his face, like a crushing helmet, a disproportionate forehead, beneath which blinked eyes so small that one never saw their gaze, and a creased mouth whose thinness revealed a love of treason. His mother's hatred procured him a mental joy that he had not yet known. He stimulated its suggestions, shared it with intoxication.

"The King of Granada is enabling a Christian to reign over the Alhambra and the kingdom!"

And that Christian might claim that she was the daughter of a Spanish Alcaide, but it was proven that she had emerged from a hovel in Seville and that the soldier who brought her had had her by the roadside. Before that slut, the descendants of the greatest families must bow down, the Zegris who were the grandsons of the sovereigns of Morocco, and the Maliques who traced their origins back to Almo-Habes, the first King of the realm of Cuco.

It was certain that in her boundless audacity, driven by her ancient habits of prostitution or by some demonic need of her body, she gave herself to men every time she could. She had been seen in the court of myrtles with the young physician Almazan, another infidel. And she had cast her eyes upon the unfortunate Tarfe, who did not enjoy all his reason. She found him handsome, he was eighteen years old and was reputed to be animated by a lubricious madness.

The most inconceivable thing was that the illustrious family of the Almoradis, to which Tarfe belonged, had conceived a pride in the fact that their imbecile child had been noticed by the favorite! What a decadence in mores! Where were the times of the virtuous Almohades, who had had musical instruments destroyed, forbidden the port to precious metals and embroideries on garments and who punished women who showed themselves unveiled with death?

Alas, since Muhamad Alhama, the arts had become flourishing, as under the Almoravides, people drank wine, women allowed themselves to be enlaced by men while dancing the zambra, and the teachings of the prophet were no longer observed! Abul Hacen, with his senile desire for pleasure, had brought those liberties to a peak. He said that he wanted to return to the traditions of the first Caliphs, who practiced tolerance and allowed woman a prominent role in the State. He wanted to resuscitate the times when Ouallada, the Sappho of Cordova, was admired the world over, when Maryem taught grammar and poetry, or Lobnah, in the pulpit of Seville, commented on the Koran before the learned men of all Islam. And under that pretext he wallowed in the arms of a creature viler than dogs.

Neither the Imams not the Alfaquis dared raise their voices against him. It was up to his son Boabdil to reestablish a virtue that he would naturally base on vengeance.

Aixa and her son had found partisans among the Zegris, who were rigid and religious men, powerful in Granada by their number and the great quantity of slaves that they possessed. Their ancient family lived in a perpetual rivalry with that of the Almoradis and since the handsome Tarfe had been noticed by Isabelle they murmured against her and sought an occasion to bring her down.

Granada rapidly divided into two camps, one of which sided with Aixa the Horra and the other with the Spaniard Isabelle. And as the Zegris had the custom of wearing a saffron-colored turban on feast days and the Almoradis wore a crimson turban, everyone, in accordance with his penchant, adopted one of those colors. The people participated in the quarrel, the suburbs were red or yellow, and Jewish merchants installed in shops on the Plaza de Bibarramba only sold scarves of those two shades.

Suddenly, destiny brought the two enemy women face to face.

In the hall of ambassadors, Abul Hacen was about to receive the extraordinary envoy of the Sultan of Egypt. After the reception, he was to take him into the music room for a secret conversation in which only the Hagib and Daoud, the Emir of the Sea, were to participate.

Then, in accordance with a ceremony imitative of that of the ancient Caliphs, the wives of the Sultan of Egypt's envoy were to be received in their turn by the wives if the Emir of Granada. It was therefore prescribed for Isabelle and Aixa to offer sorbet and rose jam to a child of twelve who was the only wife brought by the Sultan's envoy.

The moon had just risen, the hall of ambassadors had emptied and the moment had come for the two women to arrive there solemnly.

Isabella had put on an immense Chinese shawl embroidered with pearls, which was a present from the Sultan of Egypt to Abul Hacen, and which had been brought to him in a massive gold chest. She had little shoes in crimson fabric whose extremities curved back and terminated in a diamond. On her fingers she had put Chinese sheaths in sculpted silver, which she had found in the Sultan's gold chest. They had belonged to the empress Nou Wen Ta Che Li and were made to enclose immeasurable fingernails. Isabelle did not have long fingernails, but the sight of the sheaths had thrown her into such a great joy that she had not been able to resist attaching them to her fingers.

A large balcony connected the dressing room where her mirrors were with the tower of Comares. That balcony was sheer on one side over the depths of the Darro and on the other over an interior garden planted with mimosas and lilies, which was known as the cypress garden because there was an enormous cypress in the center that was reputed to be as old as the Alhambra. A wisteria with thick branches overhung the balustrade of the balcony on the side of the garden and overflowed in a torrent of flowers whose perfume mingled sweetly with the fresh air coming from the shade.

Playing with the silver sheaths on her fingers, swinging a flap of her Chinese shawl, Isabelle took a few steps along the balcony and gazed at the narrow white streets of the Albaycin that unfurled facing her on the flanks of the fill. She seemed to be looking for something. She leaned over a little, and suddenly stepped back, leaping on her feet while laughing all alone and waving her shawl in the air. She had perceived a little red flame on the terrace of a distant house, which had been lifted up three times, like a signal.

At that moment someone went past her on the balcony. It seemed to her that a scornful snigger departed from that figure silent emerged from the stones.

Annoyed to have been surprised, and desirous of knowing by whom, Isabelle took a step forward, seized a corner of the veil of the nocturnal stroller and said: "Who are you?"

Aixa slowly lowered the veil that hid her face, showing her features, in which she had assembled the immense sum of the scorn of which she was capable, and, dreading allowing herself to be seen thus, suddenly spat on the ground in the direction of her rival and continued on her way.

She took three or four steps in an infinite jubilation. She was fearless, believing in the cowardice of her rival. She received a mighty slap from Isabelle's hand on her ear, from behind, while the Chinese sheaths stung her cheek. Instinctive-ly, she parried a second blow by raising her arm.

She did not think of striking. Her dignity did not permit her to do that. She murmured: "I've just walked over the vilest of ordures."

But Isabelle, drunk with fury, careless of Aixa's tall stature, which surpassed hers by a head, barred her route and, very close to her, in a low voice, she recited in Spanish all the insults she had learned in Seville.

Aixa did not understand, but the forcefully thought words acted on her sensibility by the mysterious magic of syllables. An earthen color covered her face and her lips began to tremble, at the same time as she was invaded by the unique idea of putting to death the execrable being she had before her.

She was physically the stronger. Isabelle, entirely given over to the satisfaction of insult, had her back to the balustrade that overlooked the Darro. An abrupt shove, and she might have fallen backwards from the height of the Alhambra. Those condemned to death had once been launched thus into the void.

Aixa delivered that push, but it was not strong enough, and Isabelle only fell to the ground, where she remained stunned for a second. She got up, and in the movement she made to rise to her feet she threw away the shawl that enveloped her and immobilized her left arm. She also cast off the sheaths from her nails. Like a launched stone she went to strike her enemy's midriff with her head, and the two of them rolled on the ground. They remained there, borne to the right and he left by their mutual fury, hammering one another with their fists, trying to lacerate one another in an enlacement that stuck them together, mingling their breath, confounding their perfumes and multiplying their hatred.

In the first shock Isabelle had ripped Aixa's silk tunic from top to bottom, and in hanging on to her she had also torn her broad bouffant trousers. She took advantage of that to be-labor the chest and the midriff, which offered themselves to her so well that she when she saw the five bloody furrows left by her fingernails she uttered a little laugh of triumph.

But Aixa had twice Isabelle's volume, and she ended up by pinning her adversary beneath her. Her turban had fallen off, her hair was uncoiled, and she perceived over her shoulder, like a cold drop of steel, a large pin as sharp as a dagger, which was planted in her tresses. She seized it, and leaned forward to put out Isabelle's eyes.

The latter had seen the flash above her; she turned her head and bit Aixa's thigh, which was within range of her mouth. She bit it desperately, putting all her force into her teeth. Pain caused Aixa to drop the pin and seize with both hands, by the nape of the neck and the gilded hair, the head whose closed jaw was biting with a delirious intensity.

She ended up freeing her leg and, as if by virtue of a kind of truce, the two women came apart and contemplated one another, crouching down.

There was no longer anything in them of royal dignity, or even feminine jealousy. Thought was no longer animating them. They were two beasts avid to bring down and bite, and to obtain the immobility of death in the other.

They contemplated one another, unkempt, deprived of their ornaments, almost naked. And suddenly, Isabelle burst out laughing—but a stifled, quiet laughter, for by common accord they were acting as silently as possible and their rage was only expressed in sighs.

"It's because your breasts are sagging," she breathed, "that you're chaste. You daren't show them. They're like empty gourds."

"All the mariners in Seville have hung on yours," replied Aixa.

"Poor old woman!"

Then, vulgarities heard in passing in the suburbs, the words of slaves surprised by chance, returned by virtue of the stimulus of outrage to the memory of the noble and virtuous Aixa and she allowed them to escape from her convulsed mouth.

She proffered them in Arabic, and Isabelle in her turn, understood them poorly.

Suddenly, the same thought crossed their minds. With a similar bound they rushed toward the glint that the large pin that Aixa had dropped was making among the stones of the balcony. They arrived there simultaneously, their heads collided, their hands mingled and the pin, launched by the shock, flew over the balustrade and fell into the Darro. They heard its fall, like a metallic laugh, music modulating their desire for death.

They resumed the hand-to-hand struggle, like lovers avid for one another. They fell down and writhed on the stone. They were panting with exhaustion. They felt their reciprocal body heat. Their sweat mingled, their skin stuck together mutually, and the disgust they had for one another added to their rage.

Isabelle's hand seized a handful of Aixa's right breast and twisted it, and that caused one to utter a gasp of pain and the other a gasp of triumph

Aixa grabbed Isabelle's slender neck and squeezed it with all her might. At the same time their knees collided and, still gripped, now naked, outside their shredded veils, they stood up momentarily, swooning against the balustrade in the midst of the violet wisteria, tumbling into the shade of the garden, still continuing their struggle.

The cypress garden was only a short drop from the balcony, and instinctively, the two women clung to one another with one hand, while the other grasped the thick branches of the wisteria. That softened their fall; they sprawled in a bed of lilies, raising a swirl of golden dust from the pistils.

A eunuch saw the scene from a window. At hazard, he seized a whip and ran out. In the moonlight, finding himself in the presence of the two slavering, bloody furies, showing their teeth and each trying to strike the other and strangle her amid the snow and gold of the lilies, he thought he was dealing with two drunken slaves, and in order to repress the prodigious scandal he whipped their wounded haunches several times.

The two women raised themselves up, howling. The eunuch recognized them, dropped his whip and fled. But his arrival and his blows had sobered the combatants Stifling the tide of their impulses, which had come from the depths of their being, they leapt over the bushes and quit the shelter of the cypress that extended its mute shadow over the ravaged lilies and dead wisteria.

When the doors of their apartments had slammed shut, Aixa and Isabelle, without even bandaging their wounds, collapsed, prey to the miserable despair that women always experience after action. Both of them were vanquished, since they were weeping. Both of them were victorious, since they had made the other weep. But, for want of being able to contemplate one another, they could neither measure their defeat not enjoy their victory.

Late into the night, in the midst of intact pots of rose jam and melted sorbets, a little black woman, magnificently clad, was found asleep in the hall of ambassadors. She retained, as she withdrew, the hieratic solemnity that befit the unique spouse of the envoy of the Sultan of Egypt, and she took away from her visit to the Alhambra the memory of a silent magic and a few hours of sound sleep in an enchanted palace whose queens were absent.

X. The Treasure of the Alhambra

When one loves a woman it is not sufficient for her to tell you that you are young; it is also necessary to render those words plausible by bringing her a few proofs of youth. Those proofs, Abul Hacen strove to furnish by means of unexpected and unreasonable actions.

On certain evening he drank beyond his capacity in order to demonstrate that wine had no purchase on his vigorous nature. He went for long excursions on horseback alongside Isabelle in order that she could admire his virtuosity as a cavalier, and he savored an infinite bliss when, on their return, she leaned toward him and, looking him full in the face, said to him: "What luck that you've remained slim. Imagine if you'd become like the fat man you were with when I saw you for the first time. I'd never have been able to love you."

It happened that the kings of Castile and Aragon sent an ambassador, as they did every year, to collect the arrears of the tribute of twelve thousand gold pistoles that, since Ismail, had been paid by the Kings of Granada to their neighbors, the Christian kings.

That ambassador was Don Juan de Vera, celebrated for his valor and beauty.

Isabelle wanted to see him and witness the interview that Abul Hacen was about to have with him. It was agreed that she would stand, invisibly, behind a little grilled window accommodated in the height of the wall.

The hagib had prepared the twelve thousand pistoles. Juan de Vera's visit was only a formality, always the same, and courteous words were exchanged in the Spanish language in order to mark the vassalage of the Moorish kingdom with regard to the kingdom of Castile.

Abul Hacen was lying on his divan with more nonchalance than usual. Aben Comixer, the Alcaide of Granada, was to his right, the Hagib to his left.

"What is it that brings you here?" said Abul Hacen imperiously, in the Arabic language, to the amazement of everyone.

Untroubled, Don Juan de Vera explained, in the Spanish language, that he had come to collect the annual tribute of twelve thousand pistoles.

Then, by a spontaneous inspiration that he attributed subsequently to Allah, but which was only due to the desire to shine before Isabelle and show her his regal power, his ease as a man and the youthfulness of his character, he raised himself up slightly, sniggered and said: "Tell your sovereign that our mint no longer casts anything but the blades of scimitars and the heads of spears." Then he turned his head and stared into space to make it understood that the interview was concluded.

Don Juan de Vera, whose mind was not very prompt to reply, remained motionless for a few seconds, then turned on his heel and drew away calmly, darting fiery gazes to the right and the left in order to substitute for the absence of an oral response and to make it understood that such an insult would soon be avenged.

Thus, to put a smile on a woman's face behind a grilled window, a virtual declaration of war had just been issued.

The rumor ran throughout Islam that the Moorish kingdom was invincible because of the fabulous treasure amassed by its kings, a treasure so great that neither that of Genghis Khan nor that of Solomon, nor the riches of the Republic of Venice, could be compared to it. That treasure permitted ships to be bought indefinitely from the Turks and the Barbary pirates, weapons from Genoa and the French, and armies of mercenaries to be raised in Morocco and Algeria.

The existence of that treasure was known to all the Moors in Spain. They relied on that wealth, which they did not enjoy, but by which they were secretly protected, and whatever his poverty, the most humble of beggars, when he looked at the Alhambra from afar, felt rich because of the mysterious reserves of gold that were contained there.

There was also another legend. Something more precious than gold and jewels was the property of the kings of Granada and reposed in the Alhambra. It was a talisman. If a few tribes from Yemen and Hira had been able to conquer the world with such fabulous rapidity, always bearing the standard of the Prophet further on, it was by virtue of a magical possession rather than by courage or numbers. For all the historians were unanimous. There was something inconceivable in the Arab conquest, something winged that surpassed the luck or energy of men. Okba had not had a considerable army when he went from the Red Sea to the Atlantic and pushed his horse into the occidental sea, regretting that it had interrupted his course. Tharek only commanded seven thousand men when he passed into Spain and had only received a few reinforcements when, on the banks of the Guadelete, he had crushed Roderic's immense army.

So many unexpected victories concealed a mystery. All the chiefs had had a veiled, unnamable and intangible object transported behind them, as sacred as Moses' Holy of Holies, as invisible as God himself. When Moussa had had an obelisk raised in Carcassonne, it was not only to attest to his progress in Narbonnaise Gaul, it was to shelter that talisman. The kings had transmitted it preciously for centuries. The Ommeyades placed it in the mosque of Cordova, the Almoravides constructed the Giralda of Seville for it, and Jacob Almanzor transported it to Granada where it remained.

That was what gave the protection that assured the immortality of the race. The Moorish people could sleep in peace. Somewhere under the hill of the Alhambra there was a hidden light, which was its genius.

Now, Isabelle the Spaniard, having heard those stories, got it into her head to possess the treasure and hold the talisman of the ancient kings in Christian hands.

The combat of the two women had thrown Abul Hacen into a great perplexity. He feared his son, whom he knew to the possessed with the love of treason. He feared the partisans that Aixa had been able to gather. On the other hand, Isabelle had sworn that she would no longer be his as long as she was not avenged, and she kept her word.

"I'll have them locked up together until they're reconciled," Abul Hacen said, several times.

But he went to Isabelle's door every evening and found it locked.

"I'm afraid of being murdered during the night," said Isabelle, the next morning. "Those who come wouldn't fail to imitate your voice." And she feigned a great terror.

One morning, he found her smiling and languid in a room overlooking the Court of Myrtles.

"I can't do without you," she said, with a movement full of desire. "And yet it's impossible to give myself to a man who refuses me the slightest proof of love."

He sensed that some demand was coming that it would be difficult to realize, and remained mute.

"I'll forgive you your weakness if you show me your treasure."

"What treasure?"

She stamped her foot and adopted a more puerile expression than usual. "The one that is hidden here under the Alhambra. It appears that you're the only one who knows where it is."

Abul Hacen's eyebrows furrowed, and he drew away without saying a word.

He came back a few hours later. She was lying on a divan, clad only in a transparent silk tunic. He trembled with contained desire.

As soon as she perceived his silhouette in the frame of the oval door she got up, took his arm familiarly and made him take a few paces, drawing him along and sketching a zambra step, while murmuring to him in a low voice: "My beloved master has come to find me to take me to my treasure. We're both going to go lie down amid precious stones."

He was about to push her away violently, rendered furious by her obstinacy. But without paying any heed to his ill humor, she stuck herself to him and sang the refrain of an ancient Arab ballad.

"In the treasure of the Alhambra

"There are the tears of our ancestors

"That have become dull pearls."

Then he considered her. She was thin and inoffensive; she was speaking as if in a dream, and between her fluttering eyelids shone a gold such as no treasure could contain any purer. He saw beneath the silk the slight undulation of her breasts, and the golden down that descended over the nape of her neck, the amber perfume of which maddened him.

Life was so rapid! Every day that passed took away a little of his strength. It was necessary to admit it to himself; he had difficulties with his sight and sometimes singular losses of memory. There would come a time when enjoyment would leave him, like the last ray of sunlight passing from one mountain to another at the moment of disappearing. Then again, had Isabelle not mentioned lying down in the midst of precious stones? Oh, what bed would be magnificent enough for that creature, which Allah had sent to him?"

"Well, so be it!" he said. "Come with me. I'll show you the treasure. Only, in your turn..."

He did not finish. She approved by clapping her hands.

They went through rooms and courtyards. They went into the Osario, which was surrounded by a high wall. It was the tomb of kings. Ali the mute was stationed there when he was not accompanying his master.

"This is the only man who is faithful to me," said Abul Hacen.

The man in question had leapt to his feet, and he preceded the Emir to a stairway closed by an enormous door, which he opened.

All three went down and arrived in a subterranean room where resin torches were fixed to the wall. Abul Hacen took one, which he lit. He made a sign to Ali, and the latter leaned with all his weight on one of the stone blocks of which the wall was made. With a dull sound, the block pivoted, drawing with it other blocks of large dimension, and unmasked an opening where there was a stairway.

Abul Hacen smiled proudly, showing Isabelle the marvelous mechanism, in the construction of which Arab engineers had long been past masters.

"It was Yussef Zeli, the builder of the Alhambra, who found that secret," he said. At the bottom of the staircase I'll show you the place where the workmen who took part in the construction are buried. It appears that Yussef Zeli was in despair at their deaths, but how else could the secret by guarded? For the same reason, later, Muhamad Alhamar was obliged to get rid of his son Hagib, whom he had been imprudent enough to bring here."

Isabelle reflected that the imprudence was greater for the person to whom the secret was revealed than the one who revealed it. She went down the steps lightly and only stopped when Abul Hacen, who was following her with difficulty, shouted to her to beware of slipping.

They suddenly found themselves before a door of black bronze. By the light of the torch Isabelle saw a hand engraved on that door similar to the one that was on the Puerta de la Justicia. Under the hand there was the design of a key.

Abul Hacen explained the symbol. "Human effort. It tries perpetually to seize the key to the mystery, always fleeing."

And that bronze door, at the extremity of the damp stairway, was sad and mute, as fatal as the subterranean powers it enclosed.

Abul Hacen had a hesitant gaze. If Isabelle had shown the slightest fear of the darkness and solitude of the place, he would gladly have gone back. But she shivered, delightfully caressed by the coolness, and breathed deeply. She rapped the bronze with her hand.

"Open it quickly," she said. "I want to see."

She did not sense the majesty of that fabulous treasure, buried under a palace, like the vertebrae of the race that lived above it.

Abul Hacen opened the door and raised the torch.

What Isabelle saw at first was confused, multiform, tenebrous and menacing. The room into which she had just penetrated was vast, to the point that she could not make out its extremities, and the walls were entirely covered with objects whose usage it was impossible to recognize.

While Abul Hacen placed the torch in a bracket near the entrance, Isabelle perceived huge masses of metal that must have been suits of armor, coffers that cast shadows and aligned pitchers, and suddenly, a fluidity of gold fell on all sides, a precious gleam that, with the light of the torch, immobilized as a sheet. It seemed to her that she was in a bath of gilded things.

Then she gazed, and could not retain a cry of admiration.

The floor was covered with mats from Samanah and Beneseh. There was a copy in solid gold, a foot high, of the ablution pavilion of Caliph El Mamoun, with its cupola encrusted with diamonds. There was a palm tree whose leaves were jewels representing dates of every degree of maturity. There were basins and crystal ewers, white gazelles whose abdomens were woven of pearls, tables of faience, silver or ebony from the land of the Zindjes, supporting trays of ivory or sandalwood, cups of agate or jade, in which radiant gems were displayed and pieces of uncut diamond. In one corner there was a heap of enamel plates and boxes of precious woods lined with silk. In another there was a superimposition of chessboards and pieces, in which every pawn was a material marvel and a masterpiece of workmanship.

Weapons could be seen shining, one of which was the famous sword Dhoul-Fikar[28] and another the shield of Amrou with the name of Allah written in seven different scripts. Standards so heavy with embroideries that it would have required several men to lift even one formed a pyramid up to the

---

[28] Dhoul-fiqar, or Zulfqar, was the sword with two points that Mohammed gave to Ali during the battle of Uhud, and which became one of the key symbols of Islam.

ceiling. An amber vase from Chahar was overflowing with camphor from Kaisour, and another in cornelian was filled with sculpted gold clasps. One chest must have contained a least seven mudds of emeralds, and another at least as many rubies, and some parts of the floor were strewn with gold dinars that crackled dully when one walked over them.

The crystals sparkled, the rubies bled, the diamonds fulgurated and large mirrors placed on the walls or supported by boxes sent back the light like so many stars, with the consequence that Isabelle thought she was passing through a subterranean Milky Way full of transparencies and luminous illusions.

"All this is yours!" she exclaimed.

And she stirred the emeralds, and made pearls stream between her fingers in cascades.

"You can take whatever you wish," murmured Abul Hacen. "Remember what you promised me."

And he drew near to her. His features were drawn, his lips trembling. He put his arms around her and tried to tip her over, but she escaped him. She could not weary of touching the silks and admiring the crystals.

"What promise?" she asked, in a distant voice.

He tried to seize her again, abruptly and kiss her on the lips, in the hope of awakening a desire in her. She understood, and nearly laughed at the folly of that hope. She slipped between his hands again.

"No," she said. "Keep your own promise."

She wanted to see and touch what no man had seen: the divine talisman that gave power, the mysterious column that had sustained the edifice of the Arab race.

Abul Hacen shivered. What was this childishness? She believed in a puerile legend. There was nothing other than the treasure he had just revealed to her.

And he started pursuing her among the coffers of jewels and the precious vases. She threw a handful of rubies at him like so many drops of blood, and a handful of sapphires like so many droplets from an enchanted spring. She flagellated him with a necklace of topazes charged with gold pendants, and as she was facing him, behind a bronze urn, she flung that necklace around his neck, so that it made a music of gems as it ran.

He begged her with puerile words and threatened her by turns. He was out of breath, and as if a magic had emerged from the surrounding objects, they both began to tremble. The furniture, the standards and the crystals had been removed from pillaged cities under the flames of conflagrations. There were precious silks that had been snatched from women as they were being raped, whose fingers had often been severed in order to remove tight rings. Those ancient murders, those past dramas, were mysteriously evoked, appearing transparently in the mirrors, and the gleam of cups changed into amorous rage in the man and panic terror in the woman.

She was about to reach the door, but she suddenly slipped and they both fell on to a bed of gold dinars. He clutched her as if he wanted to crush her, but she clawed his face, to the point that he felt blood running into his eyes; she crawled beneath him and escaped again.

They had both lost their reason.

She took the sword of Dhoul-Fikar and raised it.

"I'll strike if you come any nearer," she said.

The Emir's fury evaporated. The supple body that he had before him weakened his entire being by virtue of he need he had to repose against its warmth.

"Well then, I'll do what you want. But you'll keep your promise?"

"I'll keep it."

"Immediately?"

"Yes. There, on the dinars and the gemstones."

Abul Hacen took a little rusty key that was attached by a ring to the key of the first door, and moved aside a Persian rug that hid a section of the wall. There was a very low door there. Instinctively, he repeated several times that Allah was the only god and that Mohammed was his prophet. Then he bent down and opened it.

He had taken in his arms a heavy object, which he turned toward Isabelle.

She only saw a mass enveloped with veils on which damp and mold had put gray crystals.

There was another argument. Isabelle thought she was being deceived. Abul Hacen did not want to recommence the struggle. In the end it was agreed that she would drop the sword that she was still holding and that she would remove a part of her clothing every time he removed off one of the veils enveloping the talisman. He believed that there were seven veils. She would be naked by the seventh.

Abul Hacen sensed the immensity of the sacrilege and his teeth were chattering. Isabelle was laughing in a hysterical fashion and at times, her eyes tipped back. At the first veil she took off her turban, at the second her slippers. Slowly with an undulation of her body, following Abul Hacen's gestures, she unrolled the long veil that enveloped her. Her breasts appeared, and then the Emir's movements became jerky and rapid. He had a desire to rip that supple, ancient, interminable silk.

In the end, Isabelle was naked. She had understood that it was necessary to finish it. Perhaps she was also caught up by her game.

The torch put red reflections on her flesh, and in the sparkle of beryls, chrysoprases and sapphires that she picked up in handfuls and poured over herself nervously, she had never been so beautiful. "Come on!" she cried, with a savage indecency.

And she let herself fall on to the ruddy fabric of a standard, extended and offered, only darting a distracted gaze at the talisman that had just appeared and no longer had any importance to her save that of a caprice realized.

Abu Hacen considered with surprise that which had been an object of veneration for so many peoples on the march, which Okba the conqueror had paraded throughout Africa, which Abderame the sage had worshiped, the reason so many men had died with a face illuminated by joy.

It was a kind of casket, the splendor of which seemed mediocre, with two flared handles and two crudely sculpted angels that seemed to be supporting its weight and lifting it up toward the sky. The casket was gold, but a gold so worn and faded that the splendor of the metal had vanished and it gave the impression of being thousands of years old, so prodigiously ancient that there could not be any similar parcel of matter in the world. Only the faces of the two angels, in spite of the times without number, had retained an intense spiritual expression.

"Well?" said Isabelle, impatiently.

Abul Hacen straightened up, dropping the divine object, which fell dully.

How sad the gold and jewels around him were! How heavy the treasure was! Isabelle's body, with pleasure and power in its form, was displayed at his mercy, a tender pink on the deep red of the standard. But it was far away, at the end of a bizarre avenue bordered by suits of armor, urns, miscellaneous objects of all dimensions whose meaning escaped him. That desirable body floated, as radiant as the stars, became as obscure as a phantom, was confused with what surrounded it; lost in the midst of a thousand lamps that were all going out, it was about to cease to exist, to be invisible.

He could no longer see it. He had gone blind.

He passed his hand over his face. It was the blood from a scratch that must have flowed. No, not blood. The malediction with which profaners were threatened, had struck him. He had been punished in the manner that he had feared the most throughout his life.

But he did not want that. There was a malign influence in the damp subterrain. That was what was troubling his sight. It was necessary to flee. In halting speech, he explained to Isabelle what had happened. He moaned like a child.

"Save me!" he repeated, beating the air with his hands.

It seemed to him that she took an infinite time to get dressed. Then, she could not detach the torch. Then there was the door that it was necessary to close. He clung to her veil, and she drew him up the staircase. The necklace of topazes that he still had around his neck made a ridiculous sound as it agitated against his belly. He stumbled several times and Isabelle clenched her teeth in order not to insult him. Finally, they arrived in the room where Ali was waiting for them, and then before the tomb of the kings.

Then, perceiving that he could see the beautiful stones of the walls again, and the divine twilight, Abul Hacen fell to the ground, put his forehead in the dust, and thanked Allah, who had pardoned him.

XI. The Temptation

It was the month of Rabi el Sani. The satiny trunks of the magnolias were whiter and their broad, polished and shiny leaves were mingled with milky flowers, as velvety as ermine.

Almazan, going through the Court of Myrtles, was breathing in the slightly sickening vanilla odor of those flowers when he heard someone call to him from one of the rooms overlooking the fountain.

A little ironic laugh rang out and he saw Isabelle de Solis lying on a divan beside a cassolette from which a heavy vapor was escaping.

"You're not afraid? You aren't fleeing at the sight of me?" she said. "I didn't know that I'd become so redoubtable."

He apologized. A thousand things solicited him. The Emir's service was very absorbing.

"As you see, I'm so bored," she said, "that I'm burning musk with the roots of the Gazan plant, which grows in the Caucasus, it appears. An old woman procured for me."

She extended her hands over the cassolette and looked at him slyly. "Do you know the effects of the Gazan plant?"

He did not know them.

"I forgot that I could scandalize you by talking to you about it. It appears that you're perpetually plunged in your books and that only science interests you."

Almazan replied that he strove to be interested in what he saw. The ideal was to discover the beauty that there was in everything.

The ideal! She started to laugh.

"Look! Would you like some crystallized ginger, or neidehs, or a little of the roasted barley liquor that they drink in this country, and which I find so poor. My ideal would be to amuse myself. Is there not a secret for that in your books?"

"Everyone has the secret of their own pleasure in the faculty of desire," he said.

She lay back in the midst of cushions, laughing again.

"Then I ought to be infinitely happy."

Then she leaned toward him, on her elbow, with her chin in her hand, and looked at him intently.

"You don't know what I desire?"

"How could I know that?"

"I would like you to carry me, as you did in Seville, on to a never-ending staircase."

The golden droplets of her eyes were tarnished between her palpitating eyelids, her teeth appeared between her redder lips, like the promise of bites, and sensuality emerged from her garments like an almost tangible wave.

He was sitting nearby and she was talking to him. She was suddenly full of sincerity and confidence. She yielded to a surge of sympathy whose cause she did not seek.

She liked pleasure—well, so what? She didn't hide it. She was merely more honest than others, that's all. She was dying of boredom alongside the Emir, and the Alhambra, with its splendors, seemed dismal to her because she had no one of her own race in whom to confide. And yet the Emir loved her to the point of fulfilling all her caprices. Had Almazan heard mention of the famous treasure of the kings of Granada? She could draw upon it whenever she wished. She had even had an ugly little casket placed in her room, a box of sorts that might be gold and which all the Arabs had considered venerable and very precious for centuries. She put her turbans and slippers in it. But what was the point of jewels and talismans if one did not have happiness?

Almazan listened to her anxiously, not knowing whether this encounter with Isabelle was an agreeable event or a trap of his evil destiny.

Sometimes she poured the roasted barley liquor into a porcelain cup and lifted it to her lips. She had made a sign to Almazan to sit down beside her, she became animated, and her voice lowered as if to give more importance to her words.

""To think that I would have been yours the first time I saw you, if you had wanted. I was afraid! You desired me—don't deny it, I understood that by your gaze—and you nearly threw yourself upon me when you set me down on your bed. I wouldn't have resisted. Anyway, if you hadn't desired me, why would you have come to Aboulfedia's house? To ask him for medical advice, perhaps? You saw me stark naked in the pool with the blue faience. I knew that you were looking at me through the mesh of the golden gauze that the ignoble Aboulfedia had placed there. It was one of his habitual pleasures, and I lent myself to it sometimes. Why? I don't know. Perhaps because I didn't know you yet. Can you explain to me how it is that one's whole life depends on meeting one man and not another? What a mystery sympathy is! I've been on the point of falling in love with a young Moor named Tarfe. He belongs to an illustrious family, that of the Almoradis, and he pleased me because he's reputed to be stupid. For stupidity attracts a woman as much as intelligence, perhaps more."

Almazan's expression had darkened. Tarfe was the horseman he had encountered on arriving in Granada for the first time, who had stared at him insolently. He had seen him again since, and the repulsion he had felt for his bestial beauty had only increased. Perhaps Isabelle had sensed that repulsion, for she persisted deliberately.

"They call him the goat, but with me he's as gentle as a lamb. We've only exchanged a few words and he's found the means of telling me that he was thinking about me and that he would wave a red lamp every evening at the summit of a terrace in the Albaycin in order to remind me of him. It's only childishness, but I have so few distractions!

It deemed to Almazan that his soul had been traversed by a dagger. There were a few scornful words hovering on his lips for the Almoradi whose folly was notorious in Granada, but he was ashamed of them and did not pronounce them.

While they had been talking, the sky had become cloudy and raindrops were making large circles in the fountain in the Court of Myrtles.

221

Almazan had risen to his feet. He explained that he could not stay any longer. The Emir might have professed the ideas of the liberal Ommeyades from whom he was descended but he would certainly take umbrage at a longer conversation.

"You don't know, then!" Isabelle exclaimed. "The Emir has left. It's a State secret that only the Hagib and I know. He's taken five hundred cavaliers and they'll ride flat out for part of the night Have you heard mention of a town called Zahara, near Ronda? It appears that its church possesses objects of great value, and the wife of my father's steward, whom I hate, ought to be there at present. Well, the Emir's going to take possession of Zahara tonight and bring me the treasure tomorrow on a mule, and the steward's wife with a chain around her neck."

Almazan shivered. So the old war of the Moors and the Spaniards, interrupted for a long time, was about to be reanimated tonight. The Catholic kings had left the refusal to pay the tribute unanswered, but the attack on Zahara could only be the first blow in a merciless war.

Isabella emptied into her cup the liquor contained in the alcazars and drank it in a single draught. Her eyes were drowned and her lips moist, as if the approach of pleasure were already making itself felt. The wind of the rising storm lifted her veils and seemed to want to remove them. Throughout her flesh there was the abandonment that the expectation of sensuality gives.

"Tonight is mine!" she said. "You can't know the joy that represents. Don't abandon me. I sense that there's a flame in you similar to mine. I admit it: I was going to give myself to the young Almoradi tonight. Amour must have rendered him intelligence, for he's bribed the eunuchs and arranged to penetrate into the Alhambra disguised as one of them. When the sun has gone down, if I respond to the signal of a lamp raised in the Albaycin, he'll come. But I don't love that Almoradi."

Large leaves detached from the magnolias were swirling, and sometimes one of them fell into the room abruptly, like a new hope on the thresholds of a commencing evening. Isabelle gave the impression of a child desirous of a toy. Her voice had become persuasive, almost pleading.

"Don't budge from your room this evening. I'll simulate a serious illness and have you summoned. Since you've cured the wound in his leg, the Emir considers you as his safeguard and that of all the people whose lives he holds dear. Nothing will seem more natural. And fundamentally, I won't be lying. I need you to cure me."

As in Seville, when he had set her down, fragile and palpitating, on his bed, Almazan had a sudden desire to embrace her. Footsteps resonated along the Court of Myrtles. A slave advanced, laughing at the force of the wind that projected her veil over her head.

"So be it," said Almazan. "Until tonight."

And he drew away,

XII. The Four Lepers

In his apartment, he learned from a slave that Christian Rosenkreutz wanted to see him immediately. He put on his cloak and, in spite of the tempest that was blowing, he left the Alhambra.

Not far from the strangers' gate, Rosenkreutz had rented a house as narrow as a cell from a weaver. He was outside his door, in the squalls and the rain, and he made a movement of satisfaction when he saw Almazan. But the latter soon perceived, when they were sheltered in the house, that he had nothing particular to say to him. He stood before him silently, and there was a great indulgence in his shining eyes.

Almazan had a desire to tell him everything, the folly of his desire and the conversation he had just had. Rosenkreutz stopped him.

"Every man has a battle to fight," he said, "that of the spirit against the flesh, and he must win it on his own, because there is no fecund victory except the one that one obtains without support. The man who goes backwards has departed before time and he will know a hard recommencement. How I want you to conquer the power that is only given to the elect, only to see in the beauty of matter the spirit that is its eternal meaning, and not the form that is only its temporary expression."

The form! The perfect form! The word evoked for Almazan the body of the woman that he could not forget. Oh, the falling curve of the shoulder, the hollow of the back, and the leg as slender as an extended stem. What was the spirit hidden behind the amber and rose of that skin?

Dusk was beginning to fall. Almazan made a movement to withdraw.

"I promised you," said Rosenkreutz, "to introduce you to Soleiman, who recovers the incarnations of men. We're very close to his house, where he lives with his three brothers in the lepers' quarter. I'll take you there."

Almazan hesitated. Isabelle might send someone to fetch him after nightfall. But the door was already open, and Rosenkreutz was going along the street.

They went through the two enclosures of the strangers' gate, walked for a while through the rain, which had become heavier, and reached the leprosarium.

It was surrounded by a high wall, of such a frightful yellow color that it seemed to be afflicted itself by the malady that it enclosed in its vast circle. The wall was pierced by a large number of doors, to permit the inhabitants, who could not leave the enclosure, to come to buy food from the merchants who flocked there every morning.

It made, by comparison with Granada, a dismal city that nothing would have distinguished from the other if a particular silence had not filled it. That silence came, not from the absence of the joy of living, for joy was as great there as elsewhere, but from the prohibition of all negotiation, the malady being supposed to be communicated more by the circulation of objects than personal contact. The great silence was even more impressive on rainy days, for then all the lepers emerged from their thresholds and held out there faces and bodies to the sky in order to be washed, attributing a mysterious curative force to the rain.

The twilight aggravated the chalky hues of the houses. There were rich ones with gardens, but by virtue of the sandy nature of the soil, the vegetation had something sickly about it; the palm trees were tumefied, and the pines secreted a more abundant resin like lymph. Dilapidated buildings succeeded one another, giving the impression of being stuck together, and their façades were cracked, ready to come away like crusts.

Rosenkreutz and Almazan slid though the long side-streets, sometimes looking at a face larger than natural, with enormous eyes, brushing blanched bodies that moved aside

225

precipitately as they approached, and they did not listen to the stammered apologies or the hoarse salutations.

A large shadow extended above them.

"This is the dwelling of the four brothers," said Rosenkreutz. "It's an old fortress that has been rebuilt by them. Their story remains inexplicable for me. The disease afflicted them almost at the same time. All four were bad men, debauched to the point that Abul Hacen's predecessor thought of banishing them from Granada. After a night more agitated than the others, spent in the company of his brothers, Soleiman had a kind of revelation. He claimed that the Prophet had appeared to him and he started to lead an ascetic life, but of a special asceticism—that of a very ancient sect of Sufis who sought divine ecstasy in the intoxication of wine. Then, intermittently at first, and then more and more frequently, he had visions of the past, and acquired the gift of reading in the astral light the previous lives of men. At the same time, the symptoms of leprosy developed in the four brothers. The Emir, who did not like them, hastened to send them here. Then they acquired this ancient castle, which they furnished sumptuously. Soleiman has accepted his destiny without complaint, while his brothers live with him in a constant rage, more avid for pleasure than ever.

The two men had traversed an enclosure in which the rain pattered on foliage they could not see. They perceived the presence of recumbent men who might have been servants, or the masters of the place. Someone recognized Rosenkreutz, for a broken voice emerged from the shadows and shouted: "He's there. You can go in."

Almazan shivered, so sinister was that great stone building and those sick men lying in the mist of shining puddles.

At the top of a long winding stairway that must have been used by watchmen and archers in past wars, they opened a door and found themselves in a room that resembled an Egyptian tomb, in the presence of Soleiman.

Sitting cross-legged, he was weeping. He did not make any movement, but his eyelids rose two or three times, and a slight sign of his swollen finger asked his visitors to wait in silence.

Rosenkreutz sat down beside him. Almazan kept slightly apart.

Finally, Soleiman spoke, but he addressed himself to himself rather than to the man who was with him.

"Khadidja! Princess Khadidja! All three of them claimed that they saw her, that she had emerged from her tomb, and they clicked their shaky teeth and trembled again with desire. But the other was a poor young woman that a Barbary ship had abducted from Corfu. The other was a Christian and she is dead! How could that be Princess Khadidja?"

On hearing these incomprehensible words, Almazan drew closer.

Tears were still running down Soleiman's face, but he emerged from his meditation. He wiped his face and he turned to Rosenkreutz, murmuring: "As the poet has said, tears are the offering of a soul in pain." Then, with a heart-rending smile, he added: "Oh, a great deal of pain."

Suddenly, he leaned forward, his face illuminated by an expression of dolor and intelligence.

"Christian Rosenkreutz, who departed from Germany and marched toward the Orient until the day when you encountered the wise men who taught you the double symbol of the rose and the cross, who has received the mission to perpetuate the truth, do you believe that the man who has killed in this life can be pardoned one day?"

"There is no pardon for sins," said Rosenkreutz softly. "There is a law of equilibrium. The effect follows the cause and their enchainment can perhaps be called pardon."

"But you would doubtless turn away if you knew that one of those you have chosen has spilled blood voluntarily."

"The only true crime is against the spirit."

"Listen. You do not know anything because you were not in Granada at that time. I lived then in the same manner as my brothers and my passions were even more frenzied. Imagine the worst. A defenseless creature delivered to four fanatics, a creature, whose face only reflected elevated thoughts, serving as a plaything for four drunken men, tortured and violated all night long, and murdered when dawn came. Yes, a slave bought in the market, but so perfect in the soul that emerged in her gaze!

"It was the most wretched of the four, the most debauched, who struck her in the heart, with no other reason than the sensuality of the crime. That was me. I remember that afterwards, I started to laugh, and I dragged her by the feet into the garden in order to bury her. Her hair was never-ending. It caught on bushes and I pulled it away, laughing. I found a gardener's spade, I dug a big hole and I threw her into it without ceasing to laugh. Then I filled in the earth, and even replaced the turf.

"When it was finished, I sat down, holding my knees with my hands, and I stayed there, bewildered, gazing at the sun, which was rising in the middle of a clump of cactus, still suppressing bursts of laughter. But the sun didn't rise for me. It was never to rise again. In its place, in the midst of the cactus, as inaccessible as moral beauty, as sad as an awakening soul, there was the face of the Prophet, who was looking at me. I recognized the one whose features are not reproduced by any image. He was staring at me, and his sadness was like a twilight. Then I fell to the ground, inanimate, and when I came round, I asked Allah, forcefully, to punish me in this life.

"That wish has been granted by bodily malady, and I await the other punishment. Perhaps it is imminent. My three brothers went to the doors of the leprosarium today at the hour when the merchants set up their ambulant stalls. Now, Princess Khadidja, the Emir's niece, also came to distribute alms to the poor lepers. And my brothers came back, prey to a sort of dementia, claiming that Princess Khadidja was exactly similar, in the grace of her face and the slimness of her body, to the young woman they had violated and I had murdered, and of whom they and I retain a different but immortal memory.

228

"I thought that a marvelous resemblance between those two creatures, the living and the dead, was going to be the new form of my pain, that it would be necessary henceforth for me to stand at the doors of the leprosarium with the beggars in order to perceive her and savor my remorse with more force. And that is why I was weeping for myself."

Darkness had almost fallen and the room was only illuminated by the gleam of nascent stars.

This is the moment when Isabelle might send someone to fetch me, Almazan thought. And he took a step forward, for Soleiman had grasped his head in both hands and was no longer moving. But Rosenkreutz leaned over him and retained Almazan with a hand gesture.

"There is one of ours behind you whose soul is tormented, and who is at the beginning of his ordeal. Have you nothing to say to him?"

Soleiman remained motionless, and Rosenkreutz, thinking that he had not been heard, was about to repeat his question when he murmured:

"I see a great maritime landscape, a city full of monuments and two beings joined by the diffuse light of desire... He is taking her away... I see other cities and the redness of the desire that envelops the man and the woman paling, becoming the color of ash... Now they have separated... He has abandoned her... There must be a great suffering in the woman, for she is writhing like a beast and the blue of her intelligence is losing its color, washing away, mingling with the brick color of bleak despair. He is very far away, he has forgotten her. There is no dolor in his life. His thought seems to be developing extremely. He must belong to the highest elite. The azure blue of spirituality radiates around him, but deep down, the little blue flame that he had left on the road has taken on a dirty hue and gone out. There is nothing more."

Almazan was only listening distractedly. He was measuring the passing time.

"So much for the former life," said Rosenkreutz, "but can you see the possibilities of events in the present life?"

A long time went by, and then Soleiman resumed in the same whisper.

"What a mysterious law it is that causes the reincarnation at the same time, for hatred or for amour, those who have hated or loved one another! There they are, side by side. They have encountered one another in the same city. Her desire to be beautiful in her previous life has rendered her beautiful in this one, and she has lost the resignation and the fidelity that caused her misfortune. She is now akin to a natural force that needs to expand. He has collected all the advantages of past efforts and the light that is around him is a blue almost as pure as your own. I see the beings in a mist, like moving lamps, but while the light that you form, Rosenkreutz, is solitary and unalterable in essence, his is dependent on another and might become, in an instant, as scarlet as passion or as brown as the love of evil."

"Can you not distinguish," Rosenkreutz said, "which of those eventualities those causes will inevitably engender?"

Soleiman swayed to the right and left such for a long time that Almazan thought that he was not going to say another word.

"No. All is veiled. There are great catastrophes. The human will can always modify what seems inevitable, but is itself a prisoner of causes. There are cities destroyed, and so much blood shed! And it is not only bodies but souls that are perishing! Evil seems triumphant. I see a kind of dark tide that is carrying fanaticism and ignorance. The spirit recoils and seems to be dying. It is the spiritual effort of an entire race that is annihilated. And what unleashes that gigantic event is perhaps the injustice inflicted on a soul, in another existence, by the man who is behind me."

Soleiman had let his head fall forward, and he seemed not to want to say any more. Rosenkreutz had stood up silently and he made a sign to Almazan to follow him.

Outside, the rain had stopped, but the wind was blowing tempestuously. The city of the lepers was deserted. They emerged from it and walked toward Granada. But Almazan was no longer hurrying.

"Have I misunderstood what Soleiman said?" he asked. "How can an action accomplished by me in another life have such incalculable consequences?"

"The mystery of causes is impenetrable," said Rosenkreutz. "A soul that has been depleted because it has been deprived of its portion of amour rolls in the infinity of lives as if it were launched by despair. It is injustice that engenders evil, and the injustice of an intelligent and just man is the most terrible thing that the world can create."

Rosenkreutz had taken his companion on a long detour along the ramparts.

"Except," he added, "that Soleiman is perhaps only a visionary who has retained old habits of drunkenness and draws incoherent images from his imagination, which he sincerely believes himself to be extracting from the astral light in which the past is inscribed.

Almazan uttered a sigh of relief.

"We know very little," said Rosenkreutz then. "Wisdom often takes the form of folly, and how can we distinguish the portion of truth that there is in the phantasmagoria of dreams?"

They had reentered Granada and had arrived at Rosenkreutz's house. The stormy night unfurled with dark clouds in the sky and Almazan calculated that it ought to be sufficiently advanced for the messenger sent by Isabelle to have knocked on his door in vain. He shook the hand that Rosenkreutz held out to him, but he did not head toward the Alhambra. He walked through the streets at random. His thoughts were crowding his brain. He felt a kind of intoxication, and the wind added to the disturbance of his mind. He had gone along the quays of the Darro and was climbing one of the slopes of the Albaycin via the street of the cutlers.

He suddenly looked up, and saw the great mass of stone that the Alhambra made, with its irregularly erected towers. At the foot of one of them, on a gallery facing the mountains, he saw a drop of red light moving, which must be a lamp. That luminous drop went up and down two or three times, and then vanished.

Almazan remembered what Isabelle had said. Irritated by his absence, she was summoning the Almoradi Tarfe.

Oh, the pleasure lost! The sensuality that one could have held tightly, and which one would never find again! Was the service of truth to which he had devoted himself imperious enough to prevent him from possessing a woman he had desired? Rosenkreutz had certainly divined his trouble and had turned him away expressly; he had stolen his hours of amour!

He started running into the Albaycin. He went along the streets at random. He went astray. Out of breath, he went back up to the Alhambra and arrived at the Puerta de la Justicia only to see two eunuchs going in from a distance. He recognized them by the magnificent red robes that had been their uniform for some time and whose ample sleeves and crimson belts were copied from those of the Sultan of Constantinople's eunuchs.

The taller of the two exchanged a few pleasantries in passing with the soldiers on guard. The other had his turban pulled down over his eyes, and Almazan recognized Tafre's silhouette, by the light of the lantern burning against the wall. He had the attractiveness and lightness that happiness gives. Then Almazan, without looking back, went down slowly toward the town. He was no longer thinking about anything. He walked for a long time, taking pleasure in making the large puddles left by the rain splash beneath his feet.

XIII. The Massacre of the Almoradis

The town of Zahara was reputed to be impregnable because it only had one gate and was backed up on two sides against high rocky corridors. When the tempest was unleashed there were no watchmen on the towers, and the ramparts were swept by large sheets of rain.

Abul Hacen and the five hundred elite men he had brought with him approached the walls thanks to the density of the darkness, and placed ladders there without the alarm being raised.

The Emir could not, as he desired, be the first to penetrate into the town. When he set foot on a ladder it almost broke under his weight. Soaked to the skin, shivering and fall of ardor, he had waited for the gate to be forced. He had then raced into the streets, looking for a fight; but the fortress was already taken, the guards on the towers massacred. Sometimes, in a square, a small group of Spaniards tried to resist. The Emir then stopped the surge of his men in order to launch himself into their midst alone, striking right and left with his scimitar. He felt a youthful folly then, and he knew that the courage of which he gave proof would subsequently be the subject of many stories that would be repeated in the Alhambra and would win Isabelle's admiration.

A single house, in which the aged Antonio de Cuerdo was barricaded with his ten children cost more men to take than the rest of the town. They had made holes in the door and fired at close range with their arquebuses.

It was necessary to burn the house, and they had a great deal of difficulty because the rain incessantly extinguished the firebrands thrown on to the roof. Then a courageous young woman, lurking like a cat behind a door, succeeded in disemboweling two Moorish soldiers with a minuscule knife. It was the occasion for a brawl; it was a matter of punishing her. Her hands had been tied and her clothes torn off. Some wanted to spare her and rape her at their ease; others preferred to put her to death right away.

But almost all the inhabitants surrendered without resistance. The sound of trumpets assembled them in the main square, where they remained while their houses were pillaged. Those who had the imprudence to stay at home fell under the blows of soldiers drunk on the extraordinary alcohol of combat. The riches that were found were immense and it took three days to heap them on to carts.

Abul Hacen appointed an Alcaide and placed a garrison in the fortress. On the seventh day he set forth to return to Granada. He felt an extraordinary joy in his victory and the vigor of which he had given proof. He occupied himself with everything: provisions, the order in which the prisoners would file four by four in the middle of his soldiers, and the manner in which a few cannons would be drawn by way of trophies.

As he was still within sight of Zahara and was climbing a hill he turned round to enjoy the extent of his power, but the long files of cavaliers with their short red jackets floating over their gilded coats of mail were not prancing to either side of the road. He did not see the noblemen under the drapery of their cloaks covered with precious stones, with the colored plumes of their turbans fluttering like fabulous insects, nor the Silahdars carrying spears and adargas. The cortege of prisoners had disappeared. The hoofbeats, the clink of weapons and the murmurs and cries were making the same noise behind him, but he saw nothing but a twilight into which darkness was rushing from all directions.

"Isabelle!" he repeated, several times.

There must be a powerful magic in the name of a woman one loves, for the mountains were replaced on the horizon, he saw the cavalry advancing, plumes shining, and, with his brow bathed in sweat, he hastened toward Granada.

All magic has two directions, every face is magnificent and baleful by turns, every thought lacerates you and enchants you in accordance with the moment that it comes to mind.

"Isabelle!" he repeated, his head in his hands—and the incantation of those syllables caused inconceivable images to crowd around him.

Before anything else, he needed to reflect, to weigh the probabilities in the balance of reason, to be prudent, wily and hypocritical.

The accusation came from Aixa, and in consequence, had every reason to be a lie. Was it not better to laugh at it? But Aixa, who was pious, had sworn on the Koran, which had never happened before. The Hagib had also sworn on the Koran that Isabelle was above suspicion, but the Hagib did not believe in anything and he had also added some sage advice about not paying any heed to anything except the commencing war.

The Almocaden who commanded the guard at the Puerta de la Justicia believed he had seen a new eunuch passing several days ago whose face he had not seen, but he did not recall with which other eunuch he had passed. The enormity of the fact, and the audacity necessary to accomplish it, proved that it was nothing but calumny. There was no young man in Granada capable of such a crime and such a folly. However, if one thought about it, it was easy to introduce oneself into Isabelle's bedroom disguised as a eunuch. But was there not a bronze door, a wall of tempered steel, around the creature with the golden eyes, and were that inviolable door and that wall as high as the stars carved in the marble and steel of his amour?

However, he had been obliged to recall that on the day he had returned from Zahara, she had had strangely weary eyes, and he had remarked bruises on her thighs, as if hands had squeezed them forcefully. He had asked her the cause of that and she had replied that she had bumped them accidentally while walking in her room in the dark. But how to explain the symmetrical character of those bruises? A double collision was impossible. Heaven and earth! There was no doubt about it! It was the fingers of the young Almoradi, Tarfe, that had opened the delicious fruit where he drank the juice of his ultimate youth.

The old men of the Meschouar and the leaders of the great families were waiting for him in the hall of ambassadors for decisions relating to the conscription of troops. In another room, there were the six provincial Walis and the twenty-four district Wazirs who needed precise orders for the defense of the frontiers. On the Plaza des Aljibes, Daoud, the Emir of the Sea, was pacing back and forth beside his saddled horse. He was counting on departing immediately for Almeria with the mission to embark there and lead the Moorish ships against the Spanish ports. The abrupt attacks whose plan was drawn up on a piece of parchment that he was holding in his hands might have incalculable results, on condition that the plan was executed without delay.

That was the important thing!

The Hagib sometimes lifted the door-curtain of the room where the Emir was now pacing back and forth, and at other times it was the mute Ali who showed his faithful face. Abul Hacen dismissed them with an imperious gesture.

Oh, if he had known! He would have examined the design of those bruises on his beloved's thighs carefully. He would have been able to recognize the undeniable trace of fingers. Now it was too late. Time, with its untiring patience, had rendered the smooth limbs their perfect whiteness.

Suddenly, Abul Hacen stopped. He fell into the midst of the cushions on his divan. His eyes were exorbitant and he bit the fabric in order not to howl. A thought had just been born in his mind, a thought wakening like a flame, a curiosity that no longer had a limit, one of those amorous curiosities that one never satisfies because they are always lost in the lies of the woman and the silence of the man.

Perhaps the bruises on the thigh were bites! It was not hands but human teeth that had designed their contours with the tender fury of lust.

He would never know! There are details that no mouth reports. There is an inviolable secret more silent than the mystery of death. King Ferdinand and Queen Isabella could prepare a formidable army entirely at their ease. The Duke of

Medina-Sidonia had just been reconciled with the Marquis of Cadiz, but what did it matter? The Sultan of Egypt was demanding a hundred thousand gold mitcals in exchange for his alliance, but so what? There was only one grave, immediate, hallucinatory problem, and that was the origin of those bruises on his beloved's thighs, those blue bruises that had turned black and then gilded like grapes, to be lost in the lunar ocean of the skin like mysterious boats laden with lust.

Life is still beautiful as long as there is doubt, but certainty is like a desolate plain where one perceives nothing in the distance but the black tower of vengeance.

The Almocaden of the Puerta de la Justicia had recognized the eunuch and the eunuch had confessed under torture that he had introduced Tarfe into Isabelle's apartment. And that fact in itself would have been trivial if it had kept a distant, anonymous, mysterious character—but Abul Hacen knew other things even more frightful.

That Tarfe, not being very intelligent, had boasted. He had given certain details and those details were circulating from mouth to mouth. The entire Almoradi family was rejoicing in the adventure.

"When he came back from the Alhambra he had bags under his eyes all the way to the chin," one of his uncles said.

"The goat has finally found his she-goat," another, whose hatred for Abul Hacen was ancient and well-known, repeated incessantly.

Abul Hacen remembered that the Almoradi family had never liked him. They were Moroccan in origin. They had fought his grandfather, and in spite of the advantages with which he had heaped them, they had remained quietly hostile Oh, why had he not relied more on the Zegris? They were rigorous, it's true, but faithful. Virtue, he could see, had its good side, and the Almohade sovereigns were not so foolish when they punished with death women who went abroad unveiled. Now he was the talk of Granada. He, who, had excited the admiration of his soldiers a few days before in the streets of Zahara, was no longer anything but an old man who had been deceived by the wife he loved with a vigorous young man. It would have been better to fall from the top of the highest mosque in Granada.

But the detestable Almoradis were about to learn to know him!

First of all, he would stab Isabelle. Afterwards...

Isabelle! The light of the dawn! Was he not illuminated by her? Did not his eyes moisten when the syllables of her name were sung? What if she still loved him? There are women who have temporary caprices. They satisfy them and they return with more ardor to the man they love. He was like that himself. Women, fundamentally, are driven by the same instincts as men.

No, he would not kill Isabelle. To know in what measure she had loved Tarfe and simultaneously to avenge himself on the Almoradis, that was the problem, and he had a simple, easy and ingenious means of resolving it.

He did not expose his plan to the Hagib. The man had a rather limited and paltry mind fixed on the interests of the realm. In addition, he had shown a monstrous indifference to Isabelle's treason. Had he not even shrugged his shoulders slightly on learning of it? The Hagib was stupid. He would act alone.

The sun would soon set. A translucent dusk was bathing the Court of Lions.

"You who are the source of my happiness, I want you to witness the punishment of my enemies."

The Emir put his arms around Isabelle with a feigned tenderness that did not leave her without anxiety.

At the back of the Court of Lions there was a room of repose full of divans, which as known as the rose room. A fountain sprang from the middle and a balcony overlooked it, which one reached by a narrow stairway. It was on that balcony that they were both sitting. Sinister silhouettes filled the room of repose.

"Why have you brought those sinister individuals?" asked Isabelle.

"I've been offended. We've been offended, you and me. The blood of the calumniators is going to flow," replied Abul Hacen.

"There's no necessity for me to remain here," said Isabelle, getting up.

Abul Hacen retained her, squeezing her wrist with such force that she understood confusedly what was about to happen, and she was afraid.

The first of the Almoradis who responded to Abul Hacen's message was Ahmed ben Alhassan, who had grown rich in commerce in jewels. He was given to flattery and humility, and the habit of bowing had eventually given his body a forward inclination.

Scarcely had he entered the rose room than he was already bowing, and that permitted Haroun the executioner to deliver a great blow of the scimitar on the nape of the neck, which almost severed his head. Then his body was pulled into a corner.

Isabelle had uttered a cry of terror, and the Almoradi who was sent in next undoubtedly heard it, for he only took a single step forward and stopped, looking to the right and left fearfully. He either recognized Haroun or perceived the body of his relative in the dim light of the room, which was only illuminated by a single high lamp placed at the back. He stepped back.

The executioner struck him with two blows that slashed his face. He whirled around, gesticulating, disfigured and bloody, until a dagger-thrust in the back had made him fall dead into the fountain, reddening the water with his blood.

An extraordinary thing happened to the valiant Ismail. He was reputed to be invincible in war and witnesses worthy of faith testified that they had seen arrows slide over him. He received three blows from Haroun without being discomfited; he drew a curved dagger that he had in his belt and, backed up against the wall, faced his enemies. They all rushed him. He had seized a large porcelain vase, with which he protected himself. His right arm, with which he tried to strike, was so badly cut that it launched jets of blood with every gesture he made.

Abul Hacen, standing on the balcony, followed the struggle, and had the desire to go down in order to join in. The Almoradi perceived him and shouted insults at him. They were lost in the din. The Emir, however, distinguished: "Miserable blind man!" and his rage redoubled, for, not knowing whether the blindness in question related to his sight or his love for Isabelle, he interpreted in both senses and received two offences.

The valiant Ismail suddenly collapsed, Haroun and his companions fell upon him. But it was only a feint. The Almoradi, seeing that all resistance was futile, had decided to kill at least one of his executioners. The one who seized him was stabbed, ravaged, opened in two, and Ismail, pierced with thrusts and already dead, plunged his tenacious blade once again into the enemy breast.

Abul Hacen stamped his feet on his balcony. It was a centenary custom to fill the room with enormous roses every morning. There were red ones, white ones and violet ones, and all of them, now soaked in blood, were spread out like the tears of beauty before the triumph of evil. The blood, the soiled petals of the flowers and the crimson cloaks of the murdered Almoradis mingled in a single red harmony, through which the silhouettes of men dislocated by fury passed like phantoms.

Isabelle had fainted, but Abu Hacen had decided to wake her up when Tarfe appeared, by shaking her by her hair and pricking her with his dagger if necessary.

For Tarfe was about to appear. To be certain of his coming, Abul Hacen had sent a written message via the faithful Ali. The scene was only organized for the death of the young man and to see what quality of dolor that death inspired in Isabelle.

Other Almoradis expired in their turn. The halls of the Alhambra filled with rumors. The Hagib, the only man who could have intervened, was absent. A eunuch who was drunk or whom fear had caused to lose his reason, started running, torch in hand, shouting incomprehensible words. Then, suddenly, through the corridors sand the gardens a kind of anguish passed like a breath, which caused everyone to fall silent and wait.

But in the rose room, where the dead were heaped up and a sanguinary fury possessed souls, Tarfe did not arrive. The mute Ali had gone to his house and had put into his own hands an amicable message from Abul Hacen inviting him to come to hear singers at the Alhambra. That invitation was only abnormal in that it was written by the Emir's own hand instead of that of one of his scribes.

Tarfe was at the foot of the staircase in his palace and his father, old Ali Hamad, was standing beside him. He showed him, not without pride, the large sheet of parchment with the Emir's seal and he picked up his cloak in order to leave. But then Ali, who had remained motionless, extended his hand. The head of the Almoradi family and his son Tarfe did not grasp the cause of that gesture at first. They considered Ali's extended hand, and they interrogated one another with their gaze. But when their eyes went to the mute's face, they understood. That face reflected the pity and sadness of simple souls, which cannot understand hatred, and sometimes tries to limit it by an invisible good deed.

Ali's arm had fallen back along his body and his face tried to become impassive again.

That was all right! He could go. Tarfe would not penetrate into the Alhambra before being informed of the danger that threatened him. Salvation often comes from a stranger who goes away without recompense and whom one never sees again.

When Tarfe arrived on horseback in the street that went from the Darro to the Puerta de la Justicia he saw an assembly

241

in which there were several Almoradis. In the middle of the group a young man of fifteen, whose lips were painted and his face made up, was speaking animatedly, raising a delicate hand whose fingernails were covered in carmine and which was holding an orange branch.

Tarfe recognized the young man as young Abdallah, the lover of his cousin, Abu Said, the debauchee.

When Abu Said, summoned like the other Almoradis by Abul Hacen, had arrived at the Puerta de la Justicia, he had declared to the guards that he was never separated from the adolescent with the handsome face by whom he was accompanied. Negligently leaning on his shoulder, he had strolled back and forth in the courtyard, awaiting his turn to be received. At the moment when he was summoned, he had plucked a branch from the orange tree and had handed it to young Abdallah with the tenderness with which another man would have given a present of a flower to a woman.

The adolescent, who was standing near the rose room, had heard a loud scream of death. He had perceived a trickle of blood under the bronze of the door. He had fled, and had been allowed to pass, no order having been given in his regard. Now, breathless and trembling, he was recounting what he had seen and heard to the Almoradis, and his falsetto voice, further broken by emotion, had something ridiculous and tragic about it.

They deliberated in order to decide what it was appropriate to do.

Moussa, supported by Tarfe, wanted them to go find weapons and attack the Alhambra. Others, more sensible, talked about leaving the city. Many Almoradis were dead. How could their servants be gathered? Which were the families on whom they could count? It was Tarfe's violence that decided the flight of all. Was not his imprudence the original cause of the evil? The essential thing was to warn the Almoradis who had not yet responded to the Emir's summons. They would take stock the following day.

The moon rose. Tarfe and Moussa found themselves alone. They departed at a gallop through the narrow streets of the Albaycin, and there was no longer anyone there but a fifteen-year-old child, sobbing against a wall.

It was only late in the night that Abul Hacen finally discovered how much he had loved Isabelle. The women known as the light of dawn thought that life was slipping away and spared neither the extravagant words nor the actions that, accomplished at the right moment, pour forgetfulness into ulcerated lovers.

When the moon was high in the sky, the Emir wanted a breath of air, and he had walked on to the terrace of the room in which Isabelle, among the cushions, was savoring a hard-earned slumber. He was like a man who has drunk a mixture of opium and nepenthe. He felt strangely light.

From the place where he was leaning he could see a door that opened to the Court of Lions. Slaves were passing through it, carrying bodies. But they seemed to be moving very far way, in a lunar world to which he was entirely foreign. Those slaves were accomplishing tasks that had nothing to do with him.

In the end, he saw a silhouette so tall that he wondered who the disproportionate individual could be, whom he did not know. The silhouette was that of the Hagib. His face was more jaundiced than usual. He was measuring with despair the dramas that the Emir's folly had engendered, and suffering from the injustice committed.

Enclosed in his thoughts, he traversed the courtyard and advanced, without seeing him, toward the balcony on which the Emir was leaning. At each step he took, very straight in his black robe, he grew immeasurably in Abul Hacen's eyes. He grew like the neglected duty, the charges of the kingdom, the inexorable effects of evil actions. He was a thin black giant, the sad Hagib meditating in the night of the Alhambra, and Abul Hacen, frightened, hastened to go back into Isabelle's room.

XIV. Almazan's Encounters in the Twilight

Almazan had a great deal of difficulty going down the street of the harness-makers. It was being searched. There were searches going on all over Granada.

A man who recognized him as the Emir's physician shouted at him, almost under his nose: "Long live King Boabdil!"

For Aixa the Horra, in accord with the Zegris, had distributed great riches among the lower orders in order that the word would go round that only Boabdil was capable of leading the war against the Spaniards successfully.

At the corner of the street of the perfumers, cavaliers of the Moroccan guard passed by. They were holding their spears in the middle and distributing solid blows with the shaft at anyone who did not get out of the way quickly enough. Their brutality had made them hated for a long time. Cries of fury burst out behind them. By the words he heard, Almazan measured the unpopularity of Abul Hacen.

Sitting outside a door, an old man who must have been nearly a hundred years old was searching with his eyes for someone who wanted to listen to him. He shouted: "Only a young man can see clearly. The Alhambra is a castle of prostitutes, Muhamad Alhamar, who was a great king, said that to reign, it's necessary to be young and virtuous."

A little further on, a man who was entirely covered by a saffron cloak and wore a turban and slippers of the same color, was announcing that all the friends of the Zegris ought to gather in the Plaza de Bibarrambla at the hour of prayer.

There was a stir in the crowd and Almazan went back up in the direction of the Puerta de la Elvira. It was not without sadness that he saw Granada delivered to factions at the moment when it would need all its strength to triumph over its enemies.

It's always thus, he thought. *It was the same in Athens, Rome and Alexandria. Cities are like men. Intelligence kills their will, and as soon as they think too much, they die.*

He heard cries and laughter, and he saw a singular cortege advancing toward him.

A traveler with a fat belly was mounted on a donkey. He was covered in dust, sweating and laughing. His spindly legs disappeared under an infinity of sacks and packages. To his right there as a pale young man who was pulling with difficulty a burden attached to him by a strap, and to his left, almost buried under withered flowers and dusty branches an equivocal brown-haired girl was walking with a slight limp.

Almazan recognized Aboulfedia. The Jewish physician stopped his mount. He did not show any surprise at encountering his disciple, but his little eyes had a gleam of satisfaction.

"You see," he said, "I'm making my entrance into Granada on a donkey, like Jesus Christ in Jerusalem, or the prophet Ibn Toumert in Tlemcen. But the prophet had made a vow always to wear a coarse woolen chemise while I, I beg you to take note, am only clad in the rarest silk."

And he insisted that Almazan feel the fabric of his chemise.

"What have I come here to do?" he said. "Lilith has summoned me, and here I am. I've brought Belial with me, as well as all the accessories of beauty and pleasure."

Almazan saw that a huge broken perfume-burner was protruding from one of his sacks, along with cushions in which embroideries alternated with rips.

"A young priestess precedes me, laden with flowers." And he indicated Rebecca, who, in spite of her lassitude, parted the flowers by which she was laden in order to smile with a toothless mouth.

"And now," added Aboulfedia, "you can take me to Lilith."

Almazan replied to him that nothing was easier than to introduce himself into the Alhambra on condition of continuing as he went to gave the Emir's favorite that symbolic name, her true name being to unpopular.

He had already seized the bridle of the donkey when a cry rang out from a street that opened to the right and a man ran forward. He was improbably thin and his head was coiffed in the black bonnet that Jews had the custom of wearing. He moved Almazan aside gently and, taking Aboulfedia by the shoulders, he said to him: "You really are Aboulfedia of Seville?"

"Yes," replied Aboulfedia. "So what?"

"I'm Anan ben Joshua, your coreligionist, and we have been living in Granada, father and son, for three centuries.

But that name said nothing to Aboulfedia; he visibly did not know his interlocutor. He was in haste to reach the Alhambra and his protectress, by means of Almazan. He pulled away from the Jew's grip, grumbling.

"I don't care about my coreligionists," he exclaimed. "Let me pass."

But the man turned toward him a face in which intelligence shone. In spite of Aboulfedia's resistance, he seized him by the neck and spoke to him in a low voice. Almazan only perceived a few words, of which he did not grasp the significance, and which the Jew repeated:

Tabernacle... Moses.... Granada...

To his great surprise, he saw Aboulfedia's face change and take on an extraordinary, almost dramatic gravity.

"Almazan," he said, "I thank you, but I'll go with my venerable coreligionist Anan ben Joshua, whom I've known for a very long time and who has just spoken to me."

Aboulfedia made a sign to young Rodriguez and the toothless girl. His donkey pirouetted and he drew away, guided by the Jew, without paying any further heed to Almazan.

When Almazan went past the great mosque it was the hour of the fifth prayer, He crossed the path of a man dressed as a Santon who wore on his shoulder the sign of pilgrims returned from Mecca. Almazan had scarcely passed him than he turned round precipitately—but the Santon had prostrated himself on the ground and was praying, soiling his forehead with the dust.[29]

Two old men passing by stopped and one said to the other: "Look at the fervor with which that Santon is making the four rika of the prayer of the night."

Almazan reflected. He was sure that he was not mistaken. That Santon was the man who had introduced himself into the room of the automata on the evening of the meeting of the Rose-Cross But he was also another individual, and his memory, infidel thus far, suddenly permitted him to receiver him in the mists of remembrance.

That Santon was a former Dominican, who had been expelled from the Order for debauchery, and of whom the Holy Office made use as a spy. He was the one who had denounced in Seville that Dutchman Van Daele and had had Felice de Hurtado burned on false accusations of heresy. Tomas de Torquemada confided inadmissible missions to him and executions for which he did not want any tribunal or judgment. If, as Rosenkreutz had said at Al Birouni's house, many Brothers of the Rose-Cross had perished mysteriously in Castile and Aragon, solely for the crime of being philosophers and scholars, it was that man who had been the agent of their death.

Almazan was about to throw himself upon him, but the spy of the Holy Office must have understood his intention, for he leapt to his feet and, renouncing his dignity as a Santon, started running alongside the great mosque. He reached the door and disappeared.

Almazan did not follow him. The presence of an infidel in the mosque would have provoked the indignation of the believers, and he would not have been able to take more than a few steps without being arrested. He promised himself to warn the Hagib that evening, or even the Emir, and he headed for the Alhambra.

---

[29] Santon is a now-obsolete term for a Muslim ascetic, who would nowadays be known as a Marabout.

He was not at the end of his surprises. As the air was stifling he went into the gardens of the Generalife, whose freshness he liked. He went alongside the Laurel Fountain and passed close to the dwarf cypress under which the nightingale had been buried.

He was struck by the sound of voices. Two forms advanced along a path. He recalled that Khadidja was jealous of the solitude of this part of the garden and, ashamed of troubling her reverie again, he hid behind the branches of a clump of bushes.

But he recognized the solid silhouette of Aixa the Horra. Walking beside her was a man of short stature with broad shoulders, whose head was covered in a brown hood. The moon illuminated his face, and Almazan saw with amazement that he was a leper.

Beneath the deformation of the lips and the nose shone an expression of baseness and ferocity. He was carrying his neck forward and his enormous head seemed to be preceding his thickest body ridiculously. He was speaking in a low voice, sometimes raising a horrible white hand.

Almazan had never seen him before, and yet he thought that he recognized him. He thought that he must be one of Soleiman's brothers. He remembered having heard it said that the four brothers were distant relatives of Aixa and that she had asked the Emir several times to release them from the leprosarium.

"You did well to come and find me," the Horra said. "You won't regret it."

Almazan did not hear the response of the leper, whose voice was hoarse and muffled, but he saw Aixa raise her hand and indicate the balcony that overlooked Khadidja's apartments and heard her say: "It's there. The spiral stairway is in that tower and ends directly opposite the large magnolia. One can go down again by the large staircase in the middle, but a woman who has an amorous rendezvous has no need to be abducted by force."

248

The two silhouettes drew away under the porticos that bordered the pool of irises. They remained sheltered for some time by the shadow of a cork-oak, like two large nocturnal raptors lying in ambush for evil, and then they headed through the rose-garden toward the communicating gate between the Generalife and the Alhambra.

What could the hateful woman and the lustful leper be planning? Almazan followed them until he saw them disappear, and continued wandering through the gardens for a long time, thinking that Princess Khadidja was in danger.

Late in the night, he went back to his apartment. He found two messages there.

The first was in Spanish and only contained the words: *What a pity you don't love me.*

The second was in Arabic, on emerald colored filigree paper that was only made in Alexandria. The characters had been traced by a calam dipped in liquid gold. The thin scroll that it formed was knotted with seven threads of almost invisible silk and of a color corresponding to each of the planets.

The message read:

Words are not necessary, nor even pressures of the hand or gazes. Spirits have their wings and they find one another unknown to their ignorant bodies. Every evening, Al Nefs and Al Hewa—desire and amour—*march alongside the Fountain of Laurels and make me signs from a distance. They know that I am behind the shutter of the window and murmur your name to me in the warm night. But even though they are Gennis, they do not murmur it with more ardor than my lips. So I was not surprised by the words that you have sent to me. I was only surprised by the quality of the messenger. If you tell me to come, let it not be with words, let no hand extend the letter, give me a sign with a ray of moonlight borne by the echo of a darbuka, and I will come.*

Almazan was confounded by astonishment. He had not seen Princess Khadidja again since encountering her in the gardens of the Generalife. He had never thought of writing to her. He had never even thought about her. What did this mystery signify?

The muezzins were already climbing the stairways of the mosques while Almazan was still meditating over the emerald-colored filigree paper.

XV. Khadidja's Rendezvous

The love that Khadidja had in her heart had multiplied of its own accord like a tree that causes a forest to flourish around it with its own seeds. All the species of good Gennis spoke to her about Almazan and those Gennis had even sent her a new nightingale, which sang on the hot nights in the magnolia near the window.

They had not only sent a nightingale. They had especially delegated the fat, caricaturish, extravagant Fatima, for Gennis have powers so diverse that they can equally direct a nightingale poet and a masseuse serving as a go-between.

How could that Fatima's words not be welcomed? It was her, her alone, the loquacious Fatima, who, by virtue of her knowledge of unguents and their influences on the human body, had removed the little tuft of hair that departed from Princess Khadidja's groin. The mark of the beast was effaced, matter had recoiled, and the milky whiteness of the skin had triumphed over hair, thanks to the most material of creatures, by the art of the gross Fatima, who resembled the monsters from beyond the deserts of Africa whose descriptions voyagers made with amazement. In truth, that contrast must be due to the Genni Al Dounia, who was reputed to be the most whimsical of celestial Gennis.

First, that Fatima had tested the terrain lightly without seeming to touch it. An allusion, a jesting word, nothing more. How prudent and sage she was beneath the enveloped of a hippopotamus! It was only a little later that it had come to Khadidja's mind like a revelation that the masseuse Fatima might have a supraterrestrial mission. She did not reflect that Fatima had long been a confident of Aixa and that it was perhaps from his conversations with that fine spy that Boabdil had obtained, in childhood, his great fondness for treason. Khadidja was such a stranger to lies that she transformed the false things that reached her into verities.

Almazan was thinking about her, and he had opened up to that gossip, that trafficker of stories, that jovial matron, that masseuse who only massaged in order to talk and make others talk. Nothing was more plausible. One did not have a choice of messengers. Not everyone could have, like her, the power to communicate her thought without a physical intermediary.

Things moved very rapidly, for, in addition to the communications made by day by Fatima, there were those, more tender and more amorous, that the faithful divine Gennis brought by night. And pure souls are very easy to deceive.

To the ordinary habit of men who absolutely want a material sign, Khadidja made the concession of writing a letter—only one—and she knew immediately that the delightful moment of the first meeting was imminent.

It was the time when the magnolia flowers seem to consume their perfumes in their calices like as many inflamed cassolettes, when the roses crowd together in the flower-beds like a host of Christian cardinals before the Pope's castle, when the cypresses file under the moon like a procession of pious Imams before the Prophet's tomb. The faces of Gennis shone behind the shutters and Khadidja, sitting on her bed, her head in her hands, meditated the charming and terrible problem all night.

How ought one to offer one's body to the man one loves? Was a traditional hypocritical resistance necessary? Was there not proof of more love in a spontaneous gift? How should one present oneself? What garments was it necessary to wear? The union of bodies would entail that of souls, but was it appropriate to hasten or was it better to remain for a long time in a state of hope, susceptible of prolonging the enthusiasm of belonging?

And it was necessary for her to recall, in order to go to sleep, that the absence of sleep slides a light ashen mask over faces at dawn.

She was not surprised the next day by the message that Fatima brought. The latter laughed to disguise her embarrassment and the audacity of her request. Why that embarrass-

252

ment? The request of the man that one loves is never audacious. Yes, she would emerge from the Generalife as that stated time, she would climb into the litter that was waiting for
her and she would go to meet Almazan.

And the day passed in the fog of an exquisite dream.
Was it necessary to put on jewels, to be as resplendent as the
sun, or was there more grace in a slim bare neck and minuscule hands ornamented by the traces of removed rings? Was it
time to pour into her hair a few drops of the suave odor that
she had composed herself and the effluvia of which had a secret correspondence with the green of her eyes, the third note
of the scale and the force of the planet Venus? So many
charming perplexities that were only resolved at the last moment, when night had fallen, when a litter went along the wall
that surrounded the gardens of the Generalife.

A green form slid into a stone stairway, brushed box-
trees, ran alongside a fountain, caressed roses with a trembling
hand, arrived at a little door through which no one ever passed
and where there was only one Moroccan guard, to whom the
green form made a sign.

The Moroccan guard opened the door, but Khadidja
turned round. How was it that the nightingale was not singing?
Was it forgetful or disapproving? And why were the magnolias letting their flowery branches fall like extinct candles from
a chandelier after a funeral ceremony? And why was that
cloud suddenly over the moon, like a fragment of crepe in an
ocean of azure? Why was the cry of that owl so unusual, so
long and so heart-rending? And why had a cone detached from
a parasol pine? And why that elongation of white pathways,
that whisper of cypresses, that languor of colonnades, that
ambient mystery, that inexpressible despair, and that anguished silence?

No, Khadidja was not hesitant, but she would have preferred the beloved gardens to participate in her delight. She
approached the fountain of irises and considered the first of
the fountain's twelve jets of water, the one that she liked most,
which she supposed to have a heart more fraternal that the

others. She would have liked that white dancer, under the dazzling cascade of its costume, to have inclined joyfully toward her, with a pirouette of approval, a crystal smile amid its broad collar of drops of water. Decidedly, the gardens were sulking. With a rapid gesture, Khadidja took one of the emerald necklaces and threw it at the neck of the jet of water. By means of that gesture she conciliated the entire population of insensate dancers.

But why did the little low door, when the Moroccan guard closed it again, make the sound that doors make that one will never pass through again?

Khadidja must have intimidated the two litter-bearers for, on seeing her, they gave the impression of being unable to believe their eyes. But they had departed nevertheless in an astonishingly rapid fashion. Khadidja heard the staff of the runner preceding the litter striking the ground of the inclined streets. How right the bearers were to hurry! The white palaces they went past gave the impression of belonging to an extraordinary city of dream, a fabulous universe in which she was wandering in pursuit of happiness.

Kaschefs making a round stopped the litter momentarily at the entrance to the street of the jewelers, but the runner showed them the insignia that he bore at the end of his staff and they stood aside respectfully.

The course was recommenced. An anxiety slid into Khadidja's soul. It was an irrational anxiety that was initially formulated as a sentiment of regret, for which she immediately reproached herself. How pleasant it would have been to be in the embalmed gardens of the Generalife at that moment, how sweet the music of the darbuka would have been over the nightingale's grave!

She lifted the silk curtain of the door. She was being carried through mute suburbs. Where was Almazan waiting for her? How far it was! There were a few negotiations at the guard-post of one of the city gates. The runner said a few words, raised his staff, and they set off again.

But where? Doubtless the porters were deaf. Khadidja had called to interrogate them but they had not heard. They continued their course impassively. Outside the city there were many houses of pleasure with dense gardens watered by canals, where the rich inhabitants of Granada went to spend the summer. Almazan must have rented one of them, or perhaps the Emir had put one of the villas he possessed on the road to Elvira at his disposal. Yes, that was it.

However, she did not recognize the road to Elvira. To the left of the road there were fields as far as the eye could see. In the distance, to the right, stood a somber mass, something like a walled enclosure.

She did not understand. But those possessed by the spirit of illusion go to the end of their folly with a blind faith. Everything would be explained. What did the place and the distance matter? Almazan was waiting for her, that was the essential thing.

They had reached a gate and a somnolent guard, holding a lantern, had just come out of a low house adjacent to the wall.

There was still time to call out, to be recognized. The idea occurred to Khadidja, but she immediately set it aside. The runner had raised his magic staff and the litter had immediately launched through the open gate with a single bound, a strange surge in which there was a triumphant joy.

At the same moment, by the light of the lantern, Khadidja has distinguished the insignia that the runner bore on his staff. It was a bronze ball on which a closed hand was crudely sculpted—which is to say, the insignia known throughout Granada as that of Aixa the Horra. And she had distinguished a face beyond the gate, the bizarre face of a crouching man, a face so sad and so terrible!

She had suddenly understood where she was. In a litter belonging to her mortal enemy Aixa, she had just penetrated into the city of lepers. She uttered a faint cry, the cry of a child, and lost consciousness.

She was woken up by a curious sensation. Something rough and damp, the nature of which she could not distinguish, was rubbing her hand and wrist. Then that indefinable thing quit her and she heard a voice above her that said: "She'll wake up in the end."

It was a singularly weak and broken voice, whose dolorous tone struck her.

Raising her eyelids slightly, Khadidja allowed her gaze to filter around her through the thickness of her long lashes.

She was lying full length on a carpet and her first distinct thought was that her veils, partly lifted, were uncovering her leg above the knee. She was about to pull them down swiftly, but the sentiment of danger retained her. Where was she? With what was she threatened?

Other broken voices spoke. There was a sound of glasses, clicking tongues and grunts of satisfaction, and she saw that there were three men considering her. Two were sitting among cushions and the third, who was speaking to them with his back turned to her, was the one who had just leaned over her and taken her hand and wrist.

But no, they were not men. She had descended, by a horrible enchantment, into the abode of the evil Gennis. She saw before her Iblis, in the triple appearance of Evil, Ugliness and the Night. She was about to endure the punishment of her sins.

Her life had always been egotistical. She had not loved the beings surrounding her sufficiently, she had only thought of the satisfaction of hr physical desires instead of elevating her spirit by ecstasy, as she had once been taught in Malaga by her master the old Sufi Abou-Lahab. She was about to enter into the circle of expiation.

But no, they were not Gennis. She remembered! The porters send by Almazan had brought her to the city of lepers. She had fallen into a trap, and it was the man she loved who had made her fall into it. She was among living lepers more redoubtable than Iblis himself, because there are certain bodily pollutions that cannot be effaced.

Suddenly, the three men who were drinking were immobilized, and the six flames of their eyes turned toward Khadidja and remained fixed upon her. They had seen the green gaze that had just become animated through the shadow of her long lashes.

A cry rang out. The three lepers were on their feet. Khadidja saw a stout form make a kind of leap and she had the same sensation of damp roughness on her neck that she had had on her hand. Her veil gave way. A hand opened it, striving to rip it from top to bottom.

Suddenly frozen by a nameless horror, Khadidja stood up at the same time, and succeeded in detaching herself. She searched with her gaze for something that might protect her from the assault of the three men. With the exception of a little table and a tall bronze lamp, the room was bare. Bringing up the fragments of her veil over her uncovered breasts, she took shelter behind the lamp and looked the hideous danger that menaced her in the face.

She he never imagined such a bestial expression on human faces. The three brothers made the same gesture with their open arms and extended white hands before them, with deformed joints and moist swellings in the palm. The eldest, the shortest, carried his head forward as if it had an enormous weight and that he had difficulty sustaining it. What aggravated that particularity were the tubercles placed around his lips, which gave them a color analogous to that of lead. The second was entirely bald and had a profound wrinkle around his forehead that made a line of demarcation, as if the upper part of his cranium, strangely high, was added to the rest of the head and susceptible of being easily lifted off. The youngest was at that phase of the malady in which the skin forms successions of dead squamae, crumbling inexorably into flakes, and, with a mechanical gesture, he passed his hand over his face incessantly to detach some crust therefrom. All three were laughing at the terror they inspired and the certainty of possession.

Together, they made a forward movement, and, with her two hands extended, Khadidja precipitated the bronze lamp against them, which collapsed noisily, plunging the room into darkness and spreading a nauseating odor of oil and burnt wick.

There were imprecations. Khadidja felt the grip of two hands under her armpits. She slid like a snake. Her hair came undone. She ran to the right and the left, bumping into the walls, pursued by the arms, which swept the air, brushed her, gripped her, let her go and seized her again. A handful of her hair was torn out with a noise of crackling sparks; she fell, got up, and ended up flattening herself against the wall, where she remained motionless.

She heard the panting of the three men, and their insults. One of them suddenly grunted with satisfaction. "I have my briquette," he said, while the others repeated: "Quickly! Quickly!"

At the same movement, Khadidja's hand, extended along the wall, encountered the handle of a door. She had perceived that door when she had darted a first circular glance around the room, but she had lost its direction. In any case, it was doubtless locked.

It was not. At the same time as the briquette, with its little star of light, illuminated three terrible visages, the door opened and Khadidja fled.

She had a few seconds start, no more, for the three brothers launched themselves on her heels, but an inconceivable surge impelled her light form. She traversed a room, descended a stairway, ran over sonorous paving-stones that had to be those of a vestibule, passed without seeing it a door that opened to a garden, climbed a stairway that the moon filled with delightful hues and almost fell into a room where a man was standing...

She was exhausted. Her heart was hammering in her breast.

"Save me!" she cried. "In the name of the Prophet, save me!"

Soleiman had heard the noise and had got up in order to go and see what was happening. He suddenly found himself facing Khadidja and his three brothers, breathless and haggard, but all the more possessed by their desire.

So this was what had awakened him from the ecstasy in which he was plunged, and in which he was seeking to confound his soul, final purified, with God! It was for this that the Prophet had appeared to him and had guided him on the path of renunciation! He had believed in the secret promise that no speech had formulated but that he had heard during the nights of spiritual exaltation: the promise of pardon.

The face of the Prophet had lied; there was no pardon.

By an inexplicable spell, a hallucinatory witchcraft, the past was revived before his eyes. As in the atrocious scene of old, he saw his brothers drunk, he saw a woman in torn garments who was looking at him with green eyes widened by fear and, with the same voice, it seemed to him, begging him in the same words.

No redemption for sins! Lust was eternal, as well as the love of making the weak suffer and shedding their blood. No redemption! No possible redemption! Like the movement of the tides, like tempests, criminal instincts come back into the souls of men who had believed themselves momentarily to be illuminated by the sun.

Well, he would abandon himself to the Law. He would reawaken he old ferocious beast asleep within him, he would kill and he would drag his victim by the feet again, he would tear out her tangled hair and he would dig a grave, laughing.

He was already laughing. He snatched a dagger from the belt of one of his brothers and threw away the sheath.

But the three panting lepers understood his intention. They remembered a similar scene. They did not want their prey to escape them. Woe betide Soleiman if he lost his reason and put his pleasure into death.

They threw himself upon him together in order to disarm him. Khadidja took advantage of that to get up. She had nothing to expect from the fourth insensate leper, who was laughing as he fought with his brothers, with a shrill and savage laughter. There was another door at the back of the room. That door gave access to a narrow stairway, which she climbed. She went up very high. The stairway was never-ending; it must be the stairway of a tower. She finally arrived in a rather vast room which the moon illuminated dimly, and she closed the door behind her. She drew the bolt and uttered a sigh of satisfaction.

But she examined the door. The wood was not every thick, and could not resist any attempt to break it down for long. Her respite would not be of long duration.

She looked at the place where she was. Against the wall there were the glints of weapons: spears, scimitars and arquebuses were lined up on all sides; that isolated room almost at the top of the tower contained the unused arsenal of the ancient dwelling.

And as blows resounded upon the door, she was stuck by a sudden thought. That door had a rather large judas-hole. It would be easy enough for her to open the judas, place an arquebus therein, and fire at the lepers at point-blank range. Her father had once taught her to handle an arquebus. She knew how to make the serpentine swing over the detonator. She unhooked one of the weapons and examined it. The weapon was an old model but in good condition. She was saved if she wanted to be.

But she did not want it. She set the arquebus down gently in a corner.

Once, in Malaga, her old master Abou Lahab had sent several days in sadness and had made a vow not to leave his house again because he had crushed a sleeping lizard while walking. It was Abou Lahab who had told her that it was necessary to traverse gardens with precaution on rainy evenings because of snails the color of earth that could not be seen. Even respiration was a danger for many small creatures. It was necessary to be incessantly careful not to destroy the life that surrounds us. No, she would not kill those lepers to save her life.

Then a great lassitude overwhelmed her. The blows that were resonating seemed to be hammering in her brain. She was so exhausted that she was obliged to evoke the horror that menaced her in order to drag herself a little further away.

There was a narrower stairway at the back of the room from which gusts of fresh air were coming. When the judas had been smashed and the door was about to be broken down, Khadidja dragged herself into that stairway and closed another door behind her.

The lepers' cry of victory, as they erupted into the armory, was followed by a howl of rage and the same sound of a lock shaken and blows struck. Followed by that tumult, Khadidja, feeling faint and aiding herself with her hands, climbed a few more steps.

Suddenly, she felt her hair flying around her head. She was enveloped by the freshness of the wind and the brightness of the sky. She had reached the ultimate terrace of the tower and all the perfumes of the gardens of Granada were reaching her from a distance like the subtle message of her past. The familiar stars were bursting forth above her head. She believed she could see the pulp of the magnolias inflating, the crazed water jets dancing, the cypresses meditating. She leaned avidly toward the night.

From the height where she was, the mute city of the lepers was merely a feeble patch of shadow. The plain of the Vega, beneath the extraordinary brightness of the moon, was like a hallucinatory sheet of silver, a mysterious lake from which the masses of hayricks surged here and there like motionless golden ships, clumps of trees like islets beaten by a silent sea, and the cupolas of houses like fabulous swans asleep for eternity.

Far away, she could see the enormous circle of Granada, with its thousand and thirty towers, where red beacons were alight like countless sad eyes. Beyond the line of the ramparts there was an accumulation of superimposed terraces, miradors, turrets and colonnades. The houses seemed to be climbing on top of one another, accumulating on the flanks of the hill of the Alhambra, all the way to the Alhambra itself, which dominated Granada, crushing it with its square framework and its towers looming up like horns.

And the entire city, with that redoubtable Alhambra, was reminiscent of a monstrous beast, like the ones that would fall to earth when the angel Israfil announced the last judgment. The livid moon sometimes caused the porcelain of a dome to shine like scales, or showed the opening of a mosque like a jaw, and an alignment of pillars like teeth. That was the terrestrial beast whose breath is suffering and which digests the love and hatred of men untiringly.

And suddenly, Khadidja saw the enormous beast move. It turned on the horizon, and sometimes disappeared, as if it had plunged into a lunar flood. Then it emerged, to run again, to make its claws sparkle, to opens its maws, to elongate its teeth. But that beast did not frighten Khadidja any more than the increasing tumult behind the door to the stairway through which the lepers were about to surge.

She was swaying with the tower in a vertiginous space. She was far away, very high amid the inaccessible azure, in a region of icy crystal and dead sapphire, in an incomparable solitude more terrible than terrestrial fears, more torturing than Hell.

Almazan did not love her. He had never loved her. She had nourished herself on the lie of her imagination, and she was about to die all alone, perfectly alone, without a thought of amour, at the summit of a stone tower overlooking a city of lepers. That was where the folly of her dream had led her, her dementia of beauty.

And then she heard, clearly and distinctly, a voice that rose above the tumult of a struggle, a voice that came from the stairway and cried: "Khadidja!"

In the distance, the ramparts of Granada had resumed their immobility. The plain of the Vega unfurled around her, immense and clear-cut under the moon, and she had sat down, with her torn garments and her scattered hair, on the granite balustrade that bordered the trace of the tower.

She listened, and she ran forward. Behind the door, neither hoarse clamors or savage cries were resounding any longer. There was only one voice, slightly anguished, but increasingly loud, which was calling her by name—and it was the voice of Almazan.

He had known! He had come to save her! Everything was not illusion in her story of amour, then; Fatima's messages were real; Almazan really had given her a rendezvous this evening and he had nothing to do with the trap that had been set for her. He loved her, and he had come to find her.

She was about to open the door, to extend her arms to him.

One more minute! Her veils were soiled and torn! She strove to arrange the pleats and to twist her outspread hair over the nape of her neck. She no longer had vertigo now. She was leaning on the stones of a tower as solid as the certainty of being loved. A great joy flooded from the depths of her soul like a wave unfurling on a beach, coming from the horizon if the sea.

Yes, yes, she would open up. She was there. There was nothing to fear.

She raised her eyes toward the sky with a thought of gratitude for the good Gennis who must be floating there, and what she saw seemed extraordinary.

The sky had many more stars than before. It was bright, it was streaming, pouring out floods of luminous heavenly bodies. And it was not distant; it was very close to her; it was descending with its planets, its constellations and its Milky Way, like a river of gems, and the crescent of its moon, like the prodigious symbol of Islam.

Khadidja had within arm's reach everything she could desire to repair the disorder of her garments, to show herself to the man she loved with an unparalleled ornamentation.

She took handfuls of emeralds and scattered them in her hair, and those starry emeralds shone with a green fire such as she had never seen. She twisted the rubies and topazes of the Great Bear into a chain and made a bracelet of them for her right wrist. She wrapped her legs in armfuls of diamonds and stuck the pole star on her forehead like a blue-tinted drop of unique light. But she required to veil her breasts the great scarf that was the Milky Way. She threw it over her shoulder and let it trail behind her like a supernatural stream.

In truth, it must have been Azrael himself who was holding out to her, from the depths of the bright and empty night, the robe of the celestial Houri of Houris, the one that summarizes the perfection of form and which has no name to be invoked.

She scaled the rim of the tower, for the divine fabric was not yet close enough.

At that moment, the door burst into shards and Almazan appeared on the threshold, covered in the blood of the lepers that he had just killed.

Khadidja smiled at him. She felt lighter than the azure. She made a gesture to seize the flap of the Milky Way that was floating alongside her, and disappeared from Almazan's sight, as if she had been absorbed by the splendid night.

"Poor Isabelle!" said Abul Hacen, when Almazan had told him the story of the death of Khadidja, when he told him how, having a presentiment that she was in danger, he had come to prowl in the gardens of the Generalife, and how, on the indications of the Moroccan guard, he had divined that Khadidja had been taken to the city of lepers, how he had found Soleiman dead next to one of his gasping brothers, and Khadidja on the terrace of the tower, hurling herself into the void.

"Those are the machinations of which women are the target," said the Emir. "Isabelle might also be deceived in that fashion. Watch over her, as you have watched over Khadidja."

Almazan was the only man for whom Abul Hacen had any affection. The affection in question augmented from that day on. But the Emir soon measured the extent of the annoyances that Khadidja's death would cause him, and its fatal consequences for the destiny of the kingdom of Granada. The taciturn El Zagal would not forgive his brother Abul Hacen for not having protected the daughter he had confided to him. When it was necessary to take back Alhama, of which the Spaniards had just taken possession, he had sent neither troops nor cannons. He had remained enclosed in Malaga and left his brother's pressing appeals without response.

Aixa the Horra, as well as her son Boabdil, had received orders not to come out of the tower of Comares again. A faithful Almocaden had been charged with the care of guarding them, and soldiers were stationed at the two doors connecting that tower to the Alhambra. From the room where he was accompanied by Isabelle, throughout the first evening of that captivity, Abul Hacen heard his son playing the flute, as he was accustomed to do interminably. He played badly, and that irritated the Emir, who as a musician.

Late into the night, the Almocaden went to sleep to the sounds of that distant flute, which reassured him regarding the possibility of an escape. In the morning, the flute was still resonating. The hours passed and it did not stop. The Emir, exasperated, sent someone to his son to beg him not to play any longer. At the same time he learned that all of Granada was in uproar because of Boabdil's escape. During the night, Aixa had made a rope with garments and he had fled through one of the windows overlooking the Darro while a slave played his favorite tunes as badly as him.

Boabdil went to join his partisans at Loxa and had himself proclaimed Emir of the Moorish kingdom. Henceforth, he had the means to satisfy his passion for treason. He entered into relations with the kings of Castile to fight with them against his father, intending to deceive them when the moment came. He sent false promises of his uncle El Zagal. He wondered how he could betray his mother, whose blind amour had saved him so many times.

He astonished the inhabitants of Loxa because he went by night, alone, to the ramparts of the city, in order to play the flute, while turned in the direction of Granada.

XVI. The Treasure of Jerusalem

The refugees from Alhama and the villages captured by the Spaniards were camped in the open air along the ramparts. A few had erected tents, others built fires alongside their carts, and others showed their rags and depicted their misery to the rich inhabitants of Granada who had come to help them.

Almazan had spent the day caring for the sick. He was getting ready to go down the Rua de Elvira in order to return to the Alhambra when he saw Aboulfedia. On seeing him, the latter quit the little man to whom he was talking precipitately. Almazan recognized that man by his singular thinness and his hands the color of wax. It was Anan ben Joshua, the scholarly rabbi of Granada.

Several times, he had encountered Aboulfedia in the Alhambra, where the Jewish physician came to see Zoraya almost every day. The favorite had introduced him to the Emir as a sort of clown, in whose company she amused herself, and he also took young Rebecca, who had adopted the title of dancer, and Rodriguez, who was passed off as a guzla player.

Aboulfedia did not seek out Almazan's company. He even avoided him. But today, he took his former pupil by the arm and started walking alongside him. His little eyes were glittering more than usual beneath his enormous brow. Almazan could not help complimenting him, smiling, on the change that must have taken place in him. He was often seen with the rabbi Anan ben Joshua. Now that rabbi, a celebrated Talmudust, was a man of an extraordinary purity of mores. If he was frequenting Aboulfedia, it must be that the latter was not as exclusively attached to pleasure as he had claimed.

"You're no longer a Christian," said Aboulfedia, "but you're not yet a Muslim. I, however, am a Jew."

Almazan looked at him in surprise. He had thought Aboulfedia above all religion.

266

Aboulfedia shook his head. "Look," he said. And with a gesture, though the Puerta de Elvira, he indicated the lamentable cortege of the refugees from Alhama, who were continuing to flow toward Granada on donkeys, mules or on foot. "The time of the Arab race is over. Its power is only apparent now. The Jewish race is going to seize in its turn the torch that will make the savages of Spain, France and England recoil."

"How will that be possible?" said Almazan, increasingly astonished. "How can that people, dispersed over the earth...?"

Aboulfedia interrupted him. "There's no dispersion but that of the spirit, and the Jewish spirit has remained one, indivisible and unalterable. How many sects are there among the Christians? How many heresies? Even the inquisitors can't count them. Aren't the whole of North Africa and Persia covered with false prophets come to replace Mohammed, and who find thousands of followers? Like a block of diamond whose facets radiate in all directions, however, the unique law of Moses has endured. Law is force. What does it matter whether men are in one country or another? The earth isn't so vast. They'll find one another when the appeal sounds."

"The appeal of the Messiah?" Almazan interjected. "Didn't you tell me in Seville that you had ceased waiting for him a long time ago?"

"The Messiah isn't necessary. Moses had foreseen the dispersion and he had given the chosen people the means to remedy it. Oh, Mohammed claimed not to work miracles. He performed one very great one, however, when he sent Abou Bekr the Truthful[30] to Egypt secretly in order to buy there everything that a petty merchant in Cairo bazaar possessed. How had he been able to divine it? Perhaps he was a magician, like all prophets, and only proscribed magic in order to make better use of it.

---

[30] Abu Bakr (573-634), nicknamed the Truthful, was the first convert to Islam outside Mohammed's family, and the Prophet's most trusted advisor.

"You don't seem to understand me. You're wondering whether my mind has gone a little astray. You've heard mention of the Ark of Israel, the Holy of Holies, which contained the tablets of the Law, for which Moses had the Temple built. Behind the five golden columns and the crimson and hyacinth veil, the Tabernacle reposed, which only the priests who had attained the third initiation could approach. For Moses had enclosed within it the force of life of which he knew the secret, the attractive power that leads the world, which the alchemists called Azoth and others the Ether, of which every man possesses a parcel, and which it is given to a few prophets to multiply and condense.

"As long as the Jews possessed the Tabernacle, they resisted calamities. It was on the family of Hillel that the task of guarding it was incumbent when the Emperor Titus burned Jerusalem and Hadrian expelled the inhabitants. A long time ago, because of wars and pillages, the Tabernacle had been removed from the Temple and replaced by an imitation of which the avid Romans made gold ingots. The Hillels guarded it faithfully in Alexandria for several centuries, but the Jewish city of Alexandria was pillaged on the orders of Bishop Cyril, and they were obliged to flee into the desert south of the Thebaid.

"What happened then? Were the Hillels massacred by the marauding tribe? Did they hide their treasure in the savage rocks, subsequently buried by the simoom, where they were unable to find it again? No one knows. The Jewish race ceased to be in possession of the heritage of Moses. For several centuries, there was no more trace of that heritage—until the moment when, by virtue of his knowledge of magic, Mohammed learned that the Holy of Holies had been bought by a merchant in Cairo from the guides of a caravan coming from the south, and he sent Abou Bekr the Truthful to buy it from that merchant.

"But the Talisman was not enclosed in the sanctuary of the Kaaba. It was confided to the warriors for the conquest. Okba and Abderame possessed it. They made use of it to vanquish. For the ineffable force that Moses had enclosed in the gold is blind and it obeys those who communicate with it via faith. For as long as the Arabs believed in it, they were the masters of the world. Now their hearts are sealed, and the force is dormant in the inertia of the metal. But suppose that the legitimate possessors of the treasure were to realize their millennial dream of rediscovering it...

"For if the Jews cherish gold with an invincible and avid amour, it's because they know, consciously or not that the genius of their prophet, the vitality of their race, their eternal soul, is somewhere in a block of gold, tarnished by time. Suppose that the Talisman were to resume its place in the reconstructed Temple in Jerusalem, in the midst of the people who have remained without alloy and whom denial has not deteriorated. That people could then resume their mission; it would be them who would rule the world."

Almazan was amazed to hear Aboulfedia expressing himself with such passion. He was about to ask him what had caused such a change when the latter stopped him. They had arrived in the middle of a narrow side-street in front of the door of a sordid house. Cries, and a kind of continuous lisp escaped therefrom.

Aboulfedia's face took on an earthen color, and anger made his lip tremble.

"They've begun to torment him," he stammered. "They'll see!"

He was about to launch himself into the house when a black and hairy form hurtled through the door, which stood ajar, dragging a chain, and hissing and chattering incessantly.

Aboulfedia received the form in his arms and covered it with caresses. It was a large monkey.

"What have they done to you now?" said Aboulfedia, rocking it. "They have vice in the skin."

In the patio of the house, in the midst of hanging laundry, Almazan saw the pale Rodriguez and the disquieting Rebecca, smiling anxiously.

"I'm teaching him to dance," Aboulfedia went on, indicating the monkey. "It's a sublime art that is in its decadence, like everything else. You see, there's no spectacle more appropriate to raise the spirits than a girl dancing naked with a monkey. I'll show you, one of these days."

And he quit Almazan abruptly.

Isabelle was dying of boredom. Her power over Abul Hacen was all the greater, for ennui gives women the mysterious attraction of profound thought.

No one in Granada was able to play the darbuka for her. It was only in Constantinople that there were suitable musiciennes and dancers. Oh, the Great Lord was very fortunate! What sadness there was in living in a little isolated realm!

She had persuaded Abul Hacen to send the Emir of the Sea himself, on the greatest galley in the fleet of Almeria, to buy six celebrated dancing-girls taught by the old professor Chosrai of Damascus. The fleet would await Daoud's return before ravaging the Spanish ports.

What was more serious was that it was also necessary for Isabelle to wait, So Aboulfedia was welcomed with joyful cries when he announced that, the following day, he would make a trained monkey dance, dressed in different costumes, with young Rebecca.

A few faithful slaves and a few eunuchs were invited, and it was decided that the performance would take place in the Garden of Cypresses, where there was a large enough lawn bordered with lilies.

The monkey's moods were variable and it was shut in a thick wooden box covered with bronze nails, carried by Rodriguez and Rebecca. There were holes in the box in order for the animal to breathe. It leapt out delightedly as soon as the lid was opened. Aboulfedia was charged with an extraordinary quantity of robes of all colors, and asked for a room where he could dress the monkey, which was a long and complicated process.

Isabelle allowed him to take possession of a room of repose that overlooked the garden and communicated with her apartments, situated on the first floor, by way of a little stairway covered with range mosaics.

The dances of Rebecca and the monkey were a great success. Rodriguez, sitting cross-legged under the wisteria that had seen the combat of the rival wives some time before, played the guzla, his figure squeezed into a doublet that showed off his hips, as wide as a woman's.

For each dance he went to put on a new doublet, by turns indigo blue, mauve and intermediate colors to China red—for, according to Aboulfedia the musician ought to have a costume in harmony with that of the dancers.

As soon as the guzla stopped, Aboulfedia, followed by his troop, went back into the room of repose to change costumes. That change was abnormally prolonged. The first time, Isabelle became impatient and went to open the door. But when they arrived at the fourth dance, having learned that a monkey has as much coquetry as a woman, she resigned herself to waiting for the final ballet, the costumes for which were Chinese.

Dusk was beginning to fall gently. Sorbets were drunk. Time passed. No one emerged from the room of repose and the room even emitted a curious impression of silence. In the end, Isabelle decided to go in there, and it was with amazement that she found it empty.

The costumes were spread over the floor in the greatest disorder along with Rodriguez' guzla; but the box with the bronze nails had been taken away.

Isabelle climbed the stairway and went through her apartments, including the bathroom and the steam-bath. There was no one there. What mysterious reason had impelled Aboulfedia to depart with his effeminate ephebe, his girl with the boyish air and his dancing monkey, in the middle of a performance that he had organized?

Isabelle went back down to the garden. She searched in vain for the key to the enigma. She raised her eyes to the heavens and saw on the balustrade of the terrace, in the violet mass that the wisteria made, a four-footed Chinese mandarin that was looking at her, and which stated chattering. It was the monkey, dressed in its costume for the final ballet.

Isabelle made a gesture, and as it ran away it climbed a eucalyptus that spread its silvery branches above the garden and the red terraces if the Alhambra.

The slaves and eunuchs began to laugh noisily, and it was at that moment that Abul Hacen appeared.

The Emir's face was grave.

He had been remorseful for some time at having left in the hands of an inestimable woman the heritage of his ancestors. It is true that his positive mind made him think that it was better to put his confidence in the number of his soldiers and the solidity of his alliances than the power of a talisman, but are there not unknown forces? Many sensible men believed in magic, and Allah manifests his designs as he pleases.

That magic must be enormous! It was nevertheless true that he had just given an audience to a dervish arrived from Mecca who had vowed all his life to recite his prayers before the ancient talisman of the Arabs. That dervish had had no pride in asking to see the talisman. He was modest and he would go away satisfied if he could place his forehead against the stone wall that sheltered the marvelous relic.

The dervish had walked through Granada and certain pious people were waiting doe him at the Puerta de la Justicia. Abul Hacen thought that it was necessary to make a few concessions to the religiosity that engenders the sacrifice so necessary in difficult times. Without giving a definitive response, he had left the dervish in the Court of Lions and had gone to Isabelle's apartment, glad to have that pretext, with regard to her as much as himself, to take back what he had imprudently given her.

Isabelle did not understand at first what it was about. A talisman? The night when he had nearly gone blind? Oh yes, she remembered. It was a very old and ugly object in which

272

she threw slippers that she no longer wore. The object had been in her bedroom for some time, and then she had had it transported here to this room of repose, where she had seen only an hour ago, where it ought still to be, buried under a monkey's costumes.

Abul Hacen raced into the room. The guzla, on which he trod, rendered an agonized sound. But the holy Ark, the divine tomb where the Tablets of the Law had rested, the cradle of tarnished gold whose handles were borne by two angels with a spirituality so great that one could not look at them without thinking of God, the miraculous Tabernacle, had disappeared.

Behind the wily and courageous Aboulfedia, carried by Rodriguez and Rebecca in the monkey's box, it had passed via the little stairway covered with orange mosaics, had traversed the corridors and courtyards of the Alhambra, to return to its legitimate possessors, the faithful followers of Moses.

In the twilight, the Alhambra was filled with an extraordinary tumult. No one knew what had been stolen but it was necessary to arrest the thieves. Cavaliers departed in all directions through the town, without even knowing who they were pursuing. And it was only much later in the night that Isabelle remembered that Aboulfedia had asked her, a few days earlier, to obtain from the Emir for one of his coreligionists a right of passage on the Emir Daoud's galley, which was about to set sail for Constantinople.

But the theft, of which no one knew the value, lost all importance by comparison with the event that followed it.

Abul Hacen, occupied in giving orders for the arrest of Aboulfedia, had momentarily forgotten the dervish who was waiting for him. He suddenly thought about him and went back to the Court of Lions, more determined than ever to show himself respectful to a holy man.

The holy man's right arm could not be seen, hidden by his robe. It suddenly sprang forth, armed with a dagger, in the direction of the Emir, and traced a flash above his head. But the Emir knew that evening that Allah did not bear any grudge against him.

In taking a step forward to strike, the dervish slipped on a paving stone and fell to one knee. He did not get up again. A guard, thinking he was doing well, dealt him a blow with his scimitar so violent that it killed him instantly, thus depriving the Emir of all that torture might have told him about the motive for the crime and the man who had inspired it.

As Almazan leaned over the man to make sure that he was dead, he recognized him, or thought he recognized him, for the blows struck by the people in the Court of Lions, which had clawed his face, had partly disfigured him. It was the fake Santon whom he had been tempted to pursue into the great mosque, the man who had introduced himself into Al Birouni's house, the Dominican once expelled from the Order by Tomas de Torquemada personally, for his indignity.

That base spy of the Holy Office had denounced and had burned, by means of lying accusations, inoffensive and disinterested scholars. There was every chance that he was the one who had poisoned Archbishop Carrillo, if the Archbishop had not died by virtue of his own imprudence. He was pursuing a work of treason and crime in Granada.

Almazan searched behind his features, beneath his beard, under the blood clots and in the already vitreous eyes for the stigmata of evil. There were none. He had an ordinary skull, the pitiful head of a man attained abruptly by death. Even the mask of the face had taken on a certain tragic grandeur.

Then Almazan was struck by a thought. That denouncer, that spy, that poisoner had just sacrificed his life—for the assassin of the Emir, within the walls of the Alhambra, had no chance of escape.

There were men fanaticized by evil just as there were men fanaticized by good, and who offered their existence to that evil in holocaust.

But perhaps it was the case that what was evil for some was not for others. There were two slopes that did not communicate, two extremely distant kingdoms, which were juxtaposed, and on the two sides, the inhabitants of those worlds lived with the illusion that their light was the sole veritable one.

That thought was odious to Almazan, but before the face of the dead man he could not rid himself of it. And that dead man as nothing but an instrument, almost unconscious. What was more terrible was that there were men of great intelligence who were evil through and through. But did they know it? Were they animated by a clear-sighted love of evil, or had they taken a different path, which was their error, but on which they believed they were marching in the truth?

He recalled everything that he knew about Torquemada, and what he had read about him in his master Carrillo's notebook.

Two bright eyes, miraculously profound, which reflect neither hatred, not pity, nor desire, nor pride, but a strange certainty that makes me shiver.

"Ever more intelligence, ever more love," said Rosenkreutz. "The rose and the cross!" But there might be minds that had arrived at a high degree of development that had for an ideal the diminution of intelligence and the killing of love.

Almazan started to walk agitatedly through the Alhambra, filled with tumult. He let himself fall on to a bench in the cypress garden. The stars were radiant and immutable, like unattainable truths.

In a tree, the monkey in the Chinese robe leaned over and threw a pine-cone.

Very high in a gorge in the Sierra Nevada, Aboulfedia and the rabbi Anan ben Joshua found a group of their coreligionists who were waiting for them with fresh horses. After descending the steep slopes at a gallop they changed them again at La Calahorra. They traveled all night and all day. They finally reached Almeria and only stopped on the harbor.

They had to embark immediately. It was their only chance of salvation, for a messenger from Granada might arrive at any moment bringing an order to the Alcaide of the city to seize them and their precious burden.

A host of mariners, merchants and petty tradesmen were cluttering the port. They asked a softa which was the galley on which the Emir Daoud was about to depart. The softa laughed at their ignorance and pointed at the harbor. At that moment, three cannon shots were fired on the Castle of Seven Towers. The crowd responded with cheers.

The Emir's galley had been waiting since morning for a favorable wind. That wind had just risen, and the galley was preparing to depart. The sails were deployed, standards were flapping, and mahones decked with banners were furrowing the port.

Aboulfedia and the rabbi saw one of those mahones casting off from a jetty. It contained a few sailors, recognizable as mariners of the Emir's fleet by their short caftans with narrow sleeves, held at the waist by a blue woolen belt. Aboulfedia hailed the mahone, brandishing a deployed parchment on which the green seal of the kings of Granada was visible.

The mahone stopped and returned to the quay, its oars raised. Aboulfedia held out the parchment to the officer in command. It was a right of passage for the bearer aboard the Emir's galley. And he got ready to descend into the mahone, followed by the rabbi.

But the officer stopped him.

The right of passage was only for a single passenger; he could not take two. In vain, the rabbi Anan ben Joshua wanted him to refer to Emir Daoud himself. It was too late. The galley was lifting anchor and the mahone only just had time to rejoin it. A single passenger! The oars were about to be lowered.

The two men exchanged a few words.

"You're the more worthy," said Aboulfedia.

"You're the stronger," said the rabbi. "Who knows what struggles it might still be necessary to sustain?"

"Death after torture awaits the one who remains. I'll stay."

"Go, I order you to do so."

And while the box was lowered, the rabbi added: "The most powerful brotherhood is at Tiberiade. Go to Tiberiade first, where Maimonides is buried. But if you don't find Samuel Halevy the talmudist there and Abraham Alfassi the commentator of the Kabbalah, go to Jerusalem, where you'll find the great Hebrew University. Where the spirit is, there is the root of the tree."

They only just had time to embrace as they separated. But they did not separate entirely. The thought of the man who remained accompanied the one who left.

For as long as he could see it, Aboulfedia followed with his eyes the gray patch that rabbi Anan den Joshua made on the quay. He was very small, very stooped, increasingly stooped. The man in whom an enormous dream lived was walking hesitantly. He stumbled; he could do no more. He had lost his black bonnet. He retraced his steps to take the sweating horses by the bridle, and he looked like a beggar who had just stolen them.

XVII. The Insensate Galley

Under the vault of the forecastle, behind the place re-served for the maneuvering of swivel-guns, two moderately large cabins had been accommodated. One was to shelter the dancing-girls that they were going to find in Constantinople. In the other, the passengers who had obtained from the Emir the exceptional favor of reaching the Orient under the protection of his arms took their place.

Those passengers were few in number. Apart from three jewel-merchants from Granada, there was only the scholar Al Birouni and Tawaz, celebrated for his immense fortune, his love of the arts and the refinements of his life.

Al Birouni was taking with him the glass bell of which he was the inventor. He was no longer attracted by anything but the mystery of submarine things. There, he believed, lived a marvelous world whose fauna had close links with human-kind. He claimed that there were fish under the sea with arms and hands, monsters with human faces, and that the world in question was illuminated by a light that became brighter the further one descended. But those luminous depths could only be attained in the distant oceans that bathed India and China. He intended to reach Alexandria, because the Sultan of Egypt was interested in his endeavors and had promised to enable him to reach India aboard one of his caravels. There he would attempt his experiment with the glass bell.

As for Tawaz, he had divided his fortune between his two sons and said adieu to them. He was going to Nichapour in Persia. His sole dream was to sit in the shade of the peach tree that let its petals fall on the tomb of Omar Khayyam in the cemetery of Hira. He would live henceforth in the small com-munity of Sufis rallied, like Khayyam, to the Ismailite doc-trine, and who came to seek ecstasy beneath the peach tree that covered him.

Next to Al Birouni and Tawaz, Aboulfedia had taken his place, with his coffer.

In the rear castle were the cabin of the Emir of the Sea, that of the galley's reis, and the one where the officers, the treasurer, the mullah, the pilots and the pages slept.

Below the deck the hundred and fifty pikemen were accumulated, along with the crates containing the violet jackets trimmed with gold, the damascened breastplates, the cashmere belts, the crimson brocade bonnets and the scimitars with golden hilts destined to dazzle the inhabitants of Constantinople when Emir Daoud made his way solemnly to the Sultan's palace.

From that part of the ship, all day long, rose an obsessive buzz of conversations and cries, which increased in the evening when the bakals made the distribution of salted meat and bread. The buzz was gradually extinguished at the hour when the stars shone through the triangular sails, caused the racks of weapons, the log-barreled culverins and the swivel-guns to sparkle. Only then did the passengers perceive, low stifled and powerful, an obscure sigh, an enormous respiration. That was the groan of the convicts who, chained in tens, their heads shaved and their muscles taut, exhaled a terrible odor of sweat, laboring without respite under the blows of overseers and panting, as if they were the galley's lungs and as if they were impelling it with their breath.

But there was another noise, more disquieting, in the galley at night. That was the footfalls of the Emir of the Sea, who was pacing back and forth on the exterior gallery or following the length of the course from the poop or the prow. In an immaculate triple turban and his long gandourah of white silk, fringed with silver, he gave the impression of a human swan, ready to take flight.

The reis at the foot of the main mast, the mariners on watch sitting on the deck and the passengers, through the partly open door, watched the distant silhouette standing on the rampart, where he was immobilized in a reverie that no longer ended. That was because, since the early hours of the navigation, it was no longer a secret from anyone that Emir Daoud no longer enjoyed all his reason.

That had commenced, it was said, at the moment of the death of Princess Khadidja. However, the Emir had loved so many women in his life, in Granada and all the other lands to which his destiny had led him: Juana de Montana, the beautiful Spanish captive for whom he had refused royal ransoms; Djemilé, the poetess of Fez who had languished for love of him and had died of no longer seeing him; The Albanian Validé and the Venetian Lucrèce had been his mistresses. Emir Daoud loved ardently and forgot quickly. The desire he had for one was rapidly replaced by the desire he had for another, No one understood how an amorous chagrin had been able to render mad a man who ought to know as well as anyone of what smoke the passions are woven.

The reis scarcely slept. It was him, in fact, who commanded the maneuvering of the *Banner of the Prophet*, but the supreme command belonged to the Emir. The latter had taken the reis by the arm as they were coming out of the port of Almeria and had confided to him with a smile that he intended to drop anchor in the town of Liampo, which was on the coast of China, in order to salute the wife of the Portuguese governor there. Since then, the reis had feared some singular determination.

And what would happen in Constantinople? How would the meeting between the Emir and the Sultan go? Was he not going to try to obtain ships and soldiers for Granada? Was the outcome of the war not dependent, in part, on his skill?

The winds were favorable, and the vessels of the Knights of Rhodes and those of the Republic of Venice were avoided. Through sunlit days and peaceful nights, the *Banner of the Prophet* traversed the Mediterranean, laden with hopes and treasures, with its white swan at the prow, outlined against the azure.

Several years later, Sultan Bazajet had the story told to him again of the interview that his grand vizier Daud-Pacha had had in his absence with the ambassador of the King of Granada, the celebrated mariner Daoud.

He wanted the names of the women that the latter had pronounced to be repeated, and a description given of the astonishment of the entire Diwan when it became evident that the Emir in the white turban had only, in sum, come to Constantinople with a magnificent escort to affirm that a certain Princess Khadidja had eyes the color of the purest emeralds.

He also wanted to be certain that Emir Daoud had shed tears when the six dancing-girls that he was to take to Granada for his master were introduced to him.

"All those that I have loved," he had said.

Sultan Bazajet was an austere man. He had proscribed music and dancing in his palace. He recommended chastity to his ministers and his generals, and every time the conversation turned to that subject, he raised his finger and said: "Remember Emir Daoud and the fate of Granada."

Alongside the glass bell and the coffer with the bronze nails, Aboulfedia and Al Birouni were now alone in the cabin of the forecastle.

The *Banner of the Prophet* was to call in at Acre, and it was there that they both intended to disembark, in order to follow their different destinies.

The minarets of Constantinople had not yet disappeared over the horizon when, close by, behind the partition of planks that separated them from the next cabin, the music of lutes had resounded. The six pupils of Professor Chosrai were singing laments for their homeland, which they were quitting forever. In very soft voices they were singing Persian poems in which there was question of beloveds as slender as the stems of palm trees, young women with faces as oval as mirrors, borne by necks of silver, and amours perfumed like roses of Ispahan and as profound as the well of Mossoul, which did not reflect the images of those who leaned over it.

The lutes of the six young women had, in addition to the four strings that correspond to the four human temperaments, the fifth string added by the musician Ziryah, which is the one that corresponds to the soul linked by blood. At the heart-rending sound of that fifth string, Emir Daoud recognized that he was taking great artistes with him, and he came to sit down with them.

He did not speak to them. He turned toward them a visage illuminated by ecstasy, and when one or other of them stopped playing, he contented himself with calling her by a name in a low voice. But that name was not their real name, which he did not know. At first, believing him to be in error, they tried to correct him.

"I'm Ghazlan..."

"I'm Honeidah..."

"I'm Mehboubeh...," they said.

But the Emir shook his head and continued to say Khadidja, Juana, or Djemilé, according to whether he was thinking in the Moorish, the Spanish or Moroccan fashion. Then they ended up getting accustomed to those names and turning toward him when he pronounced them, so that he was soon able to believe himself surrounded by the women he had loved, and cradled by the music of their lutes.

It was the evening of the third day of the month of Shaban, and the heat was overwhelming. A dense green-tinted vapor was trailing over the water, which seemed sick, as if afflicted by a putrescence rising from the depths. There was not a breath of wind. The galley was advancing by means of oars and it gave the impression of cleaving through a heavy and putrid mass. Phosphorescences palpitated in the distance and flying fish made vague luminous streaks. The oarsmen seemed ready to expire at every effort, and the human odor that exhaled from the convicts' benches was like a palpable mist. An anguish devoid of any apparent cause, born of the immobility of the sea and the occult presence of death, gripped all souls.

After having wandered around the deck, Al Birouni went back down the few steps that connected the exterior gallery of the deck with his cabin. He saw his traveling companion Aboulfedia leaning over the mysterious box over which he had never ceased to watch jealousy since the departure from Almeria. The lid was raised, and Aboulfedia was lost in mute contemplation.

From the top of the steps, Al Birouni looked at the box. Since the departure he had wondered what the panting and haggard Jew might have to transport that was so precious. Now, he could see it. It was a solid gold object, but a strange gold, prodigiously ancient, which gave off a supernatural radiance. Al Birouni started slightly with surprise. The lid of the box closed again abruptly, and Aboulfedia closed the catches.

Al Birouni came down the steps quietly, sat down cross-legged, and began to reflect.

He had read in Flavius Josephus and other Jewish and Arabic historians the description of the Holy of Holies enclosed by Moses in the Temple of Jerusalem. He knew the Arab legends about the Talisman transported by the first Moorish conquerors and enclosed in the Alhambra. He had made connections between the two sacred objects of those different races. He recalled that he had heard mention of a Jewish brotherhood whose objective was to search for the ancient Tabernacle in Spain. And the conviction came to him abruptly that the fat man with the little eyes had discovered it in Granada, had stolen it and was taking it to the land that had been the cradle of the Jews.

Al Birouni knew that an initiate like Moses could enclose an active magnetic force in metal for centuries. On that force the Arabs had been able to draw since the early days. If it were stolen from them at a critical moment, what would happen? The Talisman that had reposed in the Alhambra ought to remain there. He would not permit a Jew to carry it away.

Al Birouni got up and prepared to climb the steps leading to the deck, but Aboulfedia, doubtless conscious of his imprudence, must have read his reflections and his determination in his eyes, for he leapt to his feet and barred his way.

They had no need to explain themselves in words; they had understood one another. Al Birouni did not try to call for help. In the next cabin, the song of the six young lute players was resounding like a prayer, like the anguishing appeal of hearts broken by amour, and that song would have drowned out his voice.

He tried to move Aboulfedia aside, but a murderous thought was shining in the latter's eyes. The two men were face to face, almost stuck to one another, silent and resolute, sensing the immense destiny of their people behind them. They were about to seize one another bodily when the noise that they heard on the deck immobilized them.

It was a muffled, fearful clamor, a long, continuous cry, the desperate appeal of men who see before them, in the most unexpected and terrifying fashion, the apparition of inevitable death.

All the mariners who escaped the tidal wave that ravaged the coasts of Syria and Palestine on the third night of the month of Shaban, which also destroyed the fortifications of the Knights of Rhodes and brought down the great lighthouse of the port of Famagusta, were unanimous in describing it as a unique wave, an irritated mountain that preceded whirlwinds, and raced from the horizon with a demonic speed over the dismal, flat, thick desert of the putrid waters.

The men who were on watch on the deck of the *Banner of the Prophet*, in the green-tinted light of the hallucinatory equatorial light, only had the time to contemplate from an extreme height, on the summit of an extravagant liquid wall, a mobile vegetation of foam. They sensed that the capsized galley climbed that summit with a velocity that ten thousand oarsmen could not have given it, and they heard a submarine roar coming from the abyss, as if there had been, far below the keel of the ship, a profound gorge from which that frightful sound was coming.

That was all for them. It was given to a few others to perceive that, as the rear castle was torn away, they were hurled liked grains of sand, amid the debris of the guard-rails and the deadlights, into the moving depths. The reis was carried away with the main-mast, on to which he was hanging. The man in the crow's nest spun away in space as if he had been projected by an extraordinary sling. The cannons flew away, with their carriages, their lifting-tackle and their platforms.

The furious, animate, multiple waters streamed over the broken deck into the crew quarters, descended in a torrent to oarsmen's benches, sweeping away the foremen and the enchained convicts. The *Banner of the Prophet* was no longer anything but a crippled pontoon in which one culverin still swung like a bronze snake, and in which an invocation of Allah or a scream of agony resounded here and there.

Then, from the forecastle, which had remained intact, Emir Daoud emerged, paler than his turban and his silk gandourah. His mind awoke from the slumber into which it had been plunged. He arrived after a long in dream in the midst of that catastrophe.

He tried to advance along the deck by hanging on to ropes, fragments of rail and pieces of mast. He understood that the waves would carry him away, turned back, and went down to the alleyway between the oarsmen's benches, which he traversed in its entire length, with water up to his knees. Having arrived at the poop, however, he observed that the helm was broken, that the galley could no longer be steered, and he heard the rumble of waves through the chambers of the hold. That rumble became louder and the water rose between the decks.

He decided to go back in order to return to the fore cabin, but the route had been too long. He had the convicts to the right and left, bound to their benches by the feet, contorted by the effort they had made when the wave had stunned or drowned them. Some of those who were dead expressed a nameless misery, others a pitiful resignation, others an impotent rage. But there were some who were still alive and who remained chained to the dead. They were struggling desperate-

285

ly to break their chains, uttering clamors and waving the stumps of oars.

When the white silhouette of Emir Daoud passed through their midst again, they extended their hands toward him in order to hang on to that living and free form, and the Emir, between those ranks of creatures stretching out at the end of a chain, between those avid tentacles, was obliged to roll up the broad sleeves of his gandourah in order not to be seized.

He walked amid the stony faces of the dead and the hateful and despairing faces of the living. The latter were howling at him, but the Emir only saw the grimaces of the cries, for the voice of the ocean drowned out all sounds with its tumult, and those silent howls were more heart-rending than the plaints.

And in the midst of those naked caryatids, to whom dolor and death gave poses of dementia, the Emir wondered whether he might be following the somber road that leads to Allah's inferno.

No, it was the terrestrial world to which he had just returned, the world where the convicts were riveted to their benches and struggling against terror while they descended into the gulf of death. Oh, to recover rapidly the music of the young Persian women, who sang the memory of amour and bore the names of the beloved!

As he finally arrived at the door of the cabin, two men were helping one another fraternally to hoist on to the deck a black box with bronze nails.

Aboulfedia and Al Birouni, sensing the ship sinking, had been tacitly reconciled, for each of the two knew that he could only count on the other to try to save the Treasure for which they had wanted to kill one another. Aboulfedia was pulling it and Al Birouni was pushing it. Between two cataracts of wind, between two breaths of the sea vomiting waves, there was a second of miraculous silence. In that second, breathless over the wood of the box that they were holding embraced, they perceived lute music, light and quavering, as distant as if the djinn that dance around wells on spring nights in the valleys of Kouhistan had commenced their round.

The galley stood up straight in the midst of a sudden din, and plunged backwards. In the coffin of the cabin, Emir Daoud fell against warm breasts and feminine faces, the rediscovered forms of those he had cherished.

And by the talismanic power contained in the eternally virgin gold of the Tabernacle, it was perhaps given to Al Birouni and Aboulfedia, who were clasping it to their bodies, to descend into the depths of the waters in the supernatural light of their realized dreams.

Al Birouni must have contemplated by that light the strange marvels of the submarine world, the sirens of fable wandering in forest of phosphorescent madrepores, incarnadine scorpion-fish charge with spines, puffer-fish inflated like bladders and similar to obese men, cephalopods with multiple tentacles with palpitating eyes, and all the monsters bearing with horror, far from the sun, the stigmata of a fallen humankind.

And Aboulfedia must have seen, appearing beyond the green infinites and the glaucous glimmer of the sea-bed, the azurescent cupola, the five columns of sittim wood and the crimson and hyacinth veils of the Temple of Jerusalem.

XVIII. The Angel of Lust

It was the month of Schouwal; the leaves of the carobs were blood red and the pepper-trees were dropping their globular berries, dried by the heat. Almazan had come to sit on the threshold of the pavilion in which he had been living for a few days, in the midst of the pleasure-gardens of Alexaras.

Abul Hacen could no longer do without him and had taken him with him, along with Isabelle, when he went to repose from the fatigues of the war in his villa outside Granada.

An enormous rose-bush that climbed up the wall of the pavilion had shed the petals of its roses, so abundantly that they formed a thick carpet on the ground. From those petals, a sudden gust of the odor of roses rose toward Almazan, mingled with a more profound perfume of scorched earth. And in the vaporous air of the night, between the golden citrus trees lining a pathway, there was a kind of apparition. He thought he saw one of the four tempters, enemies of the soul, described by Muslim mythology: Al Nefs, the lustful angel, who has the form of a woman and an adolescent at the same time, who draws down by the spell of sensuality.

Still penetrated by the reading he had just undertaken on the religion of Mohammed and its superstitions, he almost uttered a cry of surprise on seeing the brother of Iblis marching toward him, the delightful angel, such as he had imagined him.

He was wearing a long blue dalmatic as supple as a cloud, floating above his short silk chemise, the color of which was crimson, like the passions it concealed. The adolescent legs were bare and the feet had minuscule slippers in a gold filigree fabric that made the sand of the pathway crackle slightly. On the infantile head was posed, by a singular caprice, the triple black turban worn by mullahs and teachers of the law, as if it symbolized that the bearer of lust is also the bearer of a certain sagacity.

288

But beneath that black turban, burnt gold hair sprang forth like a flame, animated by a life of its own, the same color as the two gilded drops that moved in the depths of the eyes, and in the stride there was something winged and intoxicating. It was by that gaze, when the angel Al Nefs was very close to him, that Almazan recognized Isabelle.

He did not have time to get up. She had sat down beside him, laughing familiarly.

"You see, it's for you that I've put on a black turban. Do I not have the appearance of a doctor thus, a commentator on the Law of Mohammed, as they say. A doctor! Fundamentally, I believe that I'd have a great deal to learn.

She picked up a handful of rose petals and threw them at him negligently.

He smiled. He felt suddenly invaded by an unexpected wellbeing, the ease that one experiences in the company of individuals that one has known for a long time, and by whom one feels loved.

He told her that he thought he had seen, for a moment, as she walked along the path, Al Nefs, the angel of lust, such as he is depicted by the Persian theologian Mirkond.[31]

That amused her greatly. She repeated several times: "That's right, I'm the angel of lust."

And she leaned toward him, to the point that he sensed the amber and musk perfume of her hair, and the youthful perfume of her breath.

Almost without thinking about it, he put his arm around her shoulder and made contact beneath the supple fabric of the dalmatic with a warm, moving, desirous carnal substance, which made him shiver.

Then she leaned against him, to the point that he had the form of her firm breast designed in his bosom, and he saw

---

[31] The full name of the ninth-century Persian historian Mirkond, or Mirkhavend, author of a book whose title translates as *The Garden of Purity*, is given by more recent sources in various forms including Muhammad Bin Khavendshah

against his own the line of her bare leg, outside the parted dalmatic.

She was talking to him now, but in a voice so low that he could not hear it. He understood. all the same. She was saying inconsequential words in which there was mention of her life, happiness and amour. Oh, how bored she was! Her greatest hope was no longer to belong to anyone but one man, the man she loved. Then she started laughing again.

"Can you imagine that when I came down the stairs to come here, I found the two eunuchs who guard me in the patio of the villa. I was holding my slippers in my hand in order not to make any sound as I walked. I looked at the eunuchs, who were asleep, lying on their mats. I had one to the right and the other to the left. And I had such a desire to tell someone that I was going to find you that I almost woke them up by dropping my slippers on their noses.

At that thought, she was shaken by tremors. She leaned her face on his shoulder. And while she said other incoherent things, he sensed that the body he had against him had suddenly become heavier, more languorous, and also warmer and more abandoned. He was holding in his arms a human form whose will was absent and communicating with the proximity of its blood the mysterious ardor with which it was charged. He yielded to the force of proximity, the law of attraction that summons one body toward another at certain moments, and drifted in the current of pleasure.

The woman's face was an oval of silver amid the burning hair. He tipped her over beneath him and immediately, when he felt his lips seized by those tender lips, perfumed like the fruits of spring, as mobile as life itself, as warm as his own heat, he understood that he was linked henceforth to the woman he held, by the fluid, eternal chain of moist lips.

With a single gesture, he ripped the crimson chemise from top to bottom, while the complaisant arms made the dalmatic slide away from the shoulders.

290

The rose petals on which they were lying exhaled the sad and carnal odor of faded things, and in the citrus trees, a nightingale that had begun to sing stopped.

Abul Hacen did not descend from the horse. The two eunuchs were prostrate, foreheads in the dust of the road. But the order to have them killed did not emerge from the Emir's mouth. What was the point? Nor was the order given to pursue the fugitives, who had departed on horseback a few hours ago. What was the point?

He had quit the siege of Loxa in order to come and embrace the woman he loved. And she had fled with a man in whom he had placed all his confidence. Thus, Allah had wished it. That news did not astonish him as much as he would have thought. It seemed to him his dolor had been hidden within him for a long time, and that it appeared to him like a landscape to a voyager on a hill when the mist rises.

He turned round. A hundred cavaliers accompanied him. The setting sun made the bulging breastplates glitter, and the diamonds in head-dresses shine. He would go to Granada, where he needed to conscript more soldiers, where his presence would calm the popular parties agitated against him by Boabdil's envoys. Action would appease his thoughts.

From the villa in Alexaras it would only take half an hour to reach the ramparts of Granada. The road was singularly deserted. The mass that the city formed in the distance seemed silent and hostile.

No trumpet resounded from any tower, as if there were no watchman to signal the arrival of the Emir and his escort. However, the Emir looked behind him and saw that one of his cavaliers was raising his banner ostentatiously.

The strangers' gate, where the road ended, was closed. Ordinarily, it was only closed an hour after sunset.

The Emir advanced toward the gate. He had taken a spear from his friend Feghani, and he hammered violently with the shaft on the oak of the gate, which resonated dully.

Anxious faces appeared and disappeared in the crenellations of the walls. People called out and responded. An awkwardly launched arrow traced a curve through the air and stuck in the ground.

And as the Emir prepared to knock again, a low and rapid voice spoke to him through a barred window that opened to the right, in one of the two towers juxtaposed with the gate.

"Lord! Make haste to flee! Your son Boadbil has taken possession of Granada. The Hagib's head is fixed to the end of a pike in the Plaza de Bibarrambla. The Alfaquis have betrayed you. The people have denied you and are crying 'Long live Boabdil!' You can no longer count on anyone."

Abul Hacen tried to recognize, through the bars of the window, the face of the man through whom the inexorable contrary destiny was being expressed. His heart was beating violently. He leaned forward on his horse.

But then that narrow window in the wall began to spin, it suddenly exploded like a sunburst, growing immeasurably, confounded with the ramparts, with the city and the evening sky. And that luminous mass tarnished, became gray, and then somber, changed into compact darkness.

"Thus Allah wishes it!" said the Emir, and turned his horse.

In the uncertainty of his soul, he did not confide to his companions that he had lost his sight, more precious to him than the city of Granada. He had made a sign to Feghani to ride ahead of him on the road to Salobrena, knowing that his horse would follow that of his companion without him giving it any direction.

But like the loss of Isabelle, this new misfortune did not bring him the despair that he would have expected. The night that fell sent gusts of fresh wind into his face, and as he went forward a great calm descended within him. It seemed to him that he had accomplished a long voyage and had finally arrived in port. He even ceased squinting while staring to the right and left in the hope that he might still be able to distinguish the contours of things. He lowered his head, closed his eyes, and perceived that he could see.

He saw the realm of the spirit, more luminous than the terrestrial realm. He saw events unfolding like a long logical chain in which everything was explicable and deducible, and in which a great harmony reigned. He was only an effect of distant causes himself. He understood everything that it had required, of wars, conquests and peoples on the march in order that the blind king who had lost his kingdom, turning his back on Granada, could ride away.

He saw the history of his race unfurl, as if in an immense, prodigious animated, living, colored tableau. In the distance, Mohammed advanced, followed by the litters of his wives, and camels destined for sacrifice, and he kissed the black stone of the Kaaba. He climbed the hill of Safa and made the assembled people an allocution, which the Koreischite Rabia repeated word for word, in a resounding voice. Abul Hacen saw the naïve and fantastical faces, the sheepskins thrown over shoulders like cloaks, and behind, between a few clumps of palm trees, the tents of the nomadic people.

Down the flank of a mountain of sand rode cavaliers who were the advance guard of Amrou, on the march toward Memphis and Alexandria. He saw Okba's soldiers traversing the Baghreb, Mousa's overrunning Spain and Gaul. Cities crumbled, others rose up with their porticos, their minarets, their bazaars and their castles charged with miradors. He saw the thousand jets of water and the magical masses of flowers of the Garden of Zohrah, the forests of capitals and cupolas of the starry fibers of the Mosque of Cordova, the stones of synagogues, and the lace of Alcazars. Ascetic prophets preached, pilgrims set forth, muezzins clamored the formulae of prayers in the sky, and Caliphs covered in precious stones received ambassadors.

Dynasties succeeded one another. The voluptuous Almoravides watched dancing girls twirl and listened to amorous verses and the music of darbukas. The austere

Almohades, in the middle of a circle of mullahs, raised crudely bound Korans in their ringless hands. Abderame the Sage rendered justice. Almanzor the cavalier traversed the plains. Al Hakem the bridge-builder scrutinized the war of rivers. In the end, Abul Hacen saw several Emirs who resembled him in their facial features. They were his ancestors the Nasrides, and among them he distinguished the great Muhamad Alhamar with his thin gray beard and his torn gandourah, like the symbol of the simplicity of his mores.

But the last of the Nasrides was a fat, ridiculous man, puffed up with pride, with eyes sparkling with lust. And in that fat man he recognized himself. For the first time he saw himself as he was, with his jaundiced jowls, his bald cranium and his enormous belly, and he almost laughed at that caricature of an Emir.

And the events that had not yet happened, but whose causes had been generated by his folly, also unfurled before his eyes. Cities were taken one by one, Christian pyres burned in public squares, he saw the grimaces of those who were tortured because they did not want to deny their faith, and the desperate expressions of those who had renounced it.

Alongside was extended the beautiful young Spanish woman for whom he had lost the kingdom of Granada, naked on a bear-skin, with her eyes closed. It was not voluptuousness that had made her close her eyes; it was in order not to see him, because of the disgust he inspired in her. And in a jacket of white fur and an ermine urban, he perceived her in the distance fleeing on horseback with Almazan, But he did not suffer from it. He no longer had any remorse.

Everything unfolded in a predictable order. Civilizations flowed from the depths of the horizon, filled kingdoms, threw forth a thousand lights. Then the lights paled. Men were born who were more refined, more avid for enjoyment, less willful, and they were swept away by new races. He, the culpable Emir, had merely been an instrument in the hand of Allah. He had served him by means of his stupidity as his ancestors had by their courage. Life was an immense tangle of causes and effects, in which everyone had his allotted place and where virtue and vice, wisdom and folly, were merged like the colors of a painting and had the same utility.

The wind that passed over him was colder now because the road was passing through mountains. The horses were weary and out of breath. The sound was audible of spears that the cavaliers were allowing to trail among the stones behind them. Abruptly disturbed night-birds fluttered their wings in the branches.

Suddenly, Feghani stopped. The place where they had arrived overlooked several valleys, and the city of Salobrena, whose Alcaide was entirely devoted to Abul Hacen, was perceptible in the distance in the mist. Dawn was beginning to break.

"You see?" said Feghani, showing him the mass of white terraces.

Oh yes, he could see. He had been blind all his life, but he could finally see. What he saw was not the sun rising over the terraces of Salobrena, it was the incomparable dawn of the truth.

XIX. The Siege of Malaga

Isabelle adapted herself poorly to the obscure life she now lived in Malaga. The house where she lived with Almazan was spacious and splendid. Gardens descended in stages to the sea, and from the terrace on the roof the peaks of the mountains surrounding the city could be seen, but she scarcely went out. Hamet, of the Zegri family was in command of the troops in Malaga, in the absence of El Zagal. Perhaps he had not forgotten his family's hatred of the former favorite. She had to fear the echo of that hatred.

In the evening, Almazan and she cast off in a boat with a triangular sail and wandered along the shore. Then she rediscovered her gaiety. She amused herself making the water spring up with her hand and throwing droplets toward the sky. By the light of the stars, those droplets fell back like a luminous cascade, and she thought about the sapphires and pearls of the treasure of the Alhambra. She fell silent, contemplating that which, in the regions of the soul, is beyond regret.

At other times the two lovers sat in the terrace of the house, huddled against one another, and listened indefinitely to a darbuka player placed amid the white laurels of the garden. Distant music came from the city. Singers went along the shore and their voices trailing in the night seemed to open invisible doors to the world of desire.

Almazan and Isabelle embraced one another then and they never wearied of the pleasure of possessing one another. But the repose that followed the caresses was always mingled with bitterness. Isabelle thought about the glory that she had lost. Her vanity, which she had developed like an appetite, no longer being satisfied, made her suffer. And Almazan remembered Rosenkreutz, whom he had abandoned without warning, his projects and his goal. To defend the spirit, to transmit the truth! Oh, how far away he was from that!

Both of them understood by their reciprocal silence the order of thoughts in which they were sunk. With a common accord they escaped from that shadow to find themselves face to face again, active and clear-sighed, avid to make one another suffer on a terrain, always the same, whose desolate curve they followed endlessly.

Isabelle talked about the men by whom she had been loved. First she threw out a name, negligently. "Him too?" Almazan questioned. She said no, quietly, turning her head away. The he took her by the wrists, it was necessary that she confess, that she tell him how it had happened, and he threatened her, he wanted her more.

She swore than she had never loved anyone but him. They both agreed that the past was an abyss over which it was necessary not to lean, in order not to be scourged by the breath it exhaled. But they were both avid to recommence, he because of the devouring curiosity that is the foundation of human desire, she for the emotion of a more intense sensuality born of an ever more furious jealousy.

It was during the most tranquil nights, under the most immaculate skies, that Isabelle evoked her past debaucheries in Seville with Aboulfedia and the suspect individuals that he gathered in Triana for his obscene celebrations.

"You've heard mention of the Sabbat," she said. "He knew the fashion in which it was celebrated in all lands. He had us put on singular costumes and there were rituals so absurd that we couldn't accomplish them without bursting into laughter. Oh, we amused ourselves a great deal, sometimes, with Rodriguez! I was always the woman who was lies naked on the altar and on whose belly the mass was celebrated. At first I had difficulty remaining serious, but as the ceremony went on, either by virtue of the heat, the mingled perfumes of incense and musk, or because of the diabolical atmosphere, my reason went astray, I no longer thought about anything, I had a desire for caresses, I received them, and I didn't know afterwards which men had made so many marks on my body in clutching me against them."

Almazan clenched his teeth. Sometimes, he threatened her. But at other times, livid, wanting to learn more, he begged her to keep talking.

Yes, the profanation added to the pleasure. Aboulfedia sculpted Christs for himself similar to the phallic divinites of paganism. The droplets of candle-wax were like sparks that stimulated bodies already excited by the murmur of infamous litanies. Rodriguez was as handsome as an angel and his villainy had a perverse attraction. She remembered the rustle of a chasuble over her loins, a drunken woman, tipped over, lips that had a taste of malediction. She had a nostalgia for the lust amid the fumes of cassolettes, in the midst of a parody of adoration.

Exhausted and furious, Almazan and Isabelle always ended up embracing one another more passionately, on the terrace that overlooked the city and the sea. But afterwards they became sad and dejected, linked by a more solid chain, separated by a more profound abyss.

By a tacit accord, they never spoke about Tarfe, but with an equal force, they both thought about him.

King Ferdinand's army was already in Besmillana, two leagues from Malaga, but no one yet believed in the possibility of a siege. Formidable enclosing walls flanked by square towers erected their mass around the city, facing the mountains. Cannons were disposed on the jetties of the port. And the port and the city were dominated by the Alcazaba, built on a rocky eminence and dominated itself by the castle of Jebelfaro, built on an even higher eminence. The two towers were connected by a covered path and were impregnable. Malaga reposed tranquilly at their feet like a clutch of houses in the shadow of two stone guardians.

The inhabitants only began to become anxious when they saw, from the height of the ramparts, thousands of cavaliers and infantrymen spreading out in La Vega, erecting their tents and banners there. Only then did they think of fleeing. Those who had boats loaded their goods into them and set sail, either for the port of Almunecar or for Morocco.

Those who did not make haste saw with consternation, on the morning of the third day, fifteen large galleys and thirty caravels blockading the bay. At the same time, the crowd stationed in the streets and the squares transmitted news that was alternately terrible and reassuring.

To begin with it was announced that the Council of Merchants presided over by the rich Ali Dordux was in the process of deliberating in the Alcazaba with the Alcaide of Malaga, Aboul Connaxa. Then the entire city sighed with relief. A deputation had set forth for the Spanish camp in order to offer King Ferdinand the surrender of the city. It was known from the example of cities already besieged that King Ferdinand was content with a declaration of vassalage and a tribute in gold. People ran to the ramparts to await the return of the deputation, others gathered before the house of Ali Dordux and acclaimed him as the representative of peace. Then, departing from the two towers, a wave of silence and terror came closer and closer, and extended over the entire city.

Hamet el Zegri, who occupied the castle of Jebelfaro with two thousand Moroccan mercenaries of the tribe of Gomeres, had descended to the Alcazaba surrounded by his soldiers as soon as he had learned of the sending of the deputation. He had put the Alcaide to death as a traitor to the Moorish cause and had himself proclaimed Alcaide in his place by the frightened Council of Merchants. As master of the army and the civil powers, he had decided on stubborn resistance.

The people did not have time to comment on that event. Fanfares resounded from all the towers, running in a circle around the city. A cavalcade descended in zigzags from the castles. Hamet el Zegri rode through the streets of the city, followed by his armed troops.

The mercenaries had black hair and were short in stature. They wore full breastplates in polished steel, and tall helmets with hooked projections that descended over their noses and removed the human appearance from their faces. Their lances were astonishingly long and they carried them very straight, in such a fashion that they resembled young trees planted in the ground, and their bucklers were sparkling metallic masses, of which they made use to crush their enemies.

Behind them, without armor, clad in brown leather and having no weapon save for a short scimitar, came three hundred cavaliers of the religious order of Rabits. They were warriors who lived in meditation and austerity in times of pace and were invincible in combat because they aspired for death. Hamet el Zegri was part of that order himself. He was bareheaded, strangely thin and seemed immeasurably tall on horseback.

He harangued the silent crowd before the port.

He promised a rapid victory. The provisions were great and permitted patience. El Zagal, who had proclaimed himself King of the realm of Granada by virtue of the death of Abul Hacen, was going to depart from Almeria with an army in order to help Malaga. Hamet el Zegri also knew, from a reliable source, that the Sultan of Egypt, on accord with the Great Lord of Constantinople, was sending an immense fleet to avenge the offenses made to the Crescent by the Spaniards. The sea and the land around Malaga would be the tomb on the enemy armies.

Those words, the sight of the troops and the faith that animated their leader reassured the inhabitants. The acclamations that had risen a few minutes earlier for the pacific Ali Dordux resounded for Hamet el Zegri the warrior.

The day passed in a glorious effervescence. The organization of district militias was begun. There was no question of anything except the predictions of a dervish necromancer named Massar, who had come from Granada and had received from Allah the gift of deciphering the future in a turtle-shell. He had seen with an extreme clarity the image of King Ferdinand with a gaping wound on the nape of his neck; and there were people at the crossroads who were offering descriptions of that wound.

Night fell. A Lombard battery set up on a hill launched its first projectiles at the city. They did no great damage. They fell on waste ground near the port. For a long time, the inhabitants, crouching on their traces, watched the ruddy curves that they traced in the sky, like prophetic comets announcing the reign of fire.

Almazan now spent his days in the cellars of towers converted into hospitals and filled with the wounded. At sunset, he went to the Alcazaba. He was part of a committee of a dozen members charged with organizing the defense of the city.

That was what Hamet el Zegri wanted—for neither he nor anyone else knew of Isabelle's presence in Malaga, and Almazan was honored as the man who had been the friend and counselor of Abul Hacen.

Almazan worked passionately. He had definitively renounced his Christian attachments and education. In any case, he was an Arab on his mother's side. He knew that in defending the kingdom of the Moors he was serving the cause of civilization and intelligence. Had Christian Rosenkreutz not come from a distant land in order to struggle by thought against the tide of fanaticism, the active evil of the Spanish people? He would approve of his conduct when he knew of it, and he would forgive him for his abrupt departure and his long silence.

The incessant activity that he deployed prevented him from thinking about Isabelle. During the day, he rejected the images that made him suffer.

But when he went along the harbor by the light of the stars in order to return home, when he followed the narrow streets between white walls, those images flowed inexorably into his soul, as alive, as precise and as torturing as ever. He hastened his steps. He went up the steps of the faience porch of his house rapidly, and immediately he shouted: "Isabelle!" his heart beating, full of anxiety, desire and the bitter hope of catastrophe that certain amours bring.

That evening, he came back later than usual. No servants' footsteps resonated in the house. No one responded to his appeal. He thought that Isabelle must be in the garden and he went through the ground floor rooms and terraces rapidly.

Through the laurels whose clumps extended toward the sea with sprays of white branches, he perceived a form drawing away.

He was about to shout "Isabelle!" again but he distinguishes that the form had a tall stature and was walking with an arrogant assurance. He ran forward. The shadow stopped and came back toward him. It was a man. Almazan knew that all his slaves had been enrolled as soldiers and were carrying cannonballs on the ramparts. He leaned forward to see the face of the unknown man. The other did the same. They were almost touching, and they recoiled with an equal horror. Almazan had recognized Tarfe.

The young man had the bestial expression that had always struck him, but a second had sufficed for him to perceive in the crease of the eyelids and the red moistness of the lips a heavy joy, the satisfaction of a sated beast.

It seemed to Almazan that a red mist enveloped him and rendered his reason obscure. He was transported into the world of jealousy and murder.

The Almoradi had not been surprised marching furtively. He had allowed the sand of the pathway to crackle without dread. That was because he scorned his rival as a man of an inferior caste, one that did not bear arms.

Almazan's fury redoubled at that thought. But he did not have time to seize Tarfe by the throat; the latter had drawn his scimitar and aimed a great blow at him with the trenchant blade.

Almazan leapt sideways and avoided the blow. He had no weapon. He looked around. There was a gardener's spade driven into the soil a few paces away. He seized it and raised it in time to parry Tarfe's second blow.

Then he started striking with all his strength with his improvised weapon. He struck with a blind rage, first attaining his adversary's wrist, then his breast, and then his head. Then he belabored a bloody mass that was lying at his feet. Then he threw the spade away and looked around at the mute gardens and the motionless sea.

In the distance, there was the sound of culverins, and sometimes a red cannonball furrowed the sky. The fires of enemy galleys blinked like evil eyes. In all directions men were on the alert, animated by thoughts of death, waiting for opportunities to kill one another. And he, who had raised his intelligence high enough to measure that murderous folly and reprove it, had just killed too, with the love of killing.

He leaned over. The young man lay there disfigured. Beside him, his scimitar was reminiscent of a blue snake with a gem-studded head.

Then Almazan felt an immense distress invade him. He strode back up the stages of the gardens and went through the house again. He launched himself into the street. He went down it, and then took another. He walked at hazard for a long time. Although windows were dark and he did not encounter anyone. As he arrived at the chains that closed his quarter, a patrol of Gomeres called out to him rudely. He identified himself and saw the grim faces relax as if in a dream and the silhouettes of the tall helmets drawing away. He reached the ramparts, went along them, and descended toward the sea..

He suddenly perceived that he had arrived near waste ground not far from his house. It was there that the dead were now buried, for the cemetery was outside the city wall. But there had been so many of them in recent days that slaves were thrown in a heap in a shallow ditch, and the layer of earth under which they lay was so thin that it did not prevent the odors of decomposition from trailing in the air in putrid gusts.

Almazan respired those odors but was not inconvenienced by them. In the unknown depths of his soul a distant thought had just appeared. He hastened his pace.

A kind of chant resounded not far away. He perceived a prostrate man touching the soil that covered the dead with his forehead. He was gesticulating with his arms and chanting plaintively. It was the dervish Massar. Intoxicated by the faith that people had in him, he now claimed to be communicating with the dead and receiving messages from them. Every evening he summoned them to this charnel-house, recited formulae, and implored and threatened them by turns.

Almazan did not stop. He hastened toward his dwelling as if pulled by an invisible chain. When he opened the door his visage was animated by a cold resolution.

Isabelle was at the foot of the staircase. She started with fright on seeing Almazan and Almazan understood from her gaze that she was aware of Tarfe's death, either because she had witnessed the fight from her window or because she had gone down into the garden after his departure.

He closed and locked the entrance door and saw her flee up the stairs toward her bedroom.

He went down into the garden to where Tarfe was lying, in the same place. He loaded him on to his back, descended heavily toward the sea and deposited the body in his boat. He climbed into it and rowed with all his strength. When he was some distance from the shore he tipped the dead man into the sea, and had the sensation of killing him for a second time. He was only perceiving the reality of things partially. It was as if he were hallucinating; he fixed his magnetized eyes on an ever more precise image.

Having returned to the land, he ran. Behind the perforated shutters of Isabelle's window there was not the roseate light that lamps make though red Venetian velvet. He told himself, however, that she could not have fled.

He arrived at her door. It was locked. He called to her by name. His voice was low and hoarse. There was no reply. He listened anxiously. Then, along with the heartbeats in his breast, he perceived a light breath coming from the bedroom. Isabelle was there, in the dark, shivering with terror.

With a thrust of his shoulder he broke through the door. He searched for her, groping, and saying: "Why have you put out the lamps? Where are you?"

She replied in an ill-assured voice, which she tried to render form: "What is it? I'm here."

He felt her, undressed and sitting on the bed. Immediately, she threw her arms around his neck and spread her perfumed hair over his face, as if she had been waiting for a long time. She dared not say: "Finally, here you are!" but she was languorous, warm, almost swooning, for fear is similar to desire.

Then he snatched off her nightshirt abruptly, and hugged a creature anxious to know whether she was about to receive amour or death. He had laid her down beneath him and, understanding her fear, he did not undeceive her. He even took her neck in his hands in order that she might believe that he was about to strangle her. She moaned softly. One of her legs was dangling over the edge of the bed like the broken stem of a flower. She seemed never to have loved him as much. And he now glimpsed in the dim light a tender, milky form, the color of sap, whose warmth burned his loins, whose beauty softened him, and he aspired a greater sensuality with the corruption of that body.

A little later, he got up, lit a lamp and opened the window. He leaned out for a few seconds toward the white laurels in the garden, toward the horizon of the sea where the Spanish caravels made patches. He was avid to question his mistress, to know for how long she had been seeing Tarfe again, to torture himself by the evocation of their caresses.

She was stark naked on the bed and he saw that she had just fallen asleep. Her breath was peaceful, and a half-smile wandered over her lips, reddened by kisses.

And as he considered her, the nocturnal wind blew into the room a moist breath in which the perfume of laurels was mingled with the odors of cadavers from the nearby charnel-house.

XX. The Putrescence of the Dead

As the months passed, hope decreased in souls. El Zagal's army, marching to relieve Malaga, had been crushed by the double effort of Boabdil's army coming from Granada and a Spanish army under the command of Gonzales de Cordoba. The fleets from Constantinople and Alexandria had not arrived. On the contrary, the Spanish galleys became more numerous and could be seen disembarking troops and provisions to the right and left of the city wall.

The Spanish camp was now surrounded by a large ditch and its surroundings were strewn with sharp spikes that prevented cavalry from advancing. Near the bridges over the ditches, the catapults and bombards accumulated like bronze flocks, and behind them, the tents, surmounted by flags and banners of all colors, were as innumerable as sand dunes in a desert modeled by the wind

Sometimes, the guards on the ramparts of Malaga, crouching behind the crenellations, saw an enormous tower rolling toward the city made with wooden beans. That tower, the work of the engineer Francisco Ramirez de Madrid, stuck to walls like an animate monster, and flying gangways and ladders sprang from it, from which swarms of enemies precipitated. Trumpets resonated, causing defenders to run from all directions. There were merciless hand-to-hand combats. But the essential thing was for the soldiers of Malaga to protect a group of men armed with large bundles of firewood soaked with resin, which they set ablaze and launched at the feet of the tower. The fire ended up taking hold. The Spaniards who had not yet leapt on to the ramparts fled in the midst of flames or were grilled on the platforms. And nothing any longer remained but the charred and rickety skeleton of the vanquished tower.

At other times, it was the besieged who attacked. Hamet el Zegri, followed by his Gomeres, succeeded in reaching the

Spanish camp during the night. Christians and Moors stabbed one another in the dark, rolling down the slopes, impaling one another on the spikes as they fought. The Gomeres came back bloody, bearing as trophies damascened breastplates, belts ornamented with jewels and exsanguinated heads that they had cut off.

But when summer came, all those in Malaga who had been given the faculty of reflection understood that the Moorish cause was doomed.

King Ferdinand's army had received immense reinforcements. It extended over all the surrounding mountains, and the long files of mules that were bringing supplies to it formed animated furrows.

There had never been a month of Schaban so torrid. The implacable heat of the sky multiplied the misery of the siege. Water ran short. The imams gathered solemnly in the Djouma mosque to ask Allah to make the beneficent rain fall on that unfortunate port of the earth. They traversed the city in procession, followed by the silent people, and they filed along the ramparts.

At the same time, behind Cardinal Talavera and priests bearing relics, an immense religious procession holding candles and singing canticles went through the Christian camp to thank God for his protection.

The sun blazed pitilessly, on the one hand on the black and yellow robes of the imams, and on the other on sparkling surplices, the miters of bishops and the gold of crosses. Between the two processions extended a blank space where there were corpses that had not yet been removed and over which crows were soaring. But neither the imams nor the Catholic priests turned their heads. The former silent at the summit of the ruddy walls, the latter singing among the tents and the standards, they followed their route as if their faith had rendered them blind.

And Allah did not grant the imams' prayers. On the contrary, the heat seemed to increase. The wells ran dry. It was necessary to put guards beside those from which muddy water could still be drawn and to ration the inhabitants. Many, who were weakened by poor nourishment, feel in the street, afflicted by heatstroke. A sentinel on a platform at the summit of the Abderame tower was seen to remain motionless for an entire day, leaning on his arquebus. Toward evening, Spanish arquebusiers who had advanced within range of him launched arrows at him without him interrupting his meditation. The sun had killed him some time before, and when night fell those who were breathing the cool air on their terraces were still pointing at his silhouette outlined in the sky.

Sometimes a Spanish cannonball set fire to a house. But the rumor went around that he heat of the sun was sufficient to provoke conflagrations on its own, and in the fiery atmosphere people lived in the perpetual apprehension of fire.

To the torture of thirst was added that of hunger. The food shops were closed. Everyone was living on what their prudence had caused them to store in their homes. The improvident begged or waited in long queues in front of the Alcazaba for distributions of food. There were some who died of starvation stoically in their homes. They were no longer seen. Their deaths only became known by the odor of decomposition that escaped their door. And as people also died of fevers and all sorts of diseases, the virulence of which had redoubled, the number of those who perished augmented to such an extent that the odor of the putrescence of the dead, filtering from thresholds, floating over terraces, and trailing through all the streets, was the odor of the city, decomposed and dying itself.

And in that extreme misery, as if it were engendered by the ferments of the corruption, a bitter and unhealthy desire developed to enjoy the flesh that was about to be spoiled.

As soon as the sun set, the streets filed with sordid murmurs. Women could not go out without risk of being knocked down and raped. Brothels were besieged. Spanish slaves and Berber dancers who devoted themselves to debauchery made fortunes in a matter of days. The high street, where many prostitutes resided, offered a singular spectacle. Women stood outside their doors beneath gem-studded combs showing through their open gandourahs bodies covered with jewelry from head to toe. The negroes guarding them, standing next to them, were similarly laden. The joy of wealth caused pride to blossom on their faces, to such an extent that a man climbing the high street thought he was walking between two rows of indecent queens, obscene idols worshiped by a corrupt people.

And that frantic thirst for enjoyment was communicated by occult means to the Spanish camp.

The knights, the men of the Santa Hermandad, the Galicians and the mercenaries were all hoping for and counting on the pillage of the city. They knew that Malaga was, next to Granada, the richest city in the Moorish kingdom. In the evening, outside the tents, they traced plans of the city in the sand. They showed one another the location of the street of the jewelers, the mosques and the palace of Ali Dordux. It was there that it was necessary to rush first.

But it was, above all, the women that they coveted. Renegade prisoners have given descriptions of the most beautiful young women. They were known by name. The soldiers played dice for them, sharing them out in advance. Zorah, the daughter of a silk-merchant who was famed in Malaga for her beauty, her chastity and her love of poetry was the most desired, after Rachel, a young Jewish girl of sixteen. And by the light of fires that made their loosened armor gleam, all of them saw in dreams the sumptuous dwellings with doors broken down, and chambers full of velvet, and beds in which, on golden brocade, they would lay down virgins trembling with fear.

One night, Almazan had a dream.

In a foggy square he saw Christian Rosenkreutz, poorly dressed and holding a staff in his hand. On his back, attached by a strap, he had a leather bag, like someone who is about to make a long journey on foot. His face was sad and his ordinarily bright eyes were veiled. Around his neck he wore the emblematic cross in alchemical gold with a thick rose in the middle, and the cross and the rose, which were not shining, nevertheless gave off a kind of supernatural radiation.

On seeing Rosenkreutz, Almazan held out his arms and ran toward him. Then Rosenkreutz turned his head slightly to one side and considered him as one considers a stranger who inspires no sympathy, and started walking with a long stride, far away. He went very quickly. He had already climbed a high mountain. At the end of an infinite road, he met other men who seemed to be waiting for him, whose faces Almazan could not make out, but all of whom wore the same emblem of the rose and the cross around their necks.

Almazan made an immense effort to launch himself forward and climb that mountain, but he felt that his body was as heavy as lead. He could not move. Something warm, powerful and delicious mobilized him.

He woke up. Isabelle had her two arms wrapped around his shoulders and her body as stuck against his. He sensed the movement of her abdomen against him as she breathed, and the air was embalmed by the human perfume by which his life was intoxicated.

What a solid chain her thin wrists made! How light she was, and yet heavy! Oh no, the man who had that warm flesh on his would never climb the mountain.

He embraced her ardently. She laughed at waking up under his caresses. As the day was born they got dressed and went down toward the sea. Everything was calm, Isabelle had never been as cheerful. At the bottom of the garden there was a little sand that formed a beach. They arrived there, and Isabelle than unrolled the long cashmere veil in which she was wrapped and kicked off her slippers, saying that she wanted to bathe. When she was naked, she ran toward the sea—but she came back immediately and called to Almazan.

There was a formless mass that the tide had doubtless cast up on the beach, and which was still half-floating. It was a human form. The fish had devoured the face, but by the crimson of the garments, which the water had been unable to discolor, Almazan recognized that it was what remained of Tarfe.

Full of horror, in the nascent dawn, he was obliged to re-load the body on to the boat and row out in order to throw it overboard as far as possible from the sea.

From that day on, they no longer went down the stair-ways of the gardens, and no longer went toward the sea.

He strove not to think any more. He knew that he had fallen and was resigned to his decadence. The desire for Isa-belle's body tormented him perpetually. He loved her with all the more fury because he sensed something in her escaping him.

One day, he quit the great market hall in which the wounded had been accumulated and went home unexpectedly. Isabelle was not there. He called the maidservants. They stammered, they knew nothing. He threatened them uselessly.

Then, filled with anxiety, he set out in search of her. The sun was more implacable than ever and the very stones seemed to be suffering. He was surrounded by a group of emaciated people who were running through the streets de-manding the surrender of the city. They recognized him as a member of the Council of Twelve and shouted to him: "Bread! Bread for our children!"

He had great difficulty escaping them.

A little further on, he heard clamors, and gesticulating women pushed him to the center of a group on the threshold of a house.

A giant with the head of a brute was brandishing the fleshless body of a little girl. He lifted that waxen mummy with close eyes over the crowd. He was a butcher who had been accused days before of having killed his child in order to eat her. Seized with rage, he had just disinterred her in order to prove the falsity of those accusations. And as the witnesses to the scene recoiled, shouting, demanding the punishment of the calumniators, the butcher sat down on the ground and started weeping like a child.

Almazan skirted the ill-famed quarter that was at the foot of the Alcazaba. The hovels were swarming with an intense life. Bodes were shining with sweat. The dervish Massar had affirmed that the extraordinary heat was an advance sign of the end of the world. That had provoked an increase in carnal desire. Through open doors, people could be seen coupling, and Almazan noticed that the groans of pleasure resembled death-rattles.

A woman threw away her jewels and asked which way Mecca was, in order to pray. A group demanded silence. The trumpet of Israfil had, they said, sounded the first blast, which was the precursory sound. It was necessary to expect the second blast, that of consternation, and the third, that of resurrection. Someone shouted that Masihal Dadja, the false prophet, had appeared, and that he was King Ferdinand. Another pointed at the sun and said that it was about to be extinguished abruptly like a candle blown out by the breath of Allah. And a negro twisted the feet of a dog in order that it would complain in human language, for on the day of the last judgment, animals would be able to speak.

A creature with mad eyes fell to the ground in a crisis of hysteria and seized Almazan by the leg, He freed himself but, in spite of the disgust he experienced, he could not resign himself to going away. He recalled the descriptions that Isabelle had given him of parodies of the Sabbat in Aboulfedia's house. He recalled the false horror of which she gave evidence, the regret betrayed by her gaze and the palpitation of her breasts. Aboulfedia had once spoken to him of that promiscuity in lust that one found in the secret cults of ancient gods. Those who had once practiced those rites aspired to recommence. Perhaps Isabelle was allowing in one of those hovels among prostitutes, surrendering herself to men whose lasciviousness was multiplied by terror and hunger.

But where to find her?

Women made signs to him and then tried to retain him. He saw nothing around him but abject, sniggering faces.

Al Nefs, the angel of lust! I remembered Isabelle with her crimson chemise, when she had appeared to him in the gardens of Alexaras under a vault of golden citrus trees. Al

Nefs was not an angel with a beautiful face, he was a demon, he was a thousand demons with frightful forms, he was the power that attracts the human spirit downwards and causes its irremediable loss.

He fled, running. He went down streets. He stumbled over ordure that was no longer being swept way and formed large heaps.

Exhausted men, sitting on those dung-heaps, did not even turn to look at him. Bands of vultures were flying overhead and alighting in clusters on the desiccated palm-trees of the public squares.

He finally reached his house. Isabelle had returned. She had a firm, hostile expression. Almazan saw with surprise that she was hiding an ivory crucifix in a box, preciously. Was it that she had gone to look for in the streets of Malaga?

That question caused her anger to burst forth.

Was she not a Christian? Was she not a Spaniard? Anyway, she had been abducted by violence. There was a curse on Malaga and the people who defended it. She did not want to be confounded with the herd of young Muslim women when the city was pillaged. She wanted to live and she was taking her precautions.

"What precautions?" Almazan asked.

She replied that Isabelle de Solis would obtain all the safeguards she required from Don Gutierre de Cardenas, one of the heroes of the war. She had known him in Seville. It was easy for her to get a message to him by night via a turncoat.

Almazan declared that he was determined to prevent her sending that message.

Then Isabelle's indignation reached its peak.

"Because I've loved you, I'm linked to you forever, and after having been the slave of a king, I should become that of a Spanish soldier, merely to have the honor of sharing your fate? Is it my fault if you're a renegade, if you can't return to Spain? It wasn't necessary for you to poison the Archbishop of Seville back then. With me, there's no point in denying it. I saw your servant, whom you also killed, the night when I sought refuge in your house in Triana. I looked through the keyhole as I went away and I understood why you hadn't taken me when I offered myself to you. It appears that you're afraid of the dead!"

Almazan remained silent. So Isabelle believed that he had murdered his protector! Perhaps that was why she had loved him. He was disgusted with himself, as if he really had committed the crime.

He went up to the terrace of the house and he stood there for a long time. The sun was setting. In the garden, a woman and an old man were drawing stagnant water from the well, with difficulty. With a clatter of wings, vultures were flying over the Djouma mosque, where a muezzin was saying the evening prayer in a hoarse voice. The air was heavy and charged with frightful odors. Everywhere in the tortured city, despair filled souls.

And he understood that his amour, by virtue of a natural law, had also decomposed, along with the breath of dead wells and cadavers abandoned to the beasts.

The end of the world did not arrive. Far from being extinguished, the sun increased its ardor. The trumpets that sounded were not the trumpets of Istrafil but those of the guards on the towers summoning the Gomeres to the ramparts. For want of nourishment and water, many soldiers could no longer get up to fight, and the Spaniards were enlarging the breaches in the walls every day.

Hamet el Zegri decided to attempt a desperate sortie with all the valid warriors that remained to him. Massar had received assurances of victory from the dead. Weapons would break against the breasts of the believers, become invincible. His certainty was so great that he offered to march bareheaded before the combatants, crying the white banner of the Gomeres. The offer was accepted, and enthusiasm returned. The city had one last frisson of glory.

Massar was the first to fall, to a stone from a sling that broke his skull. The Gomeres fought with frenzy, but were overwhelmed by numbers. Hamet el Zegri sought death in vain. He came back covered in blood, desperate. Nevertheless, he was able to save the white banner.

Then it was as if the city emerged from lethargy. Delegates of the quarters and the trade guilds slid furtively toward the house of Ali Dordux. It was necessary to offer the surrender of the city. Ali Dordux had done it himself. He had already sent emissaries to King Ferdinand. He had proposed to open a gate to the city treacherously, to deliver Hamet el Zegri, his Gomeres and the renegades on condition that the inhabitants of Malaga would have their lives spared and their property would be respected. King Ferdinand had replied that city must be surrendered without conditions, that it would be pillaged, and that its inhabitants would be reduced to slavery.

When Almazan arrived at Ali Dordux's door, where the Council of Twelve was in session, he was refused entry. When he was astonished, and took as witnesses several notable merchants who were there, they turned away. He understood The Spaniards would doubtless treat him as a renegade, and in order not to have to defend him, the inhabitants of Malaga were hastening to abandon him.

He headed for the castle of Jebelfaro in order to join Hamet el Zegri. On the way, he saw people weeping in doorways. Others were praying with grim resignation, prostrate in ordure. They had just learned of the King of Spain's response.

But Almazan could not reach the castle. The vaulted gallery that departed from the Alcazaba and which led there had its heavy doors closed. Hamet el Zegri had locked himself in with his last Gomeres and no longer wanted to communicate with a city that was planning to surrender.

Almazan went home. Isabelle was waiting for him impatiently. She threw her arms around him. She was tender and full of ardor. She immediately drew him into the garden. There was a fisherman of the neighborhood who was also waiting for him. The fisherman was a brave man named Reduan whose forearm had been broken by a cannonball at the beginning of the siege and whom Almazan had treated and healed. He had just come to make Almazan party to an escape plan that he had conceived with two other fishermen.

They had noticed that large flat-bottomed mahones were perpetually furrowing the sea around the Spanish galleys, carrying troops to the shore, bringing water and provisions to the ships. Those mahones all had a red beacon light in the prow. Now, he possessed a mahone of the same form. As soon as night began to fall, he would embark on it. He would come along the coast and then, hooking a red light to his prow, he would row straight toward the Spanish fleet. He hoped, by favor of the darkness, to be confounded with the supply boats and get through the enemy line. Afterwards, he would deploy his sail and, if Allah protected him, he would reach Almunecar, or even the Moroccan coast.

He offered to take Almazan and Isabelle with him. The latter had already accepted, and a small box containing her effects was already prepared, as well as a casket containing her jewelry.

The immutable sun was about to disappear into the sea and a fiery breeze carrying dust and miasmas, was rising heavily. Reduan declared that the breeze would permit them to reach Africa during the night. It was agreed that in an hour, he would be at the bottom of the garden with his mahone.

That hour of waiting on the terrace of the garden passed very quickly. Isabelle placed her head on Almazan's shoulder several times, fixing him with her eyes of slightly ambered gold. She asked him to forget the bad words she had said to him. Was he not the only man that she had ever loved?

But her nerves were shaken. She was trembling, she had sudden alarms. She ran toward the entrance door of the house, opened it and looked out into the street anxiously.

Since the morning the cannons no longer resounded, either on the side of the besieged or the besiegers, and there as something sinister about that silence. At a given moment, Isabelle huddled against Almazan and begged him, in an infantile voice, to take her away and always keep her with him. Then, suddenly, she disengaged herself, wiped her eyes and listened once again for footfalls.

In the end, there was a splashing at the bottom of the garden and a whispered appeal. The mahone was there. Almazan took Isabelle's box and they went down. They had already taken their places beside the three men when Isabelle leapt ashore, lightly. She had forgotten the casket containing her jewels.

She disappeared into the laurels. She did not come back down. The fishermen became impatient. It was at the beginning of the night that it was necessary to attempt the chance, because there was a coming and going of boats then that ceased thereafter.

Almazan ran back up the stairways of the garden and then those of the house. He went as far as the roof terrace. He went back down. Everything was deserted. The casket of jewelry that he had noticed on the bed in the bedroom was no longer there.

Then, gripped by a presentiment, he went to the door to the street. It was only necessary to push it. That was the way that Isabelle had just fled. She had fled voluntarily, because if there had been violence, she would have uttered a cry that he would have heard. He recalled her last words of love. What a mystery the heart of a woman was!

He traversed the garden again. The three fisherman would take their chance without him. He embraced them. All would be well. The Prophet would guide them safe and sound to the Moroccan shore. He would stay. He did not merit liberty.

At the corner of the street of the armorers and the marketplace, Almazan was jostled by a man who was staggering.

"Ali Dordux has just yielded the Abderame gate," he said. "The Spaniards are in the city."

The man sat down on the ground, as if he were relating the story of an event. But he vomited a flood of blood and began to gasp.

Almazan heard a sound of footfalls and clinking weapons. He only just had time to slip into a doorway. Spanish soldiers, holding their arquebuses in the middle, were running toward the street of the jewelers.

There was a detonation, and then several others, and in all directions rumors resounded, cries of fright and the sound of axes striking the wood of doors.

Without knowing where he was going. Almazan went down the street of the armorers. His mind was blank. He was not suffering and he was not astonished. The misfortune of others was in conformity with his own misfortune.

Above him, on the balcony of a stone house, he heard a heart-rending scream. A semi-naked woman was trying to climb over the balustrade of the balcony and throw herself into the street. Her brown tresses were hanging down and her breast was crushed by the stone. As she was about to swing over, two men surged forth behind her. One seized her under the armpits, the other by the legs.

They repeated: "We won't do you any harm! On the contrary!"

There was a third who lifted a lantern, and by its light Almazan saw an expression of idiotic gaiety on his face.

A few paces further on a sort of colossus who was carrying an immense two-handed sword under his arm, was holding his neck, from which blood was running, and he shouted: "Bring him here. He's traversed my neck with his teeth. Since he's a wolf, I'll treat him like a wolf and nail him to his door. He'll serve as an example to others."

From the interior of the house someone threw him a thin child about fifteen years old, who struggled.

The man with the big sword drew a dagger from his belt, seized the child by the wrist twisted it, and with a single blow in the middle of the hand, he pinned him to the wood of the door.

At that moment, a mercenary wearing a Galician uniform came out of the house opposite. His eyes were shining in a cunning face. He was dragging three young women in nightshirts, attached to the same rope. He took two of his companions as witnesses, one of whom was in the process of loading a chest on to other's back.

"Look at these pagans. They're three sisters. Chained to the same halter like she-donkeys! No one can dispute that they're mine. I'll sell them at the price I wish. Here, feel what soft skins they have!"

He tore the silk gauze chemisette off the first and shoved her forward brutally in order that his companions could palpate the young body.

But he went sprawling four paces away, his belly opened. The man with the big sword, who turned round to look at the young women, received a dagger-thrust in the right eye, which caused him to collapse.

Almazan had sprung out of the shadows and he lashed out like a madman. What he had just seen had removed all prudence and all reason. Imprecations resounded. Swords whistled around him. He delivered other blows, and launched himself forward at random.

He climbed one street and descended another. The force that animated him made him strike and pass on. Through the darkness, howls of rage followed him. He perceived faces on all sides that all expressed the same bestial lust, arms open to seize women.

Confusedly, he thought: *Al Nefs! The demon of lust who doomed me! It's him who's expanding, him who's unleashing, with wings, mouths and tentacles, a multiple, monstrous, infinite life.*

He was fighting against Al Nefs. A strange power rendered him light, winged invincible.

Desperate appeals emerged from a house. He penetrated into it, leapt over cadavers and saw, by the light of a bronze lamp, a man crouching over a woman he was raping. He had a sparkling helmet and a bulbous breastplate. Almazan plunged his dagger into the base of his skull between the helmet and the breastplate, and, as a Spaniard who had followed him took

319

aim with an arquebus, he turned the blow aside and threw the bronze lamp in his face.

He resumed his course. In a small square he vaguely recognized an old man with a long white beard. He was standing on the threshold of his house, lifting up a little lantern and smiling as he repeated: "I knew it! It's the end of the world!"

Perhaps he had lost his reason. A cavalier traversing the square leaned over in his stirrups in order to examine him. He was wearing a supple coat of mail, a short violet velvet cape, and his features had something sad and grave about them.

"It's the end of the world!" the old man said to him, softly.

The cavalier shrugged his shoulders, and negligently struck the old man on the head with the shaft of his lance.

Almazan leapt on to the horse behind him, seized him around the body, unsaddled him and rolled on the ground while laboring his face with his weapon. Soldiers who emerged from a side-street launched forward and attempted to pierce his breast with the points of their halberds, but the horse reared up in their midst and Almazan resumed his course, followed by a clamor of rage.

Fires were lit here and there. He ran, followed by the footsteps of those pursuing him, through a world of hallucination and phantoms. He was carrying the light of vengeance in a fantastic city.

Fugitives emerged in a crowd from a mosque. He cut through them and also traversed a group of Spanish soldiers seized with panic, who shouted to the others: "Look out! Here come the knights of Santa Hermandad! They're putting incendiaries to death."

He stopped at a crossroads, struck by a name that he had heard in Isabelle's mouth. One soldier said to another: "It's Don Gutierre de Cadenas! He's come to plant the standard of Santiago and the banner of the kings on the tower of the Alcazaba."

He saw a young man with blue eyes go by in the midst of an escort, clad in white armor with a white decoration on his helmet that resembled the archangel Michael, such as he is represented in the illuminations of Christian missals.

He did not stop.

He was covered in blood and he had the sensation of carrying in his fist, with his chipped dagger, a sort of purificatory flame. He did not weary of striking. He sought to give the wound that saves men. It was the lust of the world of which he wanted to puncture the heart.

Arquebuses fired on his heels. He heard crossbow bolts whistling. He sometimes passed through the same streets, falling upon the same groups. Howls went up then: "There he is!" But he was pushed forward by an interior law stronger than his will.

He traversed sheaves of swords without being touched by them and he disappeared into the darkness when anyone tried to seize him, as if he were an animate parcel of that shadow full of fear.

And suddenly, at a crossroads, in front of him, near enough to touch, like the personification of the nocturnal lust that he was pursuing, a naked creature of extraordinary loomed up, splendid, whose skin was flamboyant, pink and white, under the glare of torches. Only a second! He had for a second a vision of beauty and pleasure, so moving that a sob shook him from head to foot. It was as if his soul capsized, and fell backwards Oh, the ideal was also shining in the matter of flesh! But only for a second.

Twenty voices cried: "Zorah! The most beautiful girl in Malaga! It's me who stripped her naked! Pass her to me!"

The torch-bearer displayed a scarred face with spoiled teeth behind the shoulder of Zorah, Zorah the chaste, who was the glory of Malaga for her poetic genius and her beauty. He was holding her by a handful of her hair and tipping her backwards slightly, which extended the curve of her breasts. And, as if from all directions, with laughter and grunts, men rushed upon Zorah. He waved his torch to the right and the left to defend his prey—but too late!

The circular flame illuminated four-footed animals, a herd of creatures half-wolf and half-pig, which were shoving one another, biting one another in order to wallow upon the fallen body of the young woman, to pollute her with their claws, their fur and their jowls.

"A voice cried behind Almazan: "It's him! It's necessary to take him alive! He has to be burned!"

He did not move. His dagger slipped from his hand. His winged force had abandoned him. He received a blow on the back of the neck. He felt someone throw his arms around his body and he was dragged away through the ordure of the street.

He only recovered consciousness the following evening. His hands and feet solidly bound, he was lying in a courtyard sealed by high walls. Some fifteen prisoners were alongside him. He recognized them as renegades. They told him what they knew about events.

Ali Dordux had surrendered one of the city gates, in exchange for liberty and the guarantee of their property for him and a few families. It was Don Gutierre de Cardenas who had entered Malaga first, but on another side, so it seemed that the place had been delivered by two treasons. The Gomeres, exhausted and starving, had forced Hamet el Zegri to surrender the castle of Jebelfaro. All day long, in the port, bishops and Castilian nobles had shared out the inhabitants reduced to slavery. It was also there that pyres had been set up and, in order to give the army a spectacle, renegades had been burned one by one. The courtyard where Almazan found himself was the one where they had been parked. He was one of the small number who remained, and who would doubtless be burned the next day.

He spent the night sitting up, too weak to remember, too desirous of death to be afraid.

The sun had been shining for a long time when the door of the courtyard opened. Men of the Santa Hermandad came in to fetch the prisoners. Almazan was finally untied. An officer pointed at him and said: "It's necessary to give that one something to eat. He's the famous Almazan. It appears that the tribunal of the Inquisition has just claimed him, and an escort of fifty cavaliers has been commanded to take him to Seville."

And the officer considered him curiously, as if considering a famous criminal.

Almazan had difficulty walking, and a soldier took him by the arm to sustain him. He could not eat the bread that he was given but he drank a little wine, which intoxicated him.

As if in a dream he traversed the captive city. The midday sun weighed upon his cranium and the smoke of pyres, in the motionless air, transported a reek of grilled flesh.

Alongside the Djouma mosque, Almazan went past a long file of young women. They were the children of the richest and noblest inhabitants of Malaga, who were being sent as a gift, as slaves, some to Jeanne of Naples, Ferdinand's sister, and the rest to the Queen of Portugal.

A little further on there was a dispute. A Castilian lord on horseback, covered in iron, had stopped in the middle of the street. His expression was savage, and an insensate flame was shining in his eyes. A cord wrapped around his right wrist was attached to the arm of a young woman whose was marching on foot beside him. She had a delightfully modest and astonished face. It was the pretty Jewess Rachel, the daughter of the money-changer Jeroboam. Jeroboam was on his knees, explaining that all the Jews of Malaga had just been ransomed by one of their coreligionists in Seville for twenty thousand gold doubloons. The sum had been paid to King Ferdinand that morning.

The Castilian lord responded that he had obtained full property in young Rachel, the previous evening, from the King himself, and that the donation was irrevocable. And as the father made as if to launch himself upon his daughter to retain her, the Castilian lord, pulling the cord, put her on the horse's back in front of him, crushed her breast against his breastplate, and departed at the gallop laughing madly.

But violence and injustice seemed to Almazan to be the norm of the world, the quotidian stone and cement of which men built their edifice. He had lost the faculty of indignation. Everything was in the order of things and contributed to unknown ends.

Nor did he make a movement when, on the road to Seville, one of his guards said, as he pointed to a closed litter preceded by a cavalier with a pennant on his lance: "Those are Cardenas' arms. That litter must contain the beautiful renegade of whom he's so fond, the one who procured him the glory of being the first to enter Malaga."

The litter had disappeared. From a little valley full of wild myrtles and palm trees a healthy odor of which Almazan had lost the memory suddenly rose: an odor that was no longer that of the putrescence of the dead. Only then did he weep.

XXI. The Torture

It was a crudely sculpted Christ, singular and horrible. It was nailed to the transversal beam of the ceiling of the immense, obscure room. But the nails were poorly driven in, the cross was adhering poorly to the bam, with the result that it shook, and seemed to be hovering in mid-air.

As the executioner's aides had tipped him on to his back against the rack and were in the process of attaching himself to it, Almazan had perceived that astonishing divine emblem above him and could not take his eyes off it.

The head was too large and disproportionate with the body, which was ctiolatcd and short, likc that of a child halted in his growth. The ignorant artist, doubtless involuntarily, had put an expression of stupidity in the physiognomy. The jaw was thick and square, the eyes were holes, holes full of dead shadow. The thorns of the crown were almost all broken, except for two, at each extremity, which gave the crown the aspect of a diabolical miter ornamented with horns, and gave the Christ floating beneath the ceiling, grating and quivering, the appearance of a bat in a dream, a bizarre night-bird ineptly crucified.

Almazan's widened gaze scarcely saw the things that surrounded him, the gripping tableau of the torture chamber about which he had thought for such a long, whose horrors had been described to him so minutely by his companions in the dungeon. He always came back to that Christ above him.

For the torture chamber was simpler and less terrible than the one he had imagined. Two resin torches on the wall did not permit him to see, at the back, the pulley that lifted patients by the arms and let them drop, breaking their joints, nor the iron pincers for tearing out the tongue, nor the mysterious instruments. The face of the executioner did not reflect a base cruelty but only a limited indifference, and a tic that the right eye had made him shake his head perpetually.

The four aides, with thickset bodies, gave the impression of four columns of matter supporting in that subterranean location the entire edifice of the prison. Like matter, they were taciturn and inanimate. And on the face of the inquisitor who had been handling his trial for months, he found the same faithful sadness, the same absence of hatred, the same desire for persuasion. That inquisitor, inconvenienced by his tall stature, doubtless timid by nature, who only drew his authority from his faith, was looking at him with the large attentive dog-like eyes. He was a dog, the executor of orders, who had been instructed to bring back a soul to the church.

Only the Christ was in anguish, up there, on which face a sculptor had once out the stigmata of stupidity.

The seconds were interminable. They were waiting for someone. Almazan's overexcited senses perceived the sound of the door turning, and, by the respect on faces, the movement of the executioner toward him and the inquisitor's respectful inclination before someone he could not see, Almazan understood, his heart began to beat more rapidly in his breast, and he began to be afraid.

Tomas de Torquemada, the Grand Inquisitor of Spain, had just come in, and was standing behind him.

It was not the prospect of torture that frightened Almazan, even less that of death. It was something that had flowed toward him in the air, something hideous and inexpressible, emanating from the being that had just entered behind him. He did not see him. Immobilized on the rack, he could not see him. But he knew that putting him to the question had been delayed because the Grand Inquisitor, Tomas de Torquemada, absent from Seville, had insisted on interrogating him personally.

Now he was there. Three paces away from him stood a little old man whose face he did not know but which he imagined sculpted in stone, an ecclesiastical Moloch who had sent so many men to death by pointing at them with his bony finger.

He remembered conversations he had had on his subject with Christian Rosenkreutz. What a mystery was the soul of that organizational genius, that precise and methodical workman, who had made the Catholic Church a machine of suspicion, of poisoning, and of burning! The machine was perfect, since no one, in all of Spain, could work on a discovery, study the sciences or approach philosophical problems, without being pursued as a heretic. What a mystery that a man could possess, with an absolute faith in his truth, such an absence of pity, such a perfect hatred of thought.

Rosenkreutz had spoken the truth. Men of elevated spirituality are incarnated in certain periods to preach philosophies and found religions. They were those named sages or prophets: Buddha, Plato, Jesus, Mohammed. But there were others who had given themselves the mission of driving humankind backwards in its progress, others who had an abstract love of evil, of entirely pure evil, which is the negation of intelligence: Nero in Rome, Genghis Khan in Mongolia, Hakem in Egypt. And this one, Tomas de Torquemada, was the most complete incarnation of intelligence lucidly organized to destroy the intelligence of which it was born. He was Satan, the Prince of Evil, in the uniform of a Dominican, with the aspect of an ascetic old man.

Almazan sensed a misery greater than that of the cords that bound him and the imminent torture. A delirious fear, a fear of the entire soul, caused a sweat of agony to flow over his brow.

Facing him, the inquisitor with the dog-like face opened his mouth as if he were about to yap. The executioner gave the impression of making him a sign, blinking his eye toward the Christ on the ceiling.

Then a voice spoke, atonal, dull, coming from afar, as if it were resonating through wadding.

That voice from another world said: "Almazan, you have been convicted on the crime of apostasy and condemned to be burned alive. Nevertheless, you can repent, and your punishment would be changed to perpetual imprisonment, for the

Church is merciful. Make therefore the complete confession that has so far been demanded of you in vain. Tell everything that you know about the order of heretics known as the Rose Cross, their relationships with the Order of Alumbrados, which we have succeeded in extirpating from Spain, and, above all, inform us as to the personality of a certain Christian Rosenkreutz, a lapsed monk from a convent in Germany who has long sojourned in the Orient and who is the founder of the impious society to which you belong."

Almazan remained silent. Long months of captivity had broken his organism. He tried to respond, but could not do it.

The voice resumed, but it became even more distant.

"Be humble, Almazan. It is your pride that has doomed you. Do not be obstinate in impiety and apostasy. It is in your interest for you to speak, and even in the interest of your companions who are in Granada and who will soon be in our hands, for God wishes the triumph of the Holy Catholic Church. Speak of your own free will, or you will be subject to the third torture of the question and will depart in the midst of suffering without having the merit of your confession."

The third torture! Almazan knew that the Council of the Supreme Audience had, on the insistence of the Pope, decided that the question could only be administered once. Torture varied in cruelty. But the third, that of fire, was far more terrible than that of the rope or that of water, which were ordinarily given. And all his strength vanished.

Yes, as the muffled voice said to him, it would be better for him to speak of his own free will. Speak? What had he to say? He did not know where Christian Rosenkreutz might be at the moment. Give names? The Spaniards would doubtless have taken Granada tomorrow. They would burn as dangerous heretics a few inoffensive scholars, a few disinterested sages devoted to the cultivation of the mind.

He shook his head imperceptibly.

There must have been a gesture behind him, for the executioner blinked, and the sad and faithful visage of the inquisitor filled with a desolate expression.

Rapidly, an aide pulled from behind a pillar a brazier, which he pushed to the extremity of the rack, from which Almazan's feet protruded. Another took his shoes off. A third approached holding a pot full of oil, with which, with a long brush, he coated him to the calves.

"One last time," said the voice, with a sigh.

Almazan closed his eyes.

He opened them a second later and his pupils capsized beneath his eyelids. Then he howled, in order to relieve himself by howling. The brazier, slowly brought nearer to his feet, reddened the flesh by degrees, and then made it swell and sizzle. Almazan had just entered into the red realm of limitless pain.

Oh, the combat he engaged was more terrible than the one he had attempted to deliver to an entire army in rut in the streets of Malaga. It was a combat in which one fought immobile, nailed to a rack, with an infernal Christ above one's head as a consolation, and in which one had as an adversary the revolt of one's own body.

He was already vanquished. There was too much suffering. He would talk. The executioner's aide pulled the brazier away slightly.

"Your pride is boundless," said the voice, in which there as a vague mildness, a slight triumph. "Return to yourself, Almazan. It's your salvation that we desire. Speak. You will not betraying anything, for we know. The Church knows everything that the thought of rebellious men nurtures against her. I can tell you the rules of the Order and the belief that it pretends to transmit. To do good. To learn the science of numbers and the unity of matter and the correspondences of the three universes. To know that the soul is reincarnated. To seek perfection through ecstasy. Ecstasy, isn't that so? That of the Greek philosophers, the Ismailites, the Albigensians, the Vaudois, of all the heretics. You can see that I'm informed. But I want to hear all that from your mouth. Speak. You're going to speak."

Almazan saw the brazier drawing nearer to his feet. The executioner had stimulated it with an iron poker. The skin became as white as parchment, sizzled and swelled again, and split.

But Almazan's suffering did not remain in his feet. It moved. It rose along his legs, it bathed him, it ran through him, it resonated noisily in his brain, it vibrated delicately in every one of his hairs.

And increasingly, the executioner, in front of him, blinked and shook his head, and seemed to be designating, above him, the grating Christ that was leaning a stupid face over his pain.

Almazan understood the exactitude of that symbol. Lying in the low room in the vacillating light of two torches in the midst of executioners and inquisitors, he was the suffering, lacerated man, a prisoner of the Church, without the hope of human pity, and he only had above his head, suspended from the vault of dogma, through the tenebrous space of the faith, the visage of the Prophet, ridiculously travestied, from whose visage the portion of the sun had been extracted, of which a divine caricature had been made.

The voice of the being, still veiled, had a quiver.

"Speak, since I wish it. I am just as good as you, perhaps better. For you do not observe the rules of the Order. They prescribe chastity. Now, are you not doomed in the eyes of your brothers? The Rose and the Cross! They are far away from you. You will never find them again. But there is still time. You can reenter the Holy Church."

Doubtless the executioner's aide who was holding the brush paraded it over his legs, for Almazan's pain increased. He was burning entirely. Every one of his nerves seemed autonomous and brought him a separate and particular suffering. His thought, however, remained active and made him see, with a strange clarity, the details of the things that were surrounding him.

He noticed that the executioner's aides and the executioner himself had their hoods thrown back over their shoulders instead of wearing them on their heads, according to custom. He examined a part of the inquisitor's face near his right eye, and was able to distinguish all kinds of memories of his childhood in the smoke of the brazier twisting in spirals in front of him. And at the same time, like a thousand vibrations of living snakes, the pain palpitated within him.

But it was too much. He had understood the mystery of the inflexions of the voice, what the man behind him wanted. It was not names, precise indications, in order to strike other victims. No, it was not a matter of that. What he wanted was to obtain a moral abjuration, the renunciation of the faith higher than all religions, the cult of the truth, that Almazan had glimpsed.

The suffering was too great. A man could not resist it with his feeble strength. Abjure? Make confessions? Well, so be it! He was about to abjure, to say everything that he knew and even more, on condition that that flame was extinguished and he was then left to rest in peace. He was ready to do penance, to beg for forgiveness on his knees, to embrace the knees of the invisible old man.

The coals of the brazier, and the oil, and the burned flesh made a smoke so thick that it extended in a sheet above him, and hid the image of the Christ. And suddenly, instead of that Christ, Almazan contemplated an extraordinary scene.

In a landscape that he had never seen, perhaps under the ruins of a temple, at the limits of a desert, three men dressed in the Oriental style were sitting on the sand, and Christian Rosenkreutz was standing before them. He was about to speak. One of the three men showed him the direction of the Occident, and he appeared to be saying: "Go, be the bearer of the truth!"

Almazan contemplated their calm visages beneath their turbans and a sky behind them of an unusual blue. Rosenkreutz made a sign with his hand, started walking—and that was all. The smoke dissipated for Almazan's eyes.

He knew what that scene was. Rosenkreutz had related it to him. It was near the ancient Palmyra, in the ruins of the temple where Apollonius of Tyana had once spent many years in meditation. The good and wise men who held the secrets of knowledge had made Rosenkreutz come from his German convent and had descended themselves from distant lamaseries in Tibet in order to charge him with transmitting in the Occident a part of the eternal truth to those who were worthy of it. And he, Almazan, was one of those. He had been chosen. But he had been chosen mistakenly. For the pleasure of the body he had quit the Brothers of the Rose Cross in Granada. And now, to escape the pain of the body, he was about to deny the truth in which he believed. Was that possible?

Almazan's flesh was sizzling, with a frightful little noise. The odor of flesh was unbearable. The inquisitor, discomfited, turned away, trying to hide his disgust. And the executioner, with his tic, designated the Christ on the ceiling untiringly.

But Almazan no longer cared about that pitiless Christ, nor the men who were around him, nor the torture of his flesh. Like a vapor drunk by the early morning sun, his soul was detached and rose toward the light of a higher thought.

And doubtless the radiation of martyrdom must have illuminated his visage, for very close to him, he heard the voice speak again, but now somewhat anguished, and coming from so very far away.

"Abjure your faith! They claim that their ecstasy is the same as that of the Christian mystics, and that at a certain height, the verities are confounded. But they lie! Abjure! Abjure!"

And the voice had a desperate tone. Then Almazan succeeded in turning his head slightly, and beside his own, as close as that of a brother, he saw another head looking at him. It was the head of the man who had made autodafés of thousands of books in Salamanca and Toledo, who had burned Jewish rabbis because they studied the Kabbalah, and Catholic scholars because they thought and expressed their thought, the head of the enemy of the Spirit, the little bald and fragile head, the immense receptacle of evil in its pure state.

And then he saw, for the first time, the bright and miraculously empty eyes, the eyes devoid of hatred, devoid of pity, devoid of pride and devoid of desire, of Tomas de Torquemada. Perhaps there was a glimmer of surprise in the distance of the pupils.

But Almazan did not see the face around those immense eyes. He did not distinguish the marble features to which they were appended. He did not see anything. He was in the presence of a void.

In that void, in the empty light of those eyes, he fixed his gaze of a martyrized man, whose soul remained invisible, like a sword a thousand times sharper than that of the archangel. The mysterious thrust gave the impression of being lost in the emptiness, but it penetrated very deeply into a subtle region in which wounds do not heal and survive those who have received them.

Then Almazan made, with all the force that remained to him, with his desiccated lips, the movement of spitting in disgust, and the darkness weighed upon him.

"He will be burned at the next autodafé," said the voice of the old man, suddenly heavy, full of an infinite sadness, while he drew away slowly, sustained by the inquisitor, as if it were his own life that had been consumed by the torture.

In the corridors of the keep a human rag with feet charred to the bone was transported, and was laid down in his dungeon with the respect he merited.

And later, when consciousness began to dawn in Almazan's mind, he heard an indescribable orchestra of delight.

Heavy as the walls were, ardent as the fire was with its power to burn and destroy, captivating as the promises of the tempter were, he had triumphed over the weight of captivity, the devouring force of the flame, and the word that halts the impetus of the runner. He was victorious.

XXII. The Autodafé

In the roseate light of the dawn, the door of the Santa Casa opened and the bells of Seville, which were ringing at full tilt, stopped at the same time. The crowd that filled the streets and was suspended from the windows of houses shivered and fell silent momentarily. The mysterious sadness that hovers over human festivals appeared heavier, more anguishing, as if the desolate souls of all the Sundays of the year were concentrated in that dawn.

And the cortege was organized with a solemn slowness. Almazan was clad in the San-Benito of yellow wool on which flames were crudely painted, and the ridiculous figures of demons. He wore on his head the rounded pyramidal bonnet known as a coroza, marked with a red cross. As his feet and legs, as far as the knees, were nothing but vast purulent wounds, he was carried on a stretcher by two Familiars of the Inquisition. To his right stood the Dominican charged with assisting him and obtaining a belated confession. But as the Dominican was aware of the vanity of his effort, he proffered his invitations to repent mechanically, without thinking about it.

"Repent, my brother, repent! Confess to me!" he said, in a low voice, as if he were chanting those formulae for an absent sinner.

The sound of horses, the indistinct murmur of the people, the groans of a few of the condemned, the appeals of the Familiars charged with ordering the cortege, the tread of the fraternities encumbering the neighboring streets, the friction of banners and weapons made a rumor both menacing and triumphant. But Almazan sensed in his soul a tranquility so great that it seemed to him that no tempest could trouble it.

He saw pass by the Charbonniers with their long pikes; the Guards attached to the tribunal of the Holy Office, black from head to toe, with black sword-hilts and stirrups; the fraternity of Saint Peter the Martyr bearing a white cross; the Dominicans bearing a black cross; the Procurator Fiscal preceded by a red cross; the Brothers of Mercy, those of the Holy Trinity, the mendicant monks, the Carmelites, the Benedictines; the Franciscans; the Augustinian Recollects; the Grandees of Spain: the functionaries of the Inquisition; and those who had come without the right, with somber garments and a great candle, driven by pride to figure as processionaries in that cortege of death.

The condemned only numbered thirty. Jaundiced creatures, emaciated by the fetid air of prisons, beneath the enormous yellow coroza, their eyes bulging in terror, rare or despair, their limbs dislocated by torture, they had the appearance of abominable puppets emerged from a realm of nightmares. Those who had repented under torture joined their hands and turned hypocritically grateful visages toward the Dominican crucifix. The courageous impenitents hoped for death ardently and sought the librating pyre with their eyes.

Behind Almazan, between two Familiars, was a woman from Triana, young and rather beautiful, who was about to be burned for witchcraft. She had heavy and mobile breasts that were visible under her robe and an animal face that caused the soldiers of Santa Hermandad to quiver with desire. One of them dropped his halberd, which made a metallic din on the pavement.

The woman from Triana, as if she were responding to an appeal, raised herself up, twisting, convulsed with hysteria and in a heart-rending voice, never extended, extrahuman and singularly sonorous, cried: "Jesus Christ! Jesus Christ! Save me!"

And the mystery of the sound of the voice troubled those who heard it to the point that many of them looked to the right and the left to see whether Jesus Christ might appear.

Someone ran forward to plunge a gag into the mouth proffering the invocation. But at that moment, at a signal given by the mastery of the Chapel Royal, all the Orders, all the fraternities and all the processionaries intoned the *Miserere*. The cortege set forth.

Insults and vociferations burst forth as Almazan passed by. Fists were waved at him. There were women who tried to reach him, spitting in his direction. The soldiers of the Santa Hermandad contained the people with the shafts of extended lances. A child succeeded in passing between them and pricked his cheek with a sharp stick.

That was because, for the people, Almazan was worse than a heretic, or even a sorcerer. He was the man who had declared several times during his trial that if he had served Abul Hacen in Granada and aided the Moors to defend Malaga, it was because he estimated Arab civilization far superior to that of Spain, where the intolerance of the Church and the cupidity of kings extended a shadow that grew denser every day. He glorified himself for having defended, under the aegis of the Crescent, the arts, philosophy and science. He was a renegade, and proud of it,

Almazan considered with surprise the faces of so many furious men, and it seemed to him that those faces were not unknown to him. He wondered where he had seen them before, and noticed that they all had a certain kinship, a family appearance, that they resembled one another. He had seen somewhere, recently, that square jaw, that thick neck and those eyes that hatred filled with darkness. He remembered. Those men resembled the Christ fixed to the ceiling of the torture chamber. They were turned toward him with the same blind stupidity.

He went forth followed by the clamors of a hundred thousand Christs as avid as the other for suffering. But now, there was no more smoke from the brazier, there was no more temptation to betrayal. The sun of the dead had just risen, dissipating within him dread, the desire for vengeance and remorse. The people could no longer frighten him. He even felt pity for them.

He was internally exalted in the midst of the tumult. He reviewed the past since the days of his youth. His life had been thus: he had cherished the spirit and had fallen into the trap of the flesh. He had delivered the battle that every man must deliver within himself, and he had been defeated. But what did it matter? The experience had still been acquired by his soul. There would be other lives to live and he would triumph in those. He was about to go through the door of fire that led there,

At the corner of a street, the part of the cortege in which he was stopped. A plank of a cart that he had not seen in front of him had given way and the books piled in the cart had spilled out into the street and were blocking it.

They were Arabic and Hebrew books that had been condemned, like him, to be burned publicly. Familiars of the Inquisition, dropping their ebony and silver staffs, picked them up in armfuls and threw them in a heap into the cart. Almazan distinguished delicate illuminations, characters that expert calligraphers had spent years reproducing on the parchment. He read the titles on the gilded bindings:

The Alchemy of Happiness by Ghazali. *The Guide to Those Gone Astray* by Maimonides. Ah! The poet Attar, the mystic Ibn Arabi and Khayyam, and all the rest! It was a little of their thought that was accompanying him through the Moorish streets of Catholic Seville, in the promenade toward death; and he thanked them all internally.

At a window of a new house, white against the shadow of the massive architecture, there was the silhouette of a woman, in the middle of a frame of gilded gauze and Byzantine velvet with mauve reflections. The unique glance that Almazan cast in that direction permitted him to see the arms of the Cardenas family on the fronton of the door and the silhouette of the woman leaned forward slightly, and the veil of silver lamé fabric that parted like two white petals, and an oval of tender flesh between the petals, like the spring pulp of the flower, and irises in which the gold was rusted, misted and extinct.

A single glance! His candle scarcely quivered in his hand and the pyramidal coroza, the grotesque bonnet of the hardened impenitent, barely trembled on his head.

337

And in the human vociferations, the brazen clamor of the bells that had resumed ringing, Almazan perceived a murmur of syllables that no mouth articulated, that no conscious soul formulated mentally, but which were nevertheless pronounced:

"I have been the terrestrial perfume of your life. When your spirit wanted to launch forth toward the heavens, I caused it to fall back into the bed where you enjoyed me. I have been your pleasure and your pain, the indecent form of the human body, the apparition under the citrus trees, the mysteries of the gardens of the Alhambra, the poison of nights inflamed by the war. I desired so much to repose in your arms! Something in you elevated me and I desired to destroy it. Nothing has been able to take away from me the desire for sumptuous fabrics, rare substances and secret debauchery, and I was sad because my breath did not succeed in tarnishing the diamond of your spirit. You have been the best of what I have had and yet I don't know whether I loved you. Adieu, my love!"

Almazan perceived the Quemadero on the Plaza de San Fernando, on to which the cortege emerged. It was a large square scaffold from which crosses emerged, pillories, gibbets and stakes, which enclosed in its masonry flanks a host of executioners, with nails for crucifying, ropes for flagellating, swords for slashing wrists, and faggots to aliment the pyres.

Around the Quemadero the masses were coming to an end. On the improvised altars, silver candelabra and golden pyxes shone, and there were metallic flashes, stones on the sparkling surplices and symbolic gems on the miters of bishops.

The faces of Dominicans could be seen, exalted by the ardor of prayer. Some had been there for two days, sometimes striking the ground with their foreheads, begging God to save the souls of those who were about to be burned. And there was a tragic and sincere dolor in their features, as if they sensed that the cause was desperate and lost in advance. A great green banner with black crepe had been planted in the ground to attest the mourning of the Church because of the sinners who were about to die impenitent. But in that ecclesiastical despair no forgiveness was visible.

Stages covered with monks and functionaries of the Holy Office surrounded the Quemadero. But there was a sense in which the entire square, with its altars, its torture stakes and its multitude of spectators was orientated toward the broad balcony of the house of the Duke of Medina Coeli. There stood King Ferdinand and Queen Isabella, surrounded by the Court, and the condemned filed before them.

Almazan was able to contemplate the brilliant Queen Isabella, with her broad, short neck, her massive stature, her plain and olive-tinted face, like the somber, arid land of Spain from which she extracted gold avidly, where she paraded iron, the feminine symbol of the tyrannical, avaricious, destructive and fanatical race. And the Christ of the torture chamber was once again in that inanimate face, which watched its subjects tortured and burned with such perfect serenity.

Facing the royal balcony was a stage higher than the others. And on that stage, surrounded by a triple row of halberdiers dressed in white, in the middle of the Procurator Fiscal, the members of the Tribunal of the Holy Office, above an entire superimposition of dignitaries, functionaries, commissioners, noble Familiars, Alcaides, there was a dominant throne. On that throne was seated the Grand Inquisitor, Tomas de Torquemada, very small beneath his miter and his pleated camail, like a microscopic drop of violet poison at the summit of the magnificent edifice of the Church.

The Grand Inquisitor looked at the ground when Almazan passed by. His miter cast a shadow. There was no face.

The mortuary and religious formalities unfolded with a sacred slowness.

The kings made the oath of fidelity to the Church. The bearer of the Holy Gospels made the tour of the Quemadero three times, preceded by the bearer of the standard of the Faith. A majordomo of the Fraternity of Saint Peter the Martyr took the sentences of the condemned from an ebony casket.

339

The latter listened on their knees. There were more masses, predications, and abjuration.

And suddenly, a supernatural silence descended over the crowd in the square and in the streets that ended there, which was as breathless as the human throats. The mothers lifted their children over their heads to show them the punishment of sinners, and the majority of the men must have desired to be executioners in order to nail and to cut, in order to transmit pain.

For the moment had come for the executioners to nail hands to pillories, to sever wrists with double-edged swords, to strangle with garrotes.

An explosion of unlimited joy, a delirium of cries, rose up to the heavens and prevented the moans of the tortured from being heard, with the result that only their contortions of pain were seen, and those grimaces were more terrible by virtue of their appearance of silence.

A single cry was perceptible, a single cry going far away, as if borne by strange wings. It was the last cry of the witch of Triana, whose gag had been removed.

"Jesus Christ! Jesus Christ! Save me!"

And the apparition of Jesus was manifest then for many eyes, and Almazan, whose turn had come to climb the Quemadero in order to be attached to the stake of the pyre, thought of the other Christ, the one that did not receive in holocaust the smoke of grilled flesh, the Essene clad in white who, according to tradition, had cried at the moment of dying: "O my Father, thou hast abandoned me!"

Beside him, the discouraged Dominican repeated, mechanically: "Repent! Confess to me!"

The executioners seized Almazan from the hands of the Familiars, hoisted him up on seeing the state of his feet, and suspended him by means of cords with enough care that he did not have to put his weight on his legs, thus sparing him an atrocious final dolor.

Almazan's heart broke for that unique mark of pity that the furious earth brought him. He would have liked to thank the executioners, but they were already crouching down some distance away to watch him burn, ignorant of their own pity.

Then, as if he were seeking a point of support before launching himself into the unknown, Almazan darted a glance at the crowd that was fixing him with its thousands of gazes.

And in those few seconds, in the midst of the extraordinary landscape of flame that the Plaza de San Fernando formed, while the pyres commenced to crackle within the flanks of the Quemadero, he finally saw the face of a man in the hallucinatory circle of evil Christs.

It was Rosenkreutz, such as he had seen him in his dream in Malaga, with a sack attached to his back by straps and a staff in his hand. He had come. Man did not abandon man. He was in the first row, and made him a sign.

Narrow columns of smoke rose up around Almazan like black candles. The stages, the windows and the balconies, and the aligned cavaliers, took on a strangely geometrical appearance around him. He was still looking at Rosenkreutz, who was waving his staff.

He was about to depart. He would reach France, and then Germany, where he had been born. He would stop there, wherever an alchemist's lamp was shining, would knock on doors in ghettos where old rabbis were poring over the mysteries of books. Everywhere, he would explain the secrets of the Kabbalah, he would extend the fraternity of the intelligent and the pure.

Toward the sky, abruptly charged with a tide of blood, like a nocturnal breath, rose a black smoke full of sparks. The human swell, the pillories, the magnificent kings, the houses and their miradors, the churches with their menacing towers and the sun setting in crimson, everything that was the varied and multiform tableau of the universe, disappeared from Almazan's sight.

It was very little. He died tranquil. The invincible spirit continued its route.

CHRISTIAN ROSENKREUTZ AND THE ROSICRUCIANS

The Life and Travels of Christian Rosenkreutz

In the south of France there are certain regions covered with pines that are periodically ravaged by fires. The pines often grow again, and one sees, a few years later, where there was nothing but calcined dust, a new forest of resinous trees. But sometimes, as if the power of the fire had descended into the very source of the seeds, the hill once covered by tresses of pines remains bare and sterile. It happens then that at the summit of the bare hill, a unique tree springs forth, strangely vivacious, which rises up alone, as if to attest the lost presence of a dead forest.

Thus, of the great Albigensian forest, cut down, burned and reduced to dust, only one man subsisted, who was to perpetuate he doctrine while transforming it. Like the solitary pine on the hill, he plunged his vigorous thought into the human soil of his time and caused it to float in the blue sky of the centuries with the foliage of books.

From the Albigensians issued, in the middle of the thirteenth century, the wise man who has been known under the symbolic name of Christian Rosenkreutz, and who was the last descendant of the German family of Germelshausen.[32] On this

---

[32] Author's note: "Almost all those who have studied the Rosicrucians have—at least in my opinion—fixed the birth of Christian Rosenkreutz in the middle of the fourteenth century. Some have even placed it in the fifteenth." He had, of course,

point there are no longer any precise details, but only a tradition. No written text exists, no historical proof. How could there be? So great was the desire to suppress the history that, not only were the bodies of the heretics destroyed, but also the stones that had sheltered them and the documents that might have been the receptacle of their thought.

In any case, those heretics understood quickly that they only had a chance of subsisting by enveloping themselves in obscurity and hiding under false names, only corresponding by means of cryptographic writings. We can only recover their history under the vestment of legend. But an individual who left such a profound trace, after such an obscure life so devoid of marvelous actions and miracles, cannot have been created by legend. Christian Rosenkreutz is as real as Jesus or the Buddha, whose more illustrious features are cited, but who have scarcely more historical foundation.

The Albigensian doctrines had spread in a fragmentary fashion in the north of France, the Low Countries and Germany. Fleeing families had traveled over the roads. Solitary men had fled, as beggars, the sunlit land where they were henceforth accursed. Many would die, but some would attain distant regions where there are no more vines, where the rivers are more impetuous and the sun less warm. There were some who reported what they had heard down there, in the low houses sheltered by the ramparts of Toulouse or in the shadow of Montségur, which still burned in their heart. And a few were

---

located it in the fifteenth century himself in *La Luxure de Grenade*.

Germelshausen, about which the author offers no comment, is a fictitious village featured in a story of that title by Friedrich Gerstäcker, which was once caused to sink into the ground by a curse but reappears once every hundred years. The young protagonist who happens to be there on the day in question falls in love with a girl from the town but is inevitably separated from her forever. Magre might have appropriated the title without knowing what the story was about.

343

understood. Little nuclei of Albigensians formed in the north around the preaching of a thin, slightly bronzed man whose face as reminiscent of that of the Saracens. Thus, the seeds thrown by the wind went to germinate in the lands to which hazard carried it.

Under the influence of an Albigensian traveler, the doctrine traversed mountains bristling with firs and flourished in the region of Rhoen on the frontier of Hesse and Thuringia. In the heart of the forest of Thuringia stood the Schloss of Germelshausen. The lords were of grim humor, half-brigands and their Christianity was mingled with pagan superstitions. They spent their time making war on their neighbors, and they did not disdain setting ambushes on the roads in order to rob travelers. They rendered a worship of sorts to a stone divinity that was worn away, and whose origin was unknown. It must once have been the fruit of some distant pillage Perhaps the statue was a Hellenic Minerva. They had set it up in the courtyard of the schloss beside the door of the chapel.

It was the middle of the thirteenth century. Germany had just been ravaged by the Dominican fanatic Conrad of Marburg, an envoy of Pope Gregory IX. The Dominican Tors was continuing his work. He was accompanied by a one-eyed layman named John, who claimed that his one eye had received the faculty of recognizing a heretic or a good Christian at first glance.[33] Almost all those who entered the visual ray of that terrible eye were marked with the sign of heresy.

Doubtless it was sufficient for him to glimpse, through its rocks and firs, the towers of the Schloss of Germelshausen to know by the color of its stones that it sheltered a nest of heretics. Perhaps a little of the force of the eternal spirit radi-

---

[33] Magre undoubtedly found the account of the exploits of Conrad Tors and one-eyed John in H. C. Lea's *History of the Inquisition*, where Lea cites Tors' invention of the "Luciferan heresy" as a significant step in the gradual expansion of the Dominicans into hunting imaginary Satanist witches as well as real heretics.

ated from the ancient statue standing in the courtyard. The landgrave Conrad of Thuringia, who had razed the small village of Wilnsdorf, decided the destruction of the schloss. He endeavored to besiege it several times at intervals of a few years. The schloss finally fell and the entire family of Germelshausen, who had rallied to the mystical doctrine of the Albigensians, who practiced its austerities, and believed in reincarnation and the consolamentum that saves reincarnations, was put to death at the moment of the final assault.

The youngest son, then aged five years, was carried through the burning schloss by a monk who had chosen a domicile in the chapel and had been struck by the marvelous intelligence of which the child gave evidence. That monk, that ascetic inhabitant of the chapel of Germelshausen, was an Albigensian perfectus from Languedoc, and he was the one who had been the family's instructor. He took refuge in a nearby monastery, where breaths of heresy had already penetrated.

It was in that monastery that that the last descendant of the Germelshausens, who was to be known under the name of Christian Rosenkreutz, was raised and educated. He learned Greek and Latin and formed a fraternal group with four other monks of the community, who resolved to devote themselves to the search for the truth. They formed the project of going to seek that truth in the source from which it had always departed, in the distant Orient.

Two of them set forth, walking: Christian Rosenkreutz, who was then fifteen years old; and one of the four monks, whom the *Fama Fraternitas* calls Brother P.A.L.[34] The pretext

---

[34] Author's note: "The *Fama Fraternitas* is an anonymous document that appeared in the seventeenth century. It is a puerile *image d'Épinal*, which summarizes all that was known in that epoch about the authentic Rosicrucians." The manifesto in question was first published in 1614 and was followed a year later by the supplementary *Confessio Fraternitatis*. An incomplete allegorical account of *The Chymical Wedding of Chris-*

345

of their voyage was a pilgrimage to the Holy Sepulcher. Their real goal was to reach a center of initiation, about the location of which they must have had precise information.

Brother P.A.L. died on the island of Cyprus, to which the hazards of the voyage had brought the two companions. Young Christian continued his route, doubtless because of the indications he had, and headed for Damascus. He took that direction because the link with the Orient, which was about to break, still subsisted. Just as Apollonius had learned from the Pythagorean groups among whom he lived the exact location of the "abode of the wise men," Christian Rosenkreutz knew, doubtless via the perfectus who had instructed the Germelhausens, that Damascus was the road of initiation.

It cannot have been easy to pass from the Christian kingdom of Cyprus into the land of the infidels. But for the man who sincerely seeks the truth, all religions are similar, and when he quit the Christian lands, Rosenkreutz put on the costume and the appearance of a Muslim pilgrim.

Damascus was then under the domination of the Mamelukes. All the scholars and poets of Persia had flocked there before the invasion of the Mongols of Hulugu. The destruction of Bagdad and Nishapur and the annihilation of their universities and libraries caused the intellectuals of the Orient to believe in a kind of decline of thought.[35] Rumors were running around of the end of the world. There had been violent earthquakes in Syria and a rain of scorpions in Mesopotamia. The Mongols occupied Persia, and the horizon was scrutinized

---

tian Rosenkreutz (1616) is generally attributed to the theologian Johann Valentin Andreae, who might have written all three. Magre's account is based on the first two documents but adds his own embellishments, in the interests of inserting Rosenkreutz into his syncretic history of magic and mysticism.
[35] Hulugu Khan's Mongols sacked Bagdad in February 1258, destroying the great library there and massacring approximately a hundred thousand people, leaving the city depopulated.

from the ramparts of Damascus with the apprehension of seeing their advance guard appear.

How astonished Rosenkreutz must have been in the city of three hundred mosques, in the midst of the erudite men of Oriental literature! What discoveries for a young man avid for learning! He read Maimonides' *Guide for the Perplexed*, Ghazali's *Alchemy of Happiness* and Mac'oudi's *Golden Meadows*. He heard the verses of Omar Khayyam recited, and strove to understand his treatises on algebra and his commentary of Euclid. He discussed astronomy with the disciples of Nazir al-Din. He meditated the Masnavi, the sacred book of Sufism and marveled at finding therein the mystical pantheism of his spiritual fathers the Albigensians. How barbaric Germany must have appeared in the bosom of the intellectual effervescence by which he was surrounded! In the presence of the great Arab civilization that was coming to its end, he understood more fully the necessity of his mission to conserve its spirit and transmit it to the men of his race.

After several years of study in Damascus, when he had acquired the greatest sum of knowledge possible for a man who has no other goal but education, he thought about a higher knowledge. He was then sufficiently mature to acquire it. The enigmatic name of the place for which he headed has been guarded by tradition. It is Damcar in Arabia, which doubtless designates a monastery in the sands, where a center of initiation was then found, and perhaps still is. Damcar was for him what the abode of the wise men as for Apollonius. He remained there for a few years, and then he went into Egypt, traversed the Mediterranean and reached Fez.

Under the reign of Abu Said Othman, in the city of six hundred fresh water fountains, which was then in its full splendor, there was a school of astrology and magic. It had become secret since the persecutions of Abu Yussuf. It was there that Rosenkreutz learned divination by the stars and certain laws that regulate the hidden forces of nature.

But he was now in haste to return to his homeland. He left Fez and embarked for Spain. That was the moment when he had to take the name Rosenkreutz, which summarized the essence of his beliefs. He entered into communication with the Alumbrados. In Spain they formed a secret society born under the influence of the Arabs, in which the sciences were studied and a mysticism was practiced derived from that of the neoplatonists. They also sought the philosopher's stone, according to the writings of Artephius.[36] The secret society in question was later to be annihilated completely by the Inquisition.

The *Fama Fraternitatis* reports an echo of the disappointment experienced by Christian Rosenkreutz. He hastened to make known the novelties that he was bringing into the realm of science and philosophy. He was counting on correcting errors and imparting lovingly what he had learned. He was greeted with laughter and scorn. At all times, partial knowledge has enveloped false scholars with an illusion of certainty that does not permit them to receive any new idea. It requires a habituation for a mediocre mind to perceive a verity that is not familiar, even if it is as luminous as the sun.

It was then that Christian Rosenkreutz understood how slowness is necessary for wisdom to penetrate into the human heart. He had to remember the persecutions that had struck excessively precocious possessors of the truth. And, while being astonished at the time necessary for the spirit to develop when it only requires a single day for a flower to bloom and a single century for a tree to grow very tall, he resigned himself to leave the acorns to the swine while retaining the pearls for the elect, while sometimes mingling with the acorns an infinitesimal dust of pearl.

He meditated on subtle philters, on the formidable secret sieves by which thought would reach the men of his race in

---

[36] Although the dates of the Artephius credited as the author of several alchemical tracts are unknown and he may not have existed at all, his name and works were familiar to Roger Bacon in the thirteenth century, a century before the (very premature) existence credited to the Alumbrados here.

rare and microscopic drops, in order that they would not be burned by them. He counted those he could initiate and saw that their number was scarcely greater than eight. He laid the foundations of an occult group so secret, whose members were linked by such a terrible oath, that the group could act subsequently in the way that he had prescribed, pursuing and attaining its goals without anyone knowing of its existence, for three hundred years, except for vague whispers.

The curiosity of superficial men who love anecdotes has suffered from that. But who could sustain that it was the egotism of a superior minority disdaining to enlighten its peers and enabling them to share its knowledge? How many men are there presently in Europe sufficiently devoid of intellectual pride to welcome an absolutely new idea? Is not that pride a barrier that forbids the new idea even from reaching them? If Christian Rosenkreutz disembarked from Fez today, would not all the academies in the world laugh if he attempted to explain that the great work, the problem of the unity of matter, is linked to the development of love in human beings? Would he not encounter, if he tried to teach, the same inaptitude to receive on the part of those he wished to inform? To aid him, without hope of recompense, would he find now, as he did then, seven faithful monks?

Christian Rosenkreutz traversed France without his passage leaving any traces there. That must have been the moment at which the mystic Marguerite Porete had just been burned in Paris, and he hastened to regain Germany.[37]

Long years had passed. Germany was penetrated by all sorts of mystical currents issued from the Albigensian heresy. There were the Brothers of the Free Spirit, who proclaimed the vanity of exterior cults and sacraments, and denied Purgatory

---

[37] Marguerite Porete, the author of the mystical treatise on divine love *The Mirror of Simple Souls*, was burned at the stake in June 1310, by which time, in terms of this count's chronology, Rosenkreutz must have been nearly seventy years old

and Hell, saying that humans are fragments of God that must, through a long series of existences, finally return to the divine essence. There were the Friends of God, who pursued liberation from desire, devoting themselves to practices analogous to those of the yoga system, and whose philosophy was copied exactly from Hindu philosophy. But the persecution of the Church was organized with a force far greater than those sects employed in their propagation.

Before the number of imprisonments and burnings, Christian Rosenkreutz had to measure the danger that spiritual enlightenment was still causing those among whom it was spread to run. He went to find in Thuringia the three monks that had been his companions in his initial studies. They formed a fraternity of four members whose number was subsequently expanded to eight. It was at that moment that the Brotherhood of the Rose-Cross had its greatest expansion, and brought together a number of true initiates that was never to be attained subsequently.

Al the members of the fraternity were German. Only the member that the *Fama Fraternitatis* designates by the initials I.A. originated from another country, probably from Languedoc.

First, Christian Rosenkreutz taught his disciples the secret writing and the symbols by means of which the adepts corresponded with one another. He wrote a book for their usage that was the synthesis of his philosophy and contained a summary of his scientific and medical knowledge. The role of the community seems to have been to act on the few men of the Occident then given to science, in order that the science in question could develop in the direction of disinterest. That time was perhaps the great turning point of our civilization. If the goal of the Rosicrucians had been attained, science, instead of being organized for material ends, might have been the source of an unlimited development of the spirit. We have seen that that was not the case.

Those who were designated by the symbol of the rose and the cross traveled the world, each having a mission to fulfill, but nothing more has ever been known of any of them. According to the *Fama*, Brother I.A. returned to the south of France, where it was perhaps incumbent on him to reignite the antique Albigensian flame. But he must have been very old. Did he succeed in rendering life to a sect in a fashion as secret as that of the Rose-Cross? Tradition only reports his death in the Narbonnaise region.

Nothing is known historically of the activity of Rosenkreutz in the last part of his life—which is to say, at the commencement of the fourteenth century. It can nevertheless be supposed, without any great fear of error, that he inspired Jean de Mechlin,[38] who preached in northern Germany and was the source of truth in Brussels on which the mystic Bloemert drew. That inspired woman achieved miraculous cures and published writings in which she advocated the liberation of the being by love. Her disciples affirmed that they saw two seraphim to her right and left, which advised her.

In all probability, Christian Rosenkreutz was the mysterious visitor of Jean Tauler, on the personality of whom there was so much discussion.[39] Jean Tauler was the most celebrated doctor of theology of his time. The scientific world of Europe came to listen to his preaching in Strasbourg. One day he was visited by a layman whose name he never revealed, and who converted him to a mystical philosophy whose ideal was the absorption of human being by the divine essence. He maintained silence for two years and joined the sect of the Friends

---

[38] "Jean de Mechlin" is mentioned briefly in the French translation H. C. Lea's *History of the Inquisition*, which Magre used as a source. In the original he is called John of Mechlin, and remains extremely obscure. The subsequent reference to "Bloemert" must be to the fourteenth-century mystic active in Brussels, Heilwege Blommaert, also known as Bloemaerdinne.

[39] The reference is to the theologian Jean Tauler (1300-1361), whose sermons were published, but to whom several more esoteric works were apocryphally attributed after his death.

of God. That sect had the same characteristics as he Albigensians. It rejected as an expression of evil the cruel God of the Old Testament. It condemned marriage. It advocated poverty as a practical means of divine realization.

Nothing is known about the death of Christian Rosenkreutz. As with Apollonius of Tyana, no location can be fixed for his tomb. It was a rule for adepts to keep their birth secret as well as their death. Was that only to avoid the violation of the sepulcher and the profanation of the body to which the Church made heretics subject? Was it to permit some of them the translation of their spirit into a new human form and in order that a secret so astonishing for the common run of men should not even be suspected?

All that has reached us is a puerile legend relating to Rosenkreutz's tomb. Two and a half centuries after his death, at the moment when the story of his existence was beginning to spread, his disciples—or, rather, some of those who would have liked to be—claimed to have found a grotto of geometric proportions in which the body of the master, still intact, reposed in the light of an artificial sun.

At all times, people have desired that those they esteem to be greater than themselves should not perish in their flesh. They attach less importance to the duration of their thought, which is, however, the sole form of their eternity. Thus, the Catholic or Muslim saints emit a sweet odor when their remains are found. The veritable sweet odor that the bodies of sages emit in the silence of the earth and the ambience of putrescence is not made of any quintessential material atom or any odorous volatilization. The subtle radiation of their soul floats in the places where they repose and impregnate them, when their body has ceased even to be dust. But it is necessary to be a sage oneself to make contact with that posthumous subsistence of being, and that perception, in enabling you to glimpse that the best do not escape the law, enables you to sense more profoundly the irremediable sadness of transformations.

True and False Rosicrucians

It was at the beginning of the seventeenth century that a sort of Rosicrucian folly burst forth. Two anonymous documents, the *Fama fraternitatis* and the *Confessio* published, in a naïve form, what the vulgar knew of the sect of the Rose-Cross, which was very little. A large number of philosophers and scholars, and also many impostors, seduced by the elevated philosophy of the Rose-Cross, claimed to be its inheritors. Secret societies were formed that rapidly ceased to be secret because of the vanity of their members, who were proud of being part of them. The majority of those groups, when they were not Lutherans, bowed down to the authority of the Church. All the alchemists said that they were Rosicrucians. Descartes attempted to make contact with the veritable fraternity of the Rose-Cross. He searched for them in the Low Countries and Germany, but he declared on his return to France that he had not been able to learn anything certain in their regard.

It has been said that Paracelsus, Francis Bacon and Spinoza were Rosicrucians, but there does not seem to be any proof. In the eighteenth century, a new grade, that of Rose-Cross, was introduced into freemasonry by the Jesuits, who had penetrated it, and Christian groups of that order were formed by them in many places. The vivacious liberty of the thirteenth-century heresies had disappeared. Those so-called Rosicrucians recognized the sacraments, studied the Old Testament as a source of all truth, and bowed down before the power of the Church and the infallibility of the Pope. That is the habitual evolution of all spiritual currents. The tree from which an excessively beautiful flower or an excessively perfect fruit emerges becomes prey to an obscure force that communicates a spoiled sap to it and causes its death.

But the true Rosicrucians continued their work. Their association had not ceased to remain hidden. Because of the voluntary obscurity of each member, no one ever knew the identity of those who were part of it. Merely by the fact that certain men declared that they were Rosicrucians, it is recognizable that they were not affiliated to the sect founded by Christian Rosenkreutz. The influence of that free spirit made itself felt in the seventeenth and eighteenth centuries in all those who struggled against the Calvinist and Lutheran tyranny, as intolerant as that of the Inquisition, and against the intransigence of the universities, which wanted to curb all minds under the intellectual discipline of Aristotle. But the messengers remained faithful to the oath not to make themselves known. The message arrived, but it was not known who had brought it.

Certain features of the life of certain men can sometimes make one think that they were the true possessors of the Rosicrucian tradition. Paracelsus practiced medicine gratuitously; his philosophy was neoplatonist; he only wore modest garments and he glorified poverty; appointed professor of surgery by the senate of Basle he burned in the amphitheater before his students the books of the old physicians that were followed blindly and which, under the pretext of respect, were an obstacle to research. Philalethes,[40] who possessed the secret of the philosopher's stone, traveled the world to care for the sick; his incessant preoccupation as to avoid the celebrity that his cures attracted. Although the Comte de Saint-Germain had a liking for precious jewels, he can be ranked, for other reasons, among the true Rosicrucians.[41] But the same conclusion can-

---

[40] Eirenaeus Philalethes was the signature employed by a seventeenth century author of several treatises on alchemy, nowadays widely believed to have been George Starkey (1628-1665)

[41] The poseur who called himself the Comte de Saint-Germain—as well as several other names—and enjoyed a spectacular but meteoric career in France in the mid-eighteenth century was co-opted by Magre into his tradition of

not be drawn for Spinoza, from the fact that his seal represent-ed a rose and he did not sign any of his works. Certain overly passionate writers have enrolled among the Rosicrucians all the remarkable minds of the last few centuries.

In 1888 Stanislas de Guaita and Papus founded a cabalis-tic Order of the Rose-Cross, with a ceremony, grade, and per-haps costumes. That, and the publicity made around that foun-dation, indicates sufficiently that the new order was not in-spired by the tradition of its first founder. One can say the same about the Catholic Order of the Rose-Cross that Joséphin Péladan founded at the same time. Those orders only had an ephemeral life. Groups can still be found today, almost all Christian, that call themselves Rosicrucian, without that corre-sponding to any initiatory reality whatsoever.

The only true Rosicrucians, the eight heirs, incessantly renewed, of the Albigensian Christian von Germelshausen, have not ceased to pursue their secret endeavor. It has been said that at the end of the seventeenth century, confronted by the increasing materialism of Europe, and as they judged the game lost, they quit the races uniquely thirsty for physical wellbeing and retired to the inaccessible solitudes of the Himalayan mountains. But a game in which the stake is divine is never lost. Perhaps they quit Europe for a time and returned. Their legend, after having fueled the conversations of all the intellectual societies of Europe, was effaced after the Revolu-tion. At present it only interests a small number of the curious. The eight sages have resumed their task in all liberty. It is true that the task has become enormous. By what means are they attempting to accomplish it?

Sometimes, little is necessary to orientate the human soul in a new direction, better and more elevated. It happens that the reading of a book suffices, or a word that is head, even a benevolent face that is glimpsed one evening and recalls the fact that goodness exists. Any of us can encounter, when the

---

supposed magicians and illuminati, and a fanciful chapter is devoted to him in *Magiciens et illuminés*.

moment comes or when he requests it forcefully, one of the eight wandering sages. Let him not be in a bad mood that day, or distracted by fatigue. Wisdom is not capricious, like fortune, but it passes by less frequently.

The Rose and the Cross

The Rosicrucians adopted the union of the rose and the cross as a symbol because that union summarizes the direction of their effort, and the effort in question ought to be that of all humans. Since time immemorial, the wisest among us have discovered that the goal of humankind on earth is to reach divine wisdom. Two routes lead to divine wisdom: knowledge and love.

The cross is the most ancient symbol that exists. As soon as the first civilizations appeared, it signified the spirit, the spirit in motion toward perfection. The rose has the meaning of amour because it is, by virtue of its perfume, color and delicacy, the masterpiece of the beauty of nature, and beauty animates love, in the same way that love transforms into beauty the elements over which it spreads. By the rose that blooms in the middle of the cross, the meaning of the universe is explained, the unique doctrine is summarized and the truth shines brightly. Humans, in order to realize themselves and become perfect, must develop their power of love to the point of loving all beings and all the forms perceptible to the senses, must extend their faculty of knowledge and understanding to the point of possessing the laws that regulate the world, and must be able to reconnect, by means of intelligence, all effects to all causes.

The person who respires the rose and savors its beauty, the person who sees the branches of the cross open toward the four cardinal points of the spirit, can be mistaken, can go backwards, and be momentarily buried by ignorance, but he holds on to the buoy in the tempest, sees the lamp on the hill, and, sooner or later, recovers the right path. Glory to the messenger who finds that salutary signal, who fixes it in the wood or on the stone in order that it is transmitted! Glory to the messenger who, by the virtue of the image, permits the truth not to be lost! He has put the number and the letter on the milestone; he has been the comfort of the traveler and the salvation of the man gone astray.

Christian Rosenkreutz had fixed the rules for the life of his disciples. The first of those rules was disinterest. Disinterest will always remain the most difficult virtue to practice. Men of whom it is said that they are disinterested and who pass among us with a vague aureole of generosity are merely those who are less avid than others. No one is disinterested. There is no example in our modern society of a man great enough to break the formidable chain of money and pass with ease and without ostentation from wealth to poverty or even from poverty to a greater poverty. As soon as the spirit has attained a certain elevation, a man understands that it is in that direction that the first step ought to be accomplished, but he does not take that step. One of the most courageous and most convinced of the virtue of poverty, Tolstoy, only decided a few hours before his death to practice the estate of the mendicant monk. That is very late.

Another essential rule was the absence of pride. The Rosicrucian must pass unperceived, must not flatter himself on his knowledge, and must remain as anonymous as possible. Modesty is as impracticable as poverty for the ordinary man. One can even observe that a stupid vanity, proud of itself, always accompanies great intellectual faculties. And that stupid vanity is considered favorably as a sign of genius.

The third rule of the Rosicrucians was chastity. At all times, sages have attached great importance to chastity. However, neither Pythagoras, nor Socrates, nor Plato, nor the philosophers of the Alexandrian school, practiced it in a rigorous fashion. Perhaps it is only a preventative measure against the excess of desires and the violence they engender.

Logically, if the pleasure of eating is not prohibited, there is no reason for that of sensuality to be. But one cannot assimilate those two orders of physical pleasure. They are, in the normal human being, as indispensable to life as one another, but while one only draws from nourishment a bodily habitude coming from a harmonious digestion, one can obtain marvelous possibilities of sensuality if it is practiced with a person one loves. It can even be a road to perfection—except that the road in question is unknown. The laws that specify how spiritual elevation can be achieved by the community of desire and its mutual satisfaction have not yet been written by any master. I have never even heard that there has been any oral information on that subject. A prudery as old as the world has stopped by its virtuous silence the flight that humankind might have been able to take by means of the portal of the flesh and sexual intercourse.

But we do not know whether the Rosicrucian symbol of the rose might contain implicitly the indication of the secret of amour that remains to be found.

The person who arrives at the supreme knowledge by means of magnified intelligence can only love beings and things whose inner workings he has penetrated, whose movements he can see, the passions of which he understands as if they were his own. The person who succeeds in reaching the sensible estate of perfect love by the emotive impulse of the heart will see the barriers of ignorance fall and will conquer knowledge by the gift of themselves to the person they love. For the two roads join at a certain height, and are only one thereafter.

The symbol is just and eternal and there is no need of any other for thousands of human evolutions. Everyone can weigh himself in his measure and find a provisional touchstone of good and evil by referring to the rose and the cross. Now, that is the question mark that looms up in so many consciences without them admitting it. What is good and what is evil? Am I right to accomplish an action that seems good from my point of view and bad from the viewpoint of others? Certainly, the rose and the cross cannot serve as a key to all enigmas, for there are too many doors in the shadows of the soul. The anguishing question, posed at least once for everyone, a thousand times for some, of knowing whether the most important thing is one's own development or helping others, whether it is better to sacrifice oneself or to impel oneself forward by study, is unresolved. But the two ever-present images provide a basis for a person who is sincere with himself.

Every time that one identifies oneself, via love, either with the ensemble of the universe known as God, with a landscape, with a human being or any other being, even a dog, one is on the path of the rose, protected by it an enriched by its substance. Every time one escapes ignorance, that one learns a fact or a law, that one permits the mind to go a little further in the knowledge of what exists, one is making progress toward the supra-terrestrial and supra-celestial place where the cross extends its four spiritual branches.

That is the message that Christian Rosenkreutz came to bring the men of the Occident. It is a message that might seem very humble to the skeptics of our race, who are convinced that they possess all knowledge and place a higher priority on hatred than love. But it was brought very humbly by a messenger who put his glory into hiding his name and who, having traveled for more than a hundred years to transmit his humble verity, left no other trace of his passage than the design of the flower open in the middle of the cross.